P9-DWA-116

DATE DUE

MY 2 '79			
FE 27 '91			
AG 9 '91			
MY 8 '93			
MY 27 '02			

STONE ISLAND

Other books by Peter Boynton

GAMES IN THE DARKENING AIR
THE EAVESDROPPER

STONE ISLAND

PETER BOYNTON

Harcourt Brace Jovanovich, Inc.
New York

Library of Congress Cataloging in Publication Data

Boynton, Peter
  Stone Island.

  I. Title.
PZ4.B794St   [PS3552.O95]   813'.5'4   73-4379
ISBN 0-15-185140-9

B C D E

For the friends who went ahead—
and for those who will follow

Peter Boynton died on January 12, 1971, in Honolulu. He had been working on the manuscript of this novel at the time and left it all but complete. I have seen it the rest of the way.

Just after his death I came across a question Peter had marked in red in Book VI of his copy of the *Aeneid*. Melancholy, tragic, whatever, its sudden fitness haunted me, and haunts me still. I ask it of him as Aeneas does of his helmsman in the underworld. "Which of the gods, o Palinurus, snatched you from us and drowned you in the midst of the seas?"

—A. WENSINGER
March, 1973

STONE ISLAND

1

Beth,

You are good to write. I need it. Yes, I do need a trip, but to none of the monstrous places you suggest. Apparently you are not reading my letters these days. (I can't blame you.) But no Vacation Lands, please. It's precisely that that I can't stand. The idea that we have arrived, that it's time to play now—and the whip cracks and the great emperors of ice cream say, Play or we'll fire you. No thank you, darling. But a trip, yes.

If I had any guts I'd go back up to the farm—if Herb hasn't sold it. I've been thinking about it. Remember though?—when you and Bill visited us, came up trailing your city things, a little warily, over granite and bog, and you settled for the fireplace as your spot? And I said, I'll take the gulls, you take the crows. And we saved drinking until evening had come and a fire was under way.

And here? Here I'm watching my tugboats again. I *am* drawn to them—and your suggestion struck a chord (you know me), and yesterday I went down to where they dock, and stood and watched. They seem to live in a small and closed society—I didn't dare go close; but they have their bars, their little waterfront apartments with the laundry out, their wives and girls, their own way of dressing, their talk, their way of standing around. I have a plan—it scares me; I'll tell you about it—later. I will.

Please get hold of Herb for me. Do try, Beth—and just *ask* him about the farm? But don't tell him to come here, please.

JOURNAL. A plan. An idea, really. All it takes is nerve, and I have that. But what do I hope to find? Be honest. Life? I want to see how they live, don't I? I want to see if it's any better down there than the way we do. I have one fear,

3

though. Not that I'll have an adventure—not even that I won't—but that I'll find something out about myself; that I *am* used up, burned out, that it's slipped on past. And that they are, too. But I am excited. Have I any clothes I can wear? I'll buy some at A & S. No, at Brustein's. And a wig. I'll go as Fifi Laverne, queen of the waterfront. Yes. And I promise that I won't just keep putting it off, like paying a bill. I promise.

THURSDAY 24. Something's up, something's happening to me. Where to go. And where, please? Someone tell me. I mean how to get *out*. But something has been nudging me all day.

When I used to draw, things were always clear to me. I knew what I could do, what I couldn't—like a swimmer, I would try for my limits, which I was aware of. Those flowers I could draw. Those buildings. People I could not. It was always slightly scary, starting to draw. But this journal—I've been at home in it; and I know why: no limits, nothing to try for, or against; it's always just gone *on*—with my letters, some of them, carbons, pasted in. And why not? Who's to see it? . . . Oh, come on, Helen. Be honest! You're writing it so it can be consumed someday; by a friend, a stranger. Everything you're putting in it (*this, too*) proves it. Stop dodging!

Sad that I don't want to draw any more. I look at flowers and there they are, perfectly indifferent, simply there—they don't need me.

But the journal—suppose I *were* actually to write, to try for something, try to get something down, some part of my life, some truth of it—I mean just to try, even to make things up —no—yes—maybe—I don't know. But to try. Like my plan. Tomorrow I'll go shopping, and I'll buy a blond wig—I promise— and suppose I make a story out of *that*. Would I even be willing to try? The famous author Fifi Laverne, darling of the Mets in her little straw hat. Oh, stop belittling.

FRIDAY 25 MARCH. I did buy them! Wig, spike-heeled shoes, piglet sweater, tight skirt, the works. I went berserk. I am terribly excited. As if I were going somewhere—on a trip—on a spying expedition (except that I'm tired of just looking on). But as if I were going to enter a new world where things are sharp-edged and dangerous, possibly poisoned. When will I dare? It will take all my nerve. But I have nerve, I'm gutsy—I can stand things.

Oh, and I watch them now, those tugs, begin to recognize certain ones. I detect a pattern that did not exist for me before. I saw them as ducks, honking, tooting, plowing along, nosing the river into teeth of white foam, below a mustache of hemp—such burly little things. Burly—I like the word—I like, would like, I think, a burly man, who would push me around in some acceptable way. Maybe I'll find one, who knows?

But how will I dare to intrude on all that? From here they mean something, do make a pattern. But there? Some lout will offer me a beer, an easy make, a score, and take me to a room, or suggest it anyway. Is that what I want? And suppose one did (I'm good-looking enough, if no girl). What then? Oh, *faw*. I know what I imagine, and it comes from bad books. You'd find them foul-mouthed, incompetent beer guzzlers, boys grown haphazardly into men, still hanging around in packs. The poor are no more worthy than the rich—they simply have less money.

But I do have the wig, the clothes—I've tried them on—I look tough as a fifty-cent steak, and marvelous.

Sunday 27

Beth,

I did it! No, wait, wait—I don't think I told you—my plan. Oh, never mind. Listen. The tugs—where they dock, where they live, and all that—I went down there. I actually did. I've been wanting to. To a place called the Paradise Bar (wouldn't you know it)—I swear I did—scared out of my wits, in a blond wig and beads, a sort of piglet sweater, as tight as I dared—spikes, the highest—simply impossible. I went in a taxi—never mind just where, but I had reconnoitered—and then walked around a little, wildly excited. I have never *felt* so *ready*. It was raining a little, mist in the air, wet streets—the tugs, the river sounds, ships hooting and moaning in the distance. And I did look the part, the new girl in town (maybe a *little* overdone, but who's perfect?). And decided on that bar. And I went in and sat at a table. Yes. Expecting—I don't know—swarms of young seamen, their wives, their families—in out of the fog, to be laughing and shouting, playing darts, drinking beer.

I sat there knowing what would happen, that one would see me and come over. He wouldn't be young—forty, forty-five—and he would say, Tell me about yourself, kid. He would have blue eyes and a cap pushed back on his head. And would introduce me to an older woman—tough-looking but with indestructible dignity, wearing an old felt hat and a sweater. And he would say, not even looking at me, Mother, this is the girl I'm going to marry. And right away she and I would know each other. Sit down, she'd say, have a beer—and to her son, Oh, go away, leave us girls alone—beat it—we got things to talk about. Get the picture? Or don't you watch TV?

Well, I sat there and I had a glass of beer. A few tough girls who knew all the men *were* in there, and a *lot* of men (I had picked a good bar), one or two of whom looked me over in the mirror. I don't know where their mothers were. They were just men. They kept saying things like Jesus and shit. I finished my beer, picked up my little bag, and walked out—infinitely let down, but somehow terribly relieved.

Well, it was a trip, of sorts. And I think it did me good to go through with it, through with something, however abortive. I may try again. Though it does scare me.

SUNDAY 27. Why did I lie to her? Though it wasn't a lie, entirely—just not quite the truth. Maybe I'll have to lie to get at the truth. But how do I tell her that *I* reneged, not him. Yes, that one did see me in the mirror and finally came over, and scared the bejesus out of me, and that it made me sick, to find how fake my little dreams had been. Me, so *covertly*, watching him and thinking, Yes, there he is—blue-shaven jaw—square— burly—oh, yes. And watching me, and catching me watching him. Coming over. (I froze, like a rabbit miles from a clump of grass.) And sitting down, after asking. Yes, just what I had dreamed about. Sizing me up, and asking, right off the bat, Are those real? And me, like a perfect nitwit, fingering my pearls, saying, These? He didn't even smile, he said, No, lady, those, not the beads. I redeemed myself, or I think, or tried to; I said, oh, those—yes— yes, of course they are—can't you tell? And him—Not these days. Are you sure? And me—I certainly am, I ought to know. And him—Well, anyway, pleased to meet you. And I said, Me?—li'l ol' me? And he said, You come on like something out of an old routine—how old are you, anyway?—I'm going on over forty myself so you can be honest. I'm forty-two, I said. Is that a wig? he asked. Well, you come on pretty strong yourself, I said. Him

6

sitting there, in a pea jacket, I think (navy-blue, blue plastic buttons)—yes, and burly. I could imagine the rest—hearing him say, What you drinking—beer?—how about a shot?—I'll buy. And then, right then, I reneged. I said, looking at my watch, I'm afraid I have to run. And he said, Run where? And I said, I've got to meet a friend, my mother—or something. But anyway, I finished my beer, picked up my purse, and skedaddled. Yes, took off, beat it—Fifi Laverne, making tracks. Him just sitting there, at the table, looking after me staggering along in my impossible heels.

Well, so that was it.

Thursday 31

Beth,

No, I'm not going to come to your party. I don't really want to see Herb just now. All he is is company and I need more than that. We had our good times (you know), but then something did absorb him, scoop him up—New York—all this—and he was *always* so intellectual. I don't mean intelligent—intellectual, and I've grown so sick of that, because I'm not, and I'm beginning to blame it all on *them*, though the blame, to call it that, can probably be tracked directly back to that terrible old man with the telescope. But at *any* rate, I need something else, something simpler. And *not* the great Tugboat Annie life (no Wallace Beerys around, I'm afraid). I hardly look at my view these days.

But don't worry about me, just let me chatter along, and don't phone. Ask Herb about the farm, if he shows up.

FRIDAY 1 APRIL. Pacing this balcony in the April cold, looking at the river again, the tugs. Burly. He was. Me and my big teats, which he admired. Fool's Day, but I'm going down again. Same bar, same table. Though probably he'll be gone by now.

Saturday 2 April

Beth,

You *are* an angel. Herb called. The farm *is* available. We came right to the point. He thinks I should go up there, as to a sanitarium (apparently you had talked to him—he knew I was with rash again). I said that it had popped into mind, that I felt like getting away, et cetera. I said that I'd write him about it, couldn't be sensible over the phone—talking into machinery makes me self-conscious. I'll let you know, of course, but meanwhile thanks, and love, as always.

SATURDAY P.M.   If I were even nervous that would be something, but squeamish is more like it. A descent, a search? But I've *got* to go look—Helen Calder, the fancy woman of the water front.

April 4 Monday

Dear Herb,

I was afraid to try over the phone, I mean explain. Probably Beth has said some of it to you anyway. She's my sounding board. It may be only the problem of growing old, of being passed by or left out, though I tell myself I *want* to be left out. Include me out—didn't we used to say? Whatever it is, I've got to make a break for it soon—I'm going under. Hence, the farm. I think I want to go there for a while. Just me. I want to try it out—maybe paint, even write. And all the clichés spring to mind—about wanting to get away from it all, to be by myself, to try a new way. Well, I do. You don't plan on using it, do you?

Anyhow, write me about it and be honest—I mean about Sally and how she might feel.

How was the Wild West?

WEDNESDAY 6.   Walked and walked, restlessly—looking for something. The trees still winter-struck and the ivy brown, but a bud here and there, a bit of forsythia, bluets in that tiny garden with the faun up by Remsen Street—the cat was out sunning itself on the wall, fat from winter.

Looking for what?

That café. It upset me, all right. So close I could lie about it and not be far from the truth. If A could have happened but B did, can we not take A for B?—or for a portion of B?

This interests me. . . .

Say that the world is now there only for us to manipulate. If they can manipulate all that, *why can't I make my life happen as I want it to?* Why must it simply *have* happened? Because my father preferred my beautiful sister, must I sulk? If A *might* have happened, in some sense A did happen. We can choose to rewrite history. Which might then, of course, have a bad ending. Who can make the future answer to our demands?

Beth,

No lectures, please. I don't make a practice of cruising the water front. But I *had* to go down there again. The tugs, a kind of life, *way* of life the sight and sound of them seemed to represent. Something clean and simple and easy. Yes, the hulking does appeal to me, as you have said before. I don't quite know why. I suppose it suggests something about maleness, something ancient, of the earth, a *kind* of power. The ideal American male may be lean, as Herb was—intellectual, elegant, and swift, and without cholesterol. Bill, on the other hand, is rotund and produces children for you, and is comfortable in bed. Right? And my father was.

These letters are just between us, aren't they? All right then —I did meet a man and I dislike myself for not having told you, though I'm going to skirt the margins even now. But I sat in that bar much longer than I admitted, because of a man who had noticed me in a mirror (I didn't tell you that, I mean the first time)—there *had* been a man and he *had* watched me, before I upped and skedaddled. And he was there again, the second time, still watching, which he did until he could tell that I was aware of him. *Every*thing, in a way, that the boats, the tugs, have suggested, down to a disreputable yet somehow jaunty old mate's cap he wore. He was off a freighter, as it turned out—a man named Mallek—or Malik. He was married. He showed me a picture of his wife, a huge, fat creature, jolly, I should think, in New London. I was immensely flattered that he wanted to pick me up, and scared silly, because obviously he meant business and was not nearly as purely brute as I had thought. Yes, I did go with him, to a room he had—sordid, almost unlit—and spent the night, feeling as though I had lost quite a number of feathers when I did get home, and terribly let down by it all, feeling unsatisfied. The vigorous, simple life I had hoped to meet wasn't there.

And he was a *good* man, too. It was not his fault. We just belonged in separate worlds. Now I can't look at the river, the tugs, the shipping. So I've got to do something.

JOURNAL. So. How much did I lie to her? Think a moment. A lot. Yes. But how could I not? Then why even tell her? Oh, because—because *some* of it was right. If it had been that other one, A, from whom I ran away, A would have occurred. But B did. If B *did* and A *could* have, can't one talk about B as though it were A? Can't I make a poem out of that—not a lie, a poem? Because I have no life now that will do.

Think of the farm, of Maine.

SUNDAY 10. I know that I'm going now. I knew it this morning as I walked in the first April rain.

Pulling up roots, those parts of me that put down even into cement, these old sidewalks. My pictures, my objects, my books —my "view"—which I've come to love again with the decision, if that is what it is.

Because there *is* no Fifi Laverne, no tough old chick who could swing in a different orbit.

Black buildings over there—window he stood against—the Chase Manhattan—yellow cubicles of light—and the sky, above and behind them, a kind of magenta now, as of rose dust held in violet smoky air—beauty of the world I am leaving. Out of squalor a loveliness.

How did I find the nerve to bring him here? (I didn't tell Beth that—lie number two.) Naked against a rose window, in silhouette, looking out at his world, that river, those ships. So odd, up here. Yes, how the manners came out. Drawn to the lights over there. Telling me, When we leave you can see us from here. Standing naked and dark—my mind dotes, at a safe distance now. Could I make a poem of it?

I went to stand by him and the lights gleamed pale over us. I said, Do you see how beautiful it is? We stood there, shy of each other. Do you like the sea? I asked. He nodded, or shrugged. I ran my hand over him. He let me. You got another of these? he said. (The drinks helped.) Standing there when I came back, black against that rose window.

My chair there, that he sat in, looking out, me sitting below him, feeling his calves, his knees, roughhewn out of flesh and grass, old wrestler's legs that spread for me. It was only me at first. He just let me. There in the chair at the window—rough hulk of him—abstracted, apart. Only gradually did he turn toward me, from the window, from the view, from that river lights floated on, from that sky grown purple and rose that buildings stood against, crisp as honeycombs with light. He left it for me with a kind of regret. A sense of duty, perhaps. He left it for a while, fucking me on the sofa.

On the sofa, my hands at his back, feeling down to the small of it, thick, flexible, involved with invisible motion. Then I see him at the window again. Out there his world, and mine. Just that we had different shares in it. Though in the morning he seemed to feel at home, told how he liked to cook, and about his wife. His old bulldog face—part A, part B—the heaviness of an older man, I saw clearly then—chest hair—those legs. He'll go with me, I can tell. I'll take him along.

Tuesday 12 April

Herb,

You're a dear to be so generous about the farm. I don't even know yet that I really want to go up there, but the thought that I can simplifies things. It's just *there*, isn't it? as you said—a matter of opening things up, plugging the leaks? I'll let you know. You *are* a dear, though, when you're not busy being important or social. There—only one bitchy aside. I'll let you know when I do. Yours, etc.

Tuesday 12 April

Beth,

Herb wants me to go ahead with the farm. The thought that I might already pleases me, has taken a shape in my mind, the shape of wood, of stone, of simple things—as if I were going to call on Sarah Orne Jewett—so ordinary and yet so exciting, almost turbulently so. Maybe only the thought of change. Change frightens me, or disturbs me anyway.

I wish I could say to you, You come, too. Not that you would. Perhaps when I'm up there, ensconced, you will visit me. Whatever, you will be in my thoughts a good deal, my one firm tie with humanity in a world I seem already to have withdrawn from. White Plains seems a million miles away, and even the Battery over there has receded, the buildings. Not a tug in sight. One freighter, nosing its way out.

Herb will sublease from me, for a while anyway, so that simplifies that. He always liked this place. Will Sally? I'm tempted to take the sofa—$1500 at Sloane's—my one real extravagance. If not, *they* will lounge on my glorious, wide-wale corduroy. In exchange for the farm.

I'm already touching things goodby—that faun on Remsen Street. I'm beginning to think I may never come back. Well, I will leave almost nothing behind. What will I find up there? Nature in place of culture, I suppose. And I will hope to survive it.

I've got to buy a car, a station wagon, I think.

I feel so free right now that I think there must be something wrong. It's as if I had forgotten some key thing—my checkbook, perhaps—and that it was almost down to the stubs.

JOURNAL SUNDAY 17 APRIL. New York—Brooklyn Heights—I'll miss seeing you, simple in the dawn—the river glittering with gulls—from my glass cage up here. Tearing bits of myself away, skin, drops of my blood on the pavement. I'm incurably *me*—can't leave *that* behind, since there *is* no new me. But transplanting will help. I must get on with it while this place still dazzles me—crystal slivers of light on a purple river. Reddish tower in blue mist—draped in its veil of cables. Under it a tug, trailing the white intestine of its steam, heads for home. . . .

JOURNAL. Deciding what to take. Books—the ones I haven't really read—*Ulysses, Finnegans Wake,* Proust—*Middlemarch, Tristram Shandy*—all good for a long winter's night; Wallace Stevens, Eliot, Roethke, Hart Crane; favorites, Stein and Virginia Woolf (sad lady), all of her—and Caroline Gordon, because I love her and knew her once—yes, Willa Cather, too (whom I don't, quite), lying quiet in Jaffrey now; Jean Stafford, who no longer speaks to me though I wished her well at that last party, Kay Boyle—all my old lady friends; yes, and Edith Wharton in her pearl choker; and the books I've lugged around since my father told me they were mine—*The House at Pooh Corner, Dr. Dolittle* (so fashionable), *Just So Stories* (so not)—*The Hollow Tree*—where a 'coon and a 'possum and an old black crow . . . That Korean bronze. Oh, heavens, I will take them all—who can leave a book behind? Like a child freezing in the snow. But I won't move Brooklyn Heights to Maine.

Why is it that the lights out there have never glowed more brilliantly, and that I think of the sea? A freighter going by.

Yes—and the journals, of course—ten *years* of words. When I glance through them now I realize I never go deep enough—the art of the journal I haven't even tried to master. But I think I know what it requires—honesty, integrity—accuracy. And yet much more than that—a real spirit—real flesh—butting against, floating along with, flying and diving in the world—even that one—this. Must something happen, as in a novel? I don't know. But me back there—simply telling about my plants, where I got them and how I learned their ways, how this one liked sun, or water, or to be said good morning to. Something arch about that. And cooking, when I got excited about *Gourmet*, trying out recipes. Would Mallek have liked to cook for me? What fun, perhaps—us growing gross together—as he and his wife have done. Odd that they, like me, had no children.

But how to write about him, take him along, when I know so little? Though I could have gotten more down, of that—like the etchings for Vollard that Picasso did, the purely sexual encounter.

Sunday April 24

Beth,

Come this Friday. Tell Bill you have to. I'll make us fifty-five martinis, build a fire in my little Swedish thing—I'll give you the scroll, and the bonsai banyan. I need you to wish me Godspeed. I'm an old freighter, and don't know where I'm heading, don't care, since it's all one river.

Something in me is singing all the time now, some mindless little hum like Mrs. McNab's. But I'll need you at the last. Two old biddies getting crocked and invoking the past. I'm in a great mood, and scared. Love—and to Bill, the children—

SUNDAY EVENING—JOURNAL. Mallek–Mendonca—one word more from old word hoard unlocked. I didn't get him right, did I? Dishonest. Trying for a poem—when it wasn't a poem.

How to write about that. His nakedness—Portuguese—from New Bedford. I had never seen that sort of man naked. So immensely *comfortable*—a great abundance of flesh—hair—stomach—its beauty, such as it was, lay in that. And the final easiness after he had drunk and looked and sat and smoked—he simply went to the sofa and waited for me. He wanted to please, was warm, was male, did what was right, finally came with great surges and swings. There *are* no very good words for it, or I don't know them yet. Except, he fucked me. And yet he, in the midst of *his* life, is a poem—sea, ships, docks—his fat wife—him sitting in bars—picking up this one here, or that, if he can—the old thrills of a conquest now and then, of a woman who wants him—as I did then.

Mendonca. Something dark there, secret yet direct—like writing on a wall.

Towers of light across the dark water. Another martini, please. I'm going away.

> *Old Stinson Farm*
> *Mims Road*
> *Orstown, Me.*
> *June 6 Monday*

Beth,

Not a letter yet—just "one for the box," as Mother used to say. I'm almost too happy to write. A million things to do to it, but the farm is here where we left it. From this desk I look out past the grape arbor to lawn a foot high that I will have to confront, at lilacs almost in bloom, at fans of iris by a stone wall.

I know how right I was to come, and each night hug myself to bed and rise each morning to think what has to be done (it's slightly manic, of course)—the furnace, the stove, a broken window, damp mattresses—things to buy (a lawn mower).

I've seen what people we knew, Herb and I. Not many. Jules Caster, Carole Bean—they're still here. Little has changed, though things do look poorer. Already, without asking around, I have the sense of a decline—houses for sale or abandoned, stores I can remember open, now empty and dusty-windowed. I don't understand it yet.

But all this fresh air blowing in from the sea. I fall into bed like a log and sleep without budging till dawn. I have a martini at hand right now to stave off exhaustion. Don't hope for me now. I don't need it any more.

JUNE 7. In town buying things. Necessities. Soap and nails, a bucket, a broom, a new mop (mice had been at the old one, so got Mouse-Nots, too, billed rather cruelly as "Mouse's Last Meal"—could have said "last supper," I suppose)—arranging for firewood—will need a vacuum cleaner—Windex, paper towels—oh, and food, of course, odds and ends. I'm still airing things out.

Seeing people who look vaguely familiar, though I don't nod. No feeling of a right to that yet. And I'm just as happy not to for now. I'm all nose, ears, eyes for this place itself—Orstown, of the Three Towns so-called—Tainesville seven miles to the north, Edsville inland from that, and this, down among islands. We're something of a peninsula and fairly remote, though everything in this part of Maine strikes me now as remote.

The light: this evening again so clear that things seemed sharp-edged, luminous, set in a kind of dust-free substance—nothing floats in it that is foreign.

> *Old Stinson Farm*
> *Orstown, Me.*
> *June 9 Thursday*

Dear Herb,

It is all absolutely right and you are to be thanked for it, and I do. The farm—just enough breakage and spoilage to swing me into action, so that I begin to think of it as mine—you know what I mean—that I'm more than just your guest.

But, oh, Maine—the sea—my glimpses of it through the spruce from that side hill (remember?)—the hundred inlets, then at Orstown the thing itself, still sheltered by the outer islands, spruce-black, looming or flat across water. It's all there—the lobster boats, like gulls in the harbor, the great cut-granite wharves, the shingled fish shacks (barrels and salt, clots of pot buoys—orange and green, blue, white, striped, dotted—remember them?—like children's toys), the houses with their sharply pointed roofs, like pricked ears, eying the bay suspiciously, the grocery and the hardware stores where we bought everything. And best of all the people. Jules Caster came over to look at the well, which had gone dry. Shaking his Yankee head. A dry year, he said, a queer one—something happening to the weather around here—ain't like it was. And so the troubles that belong with being here begin, and I brace for them. More than just something to do, they fit me in, hammer and saw me into the pattern of things. I *will* belong.

Good luck to you and yours.

JOURNAL SATURDAY 11 JUNE. From here at my desk, with my things about (my Korean bronze, my scrimshaw tooth), through this window a morning fog thins and drifts, opens, closes, letting the stone wall emerge, then hushing it back into gray obscurity. I don't like them when they stay too long—nobody does—but a morning of it, or a day, changes perspectives, adds a seriousness to things, an intimacy. That wall, appearing, disappearing like that, turning on and off—I become more aware of it, of its bread-loaf stones, of a patch of blue-green lichen here and there, leprously beautiful. And I think of stone being eaten away—of time and perishing things. Fog has to do with the sea, with deaths and promises. I'll drive into town to look at the water, the boats, in a while.

I need things anyway. Latches for the screens, flashlight batteries, food—fish tonight, and a fire, and a martini—maybe two, or three (Saturday night)—and the first page of *Finnegans Wake*. I'm going to set myself a page a day.

JOURNAL—SAT. EVENING. Haddock in the oven, a fire—not that it's cold, but not that it's not, either—the *Maine Coast Fisherman*, because I've got to learn the names of things around me here, the kinds of boats (what's a Jonesport, what's a Friendship sloop?), the tides. Fog still around. It's been around all day, but it's thicker now and damp—through my window I could reach out and pick off chunks like angel food cake.

Jules is finished with the well—only a matter of pipes and pump, it seems, after all—it had not gone dry. His next project, while I've *got* him here, leaks and things in the kitchen—he'll come Monday. Meanwhile, I'm settling in, finding my way. Torn already between wanting to drive and to walk, to explore, to look—it is all so filled with promise—like Venice with Father that time—you didn't know which way to start off or for what. But I must let it happen, not rush at it frantically. I will.

Saturday 11

Beth,

Just another note to say that by God I am here. Though at moments I still don't believe that I am. Too sudden, too different. I keep saying, I did it—I've actually flown. Flight is still my metaphor. Can hardly remember the drive up, pursued by furies, guilts, anxieties. But—by God, I am here—getting myself together, trying to learn that I am.

No more for now. Much love.

SUNDAY 12 JUNE. Walked into town this morning through a thin and blowing fog. Can I describe it?

From town I'm the third farm out along Mims Road—the Williamses', the McFarlanes', then me. Their houses are white, with porches and barns, trucks, tractors, heaps of cut wood —pasturage, stone walls, and spruce—and in the fields great clots of granite erupting from sparse grass. A tough world to hack a farm out of—those fields their ancestors cleared, for cattle or sheep. The spruce are everywhere, and often gray with a lichen that looks like Spanish moss.

And though I looked the other way, an eyesore or two just on the edge of town where the houses begin—an aluminum trailer that made me cringe was up on concrete blocks in a meager, token yard—a mobile home—they're coming in—I think by the thousand now. Yes, and down the road from it (not nearly so bad, but bad enough) two of those wooden boxes, one a chemical yellow, the other a pale, depthless green, looking sudden, foreign, perishable, but very cockily there. I'm afraid even Maine won't keep all that at bay. What will there be to look at fifty years from today?

But then, over the brow of a hill, so that suddenly, walking over a rise, you see water and boats below, and beyond that the islands. Orstown itself appears, and surprises you. You see white houses, sense an openness that has to do with sunlight, water, boats (when there is sunlight)—you see small fences, stone walls, granite pouring out from flowers, grass, flowing down the hill. And not all the spruce are gone, just those forests of them that surround us inland. They stand at corners here—help shelter a house, form a hedge—add a note that is almost Japanese—tough, indestructible, like the place itself. Grass everywhere, some wild, some clipped, but a neatness to things.

What to tell myself about it? That it's a fishing village and not a seaport town. No founding fathers, picturesque details involving Puritan squabbles with Indians, famous town drunks, or mad poetesses. None of your great captains' houses here. A working town of coastal Maine—remote, unimportant, exposed. But the fog thinned for a moment and the harbor, the islands, took my breath away—a fleet, as of ships out there, anchored to the dark foundations of the world. Then it blew in again, vague furious ghosts that raced past me along the street and up the hill, as if I had seen enough of the present for then and must think of the past.

Oh, yes, half the town looks abandoned now. Prosperity seems to have slipped away and with it skimpier folk who depend on that. Because what is left is sober, serious, and heartbreakingly beautiful—of a beauty difficult to define—an antique bareness of statement—stone, water, wood—of houses lived in, used, patched and repaired, and repaired again, with odd touches of recent paint that among the gray and silvering shingles, the rippling of white old clapboards, seem gaily frivolous, as do certain houses that are not white (as I approached, a yellow one glowed through the fog and seemed radiant)—as do the laundries blowing in the damp gray air—as will the flowers soon to come, the hollyhocks, the petunias.

In my denim skirt, my bandanna, my flat shoes—walking through town. And I imagine them—them as saw me from their cars that passed—saying to each other, There's that new woman —got the old Stinson farm up the hill—and wonder if they resent me, if I intrude. I feel strange among them and perhaps always will; they've earned this place, I've merely paid for a patch of it—not even that. And I pass the post office (I've already been there looking for mail) with its massive granite steps, its clean white clapboards, and its porch, its bench. And pass the lane that leads down to the cannery, whose roof I can see and the gulls perched along it—a sardine boat is in, tied to its wharf, picturesque in the fog. I am walking along Water Street, which follows the shore; and when the old and sometimes paintless wooden buildings of the stores give way to shingled houses (tiny, weathered, neat) I can see wharves and the harbor beyond, and since it is Sunday most of the lobster boats are at their moorings. Heaps of lobster traps in yards—a sense of things used or broken, lying around—seafaring, fishing things—gear—skiffs— and rope, twine, nets. It is all timeless and weathered, rickety and permanent, in a timeless and blowing fog.

And up the other hill, out of town, in the fog, I went, and passed the white clapboarded school with its jungle gym, its swings, and its weed-grown playground—where they learn what they learn. To read, I suppose, and arithmetic—not much about history, or art. What is it that they need to know here anyway? I pass by, feeling baffled at my own ignorance.

And up there, beyond the school and a church across from it, the road branches, as roads will, and to the right wanders off into spruce, and you realize that more houses than you had thought were here are around, though the yards are poorer than those below, the houses often only tar-paper shacks, teeming with children—piles of cut wood, battered and rusting cars. So that, Why this, why this? you wonder, at such poverty those few steps up from the water. Why do some and not others, these, prosper?—whose *are* all these children and what will become of them? Do they go to that school? I don't understand, though sense something natural here, not to be warred on. I keep to the left, knowing that the road will duck, wind, and return to the water.

It rounds a gray shoulder of granite over which crusts of lichen grow, scabrous and beautiful, like the poor, and a kind of blueberry, two or three inches tall, tufts of stiff grass, and tiny plants I don't recognize that make a garden I want to pick the dead leaves from, and the crumbs of broken rock. Up here the stone seems alive to me—the way the granite flows out from under things to move, it seems, toward some distant goal, bearing this life along with it.

Past it I see open fields and then a cove they run down to that has boats in it, and a wharf and shed fixed to the granite shore (the fog has thinned for a moment to reveal them, is blowing past). And then, as the road bends, I see a long white house that rambles off into sheds and a barn. Three cars are out in the yard: an old Chevy sedan, a truck made from the cut-down body of a Buick, and a jeep. Garish and beautiful, an Old Glory hangs damply from a white pole. A lawn flows away to a path that joins the fields, and I see the wharf and the cove again. And for an instant I see the landscape as moral, things getting along, being proper together, helping each other out.

I pass a mailbox: on it in firm black lettering the name HALE— and something in me smiles at that. Yes, the Hales—substantial people, obviously—real coastal Maine. The house is probably 1840, or in part. And would you say that they thrived, they prospered? You might learn that there wasn't much cash around but that their credit was good. Hale would be a lobsterman, of course; and out in the cove I see his boat; it has a mast at its stern, sail up (triangular patch of orange-brown canvas), and beyond it a string of mustard-yellow dories afloat in the fog with sheers so long and classical they seem to be the perfect boat and immune to change —as perhaps the Hales are, too, belonging to history and wearing it as naturally as work clothes. Fog blows in again, the dories thin to mustard-yellow strokes of a brush, the stern of Hale's boat shifts —I see only its keen bow. The flag stirs as I pass the house, wishing that someone would ask me in. No lights are on, but in daylight here they almost never turn on lights. I want to be called in, I want to tell them that I like their name, and the way the house and the yard and the cove all fit together. I want to say, This is right—what you've arrived at is right—you've struck a balance here —mankind will not do better. Oh, that's not what I want to say— I want to say, Don't move, stay right there.

I pass by and in fifty yards I enter spruce, dark, tragic, eclipsing all but the memory of the cove. The road winds among massed rick, dark lichened trunks, a landscape by Salvator Rosa in miniature, romantic, slightly deranged (where is the sea?), divides, and I take the right this time, an inland road that will wind back, join, eventually, my road.

And come on fields again, and unexpectedly, the way you do down here, a smaller, poorer farm than the McFarlanes', or my own. And I pass by it being barked at by a short-haired, energetic dog (not unfriendly—rather interested, in fact, though I snub it), and see, back behind some tall lilac, a boat up on supports—where it has been for years, you guess (the paint seems brittle and old)— yes, and some lobster traps—there to catch field mice now. Juniper grows very low in a field and extends itself over rock like a green fan. Cattle have made paths through it.

And then, as suddenly as the bay and the islands had appeared, I come on a field of lupines, and, surprised, my heart lifts in astonishment. Pink, pale purple, blue—I remember now, they *are* up here, this month, as perhaps nowhere else. I want to paint them. And farther along I come on a house with fields filled with them on both sides of it—like small, stately women from long ago, dressed in their Sunday best and gathered for some occasion—perhaps the end of the world. And, My, I think, they suit a white house, a stone wall, as grandly as delphiniums do. Why don't I have them? And I think, Perhaps you have to earn them in some way, be here a while.

Strands of fog—but it was clearing, a pink and blue light was taking its place. Crows were cawing away, gulls adrift in the air. New York, for a while, kept popping into mind. I saw it, though, as separate from myself, on a postcard left on a sofa somewhere. . . . I have described my walk.

———

NOTE: Yes, bits of N.Y. around, and Mendonca (Mallek?), too. I see him as if through water, some medium that wavers, distorts. I see parts of him—then see him only as a name, a word—words. At moments I simply know that he's there.

I've let him in once. Then threw the page away. Rather rude of me, I suppose.

TUESDAY 14 JUNE. A sunny morning, as if fog had never been, did not exist. I called Mrs. Bean to ask would she be in if I dropped by about ten. She would, indeed, she said, and sounded pleased—had meant to call but doesn't have a car—foot bothering her—et cetera. I forget how we met—with Herb, I think, who might have bought lobsters from her husband (who I hear is no longer with us—Ellsworth?)—yes—and at that church sale where we got those quilts.

I walked down as I had Sunday and noticed so much more, seemed to see and hear things, bird song, tiny plants, as well as the bone and bulk of this place. And because I was going somewhere I felt appropriate; I was taking a step that I needed to—because I don't know her well, or much of anybody, and will need to. A foray on all of this.

And then coffee in that white kitchen of hers; being up the hillside a little, you can see the islands from it. A fresh morning breeze was wrinkling the water, tin-foiling it. Her kitchen is pure joy and typical, I guess, of down here ("down" meaning up, or east). They think of themselves as "down East," probably downwind from Boston or Cape Ann.

Mrs. Bean's kitchen—my impression is of "white and shiny." Thick-as-porcelain white paint covers everything—it would chip, you feel, like enamel, and is there to preserve as well as cheer up. On the floor a white-and-gray linoleum, and on the table and sideboards white-and-red oilcloth, though a kitchen range black as a crow shines so, you feel it, too, is white, and makes me smile at something a black friend once said. Mrs. B. cooks on it and warms herself there when the fogs are in or it's rainy. Glass things along the window sills, tiny bottles, Sandwich marbles in glass cups that sparkle because many are chipped, though she has some real beauties. A couple of Boston rockers are near the stove; she's braided mat seats for them and I learn later why they look slightly odd to me. They like light up here, and gay colors; it's their way of confronting all that: what lay outside her windows—the unconquerable, immediate forces of nature.

Yes, hers is a lobsterman's kitchen, mine more an inland one and more typically New England, *old* New England. A sense of sea things, fishing things, surrounds hers—out on that side porch, her kitchen porch, you see ropes and buckets, pot buoys, gear, used up, deteriorating, like almost everything else up here, or ready to be fixed and used again—they make do. Ellsworth's old things, her husband's, which she keeps as he left them. I don't like to throw them away, she says. They keep, they save, they make do—and things look it, somehow, or not department-store new (there's no department store, unless you drive to Bangor). I am a farm. She is a fisherman's house, quite small, very tidy, and both old and somehow new-looking—everything painted and painted again, with leftovers, you gather—all snug and reflecting care and pride. So isolated they are—in the old days they moved back and forth by water—that was a road out there. They still use it, though our land roads have destroyed the coastal shipping (as they might destroy it all in time); but to visit cousins, family, here and there, they'll still take the boat, if they have one, as often as the car. It's closer by water—a hundred miles by land (up one peninsula, down another). Yes, and a few still live on islands.

A swarthy little woman, somehow speckled—we had a nice chat. I think she liked it that I called her and stopped in. And I learn a little more about this place from her. She doesn't want to hear about *my* life yet, though I think some of that will come later (they're curious but reticent, friendly but reserved, and really, when you do get down to it, more concerned with themselves than with strangers; you wish that *we* were, sometimes). I asked about families, the ones for whom places, coves, the islands, are named, and about the Hales, that house I passed at Goose Cove. And she knew, she knew, and told me a little.

We're not old down here, the way they are in Wiscassett or Castine, you know. Now, they're *real* old. We're lobstering, and that come later. Though everyone's fished off here since the Year One, you hear. But lobstering don't make a body rich—it was shipping done that, and the mills and the boatyards built them fine houses. With us it's mostly make-do, though some flourishes and some fails, like that shanty crowd up on the hill on what we call "Sunset Boulevard."

And the Hales? I say. I walked past their house the other day and it looked like a fine one. Do they flourish?

Ethel and Elmo? she says. Yes—I'd say they do—or anyway used to—or for here. Ain't rich, you know, but Elmo's got a fine boat and Ethel works at the selling of real estate, or claims she does, and they got that house and good land, good property.

What are they like? I ask, thinking "Elmo Hale," savoring the name.

Ethel and Elmo? She thinks a moment. Elmo's a good worker, keeps at it regular—him and my Ellie always got along good. Me and Ethel, too, though I ain't seen much of her of late, kind of spindly—in and out of good health. And you don't with everyone, you know, I mean get along, even here, where you ought to.

I watch her fish in the oven for a crumb cake. Four of her fingers are bandaged, wrapped in adhesive tape—her work at the canning factory cuts them, as it hurts her feet.

Leftovers, she says, bringing the cake—Ellie used to like a crumb cake.

I praise it—it's good—very short and not sweet. I ask if she minds if I smoke; which I like to with coffee, I say.

Heavens no, she tells me. Ellie smoked like a chimney.

Then I ask, He's gone, I heard—is that so?

She nods. Out there, she says (nodding to her right at the window). They never did find him, poor dear.

I express what sorrow I can, I commiserate, and she nods, waves a hand at it. I wouldn't accept it for a while, she says. I'd wait for him. I do now. But he's gone. It's common around here. One thing or another catches them—can't swim, you know, in them boots and things. Tides—ledge—one thing or another—and Ellie did drink. The men do, quite a few of them. Can't blame them, you know—it's hard out there, all alone—it's a hard life—up at four, coming in sometimes at dark—storms, and their gear stove up, washed away. Yes, they'll drink, even out there, like for company.

She isn't a gossip, or not with me yet, but one does tend to talk about people, and I get her to, and she doesn't mind; it gives us a subject we can both sink a tooth into, though I mostly listen. And she salts it up a little.

I learn that quite a few are mad down here, though she doesn't call it that, she calls it queer. Quee'ah. And why not? she asks—they are everywhere else from all you gather. And says that adultery

23

flourishes between hedgerows, or that at least there is a strong undercurrent of all that, not always visible to the naked eye. We're lively folk, she says, though we might look quiet to some, and it'll get out—Ellie himself—I know. They need a place to go sometimes, and they'll find one. What she means is, I think, that apart from work there isn't much to do. Or maybe what she means is that they're just like everyone else, the rest of us, churchgoers though they are, but that you don't expect it here. And I've wondered, of course, what lies behind the hard-work, weathered surfaces, within these small and quiet houses way down here. We're led to believe, by the lovers of the picturesque, that all is sweet, all sound. Not so, apparently. About farther inland one hears stories with a tone to them that would have been familiar to a Greek. I allude to this, indirectly, and find her nodding. Yes, so you hear, so the gossip is. Turn over a log and look to find all manner of crawling things under it. More coffee? she says, and I hold out my cup.

Yes, I've been looking at them with my inquisitive stranger's eye (at the men, naturally)—and see two types, in general: lean New Englander with his bony, taciturn face, often austerely beautiful so that you want to draw him, catch that line of forehead, cheek, and jaw, that angular long body bound with sinews under cloth, rough, patched, yet somehow elegant; and the other English country type (though I've read it is Norman), round-faced, rubicund, rotund—or burly (my word), tramping along in great rolled boots and oilskins of a bilious yellow. A type. Usually dark-haired. I fancy them. And the others fall in between somewhere as they mix and mingle. The lean ones look at you out of pale smoked-blue chips of glass, and their nerve ends, you imagine, lead down to the neurotic. The others, the large, slow-moving ones, seem to live in the flesh, immune to surface temperatures—to thrive as indigenous plants, to have roots that go down and down. But these are fine people, serious, involved with labor, with work; which they have to be to survive up here (*down* here). I'm one of your burly types myself, come to think. And could stand some proper work. I'll get at that garden, at that barn.

Standing to go, I admired the braided chair mats and she was pleased.

Guess where they come from, she says. Those was the ribbons from Ellie's memorial wreaths, and some others I had—couldn't bring myself to throw them away.

My bottom suddenly tingles, but I admire them with redoubled intensity. Make do—everything used to the nub.

THURSDAY 16 JUNE. Out of a mackerel sky last evening (barred, finally; red and black) rain today. It's splattering now from a gutter onto the granite flags by the grape arbor—a bright, cheerful sound. Sharp and metallic, it clatters down like a falling of silver spoons. A chance to do lady chores and not miss too much. So I cleaned and scrubbed at things that needed it. Cleaned out the stove in the upstairs sewing room, where I might paint someday.

I get to know this house better for tending it. I want to belong to it, as others in their times have—learn which creaks are which in the various weathers. Did winter find them out? Who, who lived here once, has perished at sea?

The old Stinson farm—most of the fields are now going back to woods. No, that's not right. It's more as if those delicate sapling spies beyond the wall were eying my ignorant apple. Yes, and to think how once, with ax and mattock, plow and hoe, they splashed that dark woods backward, then themselves sank impotent down the silent cold eclipse of time and the forest. I'll charge out there one day myself and have a go at them. My barn, too— where, here and there, a shingle slithers groundward, a board snaps loose. A farm, a real one, one to make a living from, breaks backs and minds up here. And the others—the majority? You see them along the roads, especially in the back country, abandoned finally, often with much of beauty about them still—a handsome cornice and a Greek Revival door. I've *got* to look in that barn, incidentally. I seem to remember things out there Herb and I once bought, old things from along Route 1, the leavings of those farms. Weren't there some humpbacked, ironbound trunks we were always going to look in again?—for love letters, or scrimshawed busks, old hats and bits of lace, old photographs? I'm leery of what might live out there. Large, energetic mice.

Things I need: Fels-Naphtha soap, and one of Mr. Bartlett's fine sprays for deodorizing old closets, musty mattresses. Some geranium slips I saw. I want a window sill lined with them. Yes, and that flint-ware glass Miss Sarah Brundage has, if I can ever catch her open—$3—which I think is not enough.

FRIDAY 17 JUNE. Evening. Yes, I'm liking this journal again. It's company—I talk to myself in it. Before or after supper.

Still gray outside. Trees blowing, a group of young birch (my spies) bend and toss, dancing to that enormous rhythm, invisible yet felt to the bone. I've built a fire against it, turned on the living-room lights. And now my fireplace irons stand in their forged shapes, my collection of wooden utensils, spoons carved, old ladies, butter molds, and along the mantel my slip-ware plates, a piece of Delft (bought at Parke-Bernet years ago). My chintz-covered chair looks sat-in under its lamp, my sofa ready to be. I neatened up the woodshed, expecting to be pounced at; I addressed myself to the kitchen's problems (never, all, to be solved). Old linoleum on the floor I'd like to see removed in favor of rugs (Jules Caster—can't come till next week)—I'll look for a tough old Bokhara.

Thinking of rain down the East River. Yes, and that other thing. It seems drunken now. Mendonca. Remote. When I consider him, I'm astonished at myself, as though I had gone on some crazy binge. I can't put it to use—I have no details that suffice, can't see him as human. That page I tore up when I did try—I don't know how to talk about it, and at moments I want to—at moments want him here, as if I had a right to him now. If B why not A—or C?

Things scudding along out there, as if breaking apart.

riverrun, past Eve and Adam's, from swerve of shore to bend of bay . . . and this wild lovely land around me now. I am on that river.

JOURNAL. Note: leave Mendonca alone—he could spoil something. Pornography.

JOURNAL. Coming to know this house, as it must be coming to know me. I want it to be as shipshape as a captain's wife would have had it. The yard, too—New England things—iris and lilac—by the wall larkspur, alyssum—and by the barn hollyhocks. A lawn glistening like emerald. Yes—I'll become a great gardener—I will, I promise.

JOURNAL. Fog blowing across the yard beyond the grape arbor—the barn, dark red, glows through. I imagine the harbor sunk in it. I'll go stand on an old stone wharf, think of history, the sea.

JOURNAL. Gertrude Hardy. Gertrude Hardy. I'm almost afraid to try to get it all down, though it shines in my mind, nearly word for word. I've been walking around with it all day. I'm afraid of the work, aren't I? afraid of missing, of doing her a bad turn.

I'll call it something. Was it Smollett who did? Fielding? Those stories he put in. "The Unfortunate Jilt." "Making Do."

God—my little fling—how it pales toward insignificance. . . .

From rain and fog, woke to a total brilliance (how suddenly it happens, like a coin flipped, a god winking one eye or nodding a blue-locked head to let it be known, That's enough). Things were celebrating, as if they had won through—birds noisy about it, gabbing—Here, *here*—see what I've found!—look at this *worm!*— left on the brown edge of a puddle.

So I made myself a fine breakfast—muffins from Bartlett's and orange juice, strong coffee that steamed in the sunlight as I poured. And knowing I would head out shortly for places unknown, I thought of Miss Jewett starting out for a walk with Mrs. Todd— to anywhere, though they always had a goal—and fancied I might find them along the road, would say, Won't you join me?—I'm out just looking at things. And in they would pile, scooping up skirts, high, sturdy shoes, a basket between them with a bottle of Mrs. Todd's spruce beer. We were going to see Mrs. Martin—the Queen's Twin, you know—won't you join *us?*

Oh, *would* I! Come back, sweet spirits, ladies, come back. I need to be one of you. Good women. They were. I am not. I am weird.

So I dusted a shell at a window sill, I watered a sick geranium. I was joining them, going to meet. And off I set.

And *had* an adventure, as they always did, nosing around. Down roads I've looked at going by.

You come out at the water's edge, almost always, of what might be a cove, an inlet, which the road might run along for a moment —gunk holes, they call them—and see granite bulging out under spruce, in a long, thick, sculpted flow. And sometimes a tiny wharf, with moorings, a boat. I begin to peer out from the dark, lichened spruce to the sea, which glimmers at me. You *see* islands out there, bay-sheltered ones, a frieze of many shapes and sizes. In a fog or mist they are Japanese, on a clear day Attic, Greek.

Yes, and down a sandy narrow lane among firs and spruce and old cut rotting stumps that moss grows around, I arrived at a cabin that seemed empty, damp, forlorn, a tiny wharf across the road from it that did look derelict—no boat; and since I had my sketching things along, I stopped and parked and walked out on the ledge. A most derelict wharf, gorgeously weathered, with a few traps piled on it, a tangle of old rope and flaking pot buoys; it stepped out into a cove of green water, much smaller than the Hales' (pilings out there boats must have moored at once). What is there about solitude—it's like standing at the edge of the grave for a moment, isn't it? safe yet aware of the inevitable. That place was like a cry of pain, muffled, indistinct.

So I returned to the car, took my things—and had squatted down on the rock, pleased as punch to have found the place— when something snapped or broke.

I had the feeling, instinctively, that she had been watching me, had finally made her presence known; though the feeling was also that she had just materialized. She wore men's clothes and had a lot of honey-colored hair drawn back in a careless bun. She just looked at me, and I, arrested, pencil in air, looked back. And eerie, somehow, or threatening, the silence across the intervening gulf—she was standing by small spruce—along a path in there. It was I who broke the silence. I said across to her, with a lifting, questioning cadence, I hope I'm not trespassing—I wanted to draw that wharf. At which she disappeared behind the spruce—and then I could see her coming around, picking her way, somewhat omin-ously, to where I sat, me hating the feeling of having intruded, and hating the thought that way up here in such a lovely, lonely place it might be resented.

And she came casually down over the rock, along smooth ledge of granite that seemed to flow out from under the roots of trees and the mossy wet black earth to the water. She came stepping her way, hands in pockets, a cigarette hanging from her lip, in-souciant, arrived, and without saying anything looked at a drawing in my box, a view of the Battery from my balcony, until I looked at it, too.

Not bad, I heard her finally say. That New York?

I nodded up at her.

Hands still in pockets, the cigarette—I saw her as good-looking —blonder than I am—lean—maybe forty-five—but that's just an impression. And no lady. I was sure of that. Not one of your Miss Jewett types, not at all.

I said, I'm sorry if I'm trespassing. Somehow I didn't think there was anyone here.

There ain't, she said—just me and the cat (which I saw had accompanied her but was keeping a sleek distance)—this is all private. I don't care much for company.

I'll leave, I said. I am sorry.

She let me hesitate a moment, then said a bit grudgingly, Oh, go on and draw—but I'm going to watch—that's the price—and I saw that she had humor, and had brought some of it with her. She sat down, saying, Don't mind me, I'm just one of the natives—ha!

And I drew; of course very badly with her watching me.

(Note to myself: take a rather handsome American woman and suggest something blighted about her—nothing quite visible—no tic or twitch—no sideways furtive glance—just something inner, *compulsive*—yes, that: held-in yet terribly anxious, *willing*, somehow, to let out. But I can't catch it, and can't do her speech—no g's to her *ing*'s, no *d*'s to her *and*'s, but I can't get it yet.)

We begin to talk. She: I haven't been there myself. I come from Dexter—ever heard of it?—well, it's about *that* big, so no wonder. I'm what you'd call summer people, too, around here.

I've quit New York, I said. I'm going to try it up here the year round.

She looked at me. Down here? she said. You must be kidding. You live by yourself?

So I did tell her a little about that, about Herb and finally wanting to get away, at which I saw her nodding. She didn't seem to mind listening, though perhaps it was more waiting than listening.

Men are jerk-offs, if you ask me, she said. Pardon the language, but it's a fact.

I know, I said. There's an assumption they all make, to wit, that they're there to run the world—and I keep saying to them, Yes, but look at it.

Yeah, look at it, she said—a fornicating mess. (That's what she said.)

But in no time, it seemed, out there on that clean, grainy, quartzlike rock, with the wharf, the spruce, and bugs we occasionally batted at (Goldarn flies), we were chatting away. About men.

Always wanting you for this or that, thinking they owned the place—though we seemed to agree that they did.

Don't get me wrong, she said—I like men—certain ones.

Well, of course, I said—who doesn't?

In fact, they, ah—come around, you know. She dropped an ash off her cigarette, rather carefully. Some of these lobstering cats—want a drink—want company.

She looked at me, and I, pencil poised, considered my pad.

And I let them, she said.

I began on a piling, trying for a long easy stroke down, but with an ear cocked, of course.

Which I suppose makes me some kind of character.

I held the pad out.

There ain't many places for a man to go down here if he wants to—and they'll drive around—drive and drive—you must of seen them—two to a car with a six-pack for company, and maybe a pint —all through these roads. Wanting somewhere to go is what they're up to. So I let them.

I would imagine, she said, when I didn't say anything, that must sort of put you off. She paused again.

Why should it put me off? I said, considering my drawing again.

Which seemed to baffle her a moment, as if she had *wanted* it to.

No reason, she said—just that most women figure there's something *wrong* with pleasing men.

They've been raised to believe they are the ones to be pleased, I said.

Right! she said—and I *let* them! Hey, I sorta like you. She's lonely, I thought. *Is* there no one she can talk to?

And heard her going on—But I won't have the kids around—no kids. It's the older ones I like. They want a place to come where they can sit and talk, have a drink—they bring it—and not get talked *about*, and I let them. None of your goddamn kids—I can't stand them.

I nodded assent, saying nobody could, that the young were unbearable—one of the reasons I had left New York—the generation gap—etc.

Which wasn't quite what she wanted to hear. Kids, she muttered, as if she had some fundamental grievance against them.

And settled in that warm, cozy little world of spruce and rock, of water and sunlight and flying things, I found myself after a while telling her about my fling—almost to hear what she would say—or what I would. . . .

So I bought this wonderful, well—costume—and went down there, scared out of my wits—and did meet a man—who watched me in the mirror for a while—
So what did he look like?
Well—big—heavy-set—
An older fellow, huh?
Yes, older.
How big?
Well—not tall, very—burly—I think you'd call him burly.
Yeah, I like them big. So go on.
So I embroidered a little, for her—she was, in a way, the perfect audience—and found myself getting it out—with interruptions—she wanting to know the details and I finally giving her a few, or making them up. What she also wanted, I learned, was company, reassurance. She was a woman who had had an experience, and one (not to make a poor joke of it) appropriate to the world she was part of, one that involved a good deal of "making do."

I can't explain to myself, I told her, why he appealed to me—at *all*. It might have had something to do with my father, whom I think I had a certain thing about.

At which she snorted. An old dad, she said, though not disparagingly.

Well—like that, I said.

But that's it, honey. Them older ones—they know, they're used to a woman—like 'em. Them kids—all skin, bones, and prick.

And all that I hadn't been able to tell Beth, or even myself, gradually came out, slightly nuttily. *She* supplied the words. I would use little blank, evasive ones, but the real ones were easy for her —she didn't give a shit.

So he ain't around now, she said, when I had finished (on a fairly high note, or for me). Too bad—he sounds nice—sort of like one of mine—I was kind of—taken by—one of your big ones. And when that one climbed aboard and started his motor up . . . She went on for a while (I was taken myself by the time she was through). . . .

TUESDAY JUNE SOMETHING. *Had* to leave off. Pages and pages and couldn't tell what they were like—too filled with my subject—total lack of objectivity, of coolness. Oh, God, how much has to be left out! Pages of the Mendonca thing thrown away (burned—I don't want them flying around on the dump like those sea gulls). The best thing, of course, is to leave out as much as possible.

At my desk window—morning now—writing on scratch paper until I get what I want, then transferring to this journal, which takes time. But if I go banging away, it ends up running all over the page like a broken egg. I made it sound as if she had blurted her secrets out. And she *did*n't.

I see her clearly enough to paint her, though.

She sits holding her knees, an American type, lean, angular, not young—looking down at water the shadows of the spruce have withdrawn from, leaving it sunlit, a black smoky green. Tide coming and her cove filling like a stone bowl. From somewhere light touches her face, lends it a radiance, and is kind to her eyes, which have crow's-feet at the corners. She has no make-up, of course. No bra on either, and I see that her breasts are small. She wears a blue workingman's shirt. She hasn't, I learn later, much of anything.

She says, You a writer of some kind?

And I lie a little again.

Have *I* got a book in *me*, she says. I couldn't write it down the way maybe you can but I've thought of it. Like you say you're interested in Maine, drive around and all. I could tell you about Maine—and not that down-East shit you hear all the time either. . . .

I can't quite spell it out, her voice—and it was important, that mixture of tones, Maine tones, her own wry, humorous, harsh inflections, and something matter-of-fact in the way she finally told me things that had happened to her—her story. I suppose she'd been working around to it. I remember her batting at flies. . . . We lived up above Dexter, she says. That's west of Bangor, you know—inland country—Nowheresville.

My mother died when I was maybe fifteen—I forget dates—but I remember her making an afghan for my birthday and she was in bed by then. I'll show it to you sometime, if you'd care to see— it's nice. She was a nice woman. And our dad cut wood, and raised potatoes and hay and what he could. It's poor country where we was—not much'll raise. But it was pretty, and we had a porch we'd sit on when the weather was nice and the chores was done, and on a good day we could see Katahdin—I could see it from my bedroom window upstairs—I liked to. And she'd have lemonade for us, or iced tea, and we'd sit out there after supper and look at the fields.

Sometimes he'd come in from logging and his back would be sore—had a cold in him from being in the weather so much. Ma had a lotion a woman around there made she would rub on him —one of my earliest recollections is of him coming in to wash, then going upstairs and she after him with that lotion, then the smell of it coming back down—camphor and pine oil and stuff. And with her sick I took up the rubbing of him myself. And then with her gone I kept on at it—he liked me to and it made me feel I was helping because we was country poor, which means no cash and a lot of making do. You might say all we had was the farm and Daddy's back.

At which she laughed, as at some not-funny private joke. One of your big country types, she said, and seemed to eye me with malice (though it wasn't that)—then added, Like that one you had —and waited a moment to see what I might say. That's why I like them big—because I liked him, the way a girl will her dad—ain't that so?

At which I shrugged, nodded, considering my drawing, then began to shade in some rocks, with her still watching me.

Yeah—*any*how, she said, he'd come in and wash up, then I'd rub him with that lotion, down in the room off the kitchen we'd put Mom in and he'd taken to using—he was missing her, as you can imagine. And it eased him—I'd rub him good—all over his back, his arms—Daddy had big arms from hoeing—and I was proud I could take up her place a little. I couldn't bring in no money, could only do chores and such, help out, and he needed the help (another laugh—a short, somewhat ugly one, again private). Yeah— like for his visiting life, you know—enter*tain*ment—he'd go to the Grange now and then. That was it. The Grange. He only had one real friend—Saul Hastings—younger than him. Them two would sit up and drink cider they'd made of a Saturday night with the radio on. That was their big time. No money for nothing else. All Daddy had was a tractor and an old truck half broke down all the time seemed like he was always fixing—fixing—fixing. But that's Maine for you, dear (de'ah)—"picturesque."

So I took up the rubbing of him as Mom had. And prided myself on it. I'd rub him all over, his arms, his back, him lying there like he was going off to sleep. And I come to like him in my hands like that, and I'd say, Turn over now, and he would. Lay your arms back, I'd say, and I'd ease that flesh, him lying there with his eyes closed letting me, and me feeling that I was pleasing him, and how good for him I was, and how good at it I was, and wasn't it good I could do this to help out.

And sometimes it seemed like I couldn't stop and like he didn't want me to—like I was healing him of something and if I stopped he'd be sick, like as long as I had him there things would be all right. Because I'd worry myself about what might happen if he should die and guessed I might have to go with Saul though didn't know if he'd take me in, me a girl and no good to him like a boy would have been. And I'd work into the bones with the grease, and knew how to—me only fifteen, around there—I'd work him an hour it seemed, turning him this way and that, getting his aches out, getting that sickness out of his bones.

And one evening after a long time of it I got tired, or sort of weak, it seemed, because he was a big man, Daddy was, and heavy and all—and lay down alongside of him, rubbing his chest, my head laying on his arm. And I found myself saying, Poor Daddy, like he was sick and missing her and I was comforting him. And then he turned and his arm come over me and I was rubbing his back and he was saying, Rub me good, honey, me saying, Poor Daddy, and his arm over me, us whispering like that—Rub me good—Poor Daddy. And I was feeling his breath on my cheek, him saying, Rub me, honey—rub me good. And I moved to get up to him so I could get at his back and we was lying together—Poor Daddy—and I was kissing him, like to comfort him—and then it seemed like he was kissing me back, had his arm around me. And then somehow he'd moved, was over me, on his elbows, whispering down, Rub me good, honey, rub me good—and I was rubbing his back with both hands, him over me whispering—and then was kissing, yes—and me all whirly inside and rubbing him. And then I kissed back, rubbing him and him holding me, and then me holding him, his body in my arms and my hands still at him because he was wanting me to and was breathing in my ear like he was running and me scared with him breathing like that, like he was sick or not him—and not me any more—just something happening—yes, and to me, so that I was scared but wanting it to, him—and him moving on me slow like something inside was hurting him—moved and moved like a kind of snake on me or I'd hurt his back. He was doing it, then, just that he'd changed and was needing me, yes, wasn't him any more, the way I'd rubbed him and all—and wasn't any more, was just holding him, scared, and him moving and moving, couldn't stop, and me scared and him going—know what I mean—it happening and me under him, not even there any more for him, him doing it—yes, and then come, I guess, come holding me, just breathing and lying on me.

Sitting there, arms hugging knees, with a rapt and faraway look, and sunlight in her hair, and me hearing this crazy torrent, listening to her . . .

So there was that—yes—and after that it got to happen regular because he wanted it to. Rub me good, honey—all over—holding him arms back for me. And got me to rub him naked one night— was just lying there when I come in—which scared me, seeing him like that, him seeming asleep—and then got to like, yes, what it did to him, and wanted to, and got on me again one night and I don't know how but got in, which did scare me, you can imagine, which I wouldn't let him do again because it hurt, made him promise not to but did, by having me rub him till I was wanting him to, and got me good, so that after that I did want him to, and he did, regular; and then it was exactly like I'd come to be his girl. . . .

I had stopped drawing and was looking over at the wharf, comforted by its clean old tangle of rope and buoys and traps, and at the green water, dancing and sparkling now with a breeze touching it—not quite able to take in, there and then, the fact, or the effect of it, that tale of illicit passion, not worn a bit thin, you gathered, by time. Some strong need she had to share or expose, express, it.

Then was hearing her again, going on . . .

Because there was that other man, Saul Hastings, that friend of his, who'd stay with us and drink cider Saturday night—slept down in Daddy's room where it was warm. And I'd sit up with them when they'd let me and listen to the talk, about land and crops, fishing and hunting, which they did together, men's talk, yes, and of women at times, though they weren't men who did talk much about women (except Saul liked some kind of dirty talk)—but mostly about their little things, their plans—the same ones, over and over. We all camped in that kitchen, you know—had the radio in there—it was where we mostly lived. Didn't have no real parlor or what you could call one—no heat—and Daddy had taken to the downstairs room we'd kept Mom in, had their big bed in it. Upstairs it was all peeling wallpaper and loose plaster we was always going to fix and never did—a hall and three rooms—I liked it up there.

Green lawn out there in glass-clear light. Why am I loving writing all this madness down? What *am* I up to? I've got to stop again. My hands are shaking. And something is missing, I'm *not* getting it. I make it sound as if she were blurting it out. It did come more and more compulsively, but it achieved a flow; and I'm leaving me out, in my role as listener, as audience—my nods of understanding, agreement, the times I held my drawing out—the sense of the two of us there—yes, and the way the sunlight came around us—the way I kept thinking, This is Maine—I'm listening to, looking at, Maine—it is like this, or like this, too; in the midst of this clean brilliance, this hurt woman—this twisted life. Though, of course, I had heard only part of it. . . .

Yes, I always liked the water, she was saying. And I liked it down here because they did. They liked to camp, liked to cook and drink whiskey when they had it, take a little boat out Saul had, set a trap or two, though you could get shot at around here doing that. Daddy was happy down here—hadn't had no time off or such except when he and Saul had gone fishing. So I kept coming here myself.

And then one by one, some excuse or another, the men got to coming around. I already knew one Saul had known—kind of an odd one—still comes around—runs a market up to Tainesville where them summer folk are. Mostly comes down to drink.

And they'd putt in—ask could they set out a trap, or did I want any fish or short lobsters. You can imagine. And one loaned me a motor for Saul's boat, a five-horse, give me some traps, showed me how to set them—and one come down in a truck— word gets around—you can imagine. So here I am.

She had stopped, rather abruptly, was just sitting there, so I said, I don't wonder they do come around, the men—you're pretty, you know. Perhaps I'll ask if I can draw you sometime, though I'm not good at people.

You think so? she said. She looked pleased. Not some old bag?

You have wonderful bones, I said. You've got lovely hair.

Well—you're not bad yourself, you know. You look like . . . what? like a German—you got nice hair, too.

I'm a fat mess—I'm digging my grave with my teeth.

Naw—it, ah—becomes you. Me, I'm all bones. Some of them

kid me about it. Like one used to come here I sort of liked—big, *fat* son of a gun—one of them lobstering cats—I got to fat you up some, dear—and I'd tell him, Screw you, you got enough for the both of us. He'd be at it half the night, till I'd tell him, Jesus H. Christ, get your rocks off or I'll be dead when you do, and he'd say, Shut your goddamn mouth, I ain't even started yet. I liked him. He used to bring a friend around—he'd sit by the stove and watch like we was two movie stars. Nutty, huh? I didn't give a goddamn—and the big one would try to coax him over—drunk, you know.

Well, there is some odd ones around—get to be what you might call peculiar down here, loners and all—like one they call Moose—Moose Delow or Dello, or something—Bull Moose—they tell me lives on an island out there—Frenchboro, I think—has a boat, a black one. Ain't all there, they say—I used to dream he'd show up here one evening, because he knows I'm here. And sometimes I wish he would, because I get nutty myself.

She flipped a cigarette away and it lit in the water with a tiny hiss, and we were silent a moment.

Well—so what do you think? she said. And when I didn't answer right away—Yeah, that I'm bad, a nut—I know.

I shook my head, not out of some sense of compassion only, but because of an odd reasonableness about her, the sense of an under-life I seemed half to recognize, down even to the shadowy figure of that Moose Delow, whose name I instantly responded to . . . Mendonca.

And felt her watching me.

You mean you believed all that? I heard her say.

I looked at her, rather taken up short, because I had, and heard her laugh, as if she had pulled a good one on me. Well, don't, she said. I'm a liar, I make things up—I tell myself stories.

She was looking at me again, sort of sizing me up, was hauling out another cigarette—and I noticed how yellowed her fingers were, mahogany, how bitten her nails. When it was lit she waved it. I probably shouldn't have told you. And then, with a bit of false humor, I get carried away. Ha ha.

After a moment I said, Which part wasn't true?—*some* of it was.

I saw her looking at her held-out cigarette, then heard her say, None of it—*all* of it. Then—You actually want to hear? You're a lady, one of these nice summer women around here—I can tell.

I'd like to hear what's true, I said, a little primly. I am nice but I don't mind the truth. (I'm trying to learn it.)

Well, I'm bad, she said. I make me *sound* okay—because it didn't happen like that.

She played with the cigarette a moment, rolled it between her fingers.

She said, He wasn't too smart, you know, my daddy. All he had was that back—and a good heart. He was lonesome, you know, like I told you. And a good man—I didn't tell you that, but he was—didn't have no mind, but he had a good heart.

I had the mind. I got gold stars in everything—I was tops in that little hick school, and always showed him my report card which he liked to see though he couldn't read—I'd point out the letters —it made him feel proud. Simple, you know.

And we'd be in that house. You should of seen it, dear (de'ah) —stuck out in those fields like somebody'd put it there to be shot at. Just us and a little radio we had—all winter.

You ever been in a winter here? she asked. Well, you wait. Snow piling up—nowhere to go—no one to *see*, except Saul when he come around—which he did—that was true.

And Daddy'd be out working at snow, chopping or hauling wood working at a garage—whatever he could to get a little work in for us. And, yes, it did happen that one time like I told you—or more or less, because I can't remember now, I been telling it to myself for so long but more or less—him wanting his back and arms rubbed and me rubbing them. Except it was me that *made* it happen—a hot-pants kid who didn't even know she was. They didn't teach that in that school I got those gold stars in—sex education.

And after it he felt bad, and wouldn't look at me or talk for quite some time. Yes, and that I thought and thought about it, you can imagine, not clear about parts of it, like what had happened to him, though had a kind of idea from being on a farm—and partly scared of it and partly wanting us to again.

And after a while I got back to putting the lotion on him, though he'd act kind of grudging at first and would say, That's enough. So I learned to be easy—and smart—and would miss times as though I'd forgot, two, three in a row. And come in on him one night—it was summer by then—him lying there in his shorts. I got that lotion, I said—I forgot. I had my nightdress on. And I rubbed him awhile, scared he'd say quit—I just rubbed his back, seeing it through my fingers in the dark in there. I was gentle and moved real slow as if to comfort him—and then worked his shoulders some. I said, Reach your arms up, Daddy, scared he'd say no, but he done it, and I worked them a little, and then down under them alongside his chest. And then I was working all over his back, and then I risked it and said, Turn over, Daddy, I'm through on your back. And after a minute he did—turning slow like he was a log not wanting to move but flopping itself to another spot, then lying with his arms back for me and his head to one side.

And then I was rubbing his chest again, rubbing down to where his undershorts was. I had him in my arms and I was in his again, and I was breathing and was scared, because what I was wanting was for him to want me like he done before, and was scared he wouldn't. It was that I was wanting, not him so much as him wanting me—I wanted him to want me. So I moved to get my arms over him more, and felt his breath at my mouth, almost touching, my mouth and his, and felt him breathing like I was, us breathing together, and his arm over me, yes, and then him, somehow—like I had slid under him or him rolled a little—and I had both my hands on his back and him over me like before, and his mouth at my ear. Then his mouth come onto mine like that was part of it, and that scared me, him kissing me like he was sucking an orange, and he come butting up into me like I once seen a goat, and hung there, and come, I could feel—come all over me.

So then I did know he wanted me though he thought it was wrong, and knew I wanted him to even though he did.

And I'd get after him, him out of the house early, coming in late, going early to his room, keeping away from me, and me thinking about him all day, knowing, or guessing, that he wanted me, and me wanting him to. And I found out little ways—like keeping away from him myself, acting like he'd hurt me in some way. And in a house like ours was you feel those things, you can hear them—I could *smell* him wanting me.

In school all I'd think about was him. He'd be in my mind like a mosquito whine you can't locate. And I'd plan not to talk when I got home.

And sure enough, I'd find him bringing me something, an arrowhead he'd found, some old Indian thing out in the field—we had a collection. But I'd keep away, wouldn't make up, and could see him watching me, following me around with his eyes—I'd catch him in a pane of glass, or the mirror over the sink, looking at me. Or he'd try to talk, say something—him without easy words, you know. Most times I did the talking for us, like tell him some little thing about school, what this one or that had said, what we'd heard about Mr. Jackson, the teacher, what girl was going with what boy—which one had got a car. Or about the hens I kept—I had names for them all and used to tell him about them, which one was sick and where they'd hide an egg. But we weren't strong on talk—you generally ain't, you know, when it's only two, three makes the difference—all you have is the same things to say, like him and Saul at the cider Saturday night. When your world's that small there ain't too much to *say*. And I'd keep my back to him and keep quiet as I could.

Till one night I heard him puttering around down in the kitchen after I'd gone up to bed. He'd been restless all evening, wanting me to talk, asking about this and that, or complaining about his back, that it was certain sore. And I heard him down there, moving about, which wasn't like him—generally he just went to bed, along about nine—didn't have no TV, you know. And after a while I heard him coming upstairs. And then in he came and I smelled it.

I brung the lotion, he said—you going to rub me tonight? It was summer still and he had on his shorts. So I let him lay down. And up there in that room, fields outside, hearing the crickets—didn't have no screens, you know—muslin curtains was all—up there in that room we knew something had come on us— no one nowhere around, just us up there where he'd never been before. We knew, could tell. Rub me, he said—rub me good. And I wanted to, but I said, Rub you good? Rub me good. All over? I said. I saw him nod. Daddy?—all over—because I did want to hear him say that. Rub me all over, he said, and I seen he was crying.

And I did—got his back, got his arms, made him turn over. And then I was rubbing his belly for him, and then rubbed in under the shorts—how did I know to do that? a girl—and his hand come down and caught at my hand—then it went away. And then I was unbuttoning them for him and it caught me again and held awhile, like a trap, my hand in his, then it went away, and there it was, like some part of him meant for me he was ashamed of.

And I rubbed him all over, him naked then—I knew I wanted something, and knew he did, too—and knew he'd know what to do if I done it right. And I did do it right and he done it, though he was afraid of it, but I wanted him to. Do it, Daddy—get on me. And he did—couldn't help it by then. And me scared but wanting him to, helping him, we doing it together. Don't let me hurt, honey—You ain't, I said, get it in me—me wanting him, and crazy, you know, because it was him, my daddy, and I was wanting him bad, and him me, and all whirly inside like before only knowing what it was of him I wanted now, yes, hot and breathing with him like we was running together, working to it—I didn't know what a man was like hot—and for me—hot for me. . . . Do you?

I saw her look at me a moment. I shook my head.

Him wanting me like that, me in his arms and him whispering me things, calling me honey, hot—he was—I didn't know, except that I had him, talking, whispering things I'd never heard, and going on me, and me under him, big, huge—he was huge—and couldn't let me go, hung on and did me again.

So I learned what love was, hot love—that it was wanting someone wanting you, and then having him. And I knew I had him then, my daddy—and later I made him say it, say it wasn't bad like he'd been thinking. Say it ain't bad, Daddy, say it, I told him, go on. And he did.

And he did—all the time, once it had happened, once we had done it together seemed like there wasn't no end to it, to him wanting me—he could screw me down to a nub—strong, you know, and hot.

And it made him happy again. I'd hear him humming out in the woodshed, out on the porch. And he got out and fixed up a guitar he'd once had—he could play it some, too. And he'd bring me little things from town he thought I might fancy. Daddy hadn't no more brain than a cat.

Sunlight in the cove and me no longer drawing, just holding the pad and she telling me, as if she'd never had anyone to, eagerly and as though the words didn't matter. Yes, she is intelligent, in a way—and him, as she said, with no power to stretch or grow. Yes, it was she who managed it, kept it alive. . . .

And of course it did happen, she says—

I guess maybe I was going on eighteen, and he'd been at me as if we was man and wife, and me at him, no pill, you know— nothing. And I said, You got to get me Saul, I said—you got to talk to him. And he didn't want to, of course, he wanted that baby for his own, but I said how could we, what would folks say, and that maybe they were already. You talk to Saul, I said—tell him he ought to come up here first, that you want him to. And I listened, through the floor grate, and heard them talking about it. And it was hard for Daddy to, him wanting me for his and wanting that child and afraid to tell Saul whose it was, and no talker anyhow—slow. Been fucking some boy, Saul said. And I heard Daddy say, I guess. Won't say who, huh? She don't like to, Daddy said. And that Saul was cunning, you know, and could sniff out a thing or two, because Daddy hadn't been with him like they used to, hadn't been listening too much, been falling asleep on him. I heard of one her own father got to, Saul said—them two just like man and wife, yes, and the mother still with them—seems like it's natural to some—not you? And Daddy said, Not me. And Saul—I would of, yes sir—teach her how it should be done—what a daddy's for—come on, Ham, certain you did. But Daddy held out on him, though later I told him myself.

And Saul went along with it. And I liked Saul, him being like Daddy, older than me and all, fat and strong—was black-haired but bald on the top (Daddy was bald as an egg, had a fringe of it left, like whaddaya callit—a wreath—them bald men's hot, you know—I read that)—and thick in the prick, he called himself—he was, too, though nothing like Daddy—and like I told you had this place. And he'd bring Daddy and me down and we liked it, we all did. And Saul did marry me and the baby was born dead so I told him whose it was one night and he said he'd figured, and after that I had the both of them, though we was quiet about it.

A cigarette flicked away.

Yes, and then Saul died and left us this place, and I went back with Daddy, and then he died and I sold the farm and moved into Dexter and went to work. I work when I feel like it now and spend what time I like down here.

Well—that's Maine for you, ain't it, de'ah? She looked at me, not unfriendly but sardonic. Woods and mean land and folks that's got to make do, and all of it pretty as a picture. She seemed to pause—but she had me now, was telling it.

Oh, you ain't heard the half of it. Fifteen years I was with that man, my daddy, and loved him—yes, and hated, too—for growing old on me. I got to see it, you know, how his flesh had grown fat like or aged, here and there, and how his face had gone loose—so I'd see him as ugly and old—me still young, you know—and get after him for it, which he couldn't help, and keep him away. And him crazy, you know, to be with me—Saul gone who'd been company for him—Saul used to fool with him some, you know—ea'ah—and him still hot for me. I've had him on his knees at my door. And then I'd go for him. I'd make him get me the cider and I'd get drunk with him, drunk as all hell, get us naked in that kitchen, and the radio going, weather from Rockland, news—get him naked in there, me, too. Let me look at you, Daddy. Oh, I knew plenty about being some little bitch and kept him satisfied—and had stillbirths—none of them come out right— four, five—and something else—and no doctor, you know—we would have had six, eight children if something hadn't been wrong. And I kept him satisfied fifteen years, mean as a two-legged cat—and him not even knowing it was wrong any more as he used to think.

Yes, and then a stroke of some sort come on him—first one, and I cared for him through it and done what I could, scared all the time—and then one other—and that one took him off. And I went plumb out of my mind and sat in that house for near a year, and him in the ground alongside of Mom—in a pretty little place not far from there—where I'd go see him and sit on the grass where they was and tell them I wanted them back.

It wasn't me she was telling it to. I was a key that had unlocked her room, with its rotten muslin curtains, maybe a shell once put at the window, pathetic, a sign of allegiance to the sea. I was a bowl into which it all poured.

So I'm waiting for that Moose Delow to show up and get back at me for all that, she said. And I'll survive it, too, and feel like he put me where I belong. And being looney, he will. Word gets around, you know—he knows I'm here.

And he'll come putting in one evening in that black boat, and I'll be standing in that door. And he can have what he wants of me —though it don't cheer me none to think of it, him so odd and all—like something out of them woods, they tell, something dark, and weird—they tell me he's big as that piling—he'll do for me proper, too, and get even for Daddy—and I've earned it, I know —he'll be something I can't bear, and I've had some rough ones out here, but I'll let him in.

Me seeing her as part of something belonging to history now, to another time, when loneliness and poverty and bad luck were commonplace and did people in, rendered them odd, slightly mis-shapen. And yet New York, I said to myself, misshaped me.

But she was through with it now—like a long drift of fog it had passed—she casual again, there on that granite ledge, in sunlight, though me seeing her from a different angle now—complex—the wornness of her clothes, her bitten nails. I was drawing again. Inventing. A and B.

Yes, we did, as the saying goes, strike it off, though I couldn't quite tell whether I liked her or just the adventure of it. So I hesitated to say, Drop around, because she didn't seem the type who did, for one thing. It was she, finally, who said for me to.

Come on around sometime, she told me—I've got some pictures and things—hand paintings. Probably junk.

I was holding my drawing out rather ruefully. Good, she said. And when I said, on impulse, Would you like it? She hesitated. Well, I couldn't take it from you, she said.

Oh, please do, I said. I'll come out and make another—and maybe one of you. And I told her my name.

Mine's Gertrude, she said—I guess I told you—Gertrude Hardy. Come around if you like. Not many people do.

Moose Delow—*de l'eau?*—like a storm out there. Sea beast. And suddenly those islands are populous with him. Seals on rocks. And he, shepherd of them, like Proteus, naked and mad. I know him. Water-fire-serpent.

How to wring the truth from him?

Answer: Hold on.

And I will someday, if I ever get that far.

I'm relieved to be through with this. So hard to catch even a glimmer of it all. Gertrude Hardy. The hand has written. How much is true?

TUESDAY 21 JUNE. Began serious garden work, finally. Weeding, mostly—clearing things out. Only that bed by the wall that has the delphinium, the iris—iris—those beautiful tough fans of green, the great purple orchid heads, too flamboyant for New England, one would think, almost tropical. Some stand now at my window looking in, tall as young horses, muzzles of velvet—wild—curious.

Jules Caster bashing around in the kitchen—getting that lino-leum up. A relief.

44

THURSDAY 23. Entry: Sitting in my car at the P.O.—letter from Beth—two girls walking by in stretch pants—one saying, And when I told her I'd got those pink pillow slips with the lace fringes, she almost shit. . . . I guessed they were sixteen. Men clomping along in rolled boots. "Oi ain't see'd hoide n' hey'a o'a" . . . muttering to each other—"hoide'n toide'n all"—untranslatable . . . language, language. I did hear "Oi'm toime toide"—sea water gargled in haired throats—didn't I? "Oi?" . . . One of them I saw as the soul of this place—grizzled, enormous, with bull shoulders and a rolling gait . . . "toime—toide" . . . wearing a gray knit cap. One of Gertrude's? (or mine?) A? B?

SATURDAY 25 JUNE. Jules busy, clattering in and out, checking pipes.

I nosed around again. Tried out a road or two. Hardly know what I expect to find, any more than I do in my page of Joyce a day. Another world, or more of this one I don't know.

I saw an island that almost broke my heart. Three of them, really, an offshore group. Uninhabited.

To think that there are still spots in this world, places, that beautiful, that untouched. Not for long. In less than a hundred years there will be fifty billion of us—or some terrifying number like that.

SUNDAY 26 JUNE. Trying to remember something Sarah Orne Jewett said about New England eccentrics, people isolated. I keep running across her in my mind—must get that book. Something about people given a better chance. Toynbee—about cultures. Same thing.

Still stunned, more or less, by GH. Mad—north by northeast. Something she said about one and a half that I had to ad-lib. My mind wandered a moment. A half? The one who watched? Her image of a log rolling over by itself—I liked that—suggestive, some-how—and right. I see an arm flop. Sense of inner abandon, a giving up—or in. Same thing? I did write Beth that I had met her, this woman, who had had a peculiar girlhood. Life with father up in Maine. No joke to me, but I was whimsical. Mendonca and me—Daddy and her—that peculiar attraction to the father, the old bulls, she called it—both possessed, oddly enough, of gentleness.

And Moose Deleau, who of a foggy night might haunt *me* anon. Must find out more about him.

Meanwhile, more gardening. Got the wheelbarrow out. (What is a barrow?) Bought a new bamboo rake, some gardening gloves. Squatting in sunlight hearing the birds.

Jules Caster almost through.

ENTRY: Funny, nasty little note from Jeremy—about had I seen a movie: 2001. And the wildest drive down B'way he's ever had, in a drunken taxi at 100 mph at night. And ending in a "Louis Soixante-neuf" bedroom, all curlicue and "cocksucker white"— told me they were all redoing like mad. That voice from the past (I must write him)—yes, and about a new book of poems by Lowell—but I don't trust his judgment.

THURSDAY 30 JUNE. Mrs. Bean does not *know* GH but has heard rumors, remarks. Asked about the Moose. Yes, him, too, though in no detail. An eccentric, out there. Then May Stinson came in and we got shunted off.

FRIDAY 1 JULY. Got the mower started (by taking it to Cauldwell's). Lost five pounds so far mowing the g.d. lawn, in sweat shirt, jeans, and sneakers. The yard looking at the moment like a recently clipped recruit, and me fallen into wicker chair, legs out, eyes glazed. But worth it. I may let the grass under the apple trees grow, beyond the wall over there. Then I will have, starting from this window, lawn, delphiniums against a wall, apple trees and tall grass, granite ledge, then spruce, or spruce and fir, to be exact. And the barn helping to frame things, hold things in.

Jules has finished—*finally*. Mrs. Bean said, He's slow, but hold a "ya'adstick" next to him and you can see him move.

But my Toro plowed on through and I felt virtuous. Kept looking back at the house, which seemed to enjoy having its out- as well as its insides attended to. A good house, with style—something between Greek and early Gothic revivals (in the romantic mind, apparently, Greek and Goth were cousins)—lots of molding —rich, heavy cornices and lintels—a veranda someone tacked on —then a string of sheds wandering out from the kitchen like afterthoughts, each one appropriate. If I ever have it painted, it'll be a dusty red to match the barn.

But how well it sits in its bowl of a yard. Whoever turned its back to the road knew what he was doing—near things and yet private, with its neat little grassed-in courtyard there for the car. Grapevines over an arbor.

Old clapboards in sunlight make a fine pattern.

I *must* go look inside, clean out, that barn.

SATURDAY 2 JULY. Fog again. It came in this afternoon like a third-act opening curtain. As dark came on I walked in it, walked up the road. A car came toward me, touched its horn going by— one of those "cut-downs"—one man in it (one of Gertrude's big ones—moon-faced). I turned to watch its profile against the lit-up fog it passed into, calling after it, Who are you?—come in for a drink—only I didn't. Sweet, and serious, the fog, about its business of hiding things, such as an old wharf.

And I thought of Mendonca, had an image of his freighter tied to a pier somewhere, in fog under wharf light, portholes dark— imagined him gone into town, lonely as I and hopeful, down some dark street that women stand along—bar town. Odd twinges of something like pain come around my heart. I would like him here.

I hear the horn from Black Horse Shoals. My fire is going. And since it's Saturday night I feel that I've earned a martini. I'll get supper with it. . . .

Drawn back to it, this desk, this mirror-window into the night of the fog—to write—thinking about Gertrude H.—yes, and that Saul Hastings (I'll leave her old dad to her), who probably told dirty things in bed; she up cold and shivering, listening down, at fourteen. Hearing what? Feeling what? Left out. He telling her father dirty things—to what purpose? To excite them both of a winter night. Can I imagine it? But *then* what?

Would I have liked rubbing my father's back? A broad one, too, Mallek's? Mallek–Mendonca here, to share a drink, this fire, this fog, then slowly to undress me, and me him. Can I imagine it? Or him of the moonface riding by—touching his horn—little merry blue eyes and a way of taking his sweet time. That car—driving up, lights flicking silently out. Can I imagine it? Indeed I can. Big jolly white buttocks rolling and heaving like a sea, little merry blue eyes looking at me, for signs of passion, as Mendonca's did, though his eyes were dark and he was trying to please, fucking me on the sofa, then on the floor.

Drunk, old girl—and bawdy, too. To bed. Those word are rich fare.

But why *can't* I use them? write about it, my Mallek–Mendonca thing? Sense of something watching—cold, critical gaze from a past I still venerate.

Oh, include—include. Mrs. McNab—the good women—Mendonca—Gertrude—that moon-face. Don't leave out, put it all in—you've written the Mallek thing, the Gertrude thing—don't harp —create.

Sunday morning (July 3)

Beth,

It's me, from the land of sunlight and fog. Fog last night, then I woke to this—early robins, a cool brilliance in the yard—and the shadows fled away.

Oh, love—not to join me yet, but how I think of you—how at times I need you, just for talk. I have very few to do that with. I'm learning already to talk to myself, for myself. Hence the journal—indispensable—a secret weapon against all that. Though I say to it only the commonplace (with occasional lapses), since my mind on which this world writes the simplest things night and day is a blank now. Nothing to write *about* except fog—rain —the sea.

I'm beginning to have a thing about the sea—you know me—like my tugboats back then—only worse, I think, more dangerous. Here, on the land, the farm, I'm cozy as a mouse in cheese—and then I think out, into green impossible silences. I don't know yet what they mean. I wait as patiently as I can to find out. It may take months or a year. See: I'm beginning to talk like that about time: a year—when probably Herb and Sal will come shouting up to say, We want it for summer vacations.

Irises are still out. They do make a display over along the wall where the grape arbor runs. I've cut the grass and it shines like a river now, so that I seem to live in a pool of sunshine and water. The lilacs have gone. I kept wanting to send armfuls to everyone. Mrs. Caster and Mrs. Bean—who "stayed the corruption and the rot" (that woman had a thing about the sea, too—I'm reading *To the Lighthouse* again now)—I'm going to have coffee with them this afternoon—saw them yesterday and said I'd stop around if okay. So let me cease now, to pick up when I get back. . . .

Hello, again. I'm fairly excited. A various and sinister (?) female named Ethel Hale was there, who knew every nook and cranny of this place, every inlet and island, and is, in fact, something of a realtor—and after me, talking islands in the most subtle way, simply because I had mentioned a beauty I'd seen. Of course I must avoid her like the plague. She has asked me to have supper Wednesday. But we all gabbled like gulls (*they* did), and a few minnows got through the nets of their talk. They gossip among themselves— let me listen, overhear. It's their substitute for books—or maybe books are our substitute for their stories, their hints and guesses.

I thought of New York, my apartment; yet nothing built there, and here everything builds. And into some mysterious future I'm going to accept. You didn't realize, did you, that your friend was a famous seeress. One always wondered what went wrong. I feel, somehow, that I escaped, though I no longer feel so frantic about those subjects—the Decline of the West. Let them blow themselves up, it would hardly touch us down here.

Yet as something here ripens and purifies, something else grows, too. That irrepressible female thing. I've never been able to talk sex with you in that point-blank way some friends do. We've never needed to. And yet—it flares up in me and at times I write it down. When my journal is sent to you some day, as it may be, you'll see, and I hope understand, and if I haven't written it well enough, read between the lines, be charitable. You are my posterity. They say women don't like each other without ulterior motives. That's not true—I love you.

Enough. The fire is flickering. My martini is gone. I'm on page seven of *Finnegans Wake*, which is further than you ever got. Wish me well and give love and regards to Bill, and to any of the children who still remember me. Write.

JOURNAL. Islands. Something that lives out there pulls at me, some huge lightness—or darkness—something that would never let go. Mindless. Divine.

Telling me he liked to please. And in pleasing becomes pleased. His body in my arms like some warm barrel, flexible, in slow snakelike rhythm, pleasing me—my moans drove him deeper and deeper—listening, moving on me, listening, listening—probing for the source, watching my face—each sound of pleased anguish a gift I made him of himself, a mirror to that need in him, an echo-

49

ing wall to his own male pleasure. Oh, leave off—*basta*—genug—for Christ *sake*!

How did it go?

Mrs. Caster and Mrs. Bean—and the "sinister" Ethel Hale of Goose Cove—who isn't really but who knows a thing or two.

I said to them, I've been wandering around. There is so much that we take for granted but never quite see.

And Mrs. Bean (Carole) in her down-East accent that is almost Virginian, Been he'ah fauty-five ye'ahs and nevah been to Bah's Neck (which meant anywhere).

And Mrs. Caster (Elizabeth) said, Jules takes me fishing now and then, but he's got his special places so we never get nowhere, not even to Isle au Haut. I want to go to a "Thu'sday night dahnce out the'ah" sometime.

And I—What I've been doing is driving down these little roads. You see islands out there, like these. You wonder who they belong to. I was telling Carole about one, and a woman I met, and wondering if any of you knew her.

I paused, or they did.

Gertrude Hardy, Mrs. Bean said. We don't know her, de'ah—we've heard a thing here and there, is all.

And Elizabeth Caster, I think, said, She's not what you'd call nice, de'ah—and I'm not one to slander.

She's dirt, one said. They gabbed a moment, until Mrs. Hale said sensibly, Why not let Mrs. Calder tell *us*?—she's the one who's met her. And to me, What's she like?

I was already feeling protective. Well, good-looking, in a way —and I thought hard. She seemed very much alone.

I waited while they sort of eyed each other, for precedence.

Elizabeth said, We hear she ain't quite right in the mind.

Good-looking? Mrs. Hale asked.

What we hear, Carole Bean said, and almost leaned forward, is that men go there—and I don't mean that she takes in boarders. It's common knowledge, de'ah.

Nice property? Mrs. Hale said.

Yes, fine property, I told her. A cove—very private. Belonged to some people named Brandon, I think—so she said. Then a man named Hastings, a cousin, whom she was married to.

I saw them listening to me. She had a child by him, who died —she works in Dexter now.

Well, she's been much talked of, off and on. She don't come to our stores, gets her mail up at Tainesville, you know—I'll say that for her.

She mentioned someone rather odd, I suddenly said—someone she called Moose Delcau, who lived on an island.

Which one? Mrs. Hale asked.

She didn't say.

Deleau?

A kind of hermit, I gathered.

Seems to me I did hear something, Mrs. Caster said. There is odd ones about—like take them Ingersoll brothers lives over by French Bend—you know them, Carole—up towards Fulsom Neck —ea'ah—peculiar, hermits, and I don't know what all.

Mrs. Bean said, Them islands used to be 'habited, you know, quite a few—to keep from the Indians, you gather, or for the fishing. Yes, folks lived out there then, same as they do now down to Isle au Haut, or Swans, or out to Matinicus—and on a few small ones, too—you'll find a camp here, a camp there. You know it, Ethel.

And Mrs. Hale—Oh, they're lived on. Mostly by summer folks now.

And me—Who owns them? You see them out there, and it never occurs to me to ask.

Families around. Or the state. Yes, families, who talk of selling them and moving to Florida. Elmo knows them, the islands.

And Betty Caster—Islands are lonely places—I wouldn't do on one at all.

And Mrs. Hale—But you take that Natalie Best, who writes, and has that aa'tist husband—says she hates to come in all summer, even for mail. (And she looks at me, sort of surreptitiously. I'm looking forward to Wednesday—partly, of course, because it will be my first meal out. I want to see her house.)

Mrs. Bean said, There's one we used to picnic on when I was a girl—you know it, Ethel—Sheep.

And Ethel: Elmo does. Elmo knows them all, from Drunkard's Ledge and York to Stonington, and east and west of that, too. Pennyless—now you take that one—Elmo used to camp out there with Richie and the boys. I've been there. It's my favorite.

And Mrs. Bean: Our dad used to take his boys out, too.

Yes, they do, Betty Caster said—Jules tells me—the men— they'll plan for it, take beer, take whiskey, take a boy or two—

fix up a fire. Yes, and get down to men's talk, you hear—you can imagine.

That's men's country, them islands, Carole Bean says. I believe they're haunted, too. They found Ellsworth's dory on Pennyless, you know (she's looking at Ethel).

That Pennyless, Mrs. Hale says—now that one's for sale. Not many are (and her head turned and she looked at me).

And I do believe that's where he is, Mrs. Bean says—and Mrs. Hale says, Yes, de'ah—and to me, What they want now is a house on shore, instead of the island.

A house on shore. . . .

MONDAY 4 JULY. A few distant pops—perhaps all that is left of what is being celebrated. I think of bunting, statues—I think of Asia and wonder how wrong we are. Very wrong? It would be terrible if we were. Shouldn't the Chinese have a Monroe Doctrine (a Manchu Doctrine)? Why can we go to their borders, or to Turkey, but no one come here, as to Cuba? Three enormous powers who have to get along (no choice), and can't. And I can find no fault anywhere. Or everywhere. What are the answers to greed and fear? Pop. Bunting.

THURSDAY A.M. 7 JULY. Supper last night at the Hales'. She *is* various. I like her. And I liked them.

A fine old house (seeing it at the cove on my walk that day, then being in it—as if I had made a bit of progress)—stretched out, with verandas overlooking the cove and a string of mustard-yellow dories, floating like marvelous birds. We ate in the dining room shortly after I arrived (I felt as if they had been waiting, it came out so promptly)—eight of us counting me: Ethel, her husband, Elmo, a friend or younger man who lives with them (Richie something), and the children, two boys and two girls, nine to sixteen, none of them very pretty but fresh as laundry.

Ethel is small and brisk and efficient, though not pushy. She moves knowingly about, tending things, letting herself be waited on when it suits her; she gives the impression that it is she who keeps things going—a nice dryness to her, a New England wit, exceedingly spare, intelligent (does she snipe at him a little?—they are such a family that of course I couldn't tell—but maybe something—in some hidden way short of temper now, or impatient with the old routines).

And him, Elmo, the husband—a Norman—black-haired, ruddy-faced, rotund, monolithic, and like his name, dressed in the proper clothes (yes, I had seen and admired him in town—and in that car, I think, in the fog)—a black-and-red checked wool shirt, khaki trousers, leather moccasins; the friend, Richie, a little like him but leaner, younger, pinker of cheek, and blond, and immensely reserved or shy—reserved to the point of speechlessness—and resembling, a little, a baroque angel: all curls and curves, a rubbery body, not fat; muscular, one would guess (I looked for tiny wings). Large babyish blue eyes that gaze without seeing you, so it seems. He goes lobstering with Elmo—is a kind of protégé, an extra son, I gather.

And the children, the girls older—Betsy?—sixteen? Not one of your shit talkers at all. A certain amount of giggling, because of me. But all of them, except Ethel, were shy at a stranger in their midst. And I did my best, I helped with things, and Ethel let me with no fuss (fuss isn't her style). I was shy myself and couldn't have said two words to the men, who didn't ignore me, it wasn't that, but simply talked together, or with the older boy, at a table by the window, nodding at what each said. They talk about motors, machinery, about weather and tides, other men, about "gear." The Hales, I should guess, are well off for around here—top drawer and old-timers. I don't understand them or these economics yet.

Ethel said, when we were at the dishes together, How is it going at the farm? Probably a little lonesome.

It was a question. I think she wanted to know about Herb—about where my husband was and all that, though she must have chatted with Carole Bean or May Stinson. So I told her, and something about New York. Unlike the others, she's a good listener, seems to like hearing things.

She asked about Gertrude Hardy.

A clattering of dishes as I tell her what I can (I avoid the father thing, which I regard as between us, GH and me).

It's a fact, she says, that some of the men go out there.

She said to me, to use her expression, Gertrude Hardy, occupation backwoods whore—so I suppose they do. I felt sorry for her.

Ea'ah—there ain't much room to stretch down here, and the men do drink and chase around, if they've a mind to, now and then. Well—it's in their nature to, even here where it's quiet most of the time—nowheres to go. And that cabin? she says—not much to it, eh?

And then I think I know what concerns her, and I say, It looked solid and all that, just terribly forlorn—yet good property, I should say. That cove never drains—it's deep water.

I could get her a good price for it, if she'd ever sell.

I might ask, I say. And we let it go at that.

Along the window sill two or three of the chipped glass marbles like those Carole Bean has caught my eye and through, beyond them, I saw the men, Elmo and Richie, a boy following, heading down a clamshell path to their landing: cut grass the late sun sweeps across, and a fine cluster of bushes in flower: pale strawberry pink of weigela (common up here and at its peak now) and the black crimson of a brier rose. Color music. Mown grass against a field of unmown that is filled with daisies now—and along a working road that leads down to their wharf and shed, posts of cut granite, reminding me that this was once also a quarrying town. I smoke and drink coffee and look down at the cove, feeling full of success.

Two of the children were watching television and I stayed a while to watch it with them—Perry Mason or something. Ethel had gotten out a piece of sewing, but I was careful not to overstay. I want to be asked back. I liked being in that family, the only real Maine one I know. I need some of that.

EVENING. Fog in again—and weirdly warm—heat from the day locked in by some freak of weather. So I walked in it, aware of a gray loveliness. I wanted to feel it on my body but was a little afraid to, or a little ashamed, as I'm ashamed, apparently, of so many things—of my need to think about men, my Mallek need, my half invention. It has been coming on me, living alone.

With Herb it was so pallid, partial, that part of things—nothing very real happened—a duty performed without joy—and I begin to know how much of that I should have had—so that I half envy GH. Admit—I do. Who can talk about it as if she *were* a whore (after many a night, I suppose, when they do talk to her, the men, and use those wonderful words—thick in the prick—suck off—fuck you).

I felt sexy in that fog—yes, and then did take my blouse off—and a few moments later my bra. Oh, wonderful—my great silken breasts. Admit—you did love yourself. I'll go naked next time. I promise. Up under the apple trees.

That looks tawdry—"great silken breasts." But why be afraid to talk about it, sex, sensuality. My body. Mallek–Mendonca's. They were fine together, doing what we did. I haven't quite the words for it—just, I think, as I have no proper words for GH yet —the incredible *ease* with which she told me what she did and wanted—seducing her father—some hot-pants kid—what did she say?—some little bitch—as if it were hardly she she was talking about but just girls in general. So frank, so direct. Sucking him off and admitting it, simply saying it.

Bawdy in the fog—bare-breasted—stroking their smooth, weighty undersides, saying, Me, me. I seemed to offer them—as if the fog, thick as it was, had a mouth—gray presence, Mendonca shadowily there, old bruisers with hairy stomachs, great legs—white—not beautiful—Gertrude's father—fucking me. A homely man, unhandsome, coarse, hair at the small of his back—yes, down to a kind of tail where the buttocks began—animal—of older man the sign—bull man—at me in slow mindless intent, lifting his head to listen, to watch . . . oh, leave it—stop. Being in the fog was good. I need more of that. I need my body, others—this world. A—not B.

SATURDAY 9 JULY. Buster the Cat. He just came in from the woods to sniff around—quite small, but cool, though shy as a shadow. And I put out a saucer of milk. I wonder if he'll come around if I keep doing it. I don't think he belongs to anyone— looked woodsy, unkempt—a coon cat. I want to comb his tail, which longs to be jaunty, raised on high.

JOURNAL TUESDAY 12 JULY. I tend my garden more assiduously than I should ever have expected. (It helps keep the fat down.) The delphiniums stand like slender blue flames by the wall—my pride—are they usually this early in Maine? Though me—I gorge. One hundred and forty, and in the mirror I am all hips and thighs and belly now—pregnant with easiness. I've always been ashamed of my wide hips, though certain men approve. I do look German, or northern, as GH said.

Minor event (major?)—Ethel Hale came around, or stopped by —I was very pleased. She knows this place—knew the Stinsons— and admired things, liked some odds and ends I have. Her house has mostly the practical left in it, or objects that have sentimental value, essentially Victorian—yes, and bits of plaster and plastic. But she, I think, could be led toward antiquing—she has the wit for it, the liking for things, the eye. Went right to some fireplace iron—Now, I like that, she said, and at a huge copper kettle green with age I had bought in Blue Hill and keep kindling in, I imagine that cost a penny. And then, just so casually, That island I told you about—the one that's for sale—Pennyless—Elmo says he'll take us out there on a picnic if you'd like. I want to see it again myself.

And then, having planted her bomb, she left.

But I like it *here!* I cried after her. I'm safe. There are the delphiniums—I'm going to clean out the barn. That cat came around, licked the saucer clean, though it could have been skunks. I'll tell her no—absolutely no. This is enough. It isn't even my house.

Well, we're going, she says, this Sunday. And I'll like that, and will not feel threatened or intimidated. She is sinister, devious— she wouldn't give *her* secrets away to the first inquirer. I like her.

SATURDAY 16 JULY. I look forward to Saturdays now. I have a routine that includes a small fire, if the weather warrants it, a good supper—generally fish or a lobster—I treat myself—and martinis— I make a sort of party of it and rehearse the week, allow a wild thought or two—at least it's narrowing down to Saturday night.

Things to do: the barn—I keep putting it off. Write Herb. Write Beth. Go see Gertrude Hardy again (I avoid it somehow, but I do want to draw that wharf—am I afraid of finding cars out there?— in the morning?).

I'm anxious about tomorrow. Ethel called to say come over at ten—tide will be right, something something—and not to bring anything.

But an air of excitement—a trip.

For a martini now—and a bowl of green olives.

Looking out at the yard as the evening darkens—myself in the mirror of the window again, afloat on its orange-silver surface —my blond hair—that holds, as if he were looking in, ghost-figure of Mallek–Mendonca—naked and dark. Is he growing less real to me?

Do I want him to? How could I keep him from gradually altering into something he is not, if I wanted to?

I would need details—certain things I could come upon in surprise, like the special blue of his shaved jaw—like that tattoo he showed me under the hair of his chest, a serpent with a rose in its mouth, the rose being a nipple—and me thinking how odd it was, how sensuous, and him pulling me to it, my mouth—ugly, at first, like a wart on fat muscular breast, and he lay holding me there till it grew rose red. A man had put it on, he told me, who had had a back covered with couples performing. It had been painful. Or a photograph—a fact—so that he would not just slip off into some vaguely imagined person I once had had a fling with.

But how to make a presence of him in this house, here at my feast? someone so real *that he would in fact be here?* Dialogue. Have him talk. Yes, but he didn't much, and it's too far away for me to hear it accurately now. So all I do have left, really, is a fairly clear image of him in the bar, the visit, his body—though that has largely become words, which I arrange in a certain way to suit myself for the pleasure they give.

But that's all I have, and my lies will only become more willful, more extreme, as the gulf widens, and I can't bear that. I *will* not let him come to infect this place. Think of tomorrow. Pray for fine weather.

SUNDAY 17. Back and exhausted, mind filled with sparkle of water, granite shores, with spruce, with islands, gulls, things flying —the Hales. Back and stricken. Pennyless. It *is* mine—and she knew, she *knew* it—they all did.

But wait, calm down—because this is serious. Things rushing through me like a tide bearing something other than wrack. Since nothing, no place, none, could have been more beautiful, not *any.* Oh, wait. Calm *down.* Talk maybe about them, not the island.

Them. Ethel looking slightly unfamiliar to me in pants, a jacket, a hat, picnicking things—needing to be helped, or wanting to be —that unfamiliar, too (but I haven't seen much of her with them, her men). They had little wooden chairs from their porch for us, Elmo and his friend Richie—Richie Hayden?—who didn't say a word, as I remember—not a word. And the boat and the children at their wharf and Elmo helping me down into it with a great warm moist palm. How grand he looked, how right (these are working people, not businessmen)—dark blue knit cap such as the Portuguese wear in Gloucester, that rolls down or up—how it suited his red face, his dark hair, and his wool checked shirt. Richie, too, so that they seemed like father and son. Elmo what?—forty-five?—an enormous country squire, yeoman of a man. Norman. Not shy but untalkative—or with females—or with me, anyhow—but there helping, watching. Them casting off.

It was all good to watch—the ease with which they handle things—ropes, machinery. A large though fast boat with one of those small masts at the stern (a jigger, they called it—I asked)—and long free lines—easing it out from the cove, then suddenly opening it up, revving it gaily—and the nice warm sense of the motor going, Elmo in at the wheel, spinning it, Richie watching—for whatever they watch for (they know every ledge, so I think pot buoys)—and Ethel and I ensconced, chattering a little, at so much to be seen, at everything. I was trying, though, to be still, to be appropriate, not a silly female out of place in their world.

The children were quiet, as I imagine they've been trained to be out in the boat—their boat—where their living comes from. They had a respect for it, you could sense, yet were very at home and knowing, even the girls, Betsy wrapped a little away in her own life.

And the land changed, seemed slowly to swirl, to rotate, as we moved out, passing a headland, a promontory—granite, flowing in vast and congealed masses, capped with wild grass, down to the water. Gulls. But they ignored us—glittering along the shore, dropping mussels, hovering a moment, following silently down. I saw Orstown come into view around a bend, surprisingly—again, looking unfamiliar. Small white houses, boxlike, neatly stacked in rows, a little like toys—and since they can't fish on Sundays the harbor filled with lobster boats, mostly white, all pointing in a single direction, like a harborful of birds. Then heading out. Towing a skiff for the landing—a tag boat, they call it.

Ethel seemed to know where she was. That's Job's, she would say, and nod at an island ahead. And then we were among them, Orstown having vanished astern—we were ringed with them—all sizes, shapes—some bare (and when I asked, Ethel said, Sheep do it—or sometimes a fire—an old storm). We could see Mount Cadillac—Mount Desert—Isle au Haut—they loomed through openings across water, very clear but, even so, blue—bluish. Pink and green islands—"adagio of islands"—going past—once so close I could see the grain of the ledge, a clump of wild iris, and a single purple

mussel shell some gull had left. Dancing water as you pass a lee
—occasionally spray at the bow.

And then we approached one—we rounded its north point,
knocking against a slight chop—and there this thing was, undulant
granite shores, a knoll of spruce, then two, with a sweep of meadow
grass that sheep must once have cleared, looking from a distance
like highland. We chugged around it, and on the far side came to
a true smugglers' cove, with a tiny beach flanked by ledge that
more grass goes back from, to a wall of rising spruce.

And I am excited. I know, but I say, Is this it? hardly daring to
hope—and see Ethel nod. Even out here the sea or brier roses
grow—at the tide's edge, by a white curve of stones, a sturdy,
cheerful pink, I see them waiting for us.

Elmo is maneuvering the boat—Richie is at the bow. He drops
anchor.

They help us into the skiff—Richie standing down in it and
holding to the edge of the boat, Elmo still on board. It will take
only us two women. And while Elmo tends to things on the boat
and the children wait, Richie rows us in, his large blue vacant
eyes looking beyond Ethel and me, beyond everything—rowing
effortlessly to the clunking sound of the oarlocks in the sunny,
watery silence of the morning, the oars quite small in his short-
fingered hands—just his arms move, back and forth—but I am
mostly watching the island.

It is large and extends itself as we come close. I lose sight of
most of it, see the roses again. And see rockweed, brown gold,
glistening on a tiny offshore crop of stone that sports a shawl of
grass and broken mussel shells and gull droppings, and which we
pass within feet, almost inches of. We glide over cold, glass-green
water into a cove where driftwood lines a shore on a mussel-shell
beach between masses of granite lichened to the silvery-pink high-
water mark and the rosebushes. Richie finds a place where we can
scramble ashore as he holds with an oar to a crack in pink rock.
Underfoot the rock feels good and crackles with the shells of
crabs and sea urchins.

We were looking for treasure or a cache or rum—and the men
were smugglers (blue rolled caps, short boots), and could have
sported one gold loop in an ear and a blue skull etched on a
brawny arm. Yes, and were Victorian, too—old picnickers—ladies
in voluminous dark skirts, laced boots—gaily ashore, being helped

by men in their picnicking hats, being handed from rock to rock —except that the men were lobstermen, and I was with them, in a family.

We explored, found what they said was Ellsworth Bean's dory —built a fire by the roots of an upturned spruce, a huge spidery thing gone gray in the weather—and had our picnic.

Oh, never mind, never mind. I'm hooked. Something has happened. I can't tell it now. Let it simmer, let it come to its boil, if it's going to.

Monday 18 July

Beth,

Something terrible has happened. I've found an island, or it has found me. I told you it would—that something would happen, some dark future present itself. And now it sits out there waiting for me. That female I told you about, the sinister Ethel Hale of Goose Cove, is the one who's responsible. I did go to supper that Wednesday, and one thing led fairly quickly to another.

For example, they were grand, the Hales—she, Ethel, small and tough and dry, in her way knowing (you would like her—some day we'll go antiquing together), her husband a lobsterman—a weather-burned and fat-smooth face, like a tomato—very knowing, too, though in a different way. Silent, he sits and listens to us, smoking a cigarette, saying, Ay-yup, now and then. Not entirely your sort, pet, though you would admire him, too. And four children, all fine—a girl of sixteen, I think, Betsy—in the sweetness of adolescence, innocence—and a young man, Richie, who lives with them, who makes Ethel a bit nervous, I have decided (because of Betsy, I wondered?). Anyway, a fine meal and visit, and good for me. But one thing did lead to another—she dropped around to tell me, very casually, that they were going on a picnic Sunday, to an island she knew of, was for sale—did I want to come?

I can't describe it, or won't. I'm its—it's mine. It's haunted, I think. By Mrs. Bean's drowned husband, who she thinks washed ashore there—his dory did. She's shown me old pictures of him. Long, lanky—a proper drowned man to drop around for a visit of a lonely night, come dripping in, green-eyed, silent, wet as the sea.

But see—I'm filled with something. Too much to let it out right now. Maybe later more.

I have a cat named Buster. Began coming around for milk I

put out. And now he has his pad by the fire, as if he owned the place. He is tiny—pearl gray and black. Cats think we're here for them. I suppose we are. I'm going to make him a little hat with a feather.

Well—I had to let you know.

Your last letter was *good*. I'm glad you're going to Nantucket (though of course I wish it were here). Get sunburned, wind-blown —have a drink for me at that cellar bar with all the anchors and nets. Keep writing. Which reminds me, or did I say, that I'm drawing again? a little, and that I met (yes, I told you) an interesting woman? one Gertrude Hardy, owns a lovely little wharf I'm going to sketch—again (I'm afraid I was a little cheap about her to you).

I've been buying marvelous old quilts—eight bucks apiece— fifty there, if you could find them. I'm already laying in against winter.

Most fondly, love. I'll let you know of developments—but I can not permit developments, so maybe not.

Did I mention a certain Moose Deleau? If not, ask me about him next—a specter, a kind of ghoul, who inhabits the islands— maybe mine.

Monday 18

Dear Herb,

Just a note to say that things are fine. I'm scampering around buying a few things, odds and ends, getting to know this place. Have met some people you and I would have liked as picturesque, typical, though they are better than that. The woman sells land and houses in an indifferent way—works on commission for a realtor here. Showed me an island. I confess to having been moved by it. She says it's for sale—but so lovely—and big—easily enough for a cabin, etc. I'm just dreaming.

I have a cat named Buster—just like his name—very coolly decided one evening he belonged here and mewed outside for milk. I think he's a Maine coon cat—with a marvelous tail and great self-assurance. Good company. Maine, as you may remember, is overwhelming—almost too much.

Fondly, etc.

JULY 21. Saw Gertrude again. Screwed up my nerve and curiosity and drove out. And she was there. I said, Hi—I'm going to try to do a better one—do you mind? And she sat on the rock with me, the ledge, as they call it, and watched and talked.

Same ceaseless smoking, and out of that same—what?—toughness?—animosity? (against what?—men?)—came her talk, about this or that. I said, Aren't you lonely out here? She said, Lonely? I like it. Wouldn't stay anyplace else. Which reminded me of Ethel's interest, and I said, You wouldn't think of selling, would you?—I don't mean to me. This place? she said, and waved a hand at it. I imagine you've had offers, I said, and she said, Plenty— they know it, the sons of bitches.

She is tough, genuine. I told her about the island and she said, after hardly a moment, as she had about my staying all winter, You'd be crazy—you'd go nuts out there. You're already a little nuts, ain't you? I hadn't even said I intended to build on it, but she knew—You think I would? Absolutely, she said. Like I do sometimes—climb the walls. Honey, you can't live alone down here unless you *are* some kind of nut. Look at me. What do you think I let them come out here for?—well, it ain't to screw all the time—who needs it?—that's just the price.

She looked at me. You'd probably get them coming out there, you know, dropping by. She shrugged. They like to—they're talkers, same as anyone—I mean like to sit around, have somewhere to go. I get all the news, you know—about who's laying who, who's beat up who. It's the young ones mostly who like to fight—the older ones—you've heard how they tell about the old salt was asked by a nice lady tourist what they did all winter, who said, Well, ma'am— in the summer we fish and we fuck, but in the winter naturally there ain't much fishing. Ha!

She paused to scratch a match on a rock, light another cigarette —puffed on it. So why don't you draw me? she said. You want to?

So I did, she talking again, and floundered badly and apologized, till she said, You ought to get one of my lobstering cats to pose for you, de'ah. They'd do it—strip right down, if you asked them right. Just tell them it's for art. I might ask Burt Beal—lives down your way somewhere. He's got a good build. She sat there letting me sketch her. A landscape you can make up; a human face, a form, you have to know. And it was odd to find how little I did know. But I tried and she said, Hey, that's not bad, when I'd finished, and I gave it to her. A fair swap.

At moments, watching her, I feel as if I were looking at a famous criminal. I guess she is famous, around here.

JOURNAL. Weather again—not good. A grayness. Wind north by northeast. Tones of pearl in the sky. Down at the harbor the water with a leaden yellow look.

JOURNAL. I'm going to start painting. Bought supplies in Bangor. I'll keep a notebook of colors for a while, try for the browns and greens of this place, the pinks and grays. The thought doth please.

JOURNAL. Down for a look at the water—the sea. I go sometimes just for a minute, as if to remind myself of something. Two arctic gulls afloat in the harbor—black-winged, superb, indifferent, as the sea itself is indifferent. The world that nevertheless we must care for.

JOURNAL. Brought Carole Bean a pie I had made—apple. We gorged on it. I feel at home in that kitchen of hers.

JOURNAL ENTRY. Walking—seeing things. Wayside flowers, piles of cut wood waiting for winter, a white, clapboarded meetinghouse —that looked back to history, part of what made these people what they are—a church that praised hard work and simple living, discouraged art as frivolous, and love that wasn't functional—knew white, knew black, but very little gray or the sweet shades in between—drove passion underground. A spare and simple beauty derived from the Gothic and the Greek—Olympian—knowing about the sea, about death. It's why, perhaps, there are no bars down here. They break them up, I'm told. Violence submerged. They're less Yankees than the inland types, the village-and-town New Englanders. Work and weather rule—necessity—they're poor, they're tough, and very religious. And underneath, as part of that, lurks the brutal, the violent—they fight bitterly. And no real way for them to play, though they love to dance, I'm told, and like what they call a musical—what Carole calls "a tune"—music at home.

The meetinghouse stands by a lane I must walk down someday. A fine cemetery of white stones behind it—urns and willows.

JOURNAL. Buster and my crows—who watch him, and I think make sport of him—who tries to ignore them in high, silken-tailed indifference. My bad angels.

OBSERVATION: One's private fantasies casually divulged cannot endlessly intrigue another. Art is required, to provide a shapeliness that points to form; form moves toward permanence, the universal.

Gertrude's story pointed that way, but not in my hands. In her account a casual brillance of effect, a sense not of the promiscuous but of the essential, the necessary. I see muslin curtains stirring in a breeze, smell the cut grass of a field coming in . . . them together in that room up there, after that first discovery—her fifteen, him in her arms, mind of a child, seduced by her and on her now, huge, giving her his body and his seed—father and daughter, suffering through that mindless hot encounter . . . the curtains stir, life—someone moans . . . the curtains cease, it grows still—a dog barks. . . .

MONDAY 1 AUGUST. A new month. I've been avoiding the journal. Other things to do. I've started to paint—just water colors, sketches, so far—to try to get at the tones of things here—the greens, the grays, the soft pinks of a distant shore. Confession: I'm trying to draw figures and can't. Don't know enough.

Letters to and from Beth. Chat letters. I haven't carboned them. She did ask about Deleau and I cursorily answered her (not being in the mood) that he was my Proteus, from whom I'd wring the truth someday. The dark side of my moon.

JOURNAL SUNDAY 7 AUGUST. Supper at Ethel's again. They all seemed easier about me being there—certainly the children did. How I love their sweet Yorkshire (I call it) voices. I got to talk a little to Betsy, who may, I think, have a thing about Richie. He doesn't seem to care about her. She trembles between girlhood and what is coming upon her, longs to confide—must be filled to the brim with bubblings of tiny daily things and dreams. Worried about a dress she was making—would the collar come out right—did I like the color? And adores her big father, who loves her back and is gentle with her. He's good with his children and settles their disputes, presides, is easy for them to come to, has a ready arm.

I come to know the house better. Slip covers over everything—white paint, as in Mrs. Bean's kitchen, Carole's (why do I always think of her as Mrs. Bean?—I like the name, I suppose). A few little treasures around—horns of deer that have been shot (they hunt, the men)—shells or stones with a scene painted on—prints of ships and photographs of a schooner that used to belong in the family and that traded up here—photos of a quarry and men standing by a huge stone to have their picture taken, all of them mustached, behatted—and a few rather odd little paintings around —very simple, very *wrong*—probably done by some member of the family once. But everything cluttered, comfortable—iron stoves in every room. Reminders of winter.

It's Elmo who says, What did you think of that island? (I haven't seen him since we went out to it.)

I liked it, I say.

It's a good one—if you like islands, he says, sitting with a great booted leg up on a knee, drinking coffee.

Do you? I ask.

After a moment he nods. They'll do. And then asks, What do you think of islands, Richie?—who is sitting across the room from us, hands in lap.

Who looks up from them, his hands, as if startled. (Yes, I would like to draw him—paint—that pink face, those blond curls. Where are his girls?)

What do you think? Elmo says, watching him.

An island? Richie says. He hasn't been listening.

Mrs. Calder here might buy and build on that island, Elmo says—on Pennyless. You think she'd be right to?

And Richie shrugs, hands in lap, says, I guess so. Then adds, surprisingly, *I* would.

Ethel's come in from the kitchen, is standing by the door holding a platter.

You would? Elmo says.

She's heard. Stay on an island? she says—you? Yes you would.

I *would*, Richie says.

Since when?

At which Richie clams up. Do they dislike each other? I wonder. Or just family things, the ins and outs.

It was a good supper, and the men stayed in and looked at television with us. They're watchers, these people; it's here to stay for them, in all their winter desolation. We don't visit like we used to, Ethel says of it—I'd rather visit than watch TV, any day.

I'm afraid of winter.

A good day—good people, the Hales.

JOURNAL. Banged my thumb with a hammer pounding a nail. Pain.

Why is pain? It seems so unnecessary, so much more than enough.

The universe rebuking us for failing in it, perhaps. Pain is punishment and the world a stern parent who will say, That's enough, one day—and bang! out we'll go. But we'll poison ourselves first.

Pain, the dark shadow of joy.

SUNDAY 14 AUGUST. Mrs. Caster and Mrs. Bean (Elizabeth and Carole), and May Stinson and me, gabbing over coffee. Carole works at the canning factory—it cripples her hands and feet but she takes that for granted. As do the others. They listen for the whistle; you hear it all over town; they set their clocks by it—seven o'clock—and then at eleven for lunch. A whistle means that a sardine boat is in, that there's work for them. It regulates their lives and is all too often silent. Hard work but they're gay about it, and grateful, and manage to have fun.

And I go to the store, the IGA, and stand gossiping with the rest of them. Part of my routine. A few summer people come and go and we nod, a little distantly (I'm still more or less one of them, even to my group). And to the P.O. where Lilly Talbot presides. People in the street nod to me, wave—the men, too, from their trucks or clomping along in their boots and caps. I haven't gotten under any surfaces yet, though I've heard more gossip, which I feel around me, somehow, their life—and their under-log life, too. The *quantities* of liquor sold at the state liquor store here—simply unbelievable; because I asked, as cunningly as I could, and the salesman, Mr. Chirtwell, said, You wouldn't believe it, Mrs. Calder, but we do $200,000 worth of business a year. My Lord!

And what *about* the summer people? Artists and such—university folk—in station wagons or VWs—beards and sweaters—that sort of folk. From Boston and New York, from various campuses—Amherst—Columbia. A few hippies (well to do). They all look familiar. It is as if we had agreed not to speak, though we do nod. Some sail, but most seem off in cabins or studios here and there along the shore.

Summer. Yes, it's summer, though it isn't seeming like the summers we used to indulge in, in a rented cottage at Jamestown, which I remember still with such nostalgia that words, names, leap to mind like tiny explosions of light—privet hedges, Main Street, the ferry to Newport, swimming at Whartons' or Mackerel Cove, picnicking at Potters', or at Beavertail in a fog—the morning fogs —fogs that we thought would not lift but then did—Daddy arriving for his two weeks. Oh, and the fun, the excitement, of that —telling about the heat and how he had missed us. Could not wait to get to the beach—Will it clear, that early-morning fog?— it would, even as you watched: light filling it, pink and then blue, then miraculously the sun—and off in the car in bathing suits to Mackerel Cove. Mother proud to have him with us, wanting to show him off to the friends we had, them talking their grown-up talk. Wet bathing things, wet towels and sand. Daddy—sweet Daddy—how I loved you on that shore, or watching you skim shale —loved it when you and Mother had friends in for a drink—sitting out on the porch—or you out mowing the yard, or with us on the rocks at Beavertail. Some snapshot of the mind I have: of you in khakis and felt hat, your old tweed coat, good shoes, looking sturdy and self-reliant, an engineering man—so that no wonder we were proud of you. You meant something different to each one of us, your three women. I suppose I was in love with you. For one whole summer I watched you secretly—though unconsumed. Though suppose that I had had to rub your back.

Yes, and the boys I knew and the absolute need of keeping up with them, fishing for crabs in the tide marsh from that bridge, or for chaugsies off the dock where the ferries came rushing in with their storms of white water, bumping and swaying the pilings —and I could; and could wrestle with them, and could join in summer fights, slingshots and rose apples, hard wild grapes that stung —smoking in a clubhouse we had—Peter Avery, yes, who had an outboard that we tried to start all summer and with whom I thought I was in love but who really loved Jane who had her own friends, was beautiful, danced so that the parents watched at the casino—all I was not. Dead now. Safely out of it.

What *was* it about summer?

Do I remember it, or only what it is like from here and now? Perhaps I only remember remembering, or my trips back, once with Herb, surreptitiously almost, to try to see it again, and seeing it not with the wild young eyes of then but with these older ones.

No, here I'm not summer folk as we were then, nor do I live that sort of summer life. Do these? I suppose they do, and that their children will look back, as I do, to that indulgent arrested time—of picnic fires, a beach, a brisk sail, a father who comes up out of the heat of a city to join his family, play with his children, and make love to his wife. Gertrude, hung in her horrors and glories—me in all that. Here in my fading summer—mid-August.

TUESDAY 16 AUGUST. On page forty of *Finnegans Wake*. Slow going. The great word-master, but does it add up? I can't tell. I feel myself sinking as into wet sand.

But I have also finished the first volume of Proust! And a novel by a man named Barth. I kept falling asleep. Maybe the others are better. Allegory tends to strike me as evasive.

But I read, read. And Buster keeps me company.

I must get at that *barn!*

THURSDAY A.M. 18 AUGUST. Wild, nightmarish dreams—I awoke from them tangled in sheets and soaking. I thought I had exorcised all that. Apparently not. It sticks, he stays. Mallek–Mendonca—and *I* sought him out, too, went looking—hideously done up—knew where to find him, apparently—down in a terrible little room, waiting for me. Watching as I came in. And then after me—all bristly, enormous—so that I *knew* what was going on. I won't have it, I won't *have* him lying in wait for me.

It's gone now, but it was bad. What the hell is wrong with me?

Fog around, too, this morning. I'll garden, then head for Bangor, stop at the junk shops along the way. I want some ironstone, anything. I'll write to Beth.

P.M. Martini. What was it? Something poking up at me. I went looking—I know. But looking for what? Have I *got* something now? Up here?

Thursday 18

Beth,

I have an idea, or one is beginning to poke its head out at me. You to come up for a week. I'll meet you in Bangor. Why not? Before the snow flies, I mean, during early fall. October will be glorious. We'll case every shop within miles. Loads of stuff around.

I mean it. Consider. I've lots to show you, lots to talk over. Bill would let you come. He would, wouldn't he? Do consider it. It may be your old chum doth need you.

FRIDAY 19 AUGUST. Surprise surprise. Guess what? Saw a cut-down truck appear in the drive. Wondered a moment, thinking of Jules Caster, who has one like it—they all do—then saw Mr. Hale get out, Elmo. No boots—an orange hunter's cap. Such a melon of a man, ponderous. Knocked at the kitchen door, the one I use.

For a moment he seemed overhearty from being slightly shy. And I said, Come in, come in, very hearty, too. I was glad to see him, though surprised at the unexpected.

And that's all it was, really, a visit. Just thought I'd stop by, see what Ethel's been talking about here, he says, in his down-East, good-humored baritone—the voice of a man quietly pleased with himself, content, sure about things, his things.

And I ushered him in. I had coffee on the stove, and yes, he would have some. And we sat in the kitchen.

He talks right along when he knows you, and apparently (because of Ethel) he's decided now that he does. It began with, How you liking it down here?—something like that (him already, in a way, presiding—and of course it is his place, his world). And we got right into it—easy. Talked about his children, a little. About Ethel. He said, Ethel thinks you like them islands. She likes to think she can sell—or is in business. It's good for her to—been hooked in at home with them children so long—we didn't have them till late, you know—Ethel's getting on to forty-six.

That was a tiny peek at them. I'm interested. Very.

And we talk. Rather at randon. And I get us a second cup. Then I say, Come—I'll show you around—and since it's still foggy out, I turn on lights, and suddenly it all looks cozy. And he admires —comes into the living room, which shrinks a little with him in it, but not away from him—it likes to be looked at.

And he looks at things. Sniffs around, picks up the piece of scrimshaw I have and asks about it. And at a drawing or two I have around (I must look for those frames). And I think, How nice to have him here.

I'll have to bring Richie by, he says, and show him all this. And he tells me about him—that he belonged to cousins who were killed in a car accident over by Lewiston—they had taken him in when he and Ethel thought they might not have children. Richie don't take to people too quick, he tells me—and adds, Kind of shy. I think: *really?*

He talks about him a while. He can draw, you know. Maybe you seen them paintings we got—them are his.

He looks at me a moment, sort of speculatively. Maybe you can help him out some—ain't had any lessons, just what he learned in the school.

We're back in the kitchen, standing. He says, Well—it's been nice, Mrs. Calder (Cal'dah). Just thought I'd stop by.

I walk out with him to his truck and he stands there a moment, looking around. Nice out here, he says. Private, yet you ain't too far from things. Kind of cozy, ain't it. Well, you come see us now —come eat with us again—Ethie'd like that. We all would.

And off he drove.

Funny—and nice, that about Ethel thinking she could sell. Nothing dumb about that one. You have the feeling, somehow, that in his slow, easy way he looks after them all, controls, presides.

TUESDAY. The weather hot and has been—over eighty (unusual, they say). The harbor lies flat, molten, and mirrors the sky.

I walked up in my woods, my spruce and fir, over long, lichen-covered outcroppings of granite—and not just outcroppings, that whole hill is granite. I don't know how the trees can find root for themselves, but they do. Their roots form a network under that thin layer of soil, which itself is mostly plant life (some moral there); mosses, rich and green as padded velvet, bunchberry and wintergreen, and lichen like Spanish moss everywhere, gray green, suggesting the ancient, the primordial; decomposing matter, old trees, fallen, rotting (would glow in the dark). Very cool and damp up in there. Many sorts of mushrooms—orange—white—the orange like bits of an old ball gown (diamonds of quartz glitter in granite). When a tree falls you can see how flatly its roots have spread out.

I'm a shore person by instinct rather than a woods one, but I like knowing what's around me, these sheltering spruce, so bunchy, terse, and so green themselves. Even up in under them I found crab shells that the gulls must have carried up, or the crows, like secret caches. Gulls and crows, white and black, light and dark—something of my own life up here.

Letter from Herb when I went to the P.O. Lilly Talbot sees it's from a man. I say, very casually, He was my husband, but she's much too trained at her job, too much an Orstown girl, to inquire directly. Others will know, though, as I suppose they do from my coffee pals (not from Ethel).

Herb worried about "student discontent." Sal is not—she refers to them, he says, as the little creeps. But it's not as easy as that, as we're learning. Something is happening.

SATURDAY 3 SEPTEMBER. Friday supper at Ethel's. All of them there, except Betsy, who was spending the night with a friend.

Ethel says, sort of briskly, It's getting to be time to buy islands; fall coming on, you know.

And Elmo says, Now, Ethel, stop trying to anchor Mrs. Calder out in the bay. She does fine here.

And I say, I wish you would call me Helen—I got tired of being a missus.

And Ethel says, I want some excitement around here—I want to see that island in good hands—a cabin on it, a wharf—then we can go visit.

Elmo says, We can go visit her here.

And Ethel—It ain't the same. And to him, and more seriously, She'll always be able to sell it. Once there's a cabin out there, and a landing, that place will double in value—easy.

And Elmo says, Course we don't know, but we're talking like she's got to swap—maybe she can keep hold of Stinsons'.

Then he says, Me and Richie's shifting a few traps around out there—you women wanna come—take another look?

At which Ethel says, Now, that might be nice. And to me, We're just talking, dear—it don't matter one way or the other to me what you do about that island. Elmo and I got a sort of joke between us.

But I say, I would like to see it again—Pennyless.

And she says, It is nice out there these days. Best part of summer's the last of it. Give us a day, she says to him.

Then we all go look at TV. Jack Benny, that old nitwit. But I do like him.

SUNDAY 4 SEPTEMBER. Contemplate, think. An island. Could I swing it? I had been thinking swap, hadn't I? unconsciously, without realizing what winter will be like. Depends, of course, on what they ask—she thinks about $5,000—three, four more for the cabin and landing—a boat—$10,000 anyway, altogether. Ten thousand dollars. I have it. With darn little left over, but enough—and it's cheaper to live up here—and I *would* be able to sell—she's sure of that. What it boils down to is, Could I live out there, in summers, as I do here?

Things do play through my mind—furtive as fish. I don't name them, don't look. Have things been going well? Pause, consider—since you asked. Have they?

Let me admit to certain gaps. How serious? Serious. Really bad? Certain Saturday nights, perhaps—good and bad—my Mallek ones —others—pages and pages burned up, and drunk to bed—when I had thought once to try to be honest. But I am honest. Honest doesn't mean just the black, it means nice things, too. I've chronicled that, I've blazed trees along the way—I told those dreams, I admitted my lapses.

Yes, parts have been bad, but in general—oh, I love this place, I do, it's worked; and who wants to be saying, Horrible—things are a mess, all the time, when they are anywhere—were even during those early blithe days at the apartment when everything sang. Black and white, and I put in more of the white. It's my nature to. Oddly enough, I am not a complainer. But *is* something secret afoot?—have I plans? Not that I know of—no—it's just something about an island, even about Jamestown, which was an island (yes—it is about that—as if, instinctively, I was going back—I was happy there). Something fierce and wild—yes, yes—oh, clean, swept bare. Wait and see. We're going again. I won't write to anyone until we have.

JOURNAL. One entry only, to be honest. Dreams again. Confusing, frightening. As if I were being driven, or pursued. The Mendonca thing—though he's taken on slightly different characteristics, is altering. I was after him—and seemed—oh—to catch him finally, catch up with, corner him. And could hear him saying, No, and could hear myself, I want to please you. Things magnified. I knew it was a dream and was hating myself for having it. I took his head in, saying, That's where you want to be, you men—his whole head, saying, See, I can, and had him inside me, as if I were giving birth to him. What have I done? I'm getting used to waking and having to stay awake.

Let me just add, touch in, the white. Lovely guileless weather . . . a silent storm of sun, and moon nights now—it rises golden and threatening, looking almost liquid, molten, as if it might drop from the sky and spread over the world like syrup. I drive around in it, stop the car, walk, look. Orange wrinkled sheets of it on the water.

Saturday 10 Sept.

Beth,

Stop criticizing me. At once. I demand that you do. No, it *isn't* easy up here (I've just been admitting that to myself), but I'm making the best of something tough and *good*, if I *can* make the best of it. And best has to mean good enough.

I must have written too much about the island (we're going out to look at it in about an hour, incidentally). No, I'm not running away, evading, and I do fit here. But it all takes *time*. You're reading between lines something that isn't there. I love it up here, I do—I swear I do. And the island—so far it's a game that Ethel and I seem to play—Elmo, too. But it is *not* a withdrawal. I can't see it that way, and I am very capable of being honest still. But, darling, I need support, not criticism. This is difficult—and I told you it would be. What that's good isn't?

Can't remember what I said—probably on one of my Saturday nights when on occasion winds do blow cold—yes, and I get in the bag and rattle around in there—but it *is* going well for me, I am loving it. And I simply can't bear the distant, nattering sounds of worry from down there—up there. I wouldn't be in New York for seven Korean scrolls.

Sorry, of course, that you can't make it yet. I won't give up hoping for that. Consider. Do.

NOTE TO MYSELF: All right—watch what you write during those little Saturday-night binges—I can't have her worrying.

SECOND NOTE: I've been dealing in the sweetly picturesque, in journal, in letters, too (apparently)—in my drawings? Okay, then, so cut that out, too. I'm tough. This place is tough. We're going to meet and I'm going to belong, and I'm *not* going to sweetly patronize it. I'm going to be honest as hell from now on.

SATURDAY 10 SEPTEMBER, JOURNAL, EVENING. Too tired to say much except that I was right. It has caught in the tangles of my heart. Was simply breath-taking, heart-consuming. Something fatal there. I will never escape (unless I hide from it, I suppose). I'll talk about it later.

An early supper with them when we got in. Potluck. Which meant in this case a chowder (Ethel had dug some clams over there, on Pennyless). Chowder and toasted cheese sandwiches. And coffee. We all live on coffee. Me sort of itching for a drink (was I the only one?) and filled to overflowing with island. I am with island. Basking in the kitchen with them, lolling around the dinner table, as though with my lovers. Yes, then, the Hales, all of them, have done this to me. This place, too, this world of stone and water.

I noticed, remembered to look at, Richie's paintings (they were the ones I had seen). Funny little things—as if a child had done them. And nice that they're up, that the Hales like them (they don't see that they're funny—they are so innocent about art, a painting, that they accept one for what it happens to be, don't expect it to be something else). Elmo says, That's our boat, and see, that's Orstown behind it—and Ethel says, I like orange—I suppose because you see so little of it—Elmo and Richie have orange floats. Richie was very noncommittal about them, would say hardly a word when I said this or that. I told him I drew and was learning to paint, teaching myself. Not quite true. Getting back to it. I am.

JOURNAL SUNDAY 18 SEPTEMBER. My dreams are all islands now. The monsters have flown.

I told my ladies, Mrs. Caster and Mrs. Bean—May Stinson, too —who launched into discourse concerning . . . you wouldn't catch me on one, or not for long—

Or not after dark. I'd be afraid of the fog.

And the lonesomeness.

Yes, islands are lonely places. Let the gulls have them.

Things wash ashore on islands—like that dory of Ellie's—probably him, too.

Now, with a man out there—

We laugh. Yes, with a man—someone to make the bed for, and pick at . . .

Carole could do with a man, I think—becoming a little too neat with just herself to look out for now, things a little too fixed and dustless.

Not that I think that every woman needs a man. Ideally, perhaps, but in the ordinary flux of things certain men, certain women, probably do better by themselves, or with other men, other women. Could I, for instance, imagine living with Beth? I don't know. For a while, perhaps—though who knows, maybe indefinitely— she would not intrude. Yes, I think I could. We would *miss* a man around—whatever it is that Bill gives her—something to push against, take care of, I suppose, control. I think women do better at living alone than men. But who knows, who knows.

SUNDAY 25, A.M. (A charitable sun in the yard outside—coffee by me—a sense of well-being. I want to write about it.)

Last night—a gala. Elmo Hale stopped around, about seven, with protégé Richie in tow. Saw them pull up in the yard, stop, get out. Elmo walking with his ponderous tread, Richie following, around to my kitchen door. Not ponderous merely—he lumbers, he rolls, but with an easiness that will do for grace—and a grand assurance.

In they came, him apologizing—explaining, really, that he wanted Richie to see this, that, or the other. My bit of scrimshaw, perhaps—my drawings. I was having a drink and felt caught in the act. And needn't have. There's nothing sheltered about them along those lines; it's just that most of their women, the ones Ethel knows, don't drink. A good church influence there. And when I said, Care to join me? Elmo sort of rubbed his hands, glanced at Richie, and said, Well, that sounds real friendly—wouldn't you say, Richie? I said, I'm afraid I don't have any beer, and he waved it away. What you got's fine. I fixed them both highballs and took them into the living room where a fire was going.

I've told Richie here when that snow flies to keep an eye on you, Elmo said. We got a jeep we rig a plow up to. Not that we'll have much snow, but likely we'll get our share.

Richie sits next to him on the couch and I'm in my armchair across from them. The fire and the lamps make us look warm. And though Elmo is almost half again his size, Richie seems sturdy enough. He lets Elmo talk. I find again that I like Richie's face. He has very startled yet staring round blue eyes that seem luminous, amazed. Elmo sits with an arm up on the sofa behind him, a leg up on a knee. I am struck by resemblances and differences. Elmo I seem to know as a type (one of the two that dominate this place); Richie is not monumental, though stocky enough— and as Elmo and I talk, I see him looking around, Richie—at a drawing I have on the wall, at three fine little black decoys on the

75

mantel, at a wooden bowl filled with shells, stones, trinkets on the table beside him. Elmo, who has been talking weather to me, seems to notice him and his arm drops down to around Richie's shoulders and he says, What you think about all this, Richie? And Richie's eyes shift to my face for a moment and express in their way a kind of, yes, shy approval and Elmo says, He likes this (to him, really)—and to me, Richie likes art—don't you, Richie? (in Elmo's mouth the word "art" (ar't) takes on slightly unfamiliar connotations—he knows the word but it is foreign, somewhat exotic, to him, or so you suppose).

I say, Would you like to see some of my drawings?—and get up and bring back a portfolio, which I lay out on the floor in front of them.

Those are some I did in New York. That's what it looked like to me from my apartment. (Shadow of Mendonca—but of so much else, too—transparent, enormous, so that for a moment I am seeing them through it—though a friendly shadow now, or a friendly feeling toward it, with them there to keep it at bay.)

Richie bends forward. I watch his hands turning pages—hands somewhere between laboring hands (broken-nailed, scarred, and short-fingered) and shapely—good hands, very strong yet suggestive of the gentle, even the feminine. I catch Elmo looking at me, a smile hidden in his face. I smile back and his own smile broadens quickly out as though it had been waiting for permission and he nods toward Richie beside him. For a moment I sense an eagerness in him to be friendly toward me.

Those are the ones I began up here, I say, as he comes to them. I see a wharf. I say, without thinking, I did two of that—it belongs to a woman I got to talking to (it comes flooding back but I barge on)—her name was Hardy—Gertrude. Do you know who she is?

Richie has turned the page but Elmo says, Out to Cobbins Cove? And when I say, Yes—she lives alone, I think—he nods. We know her. Then adds, mischievously, Richie here used to court her some. At which Richie looks up at me, and after a moment shakes his head, and the corners of his mouth go down. He did, though, Elmo says.

The new drink I have brought him is mellowing Elmo, who says, broadly, again, He did—to me, though watching Richie, who just shrugs. He has turned to some figures I have been trying. They're pretty bad, I say—I can't do figures. And because I have a new drink myself, I say, I need to draw from life, from a person

—need someone to sit for me. At which Elmo, who tends now to barge in, says, Maybe Richie here will—and then, Going to sit for the lady, Richie?—who, since he's having a second drink, too, says, to me, *He* will, with a sideways nod. Who says, Well, I *might*—and cocks his arms and head in mimic of posing. Elmo has a streak of humor in him that is native, like suppressed exuberance (wa'al, oi moight).

Yes, like that, I say, and smile at Richie, who is suddenly engulfed again by one of Elmo's huge arms—animal good humor lodges in him as in a cave, though he is not kittenish, just feels fine.

I liked yours, I say to him—the ones I saw at the house; and he shrugs, says, They ain't much.

He writes, too, Elmo says—writes poems.

You do? I say—and see him nod.

And just that, the nod, seems to tell me so much more about him, and I see him as a person reaching out or fumbling toward something. He looks at me, eyes large, luminous—and suddenly I imagine him, with his husky round body and curls, as chubby, innocent, and perhaps angelic, and feel a wave of sympathy, even love, for him.

Would you go drawing with me sometime? I suddenly ask—and after a moment hear Elmo tell me, Sure he will. Would *you*? I say—and he nods again. And we seem like his parents for a moment.

They don't stay long. I sense they are out gallivanting, or that Elmo is, and bring him a third drink, which he accepts without comment. And we gab a while longer, and having finished it he rises. Well, let's leave the lady to her own, he says.

I liked having them here. And I wish he *would* come drawing with me.

My face in the silvery-smooth black windowpane—lamplight across it. I'm imagining Richie and me together, drawing Elmo, who is posing for us. I imagine Elmo in some mysterious way to resemble my father. I am interested in his body, though I do not mentally undress him—I am aware of limbs and flesh, of proportions—and curious. About Richie, too.

SATURDAY 1 OCTOBER. Walked into town and around by the inland route home. Noticing things. Summer going out like a tide, the seasonal ebb, taking things with it—the sweet time of the year, for one. A clarity of light seems to have settled over the houses of this place, and with it, or do I imagine, a silence, a quietude, suggesting a pause, a balancing, or things coming into a new and more serious focus.

Yes, and around me in the fall sunlight the lives of these people, their houses, their yards, their boats, the ones on shore, too, drawn up, resting, or finished with the sea.

How good—how *good* it is to walk. How many flowers you see. How they love flowers—petunias—gay, and brave—flaunting their pinks and whites against a wall—braving it out in the face of this great thing coming toward us.

Letter from Herb—a horror tale. He says that he knows something now—has heard (a friend from Brussels, I think, has written him) that we have now, at the rate things are going, thirty-five to fifty more years. That the ocean, which gives us 80 per cent of our oxygen, is *already* so polluted that that oxygen cannot be forthcoming—and there is no turning back (I mean even if we wanted to, which we don't). Result: *universal suffocation.* Not the *bomb,* not even the population bomb—mere ecological breakdown—ecological doomsday: thirty-five years away. This from a gathering there, in Brussels, international. News not yet released (though the findings are in). It sounds fantastical; he assures me it is not, that it is sound prediction, computerized, actuarialized, verified. It has already happened. Government concern, student seminars, angry citizenry—too late—it has *happened,* we've "blown it."

I do look at fall with a special love, a commiseration for all that must die; and not seasonally, as it should, with the promise of spring rebirth, but with a finality now that exceeds any sense in Greek drama of absolute tragedy, equivalent only to Revelation, that last book of the Hebrews. They were right, we did not care for the garden, the given. A moon for the misbegotten—why we seek it out—as though to visit, while we can, our own grave.

I'm depressed. I wrote him jokingly back something about the mask of the red death and that I had given up dancing. Yet added, I know, I know—*that's* why I'm looking, like a spy, at all this, all these, who are innocent, who are not *of* it.

They've been crying doomsday since the Year One, though—can it now be that close? We are cunning, infinitely, and resourceful.

MONDAY 3 OCTOBER. Out in the yard last evening I heard geese going over, their cries faint and far up, mysterious. They gave me the sense of being left behind. I imagined them winging their way over New York, and the city a heap of spilled jewels on black velvet below them, the East River dark—and then the sea. My coffee ladies are glad I'm staying. You'll like it here, they said. The summer folk never see this place when the weather's around. They leave with the birds, or before.

Jules Caster over to put the storm windows on. He said, Gets a mite nippy down here—you'll be glad you got them. They were in the barn. I didn't know we had them. I wonder what else is out there. It would be nice to find an old Tiffany glass shade. I want one for the kitchen, but not for five hundred, or whatever, now. What keeps me out of the barn? Pure laziness. Mice. Things that scurry and are quick.

WEDNESDAY 5 OCTOBER. Letter from Beth. She cannot make it. Twins sick, Bill in a stew over something. Was I terribly disappointed? Yes, I had been looking forward to her. We would have had such a time. I could have shown her the Hales. And she's all I miss of New York, except that at times my old view floats into mind like a mirage, the buildings, the bridge, yes, and the tugs on the river. My old flame. I've been good about that.

I'll write her that it doesn't matter. I'll be good about that, too. But, goddamnit, I did want her here, I wanted her to see all this so that she could understand my letters, read between the lines. I wanted her good company.

OCTOBER 13. Glorious day. I see that the birches are yellow. Had coffee with the girls, who are beginning to collect things for a church bazaar—anything they can get, which isn't much. There isn't much left over here. It's all used till broken; then mended, painted, used again. Quilting's their art. They make do with scraps and love color and old bits of elegance—velvets and satins, whatever they can find. They say they'll teach me how. A quilt will probably take a winter. No velvet for me—I want geometry, and cotton.

But such a day. One of your crystal ones you could snap with a fingernail and make ring. So I drove out to see if Gertrude had

79

gone with the geese, and she had. At least the windows were boarded up, though you couldn't have told otherwise.

What do I make of that? I don't know, exactly, but I like her, worry about her—a touch of the tragic—as if she had been stabbed with an icicle that had slowly frozen her heart. No, that's not it. A woman who needed things that were not available. What does she do all through a day, how does she spend her time? How often do the men come there? I gather that she only encourages certain ones. Cars driving up, lights flicking silently out.

And also stopped by to see Ethel, feeling slightly abandoned by Beth. Said to come by for supper when I told her. Heavens, she is good. Various, yes (and I'm beginning to think I may know why), but *good*, solid, *of* this place, rock in her bones and good sea-water blood. I wanted to talk about Gertrude, but refrained.

But it was good to be there again with the children around and their sweet accents—Dorset? or Cornwall perhaps?—where they all once came from. I like it how Elmo calls them all "dear." They do up here. To Richie, at the table, No, de'ah, John ain't ready for her yet. They call everybody they know dear.

Ethel and I talked in the kitchen over the dishes. She quilts, too, in another group. Though I'm afraid of it, the winter, I tell her I'm looking forward to it, too, and she looks at me a moment, then says, Well, it's hard, but we manage, we get through—and you will, too, I expect—and we'll help.

She says I'm to have Thanksgiving with them; and I said, Now there *is* something to be thankful for. I must do something back for them sometime. Have them to dinner perhaps—a good steak, mushrooms, the works. So far I haven't done a thing, simply gorged myself all summer on one huge casserole after another.

16 SUNDAY A.M. Dreams again. Oh, God, I thought they were gone. Mallek. I think it was—he was posing for me, back to—enormous weight-lifter muscles, like stone, though misshapen—too much—that I was drawing—and then he turned and it was Elmo, or partly, with an expression that is a cloud over this morning still, a leer, somehow, that cheapened me. You want to see me, don't you? he said. What happened? It was vague—he exhibited parts of himself. I had drawn for Mallek—and then it was only Mendonca again (I knew by the tattoo), but they seemed to know each other.

But a morning now like a bowl of sunlight. I look out into it as into a crystal that contains my future. I must order wood—three cords, at least. I'll burn a lot this winter. The nights are already cold. I plunge into bed as into a bank of snow and hold still till my body warms the sheets. Country New England—somehow luxurious. Aware, if the light is enough, of my bits of cut glass at the window, glittering like ice, my rag rugs—the sheltering angle of the ceiling over me.

Looking out into the clairvoyant sun—watchtowers of spruce beyond—my beautiful yet dangerous world, beginning its long and brilliant slide into winter, death.

P.M. They've just left. They had been driving around, I think, on a Sunday afternoon—I begin to realize they do. And in they wheeled—me in the kitchen, peeling potatoes, onions on the sideboard, a filet of haddock to be baked, beginning to consider drink time since it was growing dark—a flame of pink cloud like an angel's wing in the sky above the black spruce and long purple shadows in the yard, the barn black. Elmo jovial, filling the doorway, the kitchen, knitted cap on, wool shirt—he seemed to troop in with Richie in tow, quiet, just there. You don't mind none, Helen—we're just stopping by to see how you are doing.

Of course I don't mind, I say. I like company, especially two such handsome men. Furthermore, it's getting toward drink time for me. What can I get you? (I don't like my tone, but I wasn't quite at ease with them.)

I fix highballs and for myself a martini on ice, catching as I do a glimpse of the evening outside, purple and pink and black, a star.

You didn't come around to paint with me, I say to Richie.

I see him looking at me, not really shy after all, just wordless, as if words were not his medium.

Elmo says, He will—and I'm going to sit for you—and cocks his arms as he had before and swells up his chest.

And because he's playing my game, I say to Richie, I have a good place to paint upstairs and maybe we will get this one (with a sideways nod at Elmo) to pose for us.

And I remember how innocently he looked at me—almost curiously. Him? he said. I wouldn't want to draw him.

And Elmo—He wants to paint Gertrude's landing.

81

She's gone, I say. I drove out there to see and her cabin was boarded up.

But Elmo does not rise to the bait, was merely himself baiting Richie, who did not rise either.

I suppose she'll be back, I say.

She'll be back, Elmo says—then Richie here can go paint her landing. And I see that they have made a joke of it, Elmo has. (Going to paint Gertrude's landing, are you, Richie?)

Well, I like her, I say. It's not easy to live alone.

Elmo says, You going to buy that island?

And I say, What do you think—do you think I should?

Islands are scarce, he says—hard to get—that's a good one.

And I say, I know—I meant how do you think I would do out there, a lone woman?

Well, he says, more seriously—you got to have the money, you know. You'd have to build, get a boat, all that.

It's the boat part that worries me, I say. Learning to run one, to land.

You'd learn—we'd help, Richie and me. And the men would see that you're all right out there, they'd keep an eye on you. And I suddenly realize that they would, in some chivalrous way.

Richie says, Me and Elmo's traps is out there. Our string runs toward Marshal, one of them.

Is that how you find them in the fog? I ask.

"Ay-yup."

What happened to Carole Bean's husband, incidentally?—did he get lost out there?

I see Elmo scratch the back of his neck while Richie looks at him. It's hard to say, he says. Never found him, you know. That's his dory on Pennyless—looked like he run out of gas—had an outboard on her, you know. They found that. Fog around. He could have been drinking—Ellie was a drinking man, at times— tucked it away.

They do drink up here, I say—don't they?

Some do, he admitted.

Not you, I say.

Well—nothing regular, you know. Me and Richie here'll have a few. Used to stay out on that island—cook up some lobsters (lob'stahs)—had a little whiskey—him and me and a man we know over to Moose Head, Nat Collins—butter and lobsters—dig a few clams—take a nip—can't beat it, he says, when it's nice out.

I should think you'd consider that island yours, I say.

Don't belong to no one, he says—won't even to you if you buy her.

Elmo is slow in some ways, not in others. I watch gray eyes in a weather-reddened face under cropped, curly dark hair, see a massive throat; hair sprouts from it like black grass.

It was nice having them here. I like it that they've taken to stopping by, though I worry, a little, about Ethel.

20 *October Thursday*

Beth,

No little care packages. I whiz up to Ellsworth or Bangor when I need things—paints, brushes, etc. What I *need* is you. Had two bad days when I found you weren't coming. I'm over it now, or mostly.

But the weather has been brilliant—early-morning frosts—the birch golden, the maples like flame in the spruce, though the leaves are going-going-gone—days like a string of crystal beads— crystal is my word for what the air is like. Marigolds everywhere. Amazing, to me, how the flowers last.

Notes from a few down there—from Jeremy—a sort of whimsical reminder that that way civilization lies and when am I coming back, that I'm missed. Phyllis wrote, too. I drop them cards, feeling, a little callously, that I have shed them.

I'm beginning to finick with a design for a quilt—blue and white with touches of red—no, not a flag—but with the faintest hint of the patriotic. Though of course *first* I have to learn how and the ladies are going to show me—or did I say? You could be an absolute angel and look for a book on it for me. There must be something.

I read a good deal, cook constantly, and brace for the winter, which I both dread and look forward to. I imagine great drifts of snow encircling the house, the huge white arms of winter hugging me to its bosom.

Enough for now. No "news." Things slowly shift and change, but so slowly as to be barely perceptible. Sorry to be such a bore today, but my mind is a blank. Love.

22 SATURDAY MORNING. Just back from Gertrude's landing with a *good* drawing of it. Spirit of her around.

I go there as to a place where an interesting crime has been committed, one that in some way concerns me, that I might, in some way, once have committed. A spectral cast to things.

And though it had changed with the season, I caught something, and something about a good deal of this coast. Spruce dark and geometric against brilliant water, a long pouring of stone, then the wharf itself—propped up on pilings somewhat askew, themselves of spruce and still shaggy. Yes, it's the water, alive with sun, the flow of granite, the dark spruce—my eyes are still dazzled. I don't think Marin quite caught that—water color won't hold it— egg tempera on board is what's needed. I suppose Wyeth. I can still hear the crows, that I like to call sea ravens (must look that up), the black angels. They inhabit the spruce, the firs. And somehow in my nostrils still the good strong smells of the coast—seaweeds, mussels, crabs, and salt.

Stinson Farm

Dear Beth,

Horrible. I *forgot* Halloween—self-centered old bag that I am. How *could* I have? The tokens, the reminders were everywhere— stuffed scarecrows out on lawns, on porches, ghosts hanging from trees in the windy weather—I just didn't suppose they'd call on *me*.

I was having a drink and suddenly heard a knock at the kitchen door. And, my God, when I opened it, there they were, a tiny band of them, in sheets and hats, masks, carrying bags—standing there like children on a *New Yorker* cover. And my heart sank like a stone. I had nothing, nothing at all—and me the new person along the road, and so few of us at that. Then I saw two parents lurking in the dark and rushed out to them.

I don't know what I said. Things like, this is a disaster, I forgot, I don't have a thing . . . but I made them come in. Come in, come in, I said, to all of them—come see my fire anyway—I don't have any candy—nothing—I forgot—but come in—let me see if I can find something. And they did, and the mothers of two tiny ones.

I had some apples. Who'll have an apple? I said. Silence. Then one of them said, I will, and held open a bag as big as he was— and we watched the apple drop in, and down—nothing in the bag—it fell like Satan through the void. Then they all took an apple. How about an onion? I said. Yes, they would have an onion, too. And a potato? I said, and we dropped those in, too. I was flying around, possessed. I found a can of anchovies. Who'd like this? I said—it's a can of anchovies. Silence. What's anchovies? one girl said. Tiny, tiny little salt fish, I said. Silence. I'll take an anchovy, she said, and held open her bag.

And that was it—no Cokes, no cider, no cookies, no nothing. Come see my fire, I said, and we trooped into the parlor to look at it, me chatting rather feverishly. And they were so darling in their funny little homemade things. I can't *think* how I came to forget, I told the mothers (nice women, large, shy). Now they have every right to bomb me out of existence (them standing there, bags in hand, watching from behind masks, listening, waiting). Oh, they won't do that, I expect, one mother said. We just live down the road, said the other. We introduced ourselves. The Williamses, the McFarlanes—me. We been meaning to call, they said—but one thing or another—you know. Yes, yes, I know, I said. Ain't this some cozy, one said, to the other, but to me, too. I ain't been here in a spell, since the Stinsons was—Rebecca —did you know them? No.

We chatted, but the children were impatient.

Oh, don't worry, both women said—they don't expect much —they're too young.

And they left, the children darting off, yipping into the dark.

So I got out the car and with a martini for company streaked into town, hoping to find Bartlett's still open, which it was. And loaded up with what he had left.

And nobody else showed up.

Well, that was my Halloween. And now I'm feeling like an absolute old fraud and failure. Shucks, as Fifi Laverne used to say, who's perfect?

Let us hope you did better.

JOURNAL. That whiz into town, clutching a martini, peering ahead through the dark—how I wanted someone along—it all pouring at me, rushing by—branches of spruce in a headlight, the road —lights at a farm. And over the brow of the hill, faint, faint in the harbor still, the last of the sunset—purple—a dash of orange. I wanted someone along—or to be back with me at the fire—on that most mysterious night of all, when the dead are permitted to roam and evil to come forth. Up here a touch of the old wildness to it— you feel it around. How could I have forgotten? Odd, a little, that the Hales did not come out.

WEDNESDAY 2 NOVEMBER. October gone. I remember of it the leaves turning, cold mornings, wind cold off the water, frost on the lawn, and more sun almost than you knew what to do with. Fog now. I welcome it as a gray reminder. And I can hear the horn at Black Horse Shoals. We have turned a corner and now walk resolutely down the road toward winter. Me with the rest of them, though not arm in arm.

Paule Loring's funny little Dud Sinker drawings of coastal Maine in winter haunt and cheer me.

SATURDAY 5 NOVEMBER. Note from Beth accusing me of not communicating (perhaps hadn't got my Halloween note yet). She knows more than you think she does. I don't really communicate, even with myself.

Amused myself, after I'd read it, wondering about happiness—decided it would be basically (a Bennington word) sexual and aesthetic, and added to that altruistic. Yes, just a small group, really—sexually attractive and handsome, interested in art, politics, very intelligent, and anxious to help others.

Chat with Ethel, whom I stopped by to see, an interesting one. She telling me that Richie would never make a real lobsterman—that something in him wanders from it; whereas Elmo, she says, gives himself to it, *is* all that, his boat, his gear, this place, instinctively. She shakes her head at his attempts to make Richie into that.

He's got to have something else, she says. You get him to paint with you, Helen. You get him away from El, or a little.

I told her they had stopped by. I said that maybe Elmo knew some of that, that he seemed to want Richie to come around by himself, maybe to draw with me.

Oh, yes, he knows, she said. El ain't slow. But what he knows and what he wants ain't the same. Elmo's selfish, you know, likes to own things. He wants Richie in tow, he wants him to work with him—he don't know yet if the boys will, and it worries him. More and more of them goes away, you know—something's changing—there might not be any of us left in a few years. Yes, I don't know that Elmo'd want Richie to *marry*, though sometimes I think he has his eye on Betsy for him. He's almost said as much, though she ain't but sixteen.

Should that have hurt? It did, a little. It was almost our first talk, hers and mine.

FRIDAY 11 NOVEMBER. This evening the first snow flew—is flying. Bits of a cold gray sky, detaching themselves, then gradually a whiteness gathering, in field, on wall—hiding the remains of fall. I stood out there thinking of N.Y., letting the darkness come around. For a while I could count the flakes, like torn-up letters from God, against the barn. They fell on my hair, my face, tiny instants of cold on my tongue when I stuck it out. And when I came inside I said I could have not one but two blue pitchers of martinis to celebrate the night—or to fortify against it. Both. I felt especially snug, and especially alone.

Yes, New York, the East River—a tug, its tiny scurrying light and the flakes curving toward it. And around me, out there, flakes falling on spruce, on bog, filling the chinks and crevices, the fissures in granite. Snow falling on a beach somewhere, filling the footprints summer left behind—old sand buckets. New York—the theaters, crowds (dark in winter garb)—or gathered in a room somewhere, drinking and talking. Do I miss all that? A little. Who wouldn't?

Yes, I'll walk out. I'll finish this, then I'll get my scarf and walk out, to meet all that, to say, Here I am—will you find me out?

SATURDAY 12. Woke to snow, the end of it. Everything white— brilliant sparkling—a fine storm (what was there to be afraid of?). I'll have more coffee, bask by my stove, read a *New Yorker*—then go in galoshes to shovel out the car. Light—how it fills this room, reflects off the ceiling now, the walls. A room of white light (imagine what Carole's must be). My barn singularly red. It was painted red for this.

EVENING. They were as good as their word. A jeep with snowplow attached wheeled in this afternoon and went to work scooping me out. It was Richie. I could see him, all whirling elbows and arms inside—did the drive, then plowed the turnaround, after which I waved to him from the path I had shoveled out to the station wagon to come in. Only about eight inches of it, though some had drifted. He got out carrying something that looked like a board. Came in wearing his knit cap and a faded red sweat shirt I've seen on him this fall, with a marsupial pouch for hands and a hood for the head. It was a painting he had; and something like a sense of well-being came over me at the sight of it—one of his. Stamping off snow.

I said, about the snow, Not that I'm not appreciative, but I could have made it out—I don't want you to consider me helpless, you know—I'm tough, and have snow tires.

I didn't have nothing to do, he said. Thought I'd bring this over.

A painting of lobster boats, all just about the same size, as if perspective hadn't occurred to him. But as boats, in profile, they had been drawn faithfully—things had an authentic look— and here and there a punt or skiff rode at a mooring. And he had used different colors—one of the skiffs was orange, one blue—and behind them, up in the air, so to speak, were some islands, a little like clouds only green. Then an odd thing happened to me. I realized, suddenly, that I couldn't improve on it, couldn't alter it for the better, had no power even to criticize: it was what it was. I was already admiring it.

It's better than the others, I said—isn't it? I saw him nod, him looking at it with me. I like it, I said. Do you?

He nodded again.

Do you like to paint? I asked.

I was watching his face. I saw something affirmative come over it, his shoulders move, hunch (his way of saying yes). Is it hard for you? I asked. I watched the way he said no, expressed it, heard him say, I just do it, saw him look at me a moment. Our faces suddenly became familiar, ordinary.

It had been done in poster paints. I said, Do you know oil paints?

Like that? he said, nodding at a bowl of flowers I had done on the wall across the room (we were in the kitchen), above a shelf of dishes by a calendar.

Yes—they give you more color, once you learn how to put them on. I think you should try them, they aren't as flat as that (nodding at his painting—we had propped it on a chair for the light). It isn't hard, after a while.

He rose and went to look at my painting. I watched him lean forward to peer, run his fingers over it. He nodded at me. When he came back, I said, If you like it I can show you how. All it takes is some practice. But I like yours. How did you learn?

With a shrug he said, I remember from school. And once in a while I do one. Then he fumbled in a pocket and brought out a piece of folded yellow paper, which he unfolded, looked at a moment, and handed to me. I could see that it was a poem, had the shape of a poem, handwritten—and grew nervous.

It was very simple, very *slim*. It rhymed. It had words scratched out but was fairly clean copy, in a childish round hand.

THE SEAGULL

I watch the seagull how it floats.
I watch it rise into the air.
I see it turn against the sun
And disappear.

I see the gull with its white wings
Is free.
I see it searching waters bare
Like me.

It sleeps on water, lives in air.
It has no troubles far or near.
If I were a gull I'd fly away
From here.

—Richard Hayden
Orstown, Maine

I said (handing it back to him), I think that's a real poem.
Keep it, he said—I got another copy.
Then I asked—Would you like to—fly away?
He shook his head.
You mean just in the poem?
Well—like something that can go where it likes, he said. Like you. I ain't been nowhere, you know—up to Bangor's about all. And on television you see places, and I get to thinking.
I like it here, I said, but everyone wants to get away, I suppose, for a while anyhow. I came up here to get *away* from so much that you see on television now. It seems to me that things are pretty much of a mess back there. Artificial, commercial—plastic —hysterical.
I wouldn't know, he said.
How old are you?
Getting on twenty-eight.

89

I get up and go to get us some coffee. Dusk is already falling outside. The snow looks blue, and I note how rich and somber the barn's red appears against it and my mind makes a painting of it. What fun to have him here, I think, as I pour and stir. He's easier, or more communicative, without Elmo. I remember the poem.

Are you going to buy that island? he asks.

It's so abrupt that I'm taken by surprise. I think a moment. I don't know, I say. Do you think I should?

I would, he says.

Why would you? I ask, rather pleased.

Oh (vaguely)—I'd like a place—somewhere to be by myself.

You'd like to be by yourself?

A shrug. Sometimes.

I'm a little afraid of it, I say—of the water, too, of a boat.

We can show you, like he said—it ain't hard.

Maybe you'd come out to paint sometime, I say (feeling as if I were pouncing on a mouse).

I see him looking out the window at the barn.

I want to paint water, and islands, I say (bustling on). Do you think you'd ever come out to paint with me?

He's suddenly vague again, but I hear him say, I might.

Might, I mumble, mimicking him, but he doesn't hear.

Oh, he says (he'd forgotten something)—they told me to ask you for supper tonight—Ethel did.

Then he's rising, pushing back from the table.

Tell them I'd like to, I say. What time?

Around six.

I hesitate, then I say, I like your painting a good deal—I really do wish you would come and paint with me here—I could show you about oils.

I see him nod.

Thanks for plowing me out, I say.

Back from Ethel's—my face at the window again—rereading my "scene."

Not really *great* dialogue but it went like that. Didn't catch the style of his speech. A matter of rhythm, inflection—like "guesso," one word—"gisso." Nor do I have his vocabulary yet; I tend to substitute my own.

Supper was fine. As usual, it was good to be with them. And an event, of sorts: Elmo was at the sink when I came in, scrubbing himself. Not embarrassed in the least. He's used to no one's paying attention. He turned, soaping under an arm, and welcomed me, nodding with his head to say, Ethel's in there. Such a mass of flesh. I had been right about the chest—a pelt of black hair. Great, comfortable-looking stomach—comfortable—yes—even fat; yet suggestive of fullness and power, maturity, a father's. Then his back as he turned again, broad, densely fleshed.

I was startled by the breasts; matted and fat-muscular, they leaped like stuffed fur bags when his arms moved. Something exceedingly sensual there to me.

At the table with all of us, I said, Richie says he'll come over to paint with me—I'm going to show him how to use oils. And when he looked at me I raised my head, coquettishly, as if daring him to deny.

He did, I said to Ethel, though I suppose he'll say that he didn't.

Richie's going to be like one of them summer artists here, Elmo said.

Well, I wish he would, Ethel said to me—pass the squash. He's good, but he needs help.

How did that jeep work? Elmo asks, reaching for rolls (and I imagine under the shirt how the breast muscles leap, fix, relax, in their haired sacks).

Worked good, Richie says.

And you were nice to help a lady out, but don't baby me.

We like to help ladies out, Elmo says.

It's that down-East hospitality they advertise, Ethel says—like chowder and lobsters. Now, have a roll before they get cold, and pass them.

I see his back at the sink, the broad curve of it, like the sway-back of a draft horse. But I won't "Mallek" him, like a bitch in heat, which I am at times. Come off it, girl—am *frequently*.

MONDAY 14. A dark, Poeish November, rain-sodden. And me with the Curse to match. Ghoul-haunted. Leaf-wet.

Went to my first quilting. A good deal of gathering and chattering. We're to meet regularly, Wednesdays at seven. I'm looking forward to it. I have my hoops.

TUESDAY 15. Rain still—washing the snow away—blue slush, brown slush. I'm remembering those walks this summer. Come a good day and I'll go for one. The town had a quiet and patient look to it when I drove in for mail. No one in sight—a car or two.

Sodden piles of dark cut wood no one has come for. Wet granite. Tall clumps of orange grass.

Friday 18 November

Dear Herb,

No, your letters are welcome. I don't get many. Beth is faithful, as faithful as I am. And I like to hear news, and the patter of your bright mind around it.

It snowed the other night and I went out in it and thought of New York—of the apartment—of the way things would look from up there. I do miss it. I loved that place and I'm glad to have someone in it I knew and also love.

You ask how it goes with me, when am I coming back, about why I did leave.

Well—as they say—it was many things. It was you and me. It was that sense of being gradually swamped by something—all that is going to make the global village—the sense of things getting too big too fast—the sense of culture without nature, as I began to put it to myself. It was commercialism, faddism, the new style, and feeling so out of touch with it (but how keep in touch with something that now changes every year?)—so out of touch with the young, who are taking over the world in a way I can't cope with, their arrogance, their assumptions, their terrible innocence and knowingness. I preferred them when they were the silent generation. No—I tend to admire them like this, if they'll only persist and not, as they say, drop out and into some other pose.

Yes, and one other thing, which is elusive, or hard to be clear about. I had begun to miss certain things, which will sound a bit sappy, but how my father used to take us all to the beaches, when they were always a surprise. The beaches—*not* one long line of shore development—a kind of innocence to things, a naturalness. I seemed to be looking for that, for something lost, or just gone. For my father, perhaps. So that I *had* to make a break for it, a try. And maybe it is gone; it may be that something I call terrible has happened, something irrevocable. Universe City. Fifty *billion* of us! As for your note of utter horror, I can't believe, or can't accept it— universal suffocation within fifty years. We, I, must go on as if that were hysterical doomsdayism, *could* not happen. (And yet, at moments, I feel that I want it to, that we all do, that we're making it happen—think—*think* of the excitement, if what you told me is true, I mean if we knew!)

I'm learning to quilt. We meet—about eight ladies and I—at the Grange Hall, and sit as close to a big potbellied stove as we can, though it's not *that* cold yet. One of the husbands comes and builds a fire for us. And we stitch and gab. I keep saying they're simple, without being quite sure what I mean. They have simple surfaces. They're staunch, they're tough, they have humor, they work. They'd look tacky in N.Y. but they look fine up here. Not much fashion about them—they're fashioned to last, to stay put—social fossils, I suppose you'd call them. And gradually I learn about this place and begin to see that it's the last of something, people living at the edge of a precariousness that is dangerous and beautiful, old-style America, what we once came from, belonged to.

You might be pleased to learn that I have abandoned *Finnegans Wake*—even my page a day. Simply too much for a lone female to handle. On the other hand, I doubt that your finely honed mind could handle it either. Maybe Sal could.

SATURDAY 19 NOVEMBER. Nothing much. Just thinking back to N.Y., my letter to Herb. I wanted to tell him about Elmo Hale, didn't I?—about seeing him at the sink. What would I have said? Something bitchy, no doubt—that it rendered me, as they say, concupiscent. Yes, I liked that great curve, didn't I, of stomach and back? I'd never thought of certain *stomachs* as having an appeal, an aura of the sensual about them. The male belly. Let me feel the words. Belly. Which implies fat, or much flesh. And a sense of the exposed, of bareness—him soaping, moving that soapy rag over his chest, then his stomach, talking (I couldn't hear)—then lifting the arm again. I could neither move nor look except at his face—I remember a kind of smile, fat, comfortable.

JOURNAL. The second quilting. Yes, I'm going to like it there, and they show me, help me out. I think I'm glad I'm not with Ethel's group.

Richie and Elmo—I do think about them. Do they *know* Gertrude? Obviously they know who she is. Has Elmo been out there,

93

perhaps? Would I be surprised to learn that he has? One of her "big-uns," maybe.

Richie—yes, I'm interested. I'll tell Beth.

Thanksgiving with them tomorrow. I'm bringing pies.

Friday 25 Nov.

Beth,

It's me again, after Thanksgiving with the Hales. I'm in love with them, as I must have said.

I'm on my second martini. And not much, actually, to report. Except that we were all there, including Elmo's mother, a former schoolteacher here (which still conveys status), and a quite old woman she lives with now in Ellsworth. They were sweet in their flowered dresses, pecked and chatted away, reminisced, appreciated, were attentive to me, as I to them. Elmo had driven over to bring them down. He drove them back, and stopped by for a drink at my house on his way home, he and his friend Richie Hayden, to celebrate, apparently, or relax.

I've talked about Richie, haven't I? admitted that I've become "interested"—quotation marks since I don't quite approve it myself, he being in the neighborhood of thirty, me beyond that of forty. But he paints, and even writes an occasional poem, and showed me one, and it was quite good, or so I thought. Which does suggest the unusual, since the painters and poets among these people tend to make tracks, or become eccentrics. Art here is "something the women do"—paint shells or bits of wood, or make quilts. The men express themselves more directly in their work. Richie is a lobsterman. He *oughtn't* to paint or write poems. It isn't quite normal.

So you can see what I mean when I say that I'm interested—a sensitive lobsterman, unmarried—to hand, so to speak. Well— that's my little excitement up here and I'll admit that it sounds mid-Victorian, and that I—may—even—be—making—it—up.

Dinner was fun. Familial. Plentiful. Untold quantities of food, of just the sort you would imagine—New England—steaming— mashed potatoes, onions, carrots, biscuits, gravy, turkey, and three pies I had made that were darn good—a mince and two pumpkins. And apple cider and coffee—and everything eaten down to the bones and the crumbs. Then the clearing away, the cleaning up, the sitting around. Stoves going.

Oh, and lots of good little things, I mean apart from Thanksgiving. I help at church suppers, rummage sales, see my ladies for coffee. I quilt, I work; I'm becoming again a marvelous cook, and have, incidentally, soon to ask a few people for supper. I don't know what to do about liquor (maybe just finesse it and pass a few joints around).

I think about you. Yes, and about the Heights. A postcard of the mind—I see it now and then imprinted against the spruce that ring my yard and look down on me—one world against another. And what I hate is the fact that they mutually exclude. Write soon. I need letters.

JOURNAL. I was fairly honest with her, wasn't I? And I'm fairly honest with myself these days. Because I want all this to be good; it isn't a fling; I'm no longer Fifi Laverne.

Their visit—piling in late after taking the ladies home. Elmo jovial again, presiding, spreading himself warmly around. He beamed—Mrs. Calder—Helen—I was both. Richie here—a kind of property of his.

I brought out drinks without asking. What did we talk about? I hardly remember. It was all physical presence that mattered. And Richie is almost dead silent between us, though in some real sense he was the one we were concerned with, referred to.

And me—did I keep to my role of bluff, good-natured lone female, a sport? I'm a little tired of it—and a little afraid of being unable to play any other, should occasion demand. But it makes us easier together. Elmo and I are beginning to feel that we know each other—nothing that I would call an undercurrent, just know, feel at home with. His initial approach to women is through good humor, good nature, a general liking for them that puts him at ease in their company. I'm seeing him as more simple than for a while I had thought—*not* devious.

Richie the silent, the boy-man. He said he might come around Sunday to be shown about oils—Elmo watching, listening, as if proud of a backward son.

SATURDAY 26. Out for a drive—through clear and brilliant air to Jonesport. Odd little place. And Beal's Island. So spare, sparse, so huddled and crouched. And yet I loved it. So *little* between them and this fierce and unrelenting world. We seem far more secure, substantial here—they more a fishing village, we more a seaport town. I have a curious impression of transparency—and of little

Old Glories out everywhere waving—and of cemeteries by the sea. Life and death at the ocean's edge. Seen from the moon, a barnacle town.

JOURNAL SUNDAY EVENING 27. An event. Richie here in the morning. I hadn't really believed he would show up. But he did.

I showed him my painting room upstairs. Jules and I had carted an old Regency-style sofa up. I have an easel, a large table, two wicker chairs—geraniums at the windows—sea shells—two good reproductions of Marin. I had painted the room white, had cleaned up the stove, a small potbellied one, shaped like a barrel. It's a happy room and warms in a minute. And we made a fire. All I did was provide him with drawing paper and a palette—white paint, black, blue, and yellow—and showed him a little about mixing them and wiping and washing the brushes—and watched him for a while before setting to work on the blue-shadows–red-barn I had started. When I went to look again he had made a picture of a wharf. I squeezed out some ocher for him. Try mixing them, I said, just to see what happens. I saw that he worked very intently. Bold, innocent. And, curiously, he did not muddy the colors. It became instantly unposterlike, alive. His preference is for the color pure.

Well, lesson number one. I said, It takes time to find out what you want to do and what you can. You don't have to paint like anyone else.

One other good thing: my own painting, barn and snow shadows, was better—for seeing how strong his own work was, perhaps. I was working in broader, bolder strokes and stronger colors. I think he'll come again. I must be careful about what I tell him— like a child, he seems to know what he wants and picks the quickest way to get there.

THURSDAY 1 DECEMBER. Dropped by to see Ethel. Would she and Elmo and Richie come to supper Saturday? She said, Oh, you don't have to have us, you know—we like having you here—it's easy for us. But I'd like to, I said. Then I can ask a few others around, my coffee ladies and all. I'll practice on you.

Well, we'd like to, she said. We never do go out, except when the stove's out.

I'm going to try a chicken thing—mushrooms and sour cream,

mashed potatoes—biscuits—fresh string beans I'll have to go to Ellsworth for.

SATURDAY 3 DECEMBER. Now, I'm not going to get stinking but I am going to celebrate. All that happened was that Elmo, whose hair was specially combed, rose to the occasion by saying, Come on, Mom, when I said, I always have a martini before supper—would anybody join me, with anything? Yes, and he stood right up and said, in his broadest, Now, I don't know about the martini part, but if you've got a little something not too strong—and that did it. I said, I make a very fine whiskey sour, a sort of punch—and to Ethel, Not very strong. And the first thing you know there we were, seated around the fire, cozy as anything. Hers *was* weak —theirs fairly strong. And even squeezed a second down them, during which Elmo gave me a wink without moving a muscle.

And we had coffee afterward—on home ground by then—and they stayed until after eleven. Food excellent—commendations. And some conversation that was more than local weather reports and doings. Ethel started it.

Well, here you are, she said—up here—in winter. Are you glad?

And that led me around to speaking my new old piece a little— about the great urban sprawl out there, global villages, megalopolis, communications, advertising, developers, revolution, the young—I just touched at this or that, but it got them going, too. Because they hear about a lot of it; they don't quite know, at first hand, but they hear, they get the news. And what it brought out in them was their own feeling for where and how they live.

They know they're to the side of it, but they feel proud of themselves, of this place, terribly independent—they don't *like* unions, they don't like to be told what they can and can't do— they *hate* the thought of an able-bodied man being paid not to work. Because they're close to nature here, in its midst—they fight with their bare hands—and haven't got time for six-hour days, limits, controls. And they're losing.

Elmo says, The boys can get more money, easier work, down in Connecticut—at the shipbuilding yards, the steelyards. It's too hard here for them now—and there ain't nothing for them to do. We'd like Davie and Ralph to stay with us, but the more training you give them, the more they want to get away. We're old-fashioned, from all we hear.

And isn't that what is going?—to be replaced by great security systems, control systems, group systems, computers, corporations? They seem to me to be clinging like limpets to something doomed, a way of life. So many places in Maine—FOR SALE—or simply abandoned. Yes, it's their independence, the way they make do, patch and repair, so that they can go out again—it's that I like. They wouldn't leave, the ones who have chosen to stay, though they'll be driven out—the taxes will get them, *are* getting them.

I said, It *is* a revolution, and perhaps it is going to free a lot of us, so that we can paint, or play, be more human, enjoy what's around us. But what I'm afraid of is that we're losing the chance for a decent way of life, of finding decent work to do—like this.

And Ethel says, It is a decent way of life. And we know it's hard—El and Richie in the season up and out at four, sometimes gone for two days, rough or smooth. Yes, it's work down here. Not much time for gallivanting. But it's our town, this is our own world, and you get so as you wouldn't trade it in on a new model.

People wanting to travel, to run off, she says—well, travel's all right, I expect, but all you do is see, visit. You can't join in since it ain't yours.

Yes, we had a nice talk—and the fire going—drinking coffee, though Elmo had himself a shot or two in the kitchen—I saw him putting the jigger down and then looking at me with a smile he hides in that big face. Good food, he said—Helen, you're quite a cook. Richie and me are going to come by tomorrow and help you clean up.

My party, my tiny success.

SUNDAY 4. They did come by. I had left some of the things just in case. And we had coffee, and then Elmo said, Go up and help Richie paint—I'll clear away—go on. So we did since he wanted us to.

Richie learns fast—and is very neat about the brushes and keeping them clean. He did the barn and the spruce and the yard out there and their truck down below. Instinctively he goes for the right colors. And little things have a fussy look to them and big things a simple look, and all of it a homemade. And after a while Elmo came up to smoke and sit and look. When you going to paint me? he says, and I knew he'd had a drink. So I say, Right now, and he looks pleased. Like this? he says—and then he says, I'd guessed as how you was going to paint me naked, and I

98

raise my eyebrows at him and a knowing, good-humored smile spreads across his broad face.

So I sketch him with charcoal as he sits, and it goes well except for the face, which I tell him I'll have to work on—and do a few small studies of it on the side and come closer. But him, in general, I get quite well and can sense how the body goes, under the trousers and wool shirt, and remember him at the sink. And I see that he likes to sit there being drawn. Not that he's vain, he's just basically pleased with himself, contented. I believe, in fact, that he would pose for me—for us, maybe. Richie, I think, would not.

And when I show him what I've done, he stands there pulling at his lower lip. Then he goes to see what Richie has done. Well, now, look at that, he says—ain't that nice? Now don't wean him away from the lobstering, he says—I need him out there.

I'm to have supper with them tonight. I'm excited about my painting, the first figure I've tried, from life, in some time, and it's good, it's sound. I must keep it simple, bold.

WEDNESDAY 7 DECEMBER. The day of infamy. And how far away it now seems.

Wars come and go, disasters lose their sharp outlines, tragedy blurs away into mere sorrow, a rusting machine, a boat on a beach, or a monument, and this place would hardly alter, one would think, in the flux of events. The people here, the men, seem a little like Wordsworth's shepherd, who lost a son to civilization but kept watching the sky.

Which is menacing right now. A leaden gray, and snow flurries. Flakes drifting, then swirled by a bit of wind over the broken grass of my lawn.

Buster stalking around and the crows making mock of him. As I throw out bread they learn to come closer, and play a kind of game with him, wheeling in over the barn, great shadowy marauders. And the little birds, the tits and juncos, and the clamorous jays—I like to think they need me now—want pumpkin and sunflower seed.

DECEMBER 8. More snow. Just lazily it's there, whitening the ground.

JOURNAL MONDAY 12 DECEMBER. Back from shopping in Bangor.

Bought a fine set of paints, brushes, palette, box, the works, for Richie—almost too much. Some simple but nice beads for Ethel, who admired some jade ones I had; red bandannas for Elmo, who I noticed uses them; and things for the children (a very nice, *young* perfume for Betsy, and a pin for Anne). It's hard not to overdo—buying for them is a treat. But I don't want to appear as Lady Bountiful. And a few tiny things for my ladies—a cactus which I'm putting into a nicer pot for Carole Bean.

I've decided to ask my ladies to lunch, Friday. I think they're curious about my place.

THURSDAY 15. Drove up to Tainesville. A lot more elegant than we; more summerized, and looking more desolate with so many things closed, so many houses shuttered up. A number of the huge old summer places I remember from Jamestown, versions thereof, preside rather pompously. A main street with several smart shops (closed) circles the harbor, which has fewer fishing boats than ours—a marina. Altogether they are more sheltered, more "up bay," though a part of the town where only the local folk live made me feel at home—down sandy lanes were small, neat houses, lobster traps in the yards, white-painted fences, trucks and skiffs resting.

You have the feeling that most of the local people caretake now, cater to summer traffic, or the summer regulars, the ones with money, estates. Oh, yes, we're more brilliant altogether—more daring, one might say—less sullied, more exposed.

Will it fade, will it pass, what we have? Are we slated for some contemporary version of all that? Oh, pray, no rash of mobile homes. But prayer, I'm afraid, is not valid now—the horrors are on the move, are heading this way. I've seen them poised in selling lots along Route 1—elsewhere. I'll die facing the enemy. But what, exactly, is the enemy? Not the rich. *Scientia*—surely that's it.

SATURDAY 17. What about the ladies? Nothing. I'm in a mood. Oh, fine, fine. Yes, it was. Crab salad, a *good* soup, muffins, a pie —I didn't overdo (why am I afraid of that?). Yes—and nice chatter by a fire. But ladies are not my dish. Quiet—shush. No, I just mean that I'm not essentially a ladies' lady, I need a good strong mix of the male in my social diet. The quilting is fine, and the morning coffee, but at the Hales' there's Elmo, whose presence is like some rich and salty perfume.

SUNDAY 18. A cold gray day, a day, so to speak, with little love in it—when who should appear but Richie, and all thought of weather vanishes. He's there to paint. So we make a fire upstairs.

Elmo's portrait, to call it that, is still on my easel and I see it freshly. I've done him with his knit cap on and the feeling is black, red, blue. I'm pleased with the proportions. I have him seated by a window—and suddenly I know how I want the whole picture—I want his profile reflected in that mirror, darkly and almost without detail, a kind of shadow. I had Richie take his place, and I sketched the shadow in.

Richie drew a boat, and a wharf with some dark little figures on it, then set right to work painting it in. I went to watch him and he worked as if I weren't there. I went downstairs and brought up a book and during a break pointed out examples of this or that—of very bold work that produces an impression rather than an exact reproduction.

I said, Why don't you try to copy this one (a Dufy of water, boats, little clouds)—just to see how it goes?

There were some Marins in the book and I talked about them a little. He liked them. But when I showed him two Wyeths he shook his head at them. What he said was interesting: I like to make up from what I remember. He liked a certain painting that had an orange sky and blue clouds. I said, All right, don't be afraid of color, and I left him looking through the book and went back to work on the Hale.

Talk with him about painting excites me. I see ways of escaping from my inability to paint a drawing, so to speak, which has always been a problem. My drawings play with the realistic, my paintings can depart, move toward color and mass—even toward using paint as paint. Shadow of Mallarmé, who told us that a century ago.

I want a drawing of Elmo as I saw him by the sink. A drawing and a painting. Can I ask him to pose? When I don't have the courage of fantasy, and a drink?

TUESDAY 20. All day making Christmas cards. Made sort of Dud Sinkerish drawings of a lobster boat coming in to a wharf with a Christmas tree tied to a mizzenmast for Beth and family, for Jeremy, for Herb and Sal, for a few others. Went up back to look for a tree and spotted a four-foot spruce I can use. In to Ellsworth to buy ornaments. Not much choice, but some nice little strings of silver balls at an antique shop. I want this place to be nice for them when they come. Ethel says to come have Christmas Eve supper with them.

Christmas lights are up and on in town—innocent old strings of yellow-blue-red-green-white bulbs hanging looped across the street in carnival fashion. Against that cold black water, those small houses and chilled streets, they seem almost wildly gay and brave.

THURSDAY 22. Snow falling and night falling fast, oh, fast. . . .

A great rich snow, huge-flaked, like our first one, soundless, a falling of feathers—as if from those geese that passed long ago. New York—walking on Madison Avenue at night in snow—almost no traffic, rubies of taillights, the streets white and trackless, and the lights from the store windows pouring silently onto the sidewalks and the flakes falling through them, casting fleet shadows. Tall buildings almost featureless. One or two black figures, muffled indistinct, and all of us curiously united by the beauty of the storm. All light at street level. Snow falling in the East River, on my balcony. I have a good fire going here. Mendonca somewhere (comfortably?) in the shadows of memory. I may invite him in.

I imagine Pennyless—and suddenly, crazily, long to be out there, my shores ringed with ice and black water, the other islands lost as in fog. Why? That way poetry lies, or madness. Me sinking into nature, vanishing like Richie's gull, grown soundless as a stone.

FRIDAY 23. Snow all day. I shoveled out to the barn and started the car, and sat in it, smoking, letting it warm so that the windshield would clear. The road plows had been by. A dry snow—suave drifts of it at a red barn's corner (glimpse of cut stone). I think of the mice in there, warm in old heaps of hay, and suddenly wonder how tiny things find food, or if they go hungry on days like this—so close to death's shadowy wall. I think of Gertrude and her father by a stove.

Back in the house warming myself at the fire—slight sense of trepidation, of being surrounded, marooned, as she was—when I heard the jeep; and then saw it pushing its way in—and my sense of comfort, of rich pleasure, returned. It was out there perhaps five minutes—then, to my disappointment, it drove off.

But then it came back, pushed around for a while, neatening the snow into blade-curved white walls I could see in its headlights, then switched them off. Dark figure getting out, black against the snow. Coming around to the lights I had turned on. It was Elmo, shaking off snow, stamping.

Richie's had a cold. Gets one a year. Be over it by Christmas.

Without asking him, I fixed us a highball, and we sat in the kitchen. I said, You looked pleased at something. He did—round and fat, beaming at me, at the snow. He and Richie are fixing their gear, are taking an outboard apart, are repairing their traps (over six hundred of them). It's fixing time.

How's my picture coming along? he wanted to know.

Would you like to see it? I said.

We went up and I showed it to him. It's not quite finished, I said, trying to see it through his eyes. I saw him nod at it. Now ain't that fine. You ain't got my face in yet. I said, Would you sit a while and let me try for it again, downstairs?

We sit in the kitchen again, he across from me at the table, and I tell him to go on with his drink but to pause from time to time. And we talk and I sketch.

Do you mind this? I ask—let me fix that drink.

I come back with it. What I want is to draw you as if you were standing at the sink washing yourself. I can't get bodies.

I feel it as a rakehell remark but he apparently does not, and from that fund of good humor he says, Anything to please a lady. The word stirs its little swirl of dust in my mind and I say, *Would* you just come by sometime?—I'd be grateful—I'd make you a pie.

A pie, he says (poi)—I wouldn't need no pie. One more of these and I'll sit in my socks for you. At which he smiles—a slow broadening of his face—And two more, de'ah, and I'll take *them* off. And I see him looking at me.

We seem to have met somewhere and my sense of the furtive vanishes, I'm instantly easier and say, Well, we can keep the socks on, but I'd be very grateful.

I work at the face a while longer—until I think I have *some* of it, then I push the notebook across to him and watch him look at the sketches.

After shoving them around a moment he says, It still ain't me yet, is it?

No, I admit. Can you tell why?

Well, he says—you got me looking like that pie.

You have a round face.

But he's right—because it's not merely round, his face—it's big-boned and strongly fleshed, could bite into a joint of beef. Faces are hard for me, I say. People are.

Richie likes that book you lent him, he says. Betsy made fun of it and he jumped her. She says, I know why you go painting to Mrs. Calder's, and he says, Why? and she says, Because she's beautiful, that's why. And now they ain't talking.

I let it pass. Do you like the way he paints? I ask.

And he says, He ain't had much learning, but he gets some of it, don't he?

He does, I say. Do you mind it—that he does paint?

I see him shrug. If a man wants to paint, I don't see why he shouldn't. Like me—now I might go make up to some lady, when I get the time.

Cigarette in hand, he rubs at his jaw. A man does what suits him. Richie, he likes to paint—me, I like to scratch around a little—I like women, you know. He nods. Ea'ah—I like women.

I like this, too, he says, lifting the glass again. Like to sit around, you know. I would like to pose for you, sometime. The big face is looking at me—no smile but the good humor is there and a kind of frankness with it—and as if he were letting me in on a secret he says, Don't say nothing to Ethel, you know.

Something there in the eyes, some sense of an offer, and I reach for the sketches evasively, shuffle them into the notebooks.

He sat through another drink, though he didn't stay long, but certain elements between us had shifted.

I stepped out with him to find that the snow had stopped and that, almost miraculously, the stars were shining. Things had a white, cold, almost breathless smell, an enormous cleanliness to them. The grape arbor was a gallows against the sky—odd reminder of summer.

SUNDAY 25 CHRISTMAS DAY. Last night at Ethel's, and Elmo bringing out a bottle of blackberry cordial and the children fixing the tree with boxes and *boxes* of old ornaments and the crumpled remains of tinsel and icicles. A child's tree, things more or less thrown on—not so many when all was said and done. Ethel somewhat indifferent to the whole process, chatting with me, sipping a little tentatively at the cordial and sort of licking her lips; Elmo

stopping little quarrels (Now what in Christ's name *ails* you—
stop that, or you'll get my boot on your ass) and helping Richie
with the lights, very much the big dad. Richie sniffled into a
bandanna and looked red-eyed, noncommunicative.

I left my things as inconspicuously as I could under the tree.
Can I catch their voices yet? Or his? "Chroist." "Moight."
"Toime." You *sense* the diphthong, the broadening—it's there,
buried in the throat. And hearing him like that—"Ye'll get moi
boot on yer ahss"—I realize again these people are hard to define.
In England they would be lower class—working people. Here
they're of a class similar, I suppose, to country people, farmers—
nonurban. At the margins only of the modern world, of highways
and city streets. And have room, still, to be what they are.

We all went to church and sang and endured the sermon—
the church filled with evergreens—lights outside at the stained
windows—white walls—a sense of New England in the snow, and
of heated bodies in a room, steaming the windows.

Elmo in a dark suit, looking stalwart, reassuring—formidable.
Richie, too, a smaller version. Ethel in a hat that makes you
realize she is both contemporary American and local Maine. Not
one female managed a bit of smartness, including me, who looked
like a visiting aunt.

And then back home under those carnival lights that hung over
the snow, bright, cheerful, irresistibly simple. The little houses
looking perched and small. Here a shingle, there a clapboard, here
white, there yellow, or red, everything very *light* in the snow. Ethel
and the girls rode in my car, the girls awake in the cold, chattering.

Ethel produced coffee and we sat around for a while with the
TV going and the tree turned on. They had presents for me, which
I took home and put under my tree—stirred my fire and had one
small whiskey.

Then Christmas morning, all sunlight and snow, the crows, the
spruce. I opened things—a package from Beth: books; and a tiny
bouquet of artificial flowers—lovely—lacquered paper, bits of colored glass; and a book from Elmo and Ethel: Maine recipes, with
fine little drawings scattered through (as this journal should have
—yes, perhaps I'll do that); a little thing the children had made:
a tiny fishing wharf with miniature pot buoys, traps, a gull, all
painted, obviously their own, exuding the charm of a child's thing.
Richie had wrapped up a new painting. I *think* it's the island,
Pennyless—green, white, and pink, viewed from where we first

landed that day. It's his, his way, but he's learned from that book, too.

And as I was bestirring, car noises outside, a jeep, and then he was knocking at the door.

He had brought back the book. Coffee. And after remarks about the picture, that I liked it, etc., and shy thanks from him for the brushes, the painting box, etc., I said what about painting for a while.

He built a fire upstairs in the painting room. I feel that he likes it up there.

I suggested that he just play with colors again, practice producing them, practice brush strokes—I even suggested that he could paint with a palette knife if he liked, and showed him.

I look at him when he can't see that I am. So intent. He seems to ignore me as he mixes and applies his paint, yet it's not that; he's engrossed, absorbed. He *is* a painter. Impossible to say whether good, but has that quality of urgency at his work. I see how his hair curls in little sculptured waves at his neck, which is round, a short column; I note how he stands, planted on what must be strong legs under paint-stained woolen trousers, how his shoulders slope. I like his hands—not pudgy but plump, and (though short-fingered) capable, finely made.

I myself worked at trying to get Elmo's face in, from the sketches I had made.

I said, Elmo stopped by and I made sketches of him. What do you think?

He came to look and seemed unimpressed.

I said, I came in when he was washing himself at the sink one day; I told him I'd like to paint him like that and he said I could. Do you think he meant it?

A shrug. He probably did.

Of a kind, I say, Elmo has a fine body. If he would pose for me, would you want to try, too?

He shook his head. And after a moment said, He just does that for you, you know—he wouldn't want me around.

Why not?

'Cause you're you, a lady, a woman—and he'll do what you want him to.

Did he know Gertrude Hardy?—I mean especially?

Ask him, he says.

Did you?

I knew her, he says—some.

Elmo said you courted her.

A shrug. And as he bends to mix paint he says, He was just talking, getting at me—at you. He likes to. You might not think it but he likes a good time, women and all, even with that family he's got. He'd pose for you—pose in the raw if you asked him to—don't give a goddamn, when he's out. He ain't like me—what you would call quiet.

We drift out of talk back to work.

THURSDAY 29 DECEMBER. My tree alight, my fire ablaze, Buster soaking in the heat—and through a martini a sense of the weather outside, brilliant as diamonds. In my mind I see snow sparkle, stars glitter green, flash, as if near. This house sustains itself against all that, creaks and snaps in the cold but holds it at bay.

2

Dearest Beth,

Greetings for the New Year. The flowers are on my desk, so fragile, yet they'll probably outlast me. And so lovely. They are a touch of you, something of your presence in this room, which I need.

No news, though I feel like talking. Not sure about what. Maybe Christmas, which involved the Hales—a family affair with children scampering, church Christmas Eve (my, how they sit in the pews, dressed up, and listen, or seem to—I love them in their "good" clothes)—presents back and forth—a giving, a getting. It knits me in. And we had snow, as I expect you did from what I read.

I'm still not getting to know many people. I think that in living here, making a living out of a place that grudges them one, even threatens them with not, they're doing something difficult to do, and have little time for excursions, play, extras—all their talk, their spare time, is somehow about that, about this place, about surviving here. There isn't room, or time, for strangers. It's wonderful here, and I love it, I do. But at times there is simply no one— no one who knows me.

But still, I am getting good at quilting, producing a beauty. We sit at a stove (which itself I love), in a sparely lit, beautiful old Grange Hall here that echoes with earlier voices, and add our own, talk stories and sew, and I love it. Homely and close, like going to market. A continual gossipy flow of talk, filled with what they are and think about and need and want. Now, back then, one will say, you could get that at Sarah Brundage's for a nickel—we still got the crocks she put it in—made her own stoppers, you know—back then they made do—it's all buy-it-and-throw-it-away now—yes, and not near so good. And it flows, their talk, in a watery way, around these beautiful and ancient shores, into, out of, the spruce, the great pointed walls of dark spruce, around houses, down their small windblown, winding streets . . . so knit into this place, this life, they are.

Beth, you would love them, too, and know just what I'm trying to say, and know why I need you, one of *us*, an ally, not to put *them* down, simply to withstand, understand, in the midst of all this that is so real and beautiful, though I am three feet under snow at the moment and about to dive into a third martini, which may permit a certain ghostlike shape to visit me (one more and I'll tell you about him—others—my companions through all this).

My casserole is baking to a brick. I need food.

Happy wishes for the New Year—to you and yours.

JOURNAL SATURDAY 7 JANUARY. The snow has a cold, sculpted look where the wind has drifted it. Long swirls around the barn, making blue shadows, and the barn in sunlight a more marvelous red even than when the rain used to darken it—drier, more brilliant. The cold has kept it, the snow.

Richie around yesterday to paint after he had plowed the remains of a Thursday-night flurry. I said, Let's both do the barn. I was pleased with mine. His work—somewhere, already, between modern and primitive, with a touch still of the child. He could see that the shadows had blue in them and somehow his white, his snow, was golden. He becomes absorbed and works fast, and what he did that I liked was to frame the barn with a part of the window we looked out from. Once he came over to look at what I was doing. No comment, he just stood there a moment, then went back to his own.

The Hale around this afternoon, on the prowl. Or it felt like that.

When you gonna paint me in the raw? he said, over a highball in the kitchen.

You really wouldn't mind? I say.

Not me, he says—I like to oblige. He's in one of his expansive moods, so I say, I'd like to paint you standing here at my sink washing yourself.

Shouldn't be no trouble to that, he says, and I go on to say, I'd want you to wear boots, I'd want a wool shirt hanging somewhere.

And he says, Well, there ain't no time like the present, de'ah, let's start *right now*. Oh, yes, there was a drink or two under that belt—no doubt. And I hesitate—then I say, I'll have to get my pad.

I see him take a long finishing pull at his glass, tilting, tilting it, see him lower it, rise, hear him ask how mine is. I say, Yes, fix me another.

Upstairs I peer out at the snow, thinking of him down there, as if our roles, almost, were going to be reversed, as if I were the one who was to pose, he waiting for me to appear. But he's the one who's been asking me to, I tell myself, he's asked me to several times. I find my pad and go back downstairs.

To find the kitchen overflowing with him. Not him. Something else. A new substance—luminous, vital. He's rolled his winter underwear down and stands at the sink, back to me, filling a glass with ice. And I feel as if I should keep away—I had forgotten how big he is, how much flesh is there, just on his back. And he turns, glass in hand, and holds it a moment, sloshing it for me, playing the ice around. Here, he says, holding it out. Then, Where you want me? He goes to the table for his own.

By the sink, I tell him. I take a long pull at my highball, put it down. (There are gaps in things, in time, in history. How did I get here?) I place a chair across the room from the sink.

I want you to stand as if someone had just come in—I want a cloth in your hand. You're pausing to talk to this person before you go on washing. I want that shirt hanging there (I nod at a latch on a cupboard).

Yes, keep your drink, go on talking—look natural. You don't mind?

I see that smile of his broaden. Mind?—I like to help a nice woman out—and he suddenly swells up his chest, which seems elastic, balloons to stretch hair, lift muscle-fat breasts. From a window a pale bluish light streams in to form almost a veil between him and me—cigarette smoke.

My pencil moves over him—almost it rather than my eyes— seems to touch, translate him. Outlines, at first.

Time passes. He's patient—drinks now and then. I'm getting it. I pause to hold the drawing out. The proportions are there. There's a sense of it all there: bones, musculature, the flesh.

We've been listening to the radio, or perhaps he has—it's been on—an almost obliging metallic murmur somewhere away from me (Gertrude flashes into mind—she and her father). I have to rest, take a break. I note that the light from the window has failed, gone gray.

Come look, I say, and he breaks from his pose, comes over to stand beside my chair.

He seems pleased. Well, now—ea'ah, ea'ah—you're getting it —that's me, all right—ea'ah.

Let me fix the drinks, I say.

I'll fix 'em.

It's his third, or fourth. He puts it away, grows increasingly genial, expansive. I ask if he thinks I should buy the island. He smells (I'm suddenly aware) sweetly of the properly human, the male; it fills my kitchen.

I guess I do, he says. He reaches for and then lights a cigarette from the pack left on the table, hoists a great leg up to a knee. It's a big thing, but we'd help you—we'd be out there to show you things—yes, and others—Bill Eaton, most likely.

And because I am still so conscious of him, I say, If I seem to be looking at you a lot, it's because in my mind I'm still drawing—don't notice.

At which he says, with a fine geniality, I like to be looked at— and seems to straighten himself, to swell, rubs a hand over his chest.

I say, I think about it a lot, that island. And I chatter.

He nods. Ethel knew. It's kind of a game with her, don't you know. There's been folks nibbling at it and she'd rather it be you.

I'm glad of that, I say.

I signal for us to start again and he rises, goes to stand by the sink, and my eyes, my pencil are on him again, questioningly, exploringly—working now toward details, though I've decided to use shadow since it's the balance and mass of him that I want.

He's been sipping at his drink and I see him watching me. He says, suddenly, unexpectedly, You're drawing my titties now, ain't you?—and a hand, big-knuckled, moves up to rub at his chest, and I feel caught out—I had been thinking how sensuous they were, the nipples, with a slightly raw look to them.

I say, I didn't realize that men *had*—titties. They do, don't they?

Some of them—and his hand holds a breast in cupped fingers, seems to lift and contain it as though it pleases him. I hear him say, Maybe I ought to be drawing *you*—what do you think?

At which I say, With my hat on we might.

At which he smiles, slowly, broadly. No, de'ah—we won't need no hat.

At which I say, Yes, but you can't draw.

Ea'ah, but I'd learn quick.

I'd have to see the drawing first. Come look.

And he does, breaks from his posture again.

Now if you was to draw me with my arm around someone, some lady, he says from beside me, looking down, we might have one of them fine pictures you see.

He goes to pour another drink, moves to the sink for ice, and I'm looking at his back again.

Drawing and all, he says, facing me again—you get to see people naked, I expect.

I never have, I say. They do in art school—they have models.

That so? Naked, eh? How would you like me like that?

I might be a little nervous, I say.

Naw. Wouldn't be nothing, de'ah.

Even this makes me nervous, I say. I'm not used to it.

I'd like to be naked for you. The glass tilts in the air. I hear him say, and it doesn't sound irrelevant, Don't worry about Ethel too much. She's having it, seems like; going through her time, and a man gets lonesome, you know—wants a woman to talk to, be with some.

My mind jumps around, settles down on my theme: You knew Gertrude, didn't you—Gertrude Hardy.

I hear him say, We all do—one way or the other.

Did you take Richie there? You said once he courted her.

A shoulder shrugs. Richie don't take much to women. Not like me (said broadly again)—I like women. Then—Don't you like men?

I nod. I do, I say.

Me?

Yes—you.

I figured you did—the way I like you.

Ay-yup—you're getting me, he says, having come over to look—and again the flesh, close to, astonishes me with a sense of its vitality, crude, brute, a beauty in ugliness as I see hair swirl in a pattern, pour into the navel. I hear his voice—You get my body good, de'ah—I *am* a *fat* one.

There was more to it, of course—about Ethel, about Richie.

He's protective. And possessive—yes, he would want to own. Perhaps me.

SUNDAY 8 JANUARY. Out driving. Passed the little lane to Gertrude's gunk hole, filled with drifted snow in which the tips of bushes showed like nerve endings and the branches of spruce lay buried. Hale and Hardy. Yes, I can imagine, him "making it" down there now and then, and her as hopelessly permissive about it—that easy, genial power—"I like women." He does—I see it now. He would frighten me. Too much.

Then down for a look at the harbor, to find it strange again in the snow—the wharves with their white-crowned heaps of lobster traps—a silent, waiting look to things as if snow, winter, were a necessary burden, the water a dark serious green around the brown pilings.

FRIDAY 13. Nothing unlucky about it. Elmo and Richie show up together. Elmo saying, Richie here wants to paint awhile and I've got errands for Ethel—I'll be back. He had coffee before shoving off. Richie and I upstairs, he building a fire.

I think about his need to paint. So little room for it here. Hardly an artist around. Why women, I think, are so enormously important here, keepers of the flame, homemakers, the family's center. Yes, up here it is a woman's world and normalcy *is* tremendously important.

Elmo came back and we sat upstairs for a while, he looking at things, then saying with a broad yet mischievous slyness to Richie, Mrs. Calder here wants to paint me naked, Richie—think I should let her? So that I had to protest, I do not and that's not fair. At which I get a look from him. I can't tell what he's told him yet.

Oh, yes, it's a game, we both know it, and he says, You want to paint me, too, Richie?—do you?—hummmm?

He has a way of cornering Richie, and Richie of eluding him. She can paint what she wants.

Well—and you think it's proper if I let a lady see me naked? he asks.

We retire downstairs to a fire and a drink.

SUNDAY 15. Odd dream. Woke from it holding it clearly in mind. I was in a strange and ugly place—a sort of city, part of one

—as if at the bottom of an excavation that was huge and still going on. Ugly, unfamiliar—sense of work around me—sense of groups of people, all strange, some threateningly. And yet I was with someone I loved and who I knew loved me.

At times we seemed to lose each other, lose touch, or contact, but always I seemed to know that that person (a man, I think) was there and that we did love each other. And the dream was a happy one.

I thought about it over coffee.

LETTER FROM BETH, in which she deplores my wayward attitude. We must live with change, control its randomness. There is no exit that will do. I wrote back: My hands are thrown up—I will not be missed.

WEDNESDAY 18. Back from Bangor with books, scraps of cloth, a fine Seth Thomas, and good steak.

THURSDAY 19. I read more poetry now, but sense that it needs to be studied—a form of "rapping," as they say—one mind offering to let another mind play with it.

This, oh, surely, is what is being lost as our culture changes—our concern for words, respect for language. And the theory—what?—that it is all too *private*, aristocratic—out of it. That books themselves lead us to wish for privacy.

Me—yes, I am involved with privacy. And already know that too much is dangerous—that my mind simply goes inward into labyrinths of self. But surely too much yapping around in packs is dangerous, too. I don't believe we're merely social animals. I would always want private minutes to read a poem, sense a fire, smell a rose, shiver at death in a snowbank, by a rotting wharf in a damp cabin.

The crowds, the incessant streaming of multitudes, covering the beaches of the world, the free and open places. Already we're being *forced* to be together.

Why did that poetry start me off? That Canadian, I suppose, that one hears about. A prophet of the new. And not just that—not him—my sense of *enormous* change, the signs of which are everywhere—not the bomb, not the moon; *population*—poison—aerial garbage—a polluted *ocean*.

The wind rises, the wind rises and howls—its litter of trash.

It may be the wind that will beat us—blind, hot, furious.
To bed, old girl, to bed—eat, eat, and then to bed—there's a
warmth to that that's good, too. A chowder.

JOURNAL SUNDAY 22 JANUARY. Dashed off a letter to Beth—
mediational.
Snow mostly gone. A warm wind. The sense of escape from it.
I went down to Gertrude's wharf, just to feel her presence, I
think. Forlorn. She seemed to stand watching me, cold, abstract,
from behind spruce. And how gray it looked, spectral. I seemed
to hear voices—warning me?

MONDAY 23 JANUARY. Chat with Ethel, who is better from whatever it was. Children at school, Elmo and Richie out somewhere.
In her kitchen we drifted into talk again about Richie. He'd like
it out on an island, I hear her say (cunning as a friendly snake)—
not that I'm making a match, you know. We both smiled. You
could stand some company, you know—I can tell.
She's knitting a muffler for someone, of red and green yarn
with bits of white.
You're a young woman, Helen, she says—something of my age,
ain't you?
I'm forty-five, I say.
And a good-looking one, too—well—do some thinking that way.
Ain't much of a talker, of course, but you seem to get along with
being quiet—I do myself.
It's a question. I say, I am good by myself, but you're right, who
wants to be alone all the time?
I hear her say, I don't know what's made him that way
—maybe hanging around with Elmo so much. El seems to own
him somehow—he's like that, you know—wants things around
him, his family, me, what he owns. El don't take to many himself, but he likes you, too.
Yes, she trusts me. So I ask, Does it bother you, that he and
Richie stop around?—do you feel left out?
She reaches for more yarn, makes a knot. I've got my troubles,
Helen, I hear her say. He feels I don't want him now, and I tell
him it ain't that and that it'll pass. And he's patient. But I like
to be alone more now—I like to look at things, and be quiet—
and when he wants me, sometimes I ain't there, if you know
what I mean.

Curious—there's almost an offer behind it. (Is there? I wonder.) She goes on: And he hangs on to Richie more, wants him around —teases him—about women and all, this and that—but wouldn't want him to go off. She picks up scissors to snip at something. Though with you, she says—well—he'd kind of have the both of you, if you see what I mean. I'm glad he's got someone he can be with, but it ain't good for Richie, El holding on to him like that.

She seems to study her work a moment. El took him to see that woman you once asked about, you know. I didn't like to say. I don't know what happened—Elmo's got a streak in him—men like him do—but I believe she took a shine to Richie and that he didn't to her—something like that. I told him to let Richie find his own— yes, and for him to keep away himself.

I see her look at me. I hear her say, And now here I am, meddling.

We both smile.

I just got to thinking, she says. No harm to it.

I drove back along the water. A fine winter day, quite warm and the harbor filled with color—bits of snow, green water, gray ice, dark under the wharves and the wharves silver—and the houses still with that shut-in waiting look. They shut me out.

Was she warning me with that about Gertrude? Or pushing me, however gently, his way? I don't know.

SUNDAY 29 JANUARY. He came around to paint. Richie. Just him.

I asked if he'd been practicing, painting at home, but he said no, they'd been doing something to the boat. It's up on shore. I decided to tell him Elmo had posed for me. I asked if Elmo had told him and he said that he had (apparently without much elaboration). So I took a leap, a longish one, feeling scared. I don't suppose you would sometime. I saw him shrug again. Couldn't tell whether negative. How would you feel if I asked you? I said.

He's squatting by the stove, encouraging a chunk of wood to catch. You mean naked, like he said *he* would?

He was making fun of us, I say. I mean with your *shirt* off, so I can see how things go. Would that embarrass you?

Poking in with a stick. Well, I ain't thought about it none.

But it might bother you? I say.

I don't know.

He's risen and gone to get out his paints. I work at the portrait of Elmo again, feeling dissatisfied with the way the face is going. The eyes—I think it's in there—small but clear, tough but friendly.

February 1 Wednesday

Dear Herb,

The letter was good to get. I seem, in a way, to have gone into hibernation here. I'm painting, I'm reading, but feel terribly out of it—yes, and still glad to be—a forty-five-year-old dropout from a world I no longer believe in. Your struggles with the frantic young sound depressing from up here. *Was* the old system so bad, so stifling? What is going out, of course, is a way of life, one that involved summer vacations, travel, politeness, neighborhoods and neighborli*ness*, family houses, a common fund of knowledge, a respect for the past. And I, for one, cannot accept the order and reason science will give us to replace it. I find myself in a universe that shares none of my aspirations or hopes or desires.

But the young—they seem to regard all change as essential, inevitable, even delightful—as if nothing were good enough to last.

No, I want this, if I can make it work, or want it for a while, and couldn't bear yet to think I don't belong up here either, since then I would belong nowhere.

Right now, though, I'm coping with winter. I go quilting. We all gossip, we rock. And have morning coffee with a lady friend or two. But I do need the sense of someone down in the city, too, so that if I did utter a yelp or two, someone might say, Stay put—the air is nasty, the traffic impenetrable, the blacks incorrigible, the highways still hideous.

Well, I *am* rambling now, but it's fun to talk to you. I miss you, you and Beth.

SATURDAY 4 FEBRUARY. Elmo and Richie stopped by this morning, on their way down to Ellsworth looking for old chain. Did I want to come along? Yes, I did.

I sat between them and worried for a while about legs—we were all thighs, though neither of *them* seemed to notice. How barren things looked except where the fir and the spruce take over, with glimpses of dark water—not a human in sight except for a car now and then, the houses looking empty—and even though it was a gray day not a light on as far as I could see. You don't turn lights on in the daytime here; it would be frivolous—or perhaps just too extravagant.

I feel companionable with them now. Elmo's talk occasionally ribald with good humor, assuming, very subtly, that I'm one of them, though he still uses the "Mrs. Calder." Mrs. Calder here, Helen, we ought to have her up hunting with us, Richie—a good cook, someone to get at that cabin. . . .

We visited junkyards. Didn't find what they wanted—drove by the Brewer Road over to Bangor.

They look fine among those town people, who seem to set them off. Elmo very confident, somehow superior, as if, in fact, he and his were what all that rusting iron was there for. We're from Orstown—announcing it, as though it established cachet. Very businesslike they were, Richie nodding, looking around, finding something over in the weeds.

And yet they are childlike, too—having so little money to spend, so little in actual cash, real funds. They live on bargains, have to make do, are poor.

Then back in the car, pleased with what they had found. Let's get a beer. Stopped at a place they seemed to know, where they could eat, too—which is part of the ritual—hamburgers, looking tiny in Elmo's hands.

Richie is feeling good, doesn't respond, except that you can tell he's listening. He likes being talked about, I should say. I feel them beside me in buttons and wool, strong shoes.

And we drive back and are gay for a while. Even Richie, who says, Let's get drunk—a remark resonant with possibilities, surprises. But we sit in an almost perfect silence of well-being, and the world passes us by—grim, sturdy, essential. A house here, there, with traces of history about it. And the terrain shaggy, and finally, perhaps, a bore (me seeing it through their eyes at last—nonromantic —solitary—grudging, remote?)—which is why they love the artificial so, the aluminum screen doors with the great initial, the bad "Mediterranean" house colors, the house trailers that are coming in (Richie admiring one—Ain't that some nice—I could have kicked him for it).

When we get home I want to ask them in, I want an evening of it, but think of Ethel and refrain.

THURSDAY 9 FEBRUARY. Housework all day. Buster's hair all over, winter must, things to be put away, dusted off, washed, cleaned.

And I felt righteous after it, and settled down, to the oncoming of the early night, with a book and coffee.

FRIDAY 10. Almost as part of yesterday's cleaning, I reread all this, the journal. Oh, dear. Yes, and oh, *dear*. So often a bore. Parts do flash out at me—no Mrs. Woolf, though bits, pieces do evoke. But, my God, who among millions has the mind that woman had, the infinite gaiety, till death itself knocked at her door and said come for a swim.

But so often I write without having enough to say. How I would love to go back and tighten it up. But is that fair, for a journal? My past speaks to me from these pages.

And yet I'm hurt by most of it. Those passages back there while I was still in Brooklyn Heights in which I announced to myself in a manifesto: I will take care, I will be honest, this will be real. And then the Mendonca stuff. I almost forget now—*Did* he exist? *Did* I bring him home? What am I worried about? Don't I *trust* art? What do I trust?

SATURDAY 11. A sobering experience, that, of rereading the past, looking at footprints to see where they've been. (Was I wrong to put that Hale thing in? Take it out, then. But what else have I?)

Flakes of snow, and I went out to them to say again, Here I am. Grape arbor—a gentle hiss of them falling, touching, sifting in.

MONDAY 13 FEBRUARY. Snow like powdered sugar around. I went out to watch them scraping their boat at Williams Boatyard, which is down a sandy road that winds past houses, fields, and spruce, to a nice bit of shore. Wharves, boat sheds, ways—and boats drawn up, though it is all fairly small—theirs in a cradle and them at it, bundled in dark clothes, scraping and calking. They seemed to be the only ones around. Elmo waved and I strolled over.

I didn't bother them, just watched. I liked seeing them work— Richie silent and industrious. I felt a touch of guilt at having so little to do myself, and envied them. I see bits of rusting iron, blackened seaweed, broken plates of old ice by the water that laps not far from us with its own dull brown persistence.

Elmo says, "A moite nippy out, ain't it"—a statement rather than a question, and I see his face, red under dark knit cap—yes, broad and strong-boned, square-jawed—and I see the eyes, small gray now, quick and alive, as separate entities while he looks at me. Then, oddly detached for that instant, I see him doubly, as the head of some great company in business suit, handsome and portly proud, and here on this shore as if on vacation from all that; and I think, Yes, in the world's scheme they are like children, whittling away at a boat, insignificant, their work so small, their possessions so few. Yes, Greek—Greek.

Perhaps a smile offshore, islands look low and flat, sunk below rising waves that are making doggedly toward us.

FRIDAY 17 FEBRUARY. Richie around to paint. We are almost pals —almosting it. Joyce's word.

His reality is persistently childlike. Things seen as if they had no history, no past. And what he makes of them is, I suppose, a less threatening world—a simpler, sweeter one. Would he live with me on an island?

I'm doing the barn again, trying for more color, or more depth of color.

SUNDAY 19. All day depressed, unreasonably. The sense of no supports, nothing to support. My plans, my favorite images, like old cans on the village dump, empty, used up. This journal a mess, sense of my life as an utter futility.

MONDAY. Still there. Yes, it is gray outside—outer and inner weather. That tissue of borrowed phrases—my life.

TUESDAY. Went down to see if they were working on their boat —not there, which depressed me, and foolishly—as though they had shut me out.

WEDNESDAY. It lifted a little, like the lid to a box. What inside? That I exaggerate, I think; that I talk, write about my life badly, blow things up, when so little actually happens, can happen. And the style—but that's it—the way things are said, the kinds of illusions language can create. One paragraph of Woolf—everything is there. And me? One woman in a small though beautiful old house, slightly stir crazy at times, and what do I make of it? What would she? Perhaps I do need an island, something outlined, like a picture frame, not to be exceeded. Yes, an island, so that there I *am*, longitude this, latitude that, under a microscope.

The quilting helped. It is always good to be with them. We

have to sit bundled up. Our fingers get cold. But we're gay. At the cookies like hummingbirds in that old hall.

SATURDAY 25. Woke to an absence of light but knew that I was better. Visitations—the spook of loneliness. I've survived it, though neither Richie nor Elmo has shown up. Martinis—a casserole— a fire, with Buster curled before it.

Mallek–Mendonca hanging around all day in some insidious fashion, wanting me to remember him, to write him down. Later I may let him in. And just the idea that I can, and may, pleases me, even restrains. Word hoard unlocked, and sudden brutish and fierce impulses swarm like birds in my mind. A becomes B. Light from this window reaches out to where legs, heavily muscled at the knees, are standing in snow.

TUESDAY 28. Still gray—a long, flat pall that must stretch from pole to pole—unblemished, untarnishable, though with a pin I could scratch it like zinc. Got the blues, they would have said some years ago. Strike up a song, someone, for the love of John Henry. Help a lady out. Come on, God, make some sun, move it up there. Nothing doing. Arctic and cold, and even the spruce looking numbed, asleep. Not a crow in sight. My black angels. Not a gull either. Lichen gray. The kind of gray no one would paint, no blue in it, no yellow. Maine flashing and sparkling in a summer breeze. No such luck, not now. The lid is on.

I've built a good fire. I'm not afraid. I'll have a martini. A book. I won't let him in, though I've seen him again—legs, standing in the snow—patiently.

WEDNESDAY 1 MARCH. That beastly February been and gone. Not many at the quilting. Too cold. Those of us who were felt virtuous —yes, and could get a bit closer to that fine stove. What a pattern the quilts make in there, and the heads bent over them, under those dim white walls, and what a music of voices. I took Carole Bean and May Stinson. I don't tell them I'm depressed.

THURSDAY 2 MARCH. For a lady depressed this is a lot of words. So am I?—really? Maybe bored? Got cabin fever?

I've polished everything in the damn house. I roam it looking for a speck. I'm a whited sepulcher. Where *are* those goddamn friends of mine, E & R?—the bastards.

I see them cozy and snug in their shack, the stove going, deer-horns and girlie calendars on the wall, mending nets or painting pot buoys, tinkering with the outboard—yes, and reaching for a beer. And it all smelling good, pine chunks burning in the stove—paint smells—terribly patient with all this—in fact, hardly noticing. Going to paint Gertrude's landing, are you, Richie? Going to get some of that, come spring? I'm going to pose for Mrs. Calder—she likes to see me, wants me naked—I know. Sitting on stools by the stove, rope in their hands, a bit of twine—booted—knit capped.

And Elmo'll show up one of these days, large, jovial, *beaming* —How you doing, Mrs. Calder?—just thought I'd drop by to see. Yes, well, screw him—get thee gone, I'm *doing* fine—and am *out* of booze. Well—now I call that pitiful, and unfriendly, too—I do. Great red fat face looking me over, with confidence, so easy smooth, so right, so bland. He'll want to get to me someday, will take his sweet time—no hurry—not him. Yes, and when he does want me, I'll say, Fuck off, buddy—when *I* wanted a little com-pany—. Yes, *non*attractive—in New York a bust—he *is* fat—who *needs* him.

What happened today? Weather is what happened. Developing animosities, resentments, is what happened.

Oh, shut *up*. You're blathering on. Have a drink.

FRIDAY 3. Coffee with Carole Bean in that white kitchen of hers that is like a rebuke. Shipshape, immaculate, it gleams like a heartless advertisement. But give me better weather and I'd call it "Maine." Now here is a perfect example of a perfect little coastal Maine kitchen.

She is a trifle nutty, but she's real, she's tough. No wit to her of your big-city type, but humor—and she's not trying to "come on." She's chopped wood, made up huge pots of chowder, quilted, sewed her own blankets, tended her husband. Yes, and gone to church, to bazaars, church sales. And joked with Ellsworth's friends drunk or sober and not blamed him, and worried about weather when weather could kill, not just depress—and did kill.

Coffee with Carole Bean. And it smelled so good, even to me from my negative world, munching resentments—the coffee, a crumb cake she was heating up. The wood stove was going, and we are so beautifully enclosed against that heartless, inhuman gray where the boats sit and the gulls float and the houses stand silent and waiting—yes, and the windows steam and frost and I rub a pane with my hand.

Yes, it was good to be there, so that I said to myself, All I needed was company. Not *all* I needed, by a long shot, but it helped just the same.

The radio is on (they keep it on for the weather, and the company). I remark that I dislike his voice, the announcer's, and tell her I seldom have it on, but that it sounds cheerful now with her. She says (they must talk about me), If you do get out on that island, don't be without it. A fog'll come in while you're fixing the coffee. Just all of a sudden and it's all around you out there. Ellie was caught in one.

Of course, if she thinks he's there, he is there, for her, as Mallek is there for me when I have to have him. A trick of the mind. Mendonca to Mallek to . . . ?

Do you suppose he's on Pennyless? I say, to hear what she will, but also because I know she likes to talk about him.

And she nods—He's there. They found his dory, you know. You saw it.

We don't inquire into the form of his being there, but I think, A knuckle bone? A tooth? I say, Well, I'm glad he is, and when *I'm* there, if I ever am, you must come visit me. We'll look for him.

You do think you might, she says, about the island.

It appeals to me, I say.

Well, I can't think why, she says, it's hard enough right here.

And I say, Yes, it is hard living alone. This last week was hard for me.

When you're used to a man around, even Ellie, you do miss him, she says—no one to fuss at, tell your day to. A person maybe shouldn't, she says, but I dream about him sometimes. I like to. We don't talk, he's just there or around, though I once heard him say, Carole, did you clean out that shed?—as clear as that. And I hadn't.

I dream about a man I once knew, I say.

Oh, she says.

The coffee is ready and she goes to get cups and pour, and to put out the cake, which we're both waiting for, rather expectantly. We like to eat.

And I realize how difficult it would be for me to try to tell her when she asks, coming back, A nice sort of man? How can I say,

A rough one, not of my class—since class, between us, her and me, is undefined.

He was on a freighter, I say.

Oh—a seafaring man she says. Ellie's cousin went to sea. We never hear from him, though freighters do come up to Belfast, and Machiasport. Do you hear from yours?

I'm not sure he would know where to write, I say, or that he even knows how to. No, I don't hear from him—directly. He was married, so perhaps it's just as well.

At which she subsides and I stir my coffee. I nibble at the cake, which is good and short; but I say, after a moment, It wasn't much of an affair, it was really just an accident that I met him at all—a brief but happy encounter.

She is perfectly willing to listen if I am to tell, yet I'm reticent. Though I suddenly long to say, He was *marvelous* in bed, bring some of my big-city talk right out. I say, We were very different but sometimes differences are what you want. My husband, Herb, and I squabbled because, in a way, we were too similar—it was what I got tired of.

She says, Well, Ellie and I squabbled, too. He'd get to drinking, staying out with men, not doing his work or his chores, leaving me alone too much. Some of the men here do.

I hear her say, Did I show you this picture of him?—I run across it in a box I keep. And she is rising. She leaves the room, still talking—her voice trailing back—things in boxes, put away, till you forget you have them; and returns, holding it, looking at it herself; and I see how closely involved she still is with him.

There, she says—that's his boat, had it built down to Moose Island, though he was a Jonesport man.

And I see, on the shiny surface, curled, split at a corner, a man beside a lobster boat on ways, a huge building behind him. Two men are with him.

That's the Benson boys, Carole says. All right when they weren't drinking, wild as hawks when they was.

They all wear caps—and I think, Yes, he's real Maine—they all are—lean and tall—and say so to her, who says, A Jonesport man, all right—never been fifty miles from home, except to hunt. They'd head for Aroostook every fall—Gody Henderson's place— Elmo and Richie, too. They all been up together.

I look at the photograph until she reaches for it, to look again herself, realizing that he would not have done for me. I might have liked him, as I like Jules Caster, but that's all.

May Stinson came in, clapping cold out of her garments, and we gabbed.

SATURDAY 4 MARCH. Bitterly, stingingly cold. Oh, this is it. Everything frozen solid, including me, though the house is warm.

How can anything out there wake from this? Gulls float in a frozen sea, at the margins of ice that extends from the shore. Water warmer now than air? It must be.

WEDNESDAY 8 MARCH. My God, to see the light again of a long, warm afternoon. Energies exhausted and winter hard on us as a steel trap. We huddled as near to the stove as we could get, quilting, but it was cold at our back in there; we could see our breath, had trouble, holding our needles. The heat from the stove seems to vanish into space a few feet from it. They say we're due for snow.

THURSDAY 9. A great storm. Snow streaming along the ground, piling in drifts—wind whistling at my eaves. I haven't been out. The snowplows have been around, flashing yellow as they went by out there. Everything white, and gone that bitter, icebound look. This, at least, is exciting, slightly frightening even.

Elmo called. You all right? he asked, shouting, as if he were addressing me through a megaphone. Ethel says come down and have supper. I'll pick you up.

Excitement—activity. Saw his jeep wheel in. Watched it nudging the snow around—back, forward, back—so brisk, so efficient. Good to watch, nice to have someone out there. It parked. Then he came in, almost in a cloud of steam—hale Hale—yes, and Hail, Hale. My animosities and resentments vanished like dirty water down a drain.

Have a drink with me, I said.

We had two.

It's a good one he said, looking out, Ay-yup, and that'll be the last of it—now spring'll be coming in.

With him there I like the snow; the way it fills up at the window sills, he fills up spaces for me.

How's the painting? he asks.

I'm working on flowers again, I say—I can't seem to finish yours.

Drink in hand he accompanies me upstairs.

The painting is pink and mauve, yellow and orange and lavender —of flowers in a white pot, on a white window sill (actually quite blue), a sea shell by it, also white (actually quite pink). The colors cheer me, I tell him. He looks at it and then nods. It is cheery, he says. Richie ain't been around a while, has he? He gets like that—mopey—he ain't been painting to home neither.

He stands looking around. The painting I tried to do of him leans against a wall—not bad—yet not good.

When you want me again? he suddenly asks, as if reminded that we had talked about it once, the possibility; and the tone, the question, has something spontaneous, uncalculating to it.

Whenever you have the time, I say, aware of his good humor and already basking in it.

I got the time now he says. He stands looking down at the painting, for the dark, mirrored profile of which Richie once sat and let me sketch him in. What about tonight, when we get back? Just don't say nothing to Ethel, he tells me, turning to go out.

Sweet sense of the illicit, swift—secret as sin.

We go downstairs, me following the swaying, clomping bulk of him.

Then out, bouncing and sliding along in the jeep in the splendid snow, which is still falling, though the wind that brought it swirl-ing and streaming to us has died into fitful gusts. Suddenly life is glittering and crisp. I peer out past the windshield wiper at the flakes rising like scraps of paper to meet us in the lights, him shadowy enormous beside me, sitting back as if the driving were nothing. Light gleams faintly on his face, shining and fat with health and good humor.

We come in, shaking off snow, to the kitchen that is steamy and warm. Boots by the stove, a row of them. Puddles of water on brown linoleum. Coats hanging from a rack.

His mother is there—Richie—all of them—excited about the storm, which is a big one. Ethel says, We got to worrying about you—you can stay here if it gets too bad.

It's quieting, Elmo says.

I say, Hi, to Richie, who in a big chair is watching television, and then bend to shake hands and reintroduce myself to Mrs. Hale (in a straight-backed Victorian Ethel has redone), whom

I had met at Thanksgiving with that older friend of hers from Ellsworth. She's been staying with them apparently. She says, I like snow. I was getting quite tired of that cold. March is a long month but it does get you to April. I'm aware that her ankles are too big.

In the kitchen the radio is giving news from Rockland and the children tell us there won't be any school—Hurray! We learn that the storm is universal, from Boston to Eastport, the whole coast blanketed, and that everything is closed; we are urged to keep off the roads. People are stuck. A certain wayside motel is jammed with refugees. I feel cozy and at home, though guilty-secreted. The feeling is strange to me, but there is a sweetness about it, a savor.

And as if to banish it, I help Betsy and Ethel bring the food in. Elmo has gone somewhere. Then he comes in as we're sitting down, saying, broadly, jovially, Too hot in here for them long johns—you women in your little fine dresses. Oh, heart—how even the rustle of a leaf can shatter your silences—though *certainly* I am not in love with him! No, but a real game is in progress, and I see him in a double light, here in his family, then at my place; and seeing Richie by a black window I wonder whether he will be told (Well, and I posed again, Richie—what do you think of that?). And to Ethel I say silently, Oh, it won't amount to *any*-thing—it's a game—it *is*. I'd be too cowardly for you to have to worry about it.

Mrs. Hale is telling us about another storm, when the snow was so high her father had to go through an upstairs window to get out and at it. We're all keyed up. Late gusts of wind heave it at the windows behind Richie, flakes dancing there a moment, looking in.

Then Ethel drops a little bomb and Elmo is instantly forgotten. She says, I meant to tell you—folks from Lewiston been in asking about property—some talk of a hotel. They asked about islands.

Then she's away, taking the coffee in.

I'm after her in a flash. As she's pouring for Mrs. Hale I say, Asking about Pennyless?

I see her nod. She moves on.

Who were they? I lean forward to ask down the table to her.

She hunches a little. Some group from Lewiston—hotel people, I think. Ginny didn't say too much.

I'm suddenly mad to talk with her, to find out. And what I realize, I think, is that perhaps I've been cornered, backed to a wall; and can't think clearly, only see it again, Pennyless, in my mind's eye, as I saw it that first time we rounded on it—sheets of pink granite, meadow grass, rising to a stand of spruce, set in sunstricken green summer water—the whole thing a dance of the elements, and I realize how much it *has* been in my mind's eye.

Well, they can't have it, I say to her in the kitchen (with a handful of plates). A hotel out there?—a sort of marina? Betsy is chattering to Anne about something.

That's some of the talk, she says.

But that's ours, I say—mine—yours—it *can't* go to them, whoever they are.

She shrugs. They got the money, she says—heartlessly.

How much? I say. How much *could* I get it for?

They can outbid you.

Yes, but if I just bought it, at what's being asked?

She takes the dishes from me, puts them in the sink. We could see, she says, and to Betsy, Go get them cups.

I long to shake her. I say, Don't you *want* me to have it—you want *them?*

It ain't what I want, de'ah—it's what you do—that counts.

Well, I *want* it! I cry—and find her looking at me.

Do you? she says.

I feel pulled up short.

I say, I don't know—no, I do—I want it—give me a day—let me sleep on it. I'm looking back at her, find her watching me. Oh, Ethel—you mean they might just scoop it up—I couldn't bear it.

The storm was still going, though it had diminished in intensity. I was somehow terribly anxious to get out, think, suddenly remembering Elmo. Yet in an odd way felt him to be part of it. We left.

He came in with me; was feeling expansive, at home—went right to the sideboard where I keep my cache and mixed each of us a drink—whiskey and water—me carrying ice to the sink. I said, Did Ethel tell you about the island—those people from Lewiston? I saw him nod. What do you think? I asked.

What do you? he said. He had planted himself at the table against a shining black window snow had piled up at.

I don't know—it's a big thing.

Well, I guess it is.

Do you think I should, really *should?*

He shrugged, reached in the pocket of his wool shirt for his cigarettes. I don't know as it's for me to advise you, Helen. It is a big thing—money involved—yes, and more than that. You'd want to build out there. You might find it too much.

We drink in silence together. I've turned the radio on.

With a long pull at his glass he finishes his drink, rises to fix himself another, looks to see how mine is.

Going to draw me? he says.

And just that helps, I'm not sure why. Let me go get my pad, I say. Yes, fix me another.

Upstairs I pause, as once before, peer out at the snow, thinking of Pennyless, snow falling on its shores, so neat, so intact, its twin crown of dark spruce and pointed firs. And I suddenly know—I know. I go back downstairs.

The shirt and undershirt have come off and flesh is revealed. The hair on his chest, shining in light, looks as if it might shock or burn if touched.

He stands by the sink again and I work on musculature, blocking in—really just notes this time—how much of a bone can be seen, or deduced, how a muscle is formed, reveals itself.

And as the drinks went down and he warmed to them, You get that island, de'ah, and we'll have some times. I'll pose for you naked.

I murmur something—pleased, in a way, though flustered.

I would now—or in the shorts if you'd like. How about in my shorts?

Oh—this is fine, I say—fine.

He's teasing, or partly. The drinks are loosening him. He's feeling fine, available—he's teasing me, us, but I realize that he means it, too, and that he might not offer again.

Well—if you *are* willing, it would help.

And with that, almost before I have finished, off come the moccasins, the socks, the pants—until there he is, immense, aglow, in blue-and-white striped shorts that he seems to fill like a grape its skin, so that you see at once how things go, what the legs are like—white, large, and hard-looking—the buttocks—the rest.

How you want me? I hear him ask—standing there, cigarette in mouth, then reaching for his drink.

Yes, at the sink, talking.

I don't quite know. By the sink again? I ask—How would that be?

Over here?

He plants himself in front of it, adjusting the shorts at the waistband and turning a little to arrange himself, with a hunching of shoulder.

And I go at it nervously, in fact appalled. Legs simply too big, too hard and white, for beauty, a fighter's legs. Abundance of a workingman's body, full and vigorous.

And he himself—so easy, pleased. He likes being there.

How I look to you? he asked once.

You look splendid, I said.

Then—I'll take these off, too, if you like.

I said, rather quickly, I really *haven't* gotten that far yet—but thanks for the offer.

It ain't no trouble, you know.

Oh—better no, I said. You're fine as you are.

Yes, but I wouldn't mind, you know.

I've gone back to my drawing, am clinging to it, in a way.

Because (and at first I hardly noticed) something was happening to him that I couldn't seem to let myself observe at first, though suddenly I did observe and knew that there was no mistaking it, hands behind him resting on sink—and knew that in a minute I would probably have to do something, break off.

I was hearing him say, I ain't ever had no one look at me like this. I like you to, Helen, I like to stand for you—the words seemingly calling it forth, the erection, still partial, tentative—and him standing there with it happening to him, talking, as if he were not aware.

Think I'm a nice-looking man?

You are, I say.

And I am nice—and like you, you know—like to help you out. And I wouldn't mind to be naked for you, de'ah, if that'd help.

Oh, this is fine, I say again—just fine.

But it ain't no trouble, de'ah. I'll just take them off and you can go on drawing me and see how a man goes, get it right—I'll just stand here.

I fend him off, ashamed of myself, even wanting him to be dressed again for me to think about it. Under the stretched cloth, it there, like a promise, or threat—which creates a silence between us. I keep drawing, wondering vaguely what would happen if he did take them off.

He managed—I suppose it was that—to stay within bounds. After I had finished, he came over to look.

Standing by me in the shorts, still enormous—you got me, de'ah
—I'm like that—the belly almost by my face a moment with its
pattern of hair. Then moving across the room to pour out more
whiskey, shorter in the bare feet.

Sits at the table with its papers, its magazines, a leg crossed,
flesh grown toward pink again in the warmth of the kitchen,
flakes of snow dancing up at the window behind him to look in,
though he's not conscious of it—at home, at ease; it's as if he
were dressed or in his own kitchen, family around. Ay-yup—when
that weather hauls around, we'll go see that island again, Richie
and us. Put some money down on her, Helen.

He sips, the little finger daintily held out. Yes, and of course
you'd be wanting a cabin out there, and a landing—them tides is
ten foot. Can't moor on granite without stoving a boat all to hell.
And we could come visit, Richie and me—bring a few lobsters,
bring some of this.

I listen, I sketch.

How'd you like that? I hear him ask.

Having you visit?

Ay-yup—it wouldn't be good to be too much alone—you'd want
company. And I'd pose for you, de'ah—pose in my bare feet. But
don't tell that to Richie or nothing.

You'd tell him, I say, feeling that we're still on ground that we
don't have a right to be on.

Not me, de'ah. Though Richie wouldn't mind. And out there,
de'ah, it wouldn't be nothing at all—we'll have our times. Ea'ah—
and we'd get Ethel out there—and the boys. They'll pull mussels,
dig clams, pick berries—I like a good feed. I want them boys to
want to be around here, I want them to stay . . . his voice going on,
with an accent, a rhythm, I can't catch—baritone, deep, rich—
that fills his chest under the arched blanket of flesh, seems to go
on in there with a rumble, to emerge as part of him, released . . .
Boys, you know—feel as they got to get away, got to move, go
somewheres else. Naw—we'll do it proper out there—I'll get them
off and we'll get a good picture for you, de'ah. I think as how I'd
like to be naked for you—and as how you'd like me to be when we
get the chance.

And he finally stretches, arms back, fisted, the muscles at his
chest lifting—easy, ogrelike—belly balloons, stretching hair—and
lifts himself by the chair arms. Ain't this been some nice—stands
scratching at the waistband of the shorts, and I flinch again. Have

to get back, he says, with a shadow of reluctance. Ethel will be worrying with all that snow. He comes around to see what I've done. Now ain't that nice. You got me looking like one of them wrestlers we see on TV.

I watched him putting his clothes back on, a reassembling of himself into another role. Until—there he was again, Elmo Hale, a churchgoing Orstown lobsterman, in his clean, unironed clothes.

We'll see you, de'ah.

Tuesday 14

Dear Beth,

I may be buying that island. I don't mean to sound flippant. I've talked to you about it, haven't I? Well, something's jelled—some people from Lewiston (see map of Maine) came prowling around looking for land, et cetera. And the Hales, both Elmo and Ethel, have urged me to spring into action. I've put money down. I've written off to my N.Y. people and Herb.

It's the whole thing. I *am* going out. It's right, I know that. This is part of that trip, that voyage we used to say I needed. It's a serious exploration.

Much love—wish me well—hope for me and all that—yrs.

WEDNESDAY 15 MARCH. It's all island with me now. Money down on it. We called the people (the Lairds), who apparently had heard that hotel types were interested and hated the idea, were *glad* to hear about me, will hold it for me a while. A relief not to have to jump, and worth the $500 "if"—

Winter has just about shot its bolt. Still cold. Rampageous. But things have cheered up. Yes, and Richie around again. I showed him the drawings of Elmo, which are good, though he seemed indifferent to them, and we went right to work with our paints, me on more flowers, though I had started to work one of the sketches into a painting. Using a palette knife for broad strokes on the back. Found I needed still more detail, more info as to the location of shoulder blades, spine.

Richie, I *think*, has been sulking. But seems to have forgotten it. I think possibly he's not very intelligent. But painted beautifully. Also, plowed around some more. Wind had taken things, snow had drifted like sand into dunes of the purest white, and only a tiny spot for the car remained clear, and Elmo's plow tracks.

He painted the barn in snow, had a marvelous sense of how it curled around corners, piled into smooth drifts—got shadows in—strong blues, greens—his barn, black and red, with odd touches of pink, or orange. I wanted to hear what he'd say about Elmo.

I said, Do you think it was wrong for me to get him to pose?

He said (with some slight sense of surprise, I think), How'd it be wrong?

It would be for you, I said.

At which he shrugged. We ain't the same, he said.

WEDNESDAY 22. Still cold but the sense of a loosening. Clouds—then sun, wind, then calm. I walk in it, blown about, red-nosed, thinking of island. The boats are going out, or more of them are, but the water looks dangerous—rumpled—very cold.

Have decided to ask Ethel and them for supper this Friday.

SATURDAY 25—MORNING. Lolling around with the mess.

It was fun. *Much* talk about the island, my getting it. Plans for the cabin, the wharf. Who to get to build it. And now is the time to start lining things up, before the spring building, the activities recommence. They recommend a certain Shirley Brawn and his boy —good solid craftsmen, reliable—not afraid to work out on an island. Oddly enough, some are, and won't.

Talk of my getting a small boat and an outboard. We'll show you about her, Elmo says, Richie and me. Ain't nothing to it.

For a moment I wondered whether Ethel weren't feeling slightly left out—then she said, I kind of envy you, Helen. What a time you're going to have with all that.

EVENING. Yes, that thing with Elmo Hale—won't it spoil the rest, like seeing him with Ethel, at his home? And what about Richie?

But, my word, it's an answer to all this—*one* answer—as Mallek was, or Mendonca. Only better since I see them all the time, not just for a fling. Or worse, because yes you do see them frequently, and need to. You are voyaging on strange seas. A is not B.

Why can't there be two Hales? An inner, an outer.

To bed. Screen before fire, glass into kitchen sink, me into cold white bed.

JOURNAL FRIDAY? There's fresh water on the island, I'm told— a great bonus. I'm sketching cabins, drawing wharves and landings.

Beth,

Mother saw her first robin today. And a cold, shivery little bird it was, maybe a leftover. But spring is on its way. We're all talking about it, the ladies and I, telling each other.

Ice dripping now, snow thawing, the lilac buds just beginning to fatten, fill up, a pinkness to the swamp maples. You can *almost* smell it. The house, I realize, has grown stuffy with me in it and the windows closed—still too soon to get at it, air it all out, but I'm putting quilts away. I peer out, hoping to see a crocus cropping up.

Yes, I have come through. I've been touched, breathed on, by an enormous if negative vitality.

Do give me your news, or just write. I have the feeling that shortly I may be scampering about and that you might lose me for a while again. Love, and all that.

FRIDAY 21 APRIL. Spring trying hard to break through, and everywhere the sense of it now; but it comes slow up here.

So much to do. Cleaning the wreckage and breakage of winter away, fixing the gutter (up on a ladder getting at old leaves). Jules Caster over with Elizabeth, she to visit and have coffee, he to take down storm windows, fix a light or two, hang a lamp that I bought for the kitchen.

The lobster boats are out, the bay dotted again with pot buoys that glitter in the sun, and the islands seem to float in air when the water is calm—a mirage.

And Richie around to paint—I guess Wednesday (they had finished up early out there).

But the land rising from the dead, unswathing. Buds stickily red in the treetops (the maple blossoms, I think), the grass turning, miraculously, from its dead dust brown to green. Caroling (sometimes just noisy) birds swooping in, returning. Mud everywhere, though who cares—it's the frost coming out, toppling some old wall. It's exciting—and the light is longer—a fond fresh sweetness over things, a radiance.

SATURDAY 22 APRIL A.M. Elmo wants to know whether I'd care to go out to the island Sunday (Ethel on the phone).

Won't cost you to look, she says, sly trader.

EVENING. Journal time. Martini time.
I've been good about Elmo, haven't I? I won't let that happen
too often—"irregardless." No, you may not pose for me. Don't
you know that I'm dangerous? And don't you know that you scared
me, letting me see what I did? as how could it not, a lone female
who tends to live in the mind?
Because, yes, he could be too much—as I'm sure that once for
Gertrude he was too much. I know his face now. *Some* of A, yes
—that second visit, and the one you had the goodness of heart to
burn—so unfair to him.
A second journal, perhaps?

SUNDAY 23 P.M.   Back, exhausted. "Won't cost you to look." I'm
afraid it has cost me everything.
Elmo in his navy-blue knit cap, wool shirt, Richie in the orange
hunter's cap he wears—Ethel to see us off (not feeling well). Then
us pulling away from the landing with a wave from her.
I don't know the island. We crept up on it—past Shepherd's
(they said), past Bear—we could see Mount Cadillac, or Scoodic,
I wasn't sure—clear as a bell—a great presence.
The islands. All shapes and sizes. Some tiny and perfect, a
single clump of spruce-crowned granite, pink and green—some
large, with sheep on them. They are alike, of a piece, as people
are, yet each is different from all the rest.
We seemed to be going by another way. Approached one, rounded
the north point of another—and there this thing was: undulant
granite shores. We chugged around it, and on the far side came to
a cove that looked familiar, a pirate's cove.
Is this it? I asked.
Elmo nodded, said rather somberly, Ay-yup—that's Pennyless.
We had come from another direction.
He let us drift and we looked at it.
Richie had already hauled up the skiff. Elmo dropped anchor.
And then, loaded to the gunwales, the three of us rowed in.
Oh, Beth, Beth, if you're reading this—and I write so much
of it for you—this *is* the thing itself, my island.
He wanted to show where he thought the cabin should be, Elmo
did. See that ledge? It was perhaps two hundred feet from the
water, to the side of the cove, and backed by spruce.

This is where Richie and me used to camp, he told me. By a fine spruce—parts of an old boat had been carried up, for sitting on (not Ellsworth's dory), burned stones, clamshells, an empty chlorine bottle, rusting beer cans, an old whiskey bottle (Seagram's) —they're not terribly neat about litter, having the feeling, I think, that here it will weather away.

Richie and me had some times here—ain't we, de'ah?

Beth—look—I'm intelligent with no great and perhaps leavening superiority, but intelligent. Which at first Herb liked, felt in position of mentor to, could, even would, instruct. Then I found that it was a game to him, or pose, and that really I must not compete too vivaciously.

Yes, I can see what's going on out there. My intelligence, like a gnome, sits back, looks out—spies an activity, spies things going on and deduces—X, Y, or Z. And looking out, as I did from my cave in Bkn. Hts., as I do from my cave here, I see, simply, that we're in for it, that it's a total revolution. And I *know* why. Technology—the irreversible process. I knew it then—and chose *not* to become involved. . . .

It was so beautiful. It spoke. Soundlessly, in sunlight, ringed with living green water, it spoke for itself. I saw my chance today.

Let me pause. Consider. Shall I try to be honest again?

Look. You met a man in a bar whose name was Mendonca— whom you took home with you. An old hulk, maybe a mate, or had been, maybe not, but so little left of him you could feed him booze, fill yourself with it, and make a kind of parody of love to an old wreck of a body shot with age and alcohol. It was the age you *liked*, the remains. A long hideous night of letting him do what he could. Queen of the water front. That first one, Mallek, you let go; you vamoosed, skedaddled, because *that* one would have laid you by the ears. Instead, you took an old bruiser—wrestler or whatever—bloated beyond recognition, and used him. Yes, and then grafted him on to that first one, made an object to contemplate of a drunken night, so that now even you don't remember what was real. A doll you stick pins in.

And now Elmo. Only he's like the first one—he scares *hell* out of you—Elmo Hale—two hundred and fifty-eight pounds and hung like a . . . whatever—you saw—and he made you an offer, standing there letting you see him, run your pencil over him, which he felt as he would have your fingers.

Your fake dreams, your cheap little gin thrills. Admit, confess! No Mallek. No Hale.

So I'll take that island. That can have me.

Though maybe Richie. Because he's shy, too. So that we would have to learn together.

What did I want, then, from Elmo Hale? Some "intimate relationship" that cost nothing, zero—him wanting me—on my terms—wanting him to want me, like GH said—and feeling that that might be all—and leading him on, thrilled that he would follow—and thrilled, thrilled that he would show me himself, an offering in the name of art, a *touch* of the erotic thrown in, that he liked me to see his bare flesh. And that I liked to. And then seeing, yes, that he's all of a piece and eager to please, ready and able.

And that woman, me? Well, life isn't good enough for her, life frightens her, always has, though she calls it disgust. She can't stand that it says, Give to me. *That's* life. And her answer?—I'll transform you into art. I know, I know. Life has to be lived through, not just talked about, made up.

So who were you just blathering about, dear? Yes, you are a fake, always accusing—words, words, nothing behind them but aversion and selfishness. Christ, *get* your little island, take that. Nothing will touch you there—not even Moose Deleau. No Mallek. *No* Elmo Hale. No Helen Calder, woman adventurer.

Saturday 29 April

Dear Beth,

This has to be one for the books. I'm flying around these days. I've bought that island. I don't know what will happen to me there. I may turn into a gull, or a crow. Keep writing, even when you don't hear from me.

SUNDAY 30 APRIL. A gentle, slightly time-consuming surprise. Old Mrs. Stinson and a daughter, Rebecca, in hats, sturdy shoes, stopped by. Were suddenly there at the door, having walked up from the town like good Mrs. Todd. It was like that, and were I that good woman Miss Jewett I would take their pictures properly.

Too much of the winter still on me, I think, so that forms of impatience lie close to the surface; they and their concerns are not, for the moment, me and mine. They seemed to be a country aunt and cousin you knew *would* pay a visit someday, and you not quite prepared, not ready.

They introduced themselves. A fine old female, fresh as the day she was born (which was in this house, on this farm) and a daughter, unmarried, large, rather gaunt, and a little weathered by time and circumstance—there to visit. Both of them wore beads.

I showed them about, or let them look. And could feel how strange it must have been for them—*both* of them born in the house. I did feel like an intruder, kept wanting to apologize.

How pretty you have it now—it's a good house—my grandfather's father built it, quite some time ago. I was born in that room (a tiny nook that I keep books and geraniums in)—the lying-in room then—before your time, de'ah (this to her daughter). Oh, yes, she said, you've a way with it.

I made them tea.

Rebecca said, We had a set brought back from Hong Kong in the seventies. We had to sell it. It was like this. We kept it over there in a corner cupboard.

And how do you find living here? Enjoying it, we hope, Mrs. Stinson said, as I poured her more tea and offered a slice of lemon (No thank you, de'ah, milk'll do).

Oh, very much, I said. I'm still a stranger, of course. But the women have been nice to me, let me quilt with them, help with the church sales—and we gam together.

Gam, Mrs. Stinson said—I ain't heard that in a while. Do you know that word, Rebecca? It's an old-time one—it was one of Uncle Jack's, he was seafaring.

Do you know the Hales?

Well, of course we do, Rebecca said—Ethel and Elmo?

Fine good people, Mrs. Stinson said.

They've been very kind to me. And then suddenly I said, Ethel's gotten me to buy an island.

There was a slight pause.

An island, de'ah?

And Rebecca, Which one?

One called Pennyless—one of the inner ones.

That set them off. I can't think why people do live on islands —and there's the outer ones, of course, that's still lived on. You been to Matinicus, no doubt—Isle au Haut—even York. Father used to tell how he'd take Mother out to pick wool on that (Mrs.

Stinson talking). They all had sheep on them then—and she'd find it on the raspberry bushes and the spruce, bits and wisps of it, and now and then they'd find a sheep the eagles had caught—you could pick it right off. And they'd take it home in a bag and she'd wash it, then make up socks and mittens for the family out of it. Folks made do in those days. Living was harder—though I don't know as it's better now.

Rebecca says, We could live on what we raised or found down here. (Rebecca must be about fifty, Mrs. Stinson what—seventy-five?)

And it seemed like there was more visiting then, Mrs. Stinson says. Folks stay home more now, watching TV. And then, with a smile at me, We gammed.

Families kept more together, too, Rebecca says. There were seven of us here—Uncle Jack and the two boys up in that room, when he was here.

Yes, and when we was visited your father'd go join them—four to the one bed—and the women up in mine, and some on the floor down here in quilts, and in there.

I can hear Jack up there now, Mrs. Stinson goes on—that voice of his, like stones in a barrel. He had tales. He died in that room.

They finished up the tea.

My, my, an island, Rebecca—think of Mrs. Calder out there.

Well, no doubt the fishing folk'll look to her, keep an eye on things and all.

Ea'ah—no doubt they will.

I offered to drive them back, but they were stopping at Mrs. Williams's down the road and said they preferred to walk, that neither of them got out enough these days.

When I was a girl we walked, Mrs. Stinson said. You met folks, chattered along the way, were called in. It was nicer somehow.

I saw them out to the road and stood looking after them. They waved back to me. I felt a pang.

I know the house better now—shade of old Uncle Jack. Maybe that's what we've lost—the uncles to cuddle up to on a winter night, the aunts, with their stories.

TUESDAY 2 MAY. A new month—which is going to be a busy one. Letter from Herb. He doesn't feel it's all that expensive. Two of my mutual funds have exploded and either would swing it, the

139

island part. Cabin, facilities—he thinks we might mortgage the farm and keep it, too. Suggests I ask Ethel's boss.

But he also, like Beth, thinks I'm running away from something, lots of things.

Yes, I will tell him, from a failed life, for which I'm learning, perhaps, to lay only half of the blame elsewhere.

Carole and Elizabeth around, having heard from Ethel.

We gabbled about the island. I show them some sketches I've done for the cabin. But they're not enthusiastic. Islands are lonely places, they repeat.

But then, as once before—Now if you was to have a man out there.

And Betty Caster—Like that Richie Hayden. Ethel says he paints with you.

The girls have given up on him, Carole Bean says. He's free pickings for someone.

And a nice young man, Betty says.

I just say, rather dryly, Don't you think he's a bit young?

Now it ain't seldom, you know, that a man'll take to an older woman, Carole says. I was older than Ellie—yes, and look at Ethel.

Yes, but I'm fifteen years older, I say.

They wave it aside. What that one wants *is* an older woman, someone to look after him like Ethel's done all these years. Why do you think he ain't struck out on his own?

Wednesday May 3

Dear Herb,

You're a good sport, though I'm not used to thinking of you as that. First the farm, and now this willingness to swap for the apartment, which may or may not be fair but seems to suit us both.

Anyway, let me say that I'm terribly happy. Later I'll send pictures. At the moment it's plans.

Yes, I am still running away. I admitted it to myself very freely the other day. But all I know is that while I've got the energy for a fast lap I'm going through with this

I don't understand it yet, I don't quite know what it means, but the springs of it run deep. What do the smart young say today?—far out? All right, let me say it.

Incidentally, I cannot bear to let that sofa go. It would be glorious in front of this great fireplace. Regards to Sal. It's probably gray with her footprints now, or long strands of gorgeous blond hair.

THURSDAY 4. Water system to be a gravity feed. The wharf will be a minor glory. Elmo indicated where it should go, according to depths, currents, etc.

SUNDAY 7. Elmo and Richie by, Elmo leaving, then later coming back for Richie, who had gone up to paint with me.

I showed him the thing I had been doing from my sketch of Elmo, the one standing at the sink, back to. It is good—done with seemingly effortless broad strokes of the knife. And for once R. seemed to admire.

And in some bitchy way I got after him about the posing, until finally he said, What do you need me for? You *got* him.

I said, I haven't *got* him—and can't always be asking him to. At which he shrugged.

At which I said, Just *some* time, when you're up here painting, you might, you know. We're friends. You could.

I watched him daubing with his brush at his paints, considering, apparently, his picture. So what do you think, de'ah? I mimicked.

He heard the mimicry—shrugged. Well—might, he said, grudgingly. And then added, I might want to try something else myself —like a man, or woman. I get to thinking about it. Not naked, though, like you got him.

He's not naked.

And I bet you've already drawn him naked, too.

I have not.

He'd probably do it.

Yes, and you will, too, sometime.

Not me.

Why not?

Why should I?

Because I *want* you to.

WEDNESDAY 10 MAY. Down to Cobbins Cove. Not yet there. I sat on the rocks and looked at her wharf. I'll find her there one of these days.

FRIDAY 12 MAY. The bright, chill remains of a spring day. Sense of it still out there, unfinished, doing something in the sky. A day to be picked like a flower, as all days ought to be. The forsythia out—butter yellow. And crocus, purple and white. A perfect brilliance.

I want the wrong things—pleasure without pain, love without involvement. I want things for nothing—a modern ailment.

The island may knit me in. Knock and it shall be opened, seek and ye shall find. Knock where? Seek where?

SATURDAY 13 MAY. Details. Arrangements.

Elmo took us over, me and Mr. Brawn and his son, to figure on exact location, lay out boundaries, etc. We placed stones at corners, measured distances.

The cove is a perfect place for the landing, though Mr. Brawn thinks we will have to sink pilings, fill up with stone, which he called grout—a fine word. Grout. Leavings. We'll get it from an old quarry island.

MONDAY 15 MAY. To Ellsworth for lumber with Mr. Brawn.

We discussed plans, costs, etc. About $3,000, he thinks. His wages are $2.50 an hour—his boy's (Harold) $1.50. Shocking, but that's what they asked for. Suggested I invest in a generator—will save much time, be able to cut on the island.

Martini. Has suddenly loosened something. And my God, I think, I'm going through with it!

THURSDAY 18 MAY. Great excitement. Toted lumber over from Wilson's Landing. A start.

Elmo and Richie arrived about nine and working like bears loaded it onto their boat, me standing by trying to look cool, feeling useless. They had gauged it for the high tide, had brought old tires along to use on the island as bumpers. We roared over and the two of them had it all on shore in an hour. I had brought cold beer and when they had finished we sat where they used to, me much moved to see it there, that yellow-white pile of fresh-cut wood.

FRIDAY 19. Decision: to build the landing first. Elmo's suggestion. Otherwise, he says, we'll be worrying about the tides. We'll build out from the shore ledge about thirty feet, though he's going to measure at low tide. Then a wharf landing built around that.

SUNDAY 21 MAY. At the IGA yesterday ran into May Stinson with a Mrs. Hutchins who had had a camp on Swans once. Would I have a fireplace? she wanted to know when she heard about the island. Very handy against weather. A Mrs. Chaney joined us. She's right, de'ah—for a place out there it's what you want.

And suddenly four or five of them had gathered, were telling me things—bottled gas for a stove—ay-yup—water—foam-rubber mattresses (no mildew to them). They like me for knowing I spent the winter here, call me de'ah now, as they do one another. Mrs. Hutchins mentioned a man named Avard something-or-other—a mason—had worked out on islands.

I had a sudden, fleeting little feeling of belonging, with them around me. Give me five years, and who knows?—five years and a husband.

In the afternoon Richie came by to paint. Thinks he wants to draw now and we talked about that.

Note: lilacs are coming out in full glory, the purple and the white—I have both.

Night comes on. A touch of fog around—a gray reminder.

TUESDAY 23 MAY. Drove over to Williams Boatyard to arrange for their pile driver and talk costs. Mr. Williams in among stored boats talking to one of his men. I picked my way toward them over ground cluttered with bits of rusting iron, rope, spikes, shaped wood, chips of granite, across tracks for some undersea railroad, weedy and barnacled, in and among the shadows of boats. They watched me approach, still talking.

And yes, he could do it. What about Friday? Before he got too busy setting out moorings, getting boats in the water. On Pennyless, eh? We heard that you bought her—a good one—ay-yup. Mr. Williams a tall, older man with a homely strong face and white hair, smoking a pipe, very pleasant.

It was fun to be among all that equipment and machinery, those boats and cradles and ways. Boats look odd to me up on land. A marvelous little old green and white schooner from Prospect Harbor made you think of ship models—polished at points to a mirror brightness. A few lobster boats were being repaired or painted. And off at the edges of things lay the derelict ones, drawn up, abandoned; unlike old cars or some old people, still with a hint of glamour about them (an old sloop, an old cabin cruiser), paint cracked and flaking, portholes and rigging gone, yet evidence of what they had been still there in the lines.

Saturday 27 May P.M.

Hello, Beth,

It's me. Getting down to a trim 135 with all this flying around. We're building. Got started on a landing yesterday. I'm dealing in pilings now, and got four beauties in. How splendid they look out there in the water when the tide comes in. Gulls have already swooped in to perch. Beginnings often resemble ends. They could be the last of one, an old wharf, rather than the start.

Elmo Hale and young Richie came whizzing out in an outboard to help, to advise. I had brought beer. Mr. Brawn, my carpenter (check that name!), and Mr. Williams, whose pile driver it is, were there. Can you *see me* directing pile-driving operations! They all know and respect one another, are hearty, efficient, know when to help, when to refrain. It's this part, the putting down of foundations, that's so important. We got a good start.

Herb has been a brick about all this—couldn't have been more helpful—and him in the middle of riots—not lashed to a barricade but gesticulating, part of it all.

Sorry to hear Bill's been under the weather. But I'm glad the children have a little black friend they bring home. I hope they're brought to his home, too.

I'm groggy with fresh air, sunlight, water. Winter was hard but the spring has flattered it away, though the nights are still awfully cold—and the early mornings pink and white, but easing themselves toward the green suns of summer.

SUNDAY 28 MAY. Richie here again. Brought some sketches he had made of their landing, of the house, of the cove. They were odd and at first I didn't know quite what to think. They were a little like Marin reduced to lines. Oh, not that much, but they went in that direction. So oddly knowing—the way he could indicate water, horizon, sky, distant trees as conventional objects you have a right to put to your own uses. Does he, perhaps, have a touch of genius?

He's growing a beard, and right now it's beautiful—copper-gold clipped wires covering a round jaw. I asked him why and he shrugged—said, Why not? The men here, a few of the fishing ones, grow them in winter, perhaps for something to do, though shave them off in spring.

I like it that he's coming around Sundays now.

No visit from Elmo in a while. It's all C, apparently—yes, because of the island, the cabin—not even A these days. And I feel better for it, too.

Took a short drive—a turn left down a rutted dirt road through scrub spruce that scratched at the car, past lichened granite, that led to a grassy promontory I had no idea was there, though I think I had seen it from the water with the Hales. From a sort of knoll the land runs down on all sides to the shore—large logs were wedged among boulders there. A terrific sense of the sea—it looks out to where the islands are merely grass and granite, some washed over by the waves, crashed up against. I had a much stronger sense of the sea itself, unimpeded—I was gazing off toward death, I felt. I could see swells out there, knew that deep water moved in its slow, thick undulations, sensed the depths.

MONDAY 29 MAY. Out with the men, practically at dawn—Mr. Williams and Shirley Brawn and a helper. Driving more piles.

Lovely, putting out there in the fresh and early morning light, seeing the lobster boats around, the islands—and molten, undulant water—gulls off cracking mussels on a rock—four of us huddled in the boat—warmly clad.

Mr. Brawn sawing up boards, getting ready for a low tide, to make a cradle in the pilings for the stone (the grout).

Mr. Williams will finish up tomorrow. Then comes the stone, if our signals are right and the weather permits.

Home tired, just from being out, from watching things happen.

Buster had caught quite a large rat. Had left it for me on the door rock. Thank you.

WEDNESDAY 31. Up before dawn to go with them, E & R. Picked up the barge over at a place near Stonington—Oceanville. Reached Pennyless with it about noon. Slow going, but who's in a hurry? Had beer along for us and they had thermoses of coffee. A glorious morn, very calm—nacreous—islands in the air—the mountains slate blue.

Richie and Elmo unloading the stone, chunks of it as big as bread and some much larger—they splashed them in and were soon wet, at which Elmo took off his shirt, then his undershirt, like wet gray skin, and I had a look at him again. Lovely to watch.

I can't get that into words. I think I'm right though—there are types, essentially two—the lean and angular, and the other—chthonic, earthborn. Handling rock became him, as it did Richie, too—blocklike arms, big hands, and a back it seemed that flesh hid the bones and muscles of, heavy, flexible.

I had made sandwiches and had deviled a dozen eggs, and when they were finished we picnicked, with Mr. Brawn and son joining us. In my mind I painted Elmo as on elbow he lounged on a rock. He belongs to sculpture—monumental.

The tide came in and covered the stone cradles, and the fresh-sunk rock gleamed under water that resembled glass. On the island, I'm aware of strong currents around me.

FRIDAY 2 JUNE. They've been building the wharf, which is coming along now fast. We whiz over in Mr. Brawn's outboard, which, like every other boat here, has the feel of a fishing boat to it.

I can see that there will be days when I don't go with them. I'm not much help. Richie promised to begin teaching me how to run one, an outboard, because I'll need to know.

SATURDAY 3 JUNE—EVENING. Elmo just gone. I fixed us highballs and, since it was cool, made a small fire. I remind him that I've got to start thinking about a boat. Does he know where I should go, what size it ought to be, all that? He says a place down near Bar Harbor will have what I want—he and Richie will take me there one day—he figures about $1,000. Well, things cost, and money seems to be going downhill these days.

I ask him, What do you think about Vietnam?

Well, not many likes it, I'd say. I figure it just ain't our business over there. You can't boss the whole world. I don't know. Seems we only like the rich countries now. Whole world seems rich against poor. It ain't like that down here—the men help each other out, and don't ask nothing for it neither.

I go to fix us another drink, and find him clumping downstairs when I come back. I hear him say, You got our Richie to drawing, I see.

Well—he kind of got himself to, I think.

Not much to them as yet, would you say?

Oh, I think they're good. They're to help with his paintings, I think.

Ain't much like yours. Now I like those. You got me good. You had Richie pose?

Not really, I say. I draw him when he's painting here. He's shy.

He nods. He is. Not like me. And then, with something of his grand, fatherly air, which the liquor inflates, he says, I'll pose in my socks for you yet, de'ah—one day.

He leaves about ten. But there *is* that undercurrent to all we say, or that undertow, and he does like to come around, have a drink, talk.

I dream of going naked on my island along the shore, picking my way, to lie on a rock and let the sun have me.

SUNDAY 4 JUNE. Gardened. Dug in the soil lustily. Iris up. Making ready for the delphiniums.

Drew up lists.

Quick dash to Carole Bean's and a brief gab over coffee.

But an event to report. Important. Richie stood for me. Not posed, it wasn't that.

We went up to paint. I brought coffee. We got things out.

And he said, out of a perfectly clear blue sky, If you like, you can draw me.

So clear, in fact, that I didn't quite know what he meant.

If you want I'll take my shirt off, like he done, he said.

I said hastily, Oh, you don't have to. Partly, you know, I was teasing you.

He just shrugged. Will if you like.

I respond, You've never called me Helen. You've never quite thought of me as a friend. You're often very standoffish. And now you're offering to help. How come?

A wordless shrugging occurs and he mumbles, I don't know, and my mind seems to waver, with us standing there, him gazing at me with his vague, emotionless eyes, round and pale blue—milky.

I hear myself saying, to them, Well, I would like it if you did. I need people to draw and can't be hoping Elmo will all the time.

I watched the fingers picking at shirt buttons. He turned away, as though modestly—the shirt came off, and then, with a bending, a lifting of arms, the undershirt—like the unveiling of white flame. Because it was, I saw at a glance, a perfect body—the skin showed you that—with the sense of a clean, supple roundedness, of the shoulders, the back.

It was mostly his back that I tried for first, seeing it as massive, of a piece, then, gradually, though broad, as complex, made up of many surfaces, shadowed and various. Hair only as a kind of bloom or fuzz, so that the chest muscles stood out in a sort of rigid clarity.

He had tacked out one of his sketches and was working paint onto it. I kept knowing how lucky I was and that in a way this was serous, expressive of confidence.

I remind him that he said he'd teach me to run an outboard someday.

I say, I don't want to take up all your time, but I could use some help.

We'll do it this week, he says, with a brush and a cleaning rag in his hands.

Yes, he's forgotten himself, that he's letting me "see."

The work on his painting is good. Something is changing in his style—no longer merely charming because childlike—there's a calculation in there—very free, still, very bold.

When he leaves, as before with Elmo, I'm tired. My eyes are too filled. And none of the sketches is any good, but I'm learning him.

THURSDAY 8 JUNE.   Wharf building. Finishing up. And a ladder is being built. It's all a big thing. I won't reckon the cost, since it was essential. Monday Mr. Brawn thinks he'll be ready to start on the cabin itself. We checked out materials. I have the lists of them—the kinds of nails, spikes, and screws, the sorts of boards, the sills, the joists, rolls of tar paper, cement, steel cable, all that. On yellow paper in a prim school hand, as if it all came from a hardware store in the nineties. Oh, I am enjoying this.

Though I feel a bit "schizzy." Out of touch with my Orstown life. I need to loiter a while, go for a walk, stand on that promontory again, facing the sea.

SUNDAY 11 JUNE.   Richie to paint again. I had been over to Ellsworth, to Blair's, and had stopped in a sporting-goods store where, rather nervily, I bought a pair of trunks—twill, and not your form-fitting sort. I said, Put these on—they're perfectly decent.

He simply looked at them, took them, and left the room. In a minute he came back.

How do they fit? I asked. I got them at that sport shop in Ells-worth—I said 36. Big enough?

He shrugged. I ain't had nothing like this on before.

Well, you've seen them in magazines.

Ea'ah—folks swimming at the beach.

Barefoot, pink white around the tan of the trunks, he went right to work. Yes, like Elmo in his way, all of a piece—rhythmically curved.

I sit off in a corner, pad on knee, and catch what I can—a leg, an arm and shoulder. And he paints as if I'm not there.

He seems to have made up his mind about something, taken another step forward. Helen?—looking around—What do you think if I don't use paint at all here—I don't want white.

I come over to look. I say, On canvas you could—here, on paper, I would use the white. The oil will bleed if you don't.

He rests. Comes over to glance at what I've been doing of him.

I'm working between realistic and geometric—making notes. I say, When you go out drawing, if you do, you might think of that, of just making notes, even notes for the kinds of color you find or want.

I don't know, he says—they seem to stay in my mind—I see them in there.

He dresses finally, and leaves, telling me he'll see me about the outboard sometime this week.

Elmo and he to haul out more lumber Tuesday.

WEDNESDAY 14 JUNE.   Fog yesterday but we hauled anyway.

Fog thickening, thinning, lifting, rolling across islands. Pennyless appeared to be holding it at bay. Could see Mr. Brawn and son, Harold, moving about.

We chugged in, past that little dab of rock I'm going to call Shawl Island because of the way the grass mantles it, avoiding their outboard, pulled up alongside. They had calculated the tide. Shirley and Harold up at the cabin site, measuring—stirring something in a flat tub.

Then Richie and Elmo set to work. The two-by-tens were already up there, for the sills. This was two-by-eights and more flooring, bags of cement, nails, tar paper, and two-by-fours for the studs. Also corner posts—eight-by-eights—back-busters, I could see, but they seemed to handle them easily. All the men carried and I toted what I could, somewhere hearing Elmo's broad voice —Watch it, Richie—he'ah, lemme git that.

Down at the wharf I saw a seal, dark, sleek head lift from the water—gaze my way with its great, soft-wet, brown eyes— then slowly submerge. Ripples for a moment in the fog, which had come in, a breeze blowing it along. It was suddenly all about us, cool, silver veils, then a substance.

Rather exciting, making it back in. Darkly, through the fog, images, outlines, of shore things appeared—a wharf, the cannery— then behind them the pointed houses, like the ears of creatures watching us. Egyptian jackal gods.

FRIDAY 16 JUNE. The end of the week. Payday. I write them out checks and try to imagine how the money will be spent, seeing a rough, hard-working hand reach out to accept it. Groceries—a little beer?

Marketing, the ladies ask me how things are going. Word has got around.

Stopped by to see Ethel. The children not home.

It was good just to sit in her kitchen in a rocker.

Why don't you stay on for supper? she asked. The Robbinses are coming. You might's well.

But I wanted to get home.

Well, come tomorrow then—it'll be the same—Richie brought me a nice haddock. You got him eating out of your hand, El tells me. What I'm hoping is that you'll get him out on that island, she adds. And what I'm betting is that you will.

We look at each other for a moment, expressionlessly.

You could do it, she says—he likes you.

Through the window I am sitting at I look out to see the boat gliding in over green water that reflects it and its triangular brown sail, Richie up at the bow to hook the mooring, a dark wall of stone and spruce beyond them. The wharf and its shed make a foreground.

Ethel has seen them, and looks out a moment with me. I say to her, Does that look pretty to you?—does it look (I hesitate)—*good*?

For a moment she doesn't reply, stands with a dish in her hands looking out. I see her glance down at me, for an instant withdrawn, contemplative. Good? She says—she nods. I know what you mean. Yes, it is good—the men working, coming home—

And that they *can* work like that—where else *is* it as beautiful, as *right?*

She nods. We see it, if that's what you mean. We get used to it but we know it's there.

My garden seemed to await me, to want to be looked at. Alyssum like foam among the stones, a few lupine (those great fields of them I saw last June are in full flare now). I haven't been here enough to visit things.

SATURDAY 17 JUNE. Out gallivanting. Off early to Ellsworth and the junk shops along the way. Looking for pots and pans, cabin equipment (why get it new?). And on my way home drove in and found Gertrude back, sitting out on her porch, with, I should certainly say, one of her "big ones."

I would have gone on, but while I was backing and turning she came down to the car. Howdy, stranger, come have a beer, meet a friend.

Yes, a big one, all right. Ran the fish market over in Tainesville. She talked about him as if he were deaf and dumb, or an object, or stuffed, perhaps. A bearlike creature who watched me with small, quick, white-lashed eyes, not unintelligent, and who said, when she'd gone inside for my beer, Where ya live? in a quick little high-pitched voice. And who said, when I told him, I know it—and then said, We call it Ortstown. Know what "orts" is? and when I shook my head said, Leftovers—garbage—and smiled.

Aw, shut up, she said, coming out with the beer.

That's an old word, he said—my mother used it.

What he means is the story, she said, handing me a beer. A captain, Abner Bass, and his wife used to live down there, in the old time—maybe you've seen it, where the house was—out on a little point of land. And they tell how they used to hear her yelling to the old man—Tide's going, Ab—throw out the orts!

At which he nods.

He don't mean no harm, she said. He ain't quite right in the mind. And he looked down at me (I was sitting on the porch steps) out of his quick blue eyes. Broad, fat chest from which gold hair at the buttons peeped out. He struck me as good-humored and unbudgeable, and somehow very odd.

I bought that island, I told her, and gave her a few details of the building of the wharf.

She's got an island, she said to him, as if he couldn't have understood. I told her she'd probably lose her mind on it.

I'm losing it anyway, I said—so it might as well be out there. How'd you like livin' on an island? she said to him.

Might get me away from the old lady, he said. Which one? One called Pennyless, I said, and saw him nod.

I know her, he said. Used to be sheep on her.

He used to haul, too, she said—was a lobsterman, in his younger days. Weren't you, de'ah? You ought to see him, she said—he's—a—remarkable. Ain't you, Hernie?

He was looking down at me and hearing her; I noted that she used a different tone when speaking to him, something closer to dialect.

I saw her put her beer can down, then move to stand behind him. Ain't you, de'ah? she said again. Mrs. Calder's an artist—she's interested in the way people look—and to me, Let me show you—and then, with him still watching me, she began to unbutton his shirt, the buttons popping back and the cloth springing apart in a wider and wider V. Ain't that something? I heard her say, him continuing merely to sit, to look at me. Let me show her, she said to him—come on. Bent over him, pulling the shirt out, unbuttoning it, pushing it back, from a chest and stomach that were encased in gold-curled hair. Which she rubbed a moment. You should feel him, she said—he's like a door mat. Show her your back, she said down to him. And then she was pulling the shirt from his shoulders, pushing it down over his arms, his back. Lean forward, she said—which after a moment he did, lifting one arm obediently, then the other, letting her strip the shirt away.

How's that? she said—and to him, Let her see, turning him with her hands and he allowing it. I was repelled, uncomfortable. He was wearing a jacket of gold fur.

Ever seen anything like that? I heard her say. I shook my head. And ain't likely to neither, she said. Ain't that something?

I saw his small, blue, quick, and lively eyes watching me. She stood with a hand on his shoulder, then came to sit on the steps with me. Mrs. Calder here's interested in local types and goings on, she said up to him—so why don't you tell us about that nutty one, the one with the mother and the dogs.

What you want to hear? I heard him say.

He's got one over in Edsville he drops in on, she said, and she's got this son—one of them backwoods types. Hernie likes to wrestle him. What's he like? she asks up.

Big, he said.

Yeah?

Like me—he rubbed a hand at his chest. Lays the old lady. You hear that? she said to me. Yeah?

Been laying her since he was twelve. Guess that's why she keeps him. He was looking down at us, first at her, then me—I couldn't tell if he was serious—rotund, almost a Buddha form. So go on.

Likes me, too, he says—she does. Likes us to wrestle.

She waited a moment, then said, Yes, and then he screws both of them—one way or the other—don't you, Hernie?

I see him shrug, looking down. One way or another, his high voice agrees.

How's that? she says to me—life in Maine. He's hairy, too, ain't he? she says, and I see him nod. And the old lady?

Bitty little thing—about that high—his hand holds out to show us.

And the boy stays with her? And when he nods, she asks, How old is he?

Maybe twenty-five now—ain't smart, you know.

She pretty?

I see him smile and she says to me, Aw, he won't talk. You should hear it though—a pack of nuts when he gets with them. And then, How's the beer?

She likes us to wrestle naked, he suddenly says.

I gather she's not too smart herself, I say.

She's had a hard life, Gertrude says—like me.

They got seven dogs, he says, and twenty-six cats. He feeds them on deer meat.

What do they do for a living? I ask.

Boy works at the sawmill—works some for me—salts fish, mops up the sheds.

For a buck an hour, Gertrude says.

And a pint, he adds.

Or a quart, she says. Then he goes home with him and drinks the half of it, knocks him around, screws hell out of the old lady—I don't know what he does to the dogs. Ain't that so, Hernie?

I said that I had to be running along.

Now don't go dropping in on her, she told him. He's liable to, she said—he roams. He's got eight children.

More than that, he said, in the quick high voice.

Come to think, she said, to me, he might pose for you sometime—he'd like to.

I gave her a raised eyebrow.

I left them sitting there and saw them wave as I drove off.

The wicked flourish like the green bay tree, whereas I live mostly in the mind—with a man who posed for me once, twice, and one who paints with me. And that is it, it really is all—you who may bother to read me.

MONDAY 19. Up at dawn. And lovely, with the light rising—my warm kitchen. I unfold like a flower with the sun touching the tops of the spruce, greening their black, then coming to visit my windows, reach in to light things on the table.

Mr. Brawn in for coffee, sitting there pencil in hand, figuring the lumber we'll need. We discussed the water situation, the spring.

Letter from Beth when we got back from the island.

Speaks about possible riots in Detroit, the cities. Not comforting, she says, to say: Not here. We are not an island. Spoke of what she called children's crusades, that the impossible young shall lead us. Spoke of the new cults, pseudo religions, around—all signs of discontent, of search, of real vitality—at least at its best. She adds, But, darling, don't make a cult of living alone—please. That is not you. And not the way these days. Nature, yes, but no withdrawals. The barricades are everywhere. . . .

Twinges of guilt, but wheels are turning now. In my mind I write back—I'm exploring, too. Don't criticize—encourage.

TUESDAY 20 JUNE. Thinking, even as I worked out there, about her letter.

But what *am* I for? Which side am I on? I seem to be against almost everything—change, technology, the young, the establishment. I seem to be only "for" the past, a time and a way that have gone.

Something has poisoned my mind, unsweetened my imagination. Possibly the past itself. As something is poisoning this world, this sea.

And if I could write properly, if I could make it sing, I'd write about how there are fewer lobsters each year, how the clam beds are vanishing, contaminated, the fish avoiding these shores. How the men can't make a living here and grow desperate, how the new taxes are driving them out. How their sons leave, go elsewhere, no longer build to last but squat in trailer "homes" that decay like cans.

There is no control, no understanding. In this incredibly beautiful world we keep thinking we can live as we always have, but this is a new dispensation and under it the old can't survive, nor the young flourish.

It would have been worth a good story. All I can chronicle is my own decline in the midst of theirs, which I can only gaze at—them, caught between two worlds. Yes, and the stately, tall white yachts will sail by, and one by one the houses they sail past will be abandoned or bought by summer people, the wharves turned, for a while, to marinas. Taxes, no work, no fish, no money—no chance. And nothing will ever be as beautiful: men working in the midst of such loveliness, as free as men will ever be, to work, to suffer, and, when their time comes, to die, having lived it well.

FRIDAY 23 JUNE. Elmo Hale, in his megaphone voice, over the phone: Want to go look at boats tomorrow?

Sunday 25 June

Dear Beth,

I've bought a boat. It scares me to death. A seventeen-foot Starcraft (aluminum), windscreen, steering wheel, remote controls, the works, with a 40 hp Evinrude that starts electrically. You drive it more or less like a car. I got everything—life preservers, foghorn, compass.

My two lobstering friends did the picking and choosing, the dickering. We launched from up the bay, and Elmo and I took it down to his wharf. You should see him at the wheel in his knit cap—such a sureness—never been in one of them before, but knew, knew—and off we flew. They're going to show me how to handle it (her) and help me with moorings and all that.

The cabin comes along. Darling, I'm actually going to have a cabin on an island of my own, and by August I'll be out there. Do wish me well.

155

My garden is more weeds than flowers, but I mow and do what I can.

Love, and all that—beaucoup—

EVENING. To make the weekend complete, Richie around to paint this afternoon. And about the posing, all he said was, You want to draw me some more? and came back in the trunks.

It still surprises me—under those scrubbed and worn and mended clothes that Rubens body—and he knows, he realizes, and under that quietness a pride.

R.'s presence up there produces a constant sense of pleasure—standing, moving about in his bare feet—an immaculate one. I do, I think, already love him—but gently. I like it that he's poor, though up here they mostly are.

Elmo came by and up and nobody batted an eye, nor was anything said, except that when we quit and Richie went out to dress, Elmo said, When you going to draw me again?

I shrugged. When you have time, I said. And he produced one of his slow smiles. It's Richie now, ain't it? he said, and I said, a little primly, perhaps, We're going to be friends, I think.

And I'm friends, too, he said. He admired the painting of himself.

R. came back, clothed; we went downstairs and I fixed drinks.

SATURDAY 1 JULY. R. as good as his word. Came around for me in the afternoon. He wasn't entirely sure of things himself, at first, saying, I ain't used to this rig (they work their outboards at the stern, directly), monkeying with levers and buttons, tinkering, jimmying this and that. But in no time he had it and off we went, putting out of the cove, then giving her the gas to fly bouncing and spraying out into an afternoon chop. Then he slowed down and was showing me things. And made me take the controls. I wouldn't try a landing but he made several, to show me—then showed me how to tie it to the raft. That bothers me, too—ropes, knots—even the simplest.

He drove me back and came in to paint, and without saying anything changed into the trunks. I said, Stand for a moment facing me—and rapidly I sketched him with brush in hand. His presence fills my eyes, produces a continuous sense of satisfaction for them, as though they had found something they had been needing and could rest now.

SUNDAY 2 JULY. Cheery visit with Carole Bean. I admire her hollyhocks, but she lets me know I've been neglecting her and I realize that my life these days is all men, all work, boating and island. And I'm suddenly mad to be gardening, tending my delphiniums, clipping grass back from the iris. We sit out on her porch and rock. I'm freshly aware of the houses, how simple and clean-looking they are—white or yellow or green, some shingled —aware of the flowers around them—I spot a Harison's yellow by a wall—the dooryard rose—one of the earliest in New England, so they say.

The town basks in summer—tall grass or neat, clipped lawn— daisies and vetch and buttercups—hydrangeas—the sense of warm stone. Carole gets up to tend a chowder she's fixing, brings back a cup of it for me to taste. Onions, potatoes, fish and clams, a spot of melting butter. Try that, she says, and waits for my response. May's coming over for supper, she says. It's a sort of question and I say, And why not me? and she says, Glad to have you.

It was nice to be with them again. We gossiped a little more.

JULY 4—TUESDAY. Bang Bang Bang again—or Pop Pop Pop. But a year has gone by. Nor has the world out there, back there, improved. Nor would my having been in it helped—in fact, let's say I'm thinning out the population. The billions will have to take care of themselves out there. Clamoring, clamoring.

Pop.

SATURDAY 8 JULY. Another boating lesson with Richie. He showed me things about the motor, the spark plugs, the choke, the controls—about the propeller and how to tilt it up, lock it. We practiced landing. Bang—I hit the dock—backed off, tried again— swung in the wrong direction, panicked! He said, Slow down— just go slow when you ain't sure.

It isn't fun for me yet. I don't have the feel of it, of how she responds to a wave, of how to maneuver.

TUESDAY 11 JULY. Studs and rafters up. Roof going on. I go over every other day. Things go more slowly now, it seems. I'm seeing my ladies again, and gardening, tending the delphiniums.

Two trips inland to look for furniture, though much will be built in—bunks, a large table, a sort of service counter to enclose the cooking area. Toilet to be a "necessary" (as I've heard it called), but I'll have running water in the cabin. A tiny bedroom. Need to find a good big iron bed. Two old wicker chairs out in the barn, which I haven't yet gone through. I will, I will.

THURSDAY 13 JULY. Stopped by to see Ethel. Just to chat. The lobstering is good, which makes the men feel good, and their families. Young David has been going with them, which pleases Elmo, she tells me. He's starting to collect little bits of gear for his own, old toggles, pot buoys.

SATURDAY 15 JULY. Another boating lesson. Elmo came with us, wanted to drive and did. We zipped out to the island, where they made me practice landing. I improve, but no style as yet; it's crash and catch hold. Hit a pot buoy and came very close (Look out!) to a ledge, which scared me. I didn't even see it—a bit of underwater stone that you simply have to know is there—and even they don't sometimes.

Richie back to paint. I dare say to him, Sometime I want you to let me draw you nude—yes—naked. Would you mind that? (I see him shrug, both shoulders lifting.) Not now—I'm not really ready, don't need it, I say; but think about it.

We leave it at that.

SUNDAY 23 JULY. A busy week. Roof on, walls going up. Mr. Brawn in a good mood despite a cold and some grumpy weather. And I screwed up my courage Friday and took my own boat along, followed them over. At moments I felt in control, though made a punk landing.

Which got us to talking about a raft, that I would need one, and a ramp, to rise and fall with the tide. They suggested I talk to Mr. Williams. I went immediately back in, landed at his wharf (bang)—and found him. Yes—he thought I ought to—standard around here. Specifications, et al.—Styrofoam floats. (Ugh!) One more big thing, but I feel good about it. Now I won't have to go bashing in among pilings.

Richie around this morning. I sketched him for a while, then went to work on my new painting of Hale-by-sink.

Who has just left, having boomed in about eight. Very genial. How's this? how's that? Had a drink, had another. Had already had several, I'd say. No posing, though very much in the mood.

It's Richie now, ain't it? he said. No resentment. Good-humored. And that's good for him, Helen—him shy and all. Not like me—all ready to go.

He's over at the sink putting water in his glass and I look at him there, in one of the short-sleeved summer shirts he wears when he's cleaned up—immense, the whole set of him there.

I say a person's got to be what he is—he's coming back with the drink to the table. We're all slow down here. Got nowheres to go.

But you like that, I say—you wouldn't want to be hurried, told when to get there.

But I would like a little loving once in a while (sloshing the ice in his drink, held in big fingers)—more than I'm getting.

It's a good-humored remark, one friend to another.

His painting's good, I say.

We like it, he says—always did. He done that when he was a kid, you know—drawed. Then: Richie's got a good figure, you know—get him to get them pants off, Helen. Be good for him.

I see his face—Well, it would, de'ah. He needs some of that. Ain't been with women, you know. And he has, de'ah—Richie got a good body.

You do, too, I say.

I see an elaborate, self-conscious shrug. I'm all fat now, he says. But I'll pose for you, de'ah—out there (nodding toward the island). I'll let you see me good, if you like. And Richie—get them *pants* off him, Helen (takes a long pull at his drink)—*I'll* get 'em off—out there.

I make us another. He drinks, sets it down, seems to contemplate the glass. Nods—says, He does what I want, that boy. And he'll stand for us, de'ah—yes, and naked—and me—I will—so's you can get that fine picture—the two of us, maybe—some fine. How'd that be? Helen—we'll have some times.

It's wrong of me, but I fix him another, not having seen him like this. And between sips he does monologues—about himself, about Richie, about "times," women, Ethel, bodies.

I done it, I told him—and would of naked if she'd asked. Yes, I would. Mrs. Calder ain't interested in that, you getting a hard on like—she needs us for them pictures—she ain't interested in no hard. She's scared of that, or I'd say. And if it *was* to—like—you just turn your back, leave her draw, I'd tell him. And you ain't going to get no hard on standing for her, Richie. I might—but not you, de'ah. I like women—women, you might say, interest me—but all she wants is to draw a man's body, I tell him. She ain't interested in no hard. You get him, de'ah—I'll help—be good to him, he ain't had none of that—we'll get him—out there. I want that boy to *learn*—needs a woman, that boy does—bad—it's all tied up in him, and I want you to help him, de'ah, and *I* will. . . .

Monday 24 July

Dear Beth,

Just a note to say hello. The only word for me these days is busy. No time for brooding (or much), or even thinking—no time for books. It's all projects—the cabin, which comes along, a raft (now being built), learning the ways and hows of my boat. I practice now by myself—scary, fun—these are difficult waters. But with a lurch and a scramble I do. And I sign checks. God, how it goes—hundreds for everything—and yet cheap, up here.

I *know* it's too far for you to come, too difficult. I just wish, that's all. Do think of a quick fall visit—just you—a long weekend. So much to show you.

Still don't "know" the island, because they're there, Mr. Shirley Brawn & Son. I can't wait for them to finish and be gone. I dream about it, dreams that tell me something is wrong, a mistake has been made—*really* quite scary. But then the old energy surges back with the morning coffee and a couple of Salems and I'm ready for it all again.

Write. Even a note. Keep in touch. Love.

JOURNAL.   Coming to know the harbor and that part of life here better. The land, the harbor—connected in their lives—the land and the sea. The wharf life—skiffs and moorings, fueling up, bringing the lobsters in—seeing the men I see in town, though I don't recognize many, at their work, their real work, running those boats—out long before I am—then racing in with the catch, about four. I like the sounds of them, the gurgle, the sputter, the roar, the high whine of the diesels—the harbor alive, awash with their wakes. One or two I do recognize now, in their boots and caps. One old grizzled fellow who may be Bill Eaton. Elmo mentioned him.

FRIDAY 28 JULY.   Elmo around, somewhat surprisingly—as I was lurching toward that third martini, the end of my week having arrived.

So I made him one, too (Let me try one of them)—and just instantly, it seemed, the wheels began to whir. With a whistle, shaking his head at it—Gets there, don't it. Sipping, testing—almost listening to it. And he asked for another. I said, Don't just throw them down as if they were old socks—these are strong.

Strong? he said.

Well, they are.

You mean I can't drink with a lady?

Well, she doesn't put away four or five at a clip. In fact—I've got a great title for a book—I'd call it "No More Martinis for Helen." It would sell, too.

I brought him a third, however.

I'm all set to pose for you, de'ah, he said. Hauled two hundred pounds today and feel good. Go get your pad.

Sit a minute, I said—just sit.

I will, I will. Richie been out? Said he was coming. I'll get him for you, de'ah. He'll pose.

But then *he* posed, he certainly did! An astonishing performance. I won't put it into words this time, but he was close to maniacal —a satyr performing alone, but for me.

SATURDAY 29 JULY. Work, which restores me. To the island—to wood and stone with friendly Mr. Brawn & Son.

Note to myself: Can I let that go on? If it's what he wants, why can't I? It isn't proper, that's why. Soon it will wind through everything. You *know* what's there—you're playing with fire. Or why not let it be that other one—G.'s? But I'm afraid of him, that one. That one wouldn't care to be drawn.

MONDAY 31 JULY. A surprise. In the form of Rufus Procter. Yes, I did know they were down here somewhere—Deer Isle. And it was fun to see him again, and odd to, in these surroundings. What are *you* doing here?—and what are *you*? Etc. At the P.O. Had just stopped to send postcards. Mimi in the car with his mother, the Dragon Lady, and one of the sons, all out for a drive.

So back they came with me for coffee and news, mostly mine. Knew Herb and I had parted.

I remember now that Herb did have this place, Rufus said.

Isn't it charming, Mrs. Procter said.

I said, You're lucky to catch me in—I'm usually out with a pile driver these days.

I can't get *over* that, Mrs. Procter said.

Rufus said, Tell her she's got to come Sunday, Mimi, who said, We're gathering—yes, you've got to. It's just us. Bobby is coming down from Boothbay.

And suddenly it seemed like a duty, an obligation, and fun.

It's a hell of a drive, Rufus said. You know how to get there, don't you? Ellsworth—Blue Hill—we're at Sunset.

Surrounded by the famous, Mimi said. Not that they'll be there.

We don't really entertain, Mrs. Procter said—and Mimi said, We estivate.

I showed them my little garden and felt proud of the lawn and the remains of the delphiniums. It certainly *is* charming, Mrs. Procter said, who was wearing an old bucket hat and looking famous and international.

Well—what do I think of that? I guess I'm going. I'll make a day of it.

TUESDAY 1 AUGUST. A new month. Where has time *gone?* Already the shadow of the season falls. Three days of fog but we've made it out to the island each time.

Elmo to pull the raft over this Saturday, and the shingles. Odds and ends. No fireplace this year but I am going to cart over a stove I've found, a real beauty—small, with doors that open. Yes, and plumbing equipment—plastic hoses, a sink. No end to it. I've made several trips by myself, toting stuff. Men are good about helping me load. They know me now at the landing and don't even smile when I come crashing in among the skiffs, stumbling about, knocking against oars and life jackets. I'm not just summer folk to them any more—word has gone round. The hideous old men, booted and aproned, bristle-jawed, hollow of eye, who work with salt and fish and damp barrels—even they, whom I no longer find hideous, know me and nod (I like and admire old Bill Eaton of the sea-broken hands, horny-nailed, who hauls out by Penny-less). And the man who sells me gas and oil—Howdy, Mrs. Calder —how's she going out there? We chat. We assemble there, Mr. Brawn & Son and I. Elmo and Richie sell their lobsters at another landing, but of course they're known, too.

Took Buster over for the hell of it. He was nervous in the boat. On Pennyless he immediately went off looking for what he could find, but did not roam far.

Carole Bean wants to go over. I suggest she come when we tow the raft. Ethel's going to. I'm no longer feeling guilty about her. I sense that she has what she wants just now, some inner life that is satisfying, or essential to her. Or am I justifying myself?

Fretting a little at the idea of the Procters, who are so *It*—so everything about Summers in Maine, summers anywhere. Money, family, that effortless, inherited style, the manner, the talk, the clothes, the opinions, assumptions, convictions. Rufus a bit of a gray sheep, for teaching (at Amherst), but Mimi redeeming him by being Philadelphia, not a Biddle but something like it. Their five children. His mother is very grand and the father just what you might expect—rich enough for his sweaters to have patched elbows, and of a New England elegance that convinces, I think, even the English. I have always felt a little defensive or on guard among them, yet withal they are immensely kind, seem to perceive at once who you are, do not mind that you are not as grand as they (might not like it if you were?).

SATURDAY P.M. 5 AUGUST. Oh, it *was* a good day. Weatherwise, everywise.

Raft over. Shingles over. Stove over. Plumbing stuff. Everything —including Ethel and Carole—Carole with her bandaged fingers suddenly looking as if she belonged on water, though she doesn't really, but she knows. Elmo in a grand good humor (but when is he not?—though this was special—women to watch him, perhaps); and even Richie looking pleasant, almost friendly. I had made what I call a terrific lunch, including deviled eggs.

The cabin, of course, looks a little sudden, self-conscious, like someone wearing Mrs. Procter's fine hat, but there were sounds of approval, almost of applause.

On shore Carole went off looking for Ellsworth's dory, or maybe him. Ethel and I let the men do what they did—which was to tie the raft and lay the ramp on it. Next step: two stone moorings for offshore lines, and fixing the pin to the wharf end. They'll haul the moorings over when they're ready. Then up went the shingles, the stove, etc. Well, I do pay them, but it seems like a lot to do for what I pay. And yet they were enjoying themselves, especially when playing around with the rope, making bowlines, or whatever. They like it when their women watch them, I think—Elmo does—even Richie seemed to show off a little, though with him it's hard to tell.

I showed Ethel the cabin. One or two suggestions, but I think she was favorably impressed. Then Carole came back (with a thighbone, I thought for a moment) lugging a bit of driftwood, and we all sat up at the cabin and ate.

Back to Ethel's for supper, all of us, and TV. Then me home, somehow anxious to sit for a moment outside with a highball and look at the stars, sniff the air, smell flowers.

The Procters. I'll have to get up early. It's a long drive. I worry about names—his sister's, who, as I remember, is about my age and will be there with a pack of children. Oh, well, all that will take care of itself.

SUNDAY P.M. Back safe and sound. I had a good time. I'll talk about it tomorrow.

MONDAY 7. Good day on the island. It comes, it comes. Working indoors now. Me continuously cleaning up after them. I miss the painting.

The Procters. My, how well they do it all. A good old family summer house down in spruce near water—verandas—lawns—boat-house—wharf—boats out at moorings—children here and there in little packs. It was a family affair, some up from the Cape, Peggy, whom I knew, up from Boston where she's doing something for a senator—Bobby up from Boothbay—all with four or five children. The admonishing of children, the letting of them alone. They're all so nice-looking, so frequently *good*-looking. There have been senators in this family, presidents of things, men on boards, trustees—they have a great effortless chic, know about boats and sailing, know the history of this place and a number of the local people, who caretake for them, whose children come to play and work.

Good simple food—with and after cocktails, Bloody Marys, highballs. Rufus looked after me. And Mimi. Nice talk with them, with Bobby and Peg and another and a friend. I told them what I was up to, and a bit about why.

Peggy said, That takes courage to try it up here alone.

I have no idea what will come of it, I said. I think of it as an experiment, a trip.

When will it touch them, you wonder? they who are at the top —not with millions, though there is a lot of money around, but with everything that money and family, training and property, can bring, and has brought. Won't they be the last to go? I think probably that they will just gradually disperse, that the children will leave, marry here and there eccentrically.

The Procters. Lanky, graceful men in old good clothes, khakis and sweaters, sweat shirts and shorts; the women with good clean faces, good bones, good eyes, good hair. I hold my own with them, I have style, too, I'm good-looking—a sort of German version of what they are (me and my big breasts, my thick long hair). I could have lived among them as a kind of aunt, a privileged one who drank too much and yet had wit and brain and a sense, basically, of manners, propriety (such as having Elmo Hale exhibit himself in your kitchen, dear?). Though perhaps I would fail, in the end, at that fine, cool New England ethic, the upper-class one, that did so successfully hold them together, make them what they still are.

WEDNESDAY 9 AUGUST. Fog in. It's been around for two days, yesterday too thick for us to go out. We went to Williams Boatyard to ask him about moorings. He said, I don't know why I didn't think about that, Mrs. Calder. And to Mr. Brawn, Yes, de'ah, I can get them for you. How's it coming out there?

The goldenrod already appearing. Things dry, ceasing to grow, my lawn somewhat brown, the grape arbor tired, a bit messy.

FRIDAY 11 AUGUST. Still fog. How it blankets these shores, battens on them like a ghoul, shrouds the wharves.

SATURDAY 12 AUGUST. Fog clearing. And it's about *time*. When it comes in and squats like that, I don't like it. Would I out there? Will I be able to make it in if it stays too long?

SUNDAY 13 AUGUST. Well, well. Hung over—rather severely—and guilt-ridden, and trying without success to remember things. That long careen through the fog last night, from Bucksport and booze at the Jed Prouty. Why do I do that? Drove up to get away for a moment, as I recall. The fog had come back in, not thick but drear. I had had enough.

Was that me singing? At the organ—knocking 'em dead with an

old hit from the thirties—Miss Laverne, on her fifth martini (Tanqueray—yes, I do remember)—doing "There'll Be Some Changes Made"—her song. The Helen Morgan of Bucksport. Oh, it was fun—those men from the St. Regis paper mill. Dancing with that young one who said, Hold me up—and I did—then danced with all of them—flung, practically, from one to the other, like an old doll. I remember saying finally, You hold *me* up. Yes, and was propositioned, too—can't quite remember by which one— one was called Butch—something Hackney—or the one from Swans Island?

They had just been thrown out of the bars in Bangor. Had put up a scrap in one, I gathered. And I loved every minute of it, so why complain now that I'm paying. New England guilt. Yes, and at the fact that I do rather put it away, the booze. And that drive back, that blind careening—ran off the road twice, to my certain knowledge, hurtling through endless pearl of fog at my headlights with glimpses of a white line, flashes of spruce, water, and toward dawn gray humps of stone sitting silent and sinister, like judges, in a blueberry barren. Roared through Tainesville, setting a new track record for blind driving. Got home about five and a wreck. Slept till noon.

So there was all that.

Yes, and then Richie around to paint. Good, though I saw him through that guilt and the remains of the hangover. Asked how I was coming with the boat and I said okay. I said, Later on show me a bowline again, and a half hitch, and he nodded. And out in the yard sunlight finally smiled on things.

MONDAY 14 AUGUST. Fog back in. Grim. Where does it come from? But we did go out. When the weather's not good I feel I ought to go with them, and do. I make coffee for us on a little camp stove. We huddle for a moment—immense helpings of sugar, of milk. I'll sit somewhere and smoke and watch, or gather things up, the shavings, the dropped nails. I began to burn up the trash, then thought to save the wood.

THURSDAY 17 AUGUST. Odds and ends. Collecting things to be lugged over.

Found a good double bed with a lovely curling headpiece of iron vines, tendrils—white, with brass knobs—with mattress, a new one, and springs. This part is fun, too, getting things—a washbowl and pitcher (white with blue rings), utensils, a couple of old rugs (not bad).

Ordered bunk mattresses of four-inch foam rubber, as Mrs. Chaney had recommended. May Stinson knows a woman who will make slip covers—the material to be a dark plaid, greens and earth yellows.

Mr. Brawn has hired two boys to dig the jakes. I'm going to have a view. Now, make it a bit roomy. I said. I had the feeling I could say anything to Mr. Brawn and he would say, Ay-yup. A sober man, father of five.

FRIDAY 18 AUGUST. Took stuff over in the boat, tagging along after them.

They're shingling now and I help a little with that, the three of us up on scaffolding, picking through shingles for the right one, making blue chalk lines (what Mr. Brawn calls a "ma'ak"), whittling around the windows, the doors. We'll shingle the whole thing, though they feel this is extravagant—they want me to paint or stain it, too, but I won't. Let the weather do that. They paint everything the minute they get it.

Mr. Brawn thinks I may need a water pump, which will work off the generator. He thinks I should go to a tannery in Ellsworth for barrels—to be placed above cabin and gravity-feed down. Another project. I'll drive over tomorrow. Also, buy more plastic hose (three-quarter-inch), two hundred feet—clamps, etc. Will have to ask Elmo for his truck. Maybe next weekend.

SUNDAY 20 AUGUST. Feeling like a woman with a new string of pearls, real ones. Oh, better than that. What is it like, when something simple and good happens to you, something you've thought about, let wander through your mind as a daylight dream? On a foggy day, too, one I had little hope for.

Richie came around to paint. And up there, me with a cigarette in mouth, getting things ready, his table, the paints, I heard him say, Would you want me without the trunks?

I seemed hardly to understand; as before, I heard, felt, myself saying, Oh, you don't have to—not quite able, I think, to take it in, realize.

I will if you like. He was behind me. I saw only his palette, his brushes in jars, a snarl of color, of pencils, of knives. I was aware of sunlight in blue smoke. I remembered what Elmo had said.

And something rose in me to meet my occasion. Without turning, I said, Well—yes—I would appreciate it.

I heard him leaving the room, as some inner turmoil began in eddies and whirls to unsettle me, unready, unprepared, having only thought about it, really hardly even thought, let the idea of it roam around by me, was about all. My account of the Hale thing had been bothering me. Yet this would be different; I already knew that. I went on laying things out, his, seeing that the brushes and rags were clean. I found my drawing pad, heard him coming back.

But it was so natural when I turned, which I did to get my chair—him already standing at the table, just the same except for the buttocks and the sense of completeness, entirety—from head to foot a single smooth garment of skin.

All I said was, Just paint and I'll make some sketches from here.

At first I could only pretend to draw, the sense of what he was doing was too strong for me to think or feel much else.

And then I could draw, a little, and was getting something, some feeling of him there, where he stood at the table, back to me, looking down at his work, holding, then dipping a brush—in sunlight tinged with blue that gave him a faint golden glow as if he were cast in some metal, a statue.

After a while I said, This is good—it helps a lot.

I heard him say, almost casually, I wouldn't say nothing to Elmo.

I said, Oh, no—I won't.

Then I added, Though I've drawn him, you know.

Not like this.

No.

Then I say, Will you tell him?

Not if you don't.

He paints, I sketch. I try for that long wonderful curving flow of shoulders-back-buttocks-thighs-calves, rhythmic, all of a piece, yet complex, since many curves make it up.

And then he turns and faces me, stands, brush in hand, and I go on drawing him while he waits for me.

It doesn't hang, it stands out—seems like a kind of mushroom in dark grass, thick-stemmed and neat, merely a part of him, not even an appendage, so that I seem to recognize it from knowing the rest of him. He doesn't frighten me a bit. Nor I him. And after a minute or two, still drawing, looking down, I say, You have a body that's good to draw—it's all of a piece, compact—you don't *look* very naked.

He seems not to be listening, to be impervious—some young prince from Greece, or from a time when a body was nothing to hide, not one like this; and I realize that he's given me something—himself. And in that soft, half-smoky, golden light, I give up my drawing to look, and for a moment find his blue eyes gazing at me, impersonally, slightly remote—the cropped beard, the immaculate, sun-shadowed body—he stands feet apart, totally at ease—beyond even that.

I'm exhausted. I say, That's enough for now. Go paint again. And he turns away, unruffled, unmoved, and looks at his painting again—dips a brush.

I leave the room saying, I'll bring us coffee, and go downstairs to make it, and sit at the table, as pleased as I have ever been, as by a marvelous accomplishment. I sit watching the coffee boil, thinking how wrong Elmo was, then knowing it had been himself he had meant with that I'll-get-him-for-you, Helen.

He has put the trunks on when I come up and is still painting—water and islands and sky.

TUESDAY 22 AUGUST. Busy all day—boats, water, carrying things—with a sense of Richie running all through it like a song. At moments I feel that it didn't happen. How do you write about music, or magic? Me a *voyeuse*? Nonsense.

SATURDAY 26 AUGUST. A week of hard work, of running, of buying things.

We're all anxious now to arrive at some end, though it will be a temporary one. Mr. Brawn says, We'll get you in, Mrs. Calder.

The "necessary" built—what's the joke?—taking the necessary steps?

Yes, and the spring dug out and the pump hooked up. All I need is a barrel now.

Stove working. Bottled gas. I'm putting in supplies. Liquor, too.

And one morning now they'll be gone and I'll be there—and terrified by the accomplishment.

But I want it, I want to.

All through this I have caught glimpses of what it will be like.

A silence—no hammers—no voices. Silence and light. Water. Rock. A wave breaking. The cry of a gull.

ENTRY. Vignette: Sitting in the car in town, looking over some bills I'd picked up at the P.O. I saw Louisa coming along. She's old and walks up and down the street, always with a grocery bag in her arm. She talks to herself. I could hear her as she approached, and looked away, but listened. . . . I should have knocked him off that bike, I should . . . so much he has to say—that Gary. Gary is a small, thin boy who pumps up and down the street all day— all he has is that bike—no fenders left, hardly a seat. He teases her. They say he takes things. I would if I were he. He has no parents.

I heard her one other time. I'd seen her up the road a little, talking with one of the old town drunks (she's one herself), and as she came by she was saying, I've got five places I can go—yes, five —and he ain't got but two.

They all sass her—make a sound like a cow as they pass—and she shakes her fist at them. One morning I saw her shaking it at the harbor. At the harbor itself.

SUNDAY 27 AUGUST. Richie here. He said, You going to draw me some more?

How easily this has happened. I was right, he had come to a decision—that I am not dangerous, a threat. I can't explain how right it is, nonsexual, as he paints and I sketch. His nakedness is simpler than his clothes, it belongs, him naked among paints and brushes, an easel, chairs, wall pictures.

I say, When you come to a resting place, would you sit in that chair for a minute? And he does. Hold your hands on your knees and look out the window. And he does. No trace of embarrassment —he simply doesn't mind, feels at home, and is liking this, as if something inner had also been shed. I say, Would you put a foot up on your knee? I stretch just that—waist, legs, the way a thigh goes, the calf muscle falls, a hand at knee and at ankle easily bracing him.

I think that next summer we should sell a few of your things, I say to him. I know a gallery at Bar Harbor—perhaps we'll start there. What do you think?

Well—can if you like, I suppose. And then says, What about you?

And I say, To be perfectly frank, I sometimes don't think mine are quite good enough yet.

His head turns. He's looking at me in what for him is surprise. Your work is fresh, you know, I say. It's original. It's already good. Mine's—oh—conventional—much better than yours in one way—not nearly so good in another. Then I say, Don't you know that?

He turns to look out the window again, saying, How would I know?

I say, Do you like your own work?

After a moment he nods. I like it—and Ethel, she does. I don't know as folks would who didn't know me.

I say, *If* they sell at all, they'll sell for about a hundred each.

He looks at me again, almost abstractly, then back out the window. Gold wires of light in his beard.

I think you may be a real painter, I say.

He doesn't even shrug.

We work together up there for two hours, then quit.

I am left for a moment with a sense of void that allows my feelings to come fluttering around the space he has occupied. Don't say nothing to Elmo. Yes, there's that (Don't say nothing to Ethel), and Elmo floats into mind like some dark promise to be kept—I'll get him for you, de'ah—for us (there was that, too).

MONDAY 28 AUGUST. Rain. No island work. Instead I worked at my sketches, filling out details, shading, articulating. Also worked at the new painting of Elmo, blocking it in. The sketches of Richie help, though his body has a very different rhythm to it, lacks that sense of the father, bull sex power—that thick genital, murderous power.

The garden wanted rain. We all did.

Thought about the Procters again. Could I have written about them? What would I say? I'd have to guess at stresses and strains beneath that superb exterior, at sufferings, at joys. What, you wonder, for people like that, is suffering? What sorts of failures do they endure?

TUESDAY 29 AUGUST. Rain. Dropped by to see Carole Bean in her cozy white kitchen. Gammed. Rain streamed at the panes, flattened the harbor.

I don't realize *yet* how poor they *are*, most of them. She with her one small fish for supper—corn bread, beans. When it's going, she works at the cannery, as Betty Caster does. $1.35 an hour, I think. And at that, work is only for two or three days a week. They blow a whistle when the herring boats come in. They all listen for it. No social security. I think she lives on about $1,200 a year—or less. Hardly enough to pay for a coffin.

FRIDAY 1 SEPTEMBER. Shingling finished (how grand, how neat). Doors hung. I brought things over Thursday—kerosene lamps I've been collecting, quilts, utensils, plates, all that. I've swept it out. I've been painting windows. A dull red—as the doors will be, the trim. Tomorrow Elmo will drive me to the tannery to get barrels, and if back in time will tote them over for me.

I can't believe that I'm almost ready to go. I feel as if a million things remained to be done.

SUNDAY 3 SEPTEMBER. Labor Day weekend. A morning singing with light. White clouds tumbling across the sky like great whales and sailing ships. A breeze. I'm making lists.

Supper at Ethel's last night. We hosed out the barrels in her yard and soaked them in baking soda. Elmo got some old cable and used it to strengthen the hoops. These are fine barrels—hogsheads—used for packing sheepskins from New Zealand. We're going to carry them over this afternoon, and some furniture.

I seem, almost, to be saying goodby to this place.

EVENING. Elmo and Richie both back here for a drink and a gab. We had boated the barrels over, and hooked up the hoses—started the pump. Hooray!—it all worked, though of course the barrels still leak, have a smell to them—but I have A WATER SYSTEM. Water from the sink taps (tasting of lanolin), and a shower. Sense of great accomplishment. Celebration.

I turn on the lamps back at the farm. Feed Buster. Elmo says, as he had once before, Let me have one of them, looking at my martini. Then, Try one, Richie.

I'm almost afraid, now that it's ready out there, I say.

Well, course you are, de'ah, Elmo says. It's like when I got my first boat—scared as all hell to take her out. But don't you worry none. We got some traps out that way, you know.

And with the drink and them with me, a sense of security, of confidence, comes back in.

How does she do with that boat? he asks Richie.

He nods. Butts the landing now and then, but she gets there.

I don't want them to leave, what I want, long for, is a night of it, but they finally do—and with them gone I go out to walk in the yard, to look at the night, sniff the air, almost to test things. But I've already decided that I won't go tomorrow. I'm using the fair as an excuse. I am scared. Scared of leaving, scared of the new, of me.

TUESDAY 5 SEPTEMBER. And a vile hangover, or whatever—mental —moral. Miss Laverne with the shakes. Whoever said I'd left her behind? Dear Beth—your old pal got picked up again—no old Mendonca either. Total debauch.

It was fear of the island, fear of loneliness—loneliness. What *wasn't* it? It was the carnival, too, the fair.

Which I had missed last year. So I went, feeling I ought to— yes, an excuse, but part of trying to fit in up here, though I do love a carnival—and did this one especially. So tiny. So poor. And why for Christ sake couldn't I have *left* it at that?

A Ferris wheel. A ride or two. Tents for eating, one for bingo. The little sideshows (canvas over cedar posts, looking homemade). The booths—darts to be hurled at balloons—ducks to be shot at— pegs to put rings around—all for prizes you hope you won't win. And off by itself a special tent with a real live barker outside, and two pitiful women—one young and deathly pale with bruised skin —the other an old fat whore, so hard, so empty with her frizzed-out red hair (me at seventy). The men stood off at a distance in twos and threes—then one by one went up for tickets and in. What happens in there? What do they do? Wiggle and waggle and take off their clothes.

Saw the Hales—joined them (Richie hands in pockets, somehow to one side of it all). Saw May Stinson and Carole Bean together—saw Jules and Betty Caster—joined them—departed. Rejoined. We tried darts at balloons. Elmo and his boys shot at ducks, and hit quite a few; or he did—the gun, a .22, looking like a toy in his hands, at his shoulder. Bang. People walked up and down under the lights, eating. The Ferris wheel (about as big as a pie) presided over our fortune. People screamed on the whirligig. Everybody ate. The fair is a big thing to them. There had been an ox pull in the afternoon. There was a shed with livestock in it.

And guess who I ran into? Gertrude H. Standing alone, hands

in pockets, smoking a cigarette. She looked marvelous and terribly alone, a pariah.

We spoke for a moment. Then I said, Come for a ride on the Ferris wheel. Why not? she said. And we did. I feel like a kid, she said, as we bought tickets—my dad used to take me to a fair we had and it was always the Ferris wheel we headed for—maybe this same one. Rising up over the fair, swaying and looking down—the sense of the sea out there in a darkness away from the lights—of the island, and me up there suddenly afraid of it all again. She liked it that I came over, talked with her. I watched, but nobody else did. I don't think she stayed long.

Then with the Hales again. Betsy off with a boy. Children running up—(Now I *give* you that dollar, de'ah)—then away, spending their few cents. But the grownups liking it as much. Visiting. Standing to chat. Seeing the men, hands in pockets, with their families, ones familiar by sight to me now—a trifle strange out of their fishing clothes, their boots and aprons. Seeing again how simple they are. The men wear open-necked shirts and look clean.

Handsome—simple (I don't mean to patronize)—yes, and ordinary, too. A few grand ones there are, such as Elmo, or old Bill Eaton (who wasn't there)—the town fathers—I saw how men came up, stood and spoke, were drawn to Elmo. I wanted Richie to ride on the Ferris wheel but didn't ask. That life not this one. We are secret, reserved, in the midst of this darkly lighted milling around. Gertrude—a sort of specter at the feast, an image which threatens me—that weather blows this way. Just wait.

I'm standing with Hales and company again, and when Ethel turns to talk to some woman, Elmo says, I seen you with Richie's girl.

Gertrude? I say—I thought she was yours.

He looks at me. What give you that idea?—how can I have two? He looks at me. Stitches in some dark garment we make together.

Anne comes up. She's won something—I see pink feathers, dyed and wonderfully garish.

Now ain't that a fine thing, Elmo says. Ethie, see what Annie's won.

Ethel turns—Anne dances away, having left it with her.

I wander off and suddenly notice the schoolhouse across the field and the empty swings and the jungle gym (remembering it from my first walk—and beyond it, serrating a mauve sky, the dark spruce. New York without lights. And for no reason I feel lost. Where am I? I say, turning to look at the fair, the wheel, at the thinning crowd. Why am I here?

Something touched me, something cold, like a cry from across water. Some sense that I should be doing something else, didn't belong. Them with their families.

It was then that I saw him (or he me), in a white shirt. Hands in pockets, he came strolling up from a darkness of parked and gleaming cars, not chewing a cigar but that type. Hi there, Mrs. Calder. The voice was high-pitched.

I couldn't place him for a moment; then it came back and I saw him on her porch again, the one with the children and the hair. Curious sense of relief, of welcome, there at the edge of the field beyond the lights. Bottles around, paper cups, the remains of things.

How you doing?

I shrug and lift my hands to show how empty they are; then I say, I like a carnival, and see him looking at it and after a moment say, You don't?

Depends, he says. Big, broad moonface of him vaguely lit by across-field lights. Come alone, did you?

The darkness presides over the silent, blue-white walls of the school, the distant hurdy-gurdy sounds, over my sense of nowhere left to go, and the scare of that other darkness that has stayed with me (wave cry, cry of far-out shore).

I've nodded, and I hear him say, Me, too.

He stands looking into the light at the turning wheel.

Ain't much, is it? he says.

Most of them have gone, I say, somehow defending it.

You leaving?

I nod again.

He stands with the light washing over him—white shirt—short, straw-colored hair; and I'm Fifi Laverne again, a girl in a bar, scared, alone; and hear myself say, Come have a nightcap with me —and see how he looks off into the light, refuses to reveal himself. So that it's I who aggress, standing at the border of a world I don't belong to. You might as well, I say—it's really all over.

I wanted the company, I didn't want to drink alone, though what I knew about him might have put me off—broad face of him now looking into the light (for her?—something better?)—brachycephalic—and even, somehow, the way the blond hair fell in the simple bangs of a boy—a face with its own innerness, and slightly mysterious, scary even. Then I see it turning to me from the light, though as if still thinking of that, and I hear his voice say, Might's well, with something of a shrug left in it, and feel a kind of tremor run through me. For a moment he reminds me of someone, and I know or guess that I'm making a mistake.

He followed me home in his truck. Came in.

He seems to feel everywhere at home, at ease. I fixed us drinks, made a fire for which he brought in logs, turned the radio on to a station that plays rock. At the sink getting out ice—he comes over—Ain't got no ginger-ale, have you?—and I feel his hand for a moment, as if innocently, on my behind. It's over there, I say, nodding. I find his great round face close to mine. He leans forward with a pouting of the lips and our lips touch and some-thing shivers in me. I'm remembering him at Gertrude's—bits of her stories.

In the kitchen we talk, I do, though I don't remember about what, just that I'm seeing him, watching how his lips seem to reach out for, pout at, the rim of his glass, how his small, short-lashed eyes shift here and there, fix for a moment on mine.

We go into the dark living room to look at the fire. After staring down into it for a while, he squats and puts a log on, then stands back up to wait as it takes hold. Then in the brightening glow of it, as in a dream, I see a hand of gold-haired fingers picking at his shirt, and after a moment of watching it and remem-bering Gertrude, I say, Wait, and put my drink down. He stands to let me remove it. I unbutton, pull the shirttails out, pull it back from the haired chest and the shoulders' gold fleece, work it down from his arms, while he stands passive. Gold fleece and his face above it, smooth and broad and round in the fire's light, and expressionless. And I hesitate, then reach out dreamingly, and my hand touches mesh of wire, crisp and dense, that seems to have obliterated the flesh, though after a moment I sense the warmth and bulk beneath.

His chest and sides—I feel at him as I might a tree, a mossed stone, my fingers curious, thrilled, repelled. I'm aware of his face lifted away as if he has nothing to do with this, and I feel at his back. Haired barrel of him—my hands wander it, feel under the lifted arms, feel over the shoulders, until they know, have grown accustomed.

In the kitchen under lights, having shown me what he is, he

sits where Elmo has sat, seeming mythic, obscene, yet the face familiar now—farm face, more of the land in it than the sea, with its straw-colored bang that slants across the broad forehead. He watches me and seems to have gained power from my approval, or my acceptance anyway.

Did you know Gertrude's father? I ask.

He nods.

What was he like?

I see his face turn, the tip of his tongue come out to lick at a lip. Hm, he says—a hand moves up to his head—Didn't have no hair.

Strong? I say.

He nods, hunches his shoulders. Were hard, he says.

What?

He were hard. He balls up an arm that is smooth and white on its underside. Weren't quite smart, you know.

Oh I say. And Saul—Saul Hastings?

He nods. Were little like me—not so hairy. At which he sits up, rubs at his chest, looks down at it, then at me. That don't trouble you none? he asks, a hand still feeling at himself so that the hair flattens. Some women likes it, he says. He knows how odd it is—why he had let me feel at him back in there. She does, I hear him say—likes to give me a shower. He's watching me. She likes to rub me, get me all soaped up, he says.

And you like her to?

I see his smile and think, These are country men; in his way this one knows everything. She likes me to dance for her, too, he says.

You dance? I say.

The smile is there.

How do you mean? I say. And see his little eyes roll up, suddenly merry, see his thick-haired shoulders shrug, enigmatic. You want me to? he says. And when I nod, he bends, pulls at the laces a moment, then works off his shoes, which I look down at—high, heavy, black. He's finished his drink, which I take from him and go to the sink, aware of the radio rock, with a heavy persistent beat to it. When I return he's down to his shorts, skin tight and white, and I see that the hair stops somewhere in under cloth and that the legs are smooth and strong.

Arms out, he moves, dances by himself to the radio, which I go to turn up. He moves—it's his own, what he does—rhythmic, flexible—sailorish, in some way—old, perhaps, from days when men did dance, on ships. Feet apart he grinds, twists, then suddenly whirls, lifts his elbows, marches in time, gay there under the light, lifting his legs. He struts erect—ridiculous but great fun. His head tilts, nods.

He comes dancing toward me, weaving his hips, stands close and blocks out the light—belly-dancing in front of me. I don't see his face, he's too close, is holding his arms up—and the belly undulates, writhes, thick-haired—until, since he wants me to, I reach out and feel the gut sucked in as I unpop a button—slow twisting of hips. I undo the second and see cloth pop back from solid hair, at which he dances away, skips, whirls, the cloth tight at the small of his back, stands back to me grinding again, whirls, reapproaches. And stands twisting slowly before me, till I reach out with both hands and push the cloth down for him. Suddenly he whirls wildly, the shorts down tight around buttocks now.

He comes dancing behind me and from there undoes my sweater, my blouse, bends to reach in—finds my breasts, fondles them—I feel hair scratching at my cheek, feel it rubbing my bare shoulders . . . he's suddenly on his knees in front of me and is reaching to suck at one. I hold his face, run a hand down his back. His eyes close, white lashes—I feel myself drawn in as he hunches closer, arms around my waist. I'm feeling his back, I'm feeling his body with my thighs, him at me, muscular, moving.

We're at the fire again. Dark glow of it on him. He stands with lifted arms and I rub my breasts at him. I push the shorts down tight as a rope around his thighs. I embrace him and my hands move at his back as he stands for me. I'm naked; he's a tree I rub myself at, him unmovable, there, arms held in air. My hands go down to encounter him, stiff and hard in the tight cloth, at which he shies away, quick, sudden. Then he's moving a little, I'm moving. We dance. In the dark light of the fire we dance for each other. I feel wanted, powerful. I'm all breasts and hips and thighs.

Where's your shower? he asks, and nods questioningly up. Going to give me a shower?

We go upstairs.

We're like children up there, naughty ones. Washing him is like giving a frisky dog a bath—he shies away, holds, turns, flexes his shoulders. I use bath oil, which I pour over us, him, till he glistens in shining gold mesh of fur, arching his chest for me, holding up his arms. He suddenly clamps them around me, goes at my mouth, holds to me, comes in with a steady thrusting I flinch at, then receive till he's in—and he has me very quickly there, oiled, sliding, sweet in my arms and thick and muscular as some great seal.

Downstairs we're naked and drinking again—I remember feeling amazed at the sight of time—I had no sense of its passage—drunk, though he is not, or only drunk with his dancing, his nakedness, rollicking, playing around me, dancing in front of the fire on knees, then holding me, clamping me to him, body that warms and engulfs, head burrowing round and hard.

He has wordless songs; he hums, he sings to himself.

Barrel of him in my arms while he rocks. I achieve, and again, as he drives me to it, over me, his body warmly scratching in my arms—rocks and rocks—getting it?—rocks—I'm in a glory—rocks—I'm wild as air—rocks, looks down at me, watches, and rocks—I claw, rip at hair, tear out patches of it—impervious he rocks. . . .

I find him in the morning sleeping on the floor, red-faced, curled up. I have a vile hangover, my head is a drum. Carnival over, I go to make coffee and clean up, while he sleeps it off. . . .

I kept falling asleep, I remember, hardly conscious toward the end, so that once he slapped me—Stay awake—his high-pitched little voice up there, intent—rocking and rocking—Stay awake—for hours, it seemed—he would rest, then go on, the singing and dancing a prelude merely. I'm a wreck. How would they say it down on the water front?—That fat fisherman-farmer fucked you proper, de'ah. I remember him watching me toward the end, hoisted up on his arms, his face pale, it seemed, and concentrated.

ENTRY. Marks like stains on my arm. The rash? I'll get calamine lotion from Burwell's, see . . . I've had it before. Nerves. From what? From that? From the lies?

WEDNESDAY 6 SEPTEMBER. I'm going out tomorrow. I've been buying supplies. Danish bacon in cans, Bovril corned beef, B & M beans, Snow's fish chowder, corn meal, flour, sugar, salt, all that. Slyly I have been storing up liquor. Lists: matches, kerosene, paper towels, cigarettes (four cartons—God). I'm excited. I want to go. Afraid of the boat, yes, but the weather promising—or so Rockland reports. Yes, and a radio I bought at the Value House up in Bangor. I wish I knew how to pray, or what to pray to.

A quick letter to Beth. Oh, she must come this fall. She will—
all but promised.

Cobwebs still from that carnival night. Was that *me?* Too much,
too much. That other me. What happened? Be honest. Who knows
what "happened"?

3

THURSDAY 7 SEPTEMBER. I'm here, drunk as a lord. Safe. Sound. I can't write. I keep touching things.

FRIDAY 8 SEPTEMBER. Yes—it's all here. I was right. My cabin, my wharf, the boat (nodding at the raft). Yes—and the island— it is silent—but the birds cry—the sea ravens, the gulls—and one that goes over and over, *Da dee—dee dee*. And something last evening that went *Grawk!*—something large. I'm not sure yet what they are.

DAWN. My tiny pine bedroom gets the first light. It came up, it rose—an *aubade*—very stately—a marshaling of light—from the east at first, but then all around me, a white opal, soft with fire. I went out to where the porch will be. Whatever makes all this, I acknowledged it. I said to it, Me, too. I could not actually say, I'm yours, though that's what I felt.

From that Ferris wheel, high up, overlooking a darkness—I saw only that and missed the light. Yes, I'm here.

JOURNAL. Doing the homely, housewifely things. Cleaning. I love to.

I need paints. Begin to make lists.

Rash almost gone.

The sounds: so early, the lobster boats—their motors over water. You can't tell where they are. Some are far off, some near. The sound—idling, chugging, as they work at a trap—then off with a low roar, a throbbing, as of exhausts under water. I had not had a real chance to listen until now—friendly, comforting—all around me, as their pot buoys are. They glitter in the early-morning sun.

Sounds of water—even more mysterious. Delicate crash of breaking wave or wavelet, like crystal shattering, tinkling—dropped from a water hand; or water thumping up under ledge somewhere, snorting, sucking with wet lips at a rock—low, thumping roar. Ceaseless pattering of water lapping along shore.

Gull cries. Plaintive—querulous. The querulous gulls. And the crows, far off—*Caa—caa-caaaaa. Da dee—dee dee dee*—sweet and prolonged—music in sun, in pure air. That one—*Graaaawk!*—whatever that one is. An osprey? A great gawk? And even from here, in the town, because the wind was from the west, the cannery whistle. Seven o'clock—and the boats out earlier.

Writing now by kerosene light, which is yellow, dim, but does. Moths around. Sound of ice in my raised glass.

In a moment I shall walk down to my wharf, sit there, listen, look, till the night breeze drives me in. Other sounds are down there—I can hear them from here. Something breaks water. Something snorts, whoozes, rolls over. A porpoise? Ellsworth Bean?

JOURNAL.   Clean as quartz, as sea water, as sand, this place.

Sitting on rock—I could become rock.

I need a flashlight.

SEPTEMBER 10.   I begin to establish a routine. I rise (not like her, the divine one, she of the shell and the honeycomb flow of hair, but nude as mother god and liking my body)—I go out to look at the islands, at the water, the light, which this morning flared across the sky in a spreading of pink wings—old Rosy-fingered Dawn. I sense an ancient glory.

And I dance for it. I don't mind that I can't; I dance even while I'm standing still.

AFTERNOON.   I'm at the journal again. With coffee, at my table looking at the sea, I talk to my few, few people (to Beth).

My routine. The making of breakfast (toast, bacon, canned orange juice). The coffee, black gold, in a pot, I take it out with me, to look around—to stare and be stared at—though maybe It doesn't notice that I'm here.

I clean. I check on things. Go up to the spring, look down into it: cool, clear, brimming. I collect moss for it, lumps of green velvet, plant them around under spruce where odd bits of crabs and urchins, mussels, clams, lie scattered.

I walk the shore, though, oddly, I'm still saving that, as if I didn't want to know it too suddenly—or as if, in part, it ought to come to me, let me know it doesn't mind.

I'm painting, and it's good to out here. I have a costume for it: a shirt, short pants (cut-offs), sandals. I would like to paint nude but am not ready.

JOURNAL. Halc-at-the-sink—two versions (one turned away from me, one toward). I think I can catch him now and that easiness of stance—and the smile, which is so secret that maybe only I see it.

I learned something from Herne the prowler (who I think is perhaps also a good father)—that a man will seek a strange woman out as for a holiday, and for her will shed his old clothes. Elmo at the sink—preparing himself before turning to me. I sense the reluctance of his loyalty there, but also the growth of need. Though in my ignorance of this place perhaps I misread and he's available to any of us who attract his eye.

FRIDAY 15. A gray one. Life is not all light. I painted, I puttered. I walked along the rock shore, to a gnarled and ancient spruce the weather has trained with careful hands to resemble itself. I want fog to come in. I want it to hide these shores for a while, a day, to cancel this obvious glory.

Read *National Fisherman* (had brought an unopened copy out) by the pale yellow moth whir of my kerosene lamps. Yes, I'll want a fireplace.

Radio on, for the news—such as it is. Switched it off—and heard Black Horse Shoals way out, with *its* news—fog.

SATURDAY 16. It did come in. Not a good one, a gray haze that silvered the water, moltened it. Lovely though. Motors out in it— they're working the traps.

I heard one close to, then saw its gray shape (because you do go to a window, or out to look when one's near). Bill Eaton's, I see (I've ambled down to the wharf), in close by Shawl Island— who waves—he knows me. Dark form of him out there (the light is behind him) working at the stern of his boat, which is small and old, and, like himself, or this place, much weathered.

And I think of old wharves, old fishing sheds, old streets, and of old men, of grandfathers—or fathers—think of mine, with whom it seems I might have been in love—indulgent, wild imaginings that frightened me at the time—but watching him out there I savor it and find it sweet to admit to some need I have that weaves through everything—not frightening now, though like the bones of

Lycidas a thing for the depths. To want something from the world that isn't there—our fate, or mine.

Dark form of him (the light has increased, the water undulates, burns like a mirror now); and I saw a dripping, silvered trap drawn up while by itself, as if trained to, the boat circled and he moved in calm aproned yellow with his catch to a tub or barrel (good, he got one), walked back while the boat still circled, bent; and saw the trap heaved over—splash!—and with a sudden beating of wings I'm after him, my clothes left on the wharf, and with beak and claws outstretched to savage him I have flown at his back. It wells up in me. I can't fend it off. I see him chugging away over molten silver into haze.

The wharf and the morning air, sun threatening to break through—and then as if following him, generationally, came a new sound—came theirs, E & R's, which I also recognized. Among my gulls, my crows, the water, these rocks, I seemed to have forgotten them, or to have shelved them, filed them away.

They came putting in and I felt pleased. Their boat is much newer, grander than Bill's, who struck me as having eluded them, slipped down some corridor back into the morning.

They tread up my ramp to the wharf—knitted caps, wool shirts, red flesh of faces, hands—and—

How you doing, de'ah, Elmo booms. Must of thought we'd forgot you.

Then, with one arm, he's hugging me, and I'm hugging back, much pleased.

Now, Richie, he says—speak to the lady, say hello to Helen here.

Oh, he doesn't have to—hello, Richie—come up for coffee, I say.

And somehow I'm asking for the "news"—as if I've been gone for weeks.

But they're just the same. Thought we'd come see how you was, Elmo says. He admires things. Richie has gone to look at my easel. Elmo sees him, rises, goes to look, too.

You're getting me, he says, from across the room. I had hidden the sketches I was working from, which had become rather over-explicit.

Don't let me forget, Elmo says—Ethel sent you out bread she's been making. She misses you.

They look around, ask how the water is, turn on the taps. Have coffee. Then they leave and I walk down with them. I'm longing to say to Richie, Come out and paint, but refrain. Elmo ducks, then hands me up bread, two heavy loaves in foil.

And out they go, chugging, moving toward a pot. And the sight of them out there, pale morning fog around, busy again (I see Richie moving about the deck), rings its changes on me. They work in that world, they and the others, and they are perishing; but they are there for now.

Soon I hear only a motor, growing remote. A gull approaches. Sees me. Turns in the fog . . .

It was she who sent them here, but they felt at home.

NEXT DAY IN SEPTEMBER. Fog. All around me now. I saw it when I woke—gray at the window. I was oddly excited, as if I knew it had come for me.

At breakfast, over coffee, I kept looking to see how thick it would be, and what I noticed was that no boats were out, and that excited me, too. And all through cigarettes and coffee thinking, if it's not too cold, I'll go out.

And then at the door it seemed almost sultry, dripping—a dog-day fog—and I furtively undressed for it.

Walking along the shore—I wore only my slippers, since my feet are not tough. It welcomed me, it beckoned, said, Come over here, let me show you things. I would see rock, water, shrouded —a gray gull—a log, wedged in a cleft of stone a storm had driven up; I came upon that weathered, twisted spruce that is Japanese and vaguely like something once human; I saw things washed up, and remembered a stretch of beach at Chilmark, where the water brings things in, things broken, used, old bits of wood, things made by men. Faintly I could hear a bell buoy awash in the waves, red iron skeleton at dance on swells that rock and lift the boats. As I stood on a rise it came in clear and thin . . . Cling . . . cling clang.

Their world, their bones that the waters rinse at Chilmark (ill-fated Mayhew's bones)—Misquamicut—or here, I thought, in a fog like time or history, that blows over beaches, sand—and remembered Jamestown, Beavertail and Mackerel Cove, at the edge of the sea-blown fog the rusting iron of a pier, a silvering of shale.

I scrambled up a flow of granite, scrambled down. I saw their things, the men's who had been here once, a bit of net, of rope, a board, and in the fog they seemed to be around, were presences. Booted and capped, wet, weathered, coarse—the fisherfolk, rough, friendly, shy.

And one in his oilskins watched me with a pale and silent face, and others stood beside him watching, too, and I saw his yellow coat pulled back and heard what he said, soft, old, and gray, and I smiled but I passed him like a thing washed up. And others— dark shapes of them. Heard voices, felt them in the air, and heard the ceaseless water lap against stone. The subtle voices of the sea.

And farther down the shore I sat on a log among them who had followed me, and thought, My island now, I've seen them, shown them myself. And theirs—yes, mostly theirs—and they stood for a moment more to let me know they'd been there. Then, though I listened, I heard only water sounds, a wave (wet crash of breaking glass), the bell, and far-off moan of Black Horse Shoals, and thought of him, mad, lonely, desperate—I called, I sang—Here here, I'm here—please come. Lap-lap of glass like water in the fog. I had a secret longing to descend, to enter it, but was afraid.

Walking back, I noticed underfoot the grain of rock—pink granite-quartz—and broken, blue-black mussel shells like the scales of some great sea monster.

JOURNAL.   It's gone, and out there now a pearl-gray morning that will clarify. Back to my routines.

The painting absorbs me. I work at it as if for three people— Elmo, Richie, and me—this is my audience.

Oh, lovely man, would you pose for me again? will I ever be able to ask you to?

EVENING.   Martini hour. A moon. Night sounds. And it's not that I'm lonely—no, call it a mood, a need. It's the way I visit, the way I meet the world, with a mind that fondles words, that makes of them real things. A rusty spike, a piece of sun-dried rope—I almost have them in my hand. I can say Herne now, just that word, and there is my bull-haired lover with his broad and old-young face. No—not it—his boy-man face—that straight blonde hair—that wide and empty look that came into it.

This is me, what I am—a nakedness almost of the crippled. Yes. So private, not to be guessed at, not to be shown to many. This is me.

Boy-man? Father? Farmer? Fat—broad-fat—with its mysterious innocence and desire—I can't get it, the face. Or that something secret in him.

He grew on me like a plant; intent, locked away, and reaching in for me—so that at moments I could feel him in my veins, him seeking me out, until what it was of him had grown dark and branching, lacy and finned as a goldfish tail, and waved in my depths—why he wanted me awake and watched me at the end, to know that he had swollen, grown, was reaching up into my womb. His face looking down—Can you feel me in there?—grown pale with the difficult and moving carefully.

Enough—too much. . . . *Lies.* Lies? Not really. Alpha, beta. Alphabet.

Will go in for supplies tomorrow. Check my list. Yes, and remember paint, and clippers for the brush.

JOURNAL. A good trip. Some unexpected feeling of confidencce about the boat. All it wants is for me to handle it; it's on my side.

Fun to come in and see the town again, the houses (point-eared), the landings stepping out. Oh, it is all so poor, so woebegone—yet so lovely for all that. I see Carole Bean's little house, her porch, and remember the marbles at her windows. My car dusty, sullen-looking, in its small, sandy-pebbly parking space along the road, by brier roses loaded now with orange rose apples. And yes, the McFarlanes' boy has been feeding Buster (seeing his empty dish). The garden looks slightly unfriendly, forgotten, and I say to it, I'll be back—wait—I'll come to weed and water you. Everything fine indoors.

I head back to town. I feel that people are watching me, but they're not. I don't visit. I buy my things and drive back to the landing.

Bill Eaton was there—grizzled, enormous. How you doing out there, Mrs. Calder? He knows me now and always waves. Must be some nice. I seen you up by the cabin.

Shy old sea monster with his gray furtive eye. A voice in the fog.

JOURNAL. I feel the air changing about me. In brilliant sun the summer is leaving. A gaudy day. Light praising the world.

Painting. Puttering around. Walked up to the knoll, the lower one, discovering wisps of sheeps' wool on spruce twigs. They were here. Up there, boats all around, white, tiny things, as if gleaning, harvest mostly over now. But I don't know the seasons yet. Have they finished shedding? And far off, the houses of Orstown, also tiny, white.

A discovery—I have a cove I didn't know about. I rounded a great whale hump of granite I had turned back from in that fog and there it was, a tiny patch of washed-in sand. Tall waving grass came down to it from spruce, and something with pinkish-purple flowers I call sea peas trailed over logs, caught up old flotsam from the sea: two fine old pot buoys—a lobster trap with faded, bristly rope and sun-bleached barnacles—chlorine bottles, sticks, things the sea had been bringing in for years.

I wanted the sun on me, took off my shirt, my bra. Pants pulled down to my thighs. I lay with my arms back for it, I spread my legs, and felt its warm hand on me. I would like to grow brown as a berry in it. I thought of men—black hair, red face, knit cap, Richie at the table, buttocks and back, boats and nets—gold wool glistening in sun, imagined him on me, jaw in air, stolidly rocking and rocking while the sun blanketed us and the roaring and snorting of distant boats at work came in.

WEDNESDAY A.M. I sketched rocks. Difficult to know what's inside, what produces the rhythm. The skin of the rock is easy enough, its texture, its obvious, crystal-flint glittering hide; but the flow, the bulge—like something once liquid and welling stopped in its tracks, the flow of cereal, frozen.

In late-afternoon-sunset-glow a martini—strong sense of the now of things around me, of the way my mind, come evening, wanders down certain paths. I think they believe I want to be by myself out here. I thought I did. Oh, I did, I do—just not *all* the time. Didn't Richie know I counted on Sunday? And thought that he did, too. Afraid of me out here—maybe that, what Elmo hinted at.

Now I remember the dancing—hands like little paws in air, a heavy, whirling leap, a friskiness . . . think of that—in gold jacket of fur he looked half-clad—in the kitchen sucking with suck-sucking lips and a blue eye that looked up at you—shoulders gold-haired. I remember him looking off at the lights, deciding. All I said was come have a nightcap with me—hands in pockets considering. Yes, and on elbows over me—with uplifted head he stares off at the

188

light, the kitchen door; the warm-haired barrel of him strongly rocks in my arms like a dog; mindless, inexhaustible, he rocks and rocks, ignoring me.

I'll see him again, let him slap me awake, on elbows over me. . . .

THURSDAY 21 SEPTEMBER. Good weather. Trip to shore. Bought stuff. Saw Ethel. Heard bits of family news—e.g., Betsy had been off visiting, Davie mowing late-summer lawns, buying paint for his pot buoys—which are to be his father's colors.

Came back in the brisk chop that, though I ducked, wet my hair. But I'm getting good at it. I practice landing. I practice tying rope.

Washed hair. Went to the cove for the afternoon sun. Took sketching pad along. Rocks *are* like bodies—difficult to indicate what is within, to catch an essential roundness—*a*roundness—an inner rhythm—as with Herne, whose rhythms involve the flexible, despite the bulk and brawn of him.

FRIDAY 22. Elmo and Richie in for a landing. We had coffee. I feel Elmo eying me in some way, or think I do—an innerness to it, to him, as to those stones—almost contemplative—nonjovial. He seems remote. I show Richie some sketches.

They've brought me a fish and two small lobsters. Elmo tells me to break up their shells afterward.

Spent afternoon painting. Elmo at the sink—facing me. It is going to be good. Less finicky, bolder—a kind of impressionism. I'm trying less for detail than for total effect—the power of him, the easiness. Another I work on, too, but don't trust—a nude. I'm afraid of it, but can't keep away. Herne working at me, rapt and intent—slap slap—Stay awake—working and working.

One martini.

I heard rain in the night drumming the roof. I think of it washing this island.

SATURDAY 23 SEPTEMBER. The channel, out from the cove where I sun, is filled at low tide with great basking whales of stone, gold, seaweedy, wet, enormous. Lying between wide, pink arms of warm granite, I am kissed by an aging sun; my breasts feel weighty, important, and again I long to be fed on. I think, sing Old Father Sea, come lie with me, as Father Sun does now. I will tend your cave—suck at my breasts, great bearded head. Wading—but who could see?—naked till the water felt at me—so cold—yet like flame.

Tonight the moon stared at me with a blind, gold eye. At night the spruce seem to wake, to move a little. They were here before I came, will be here after. I went and stood under them in the dark, to accustom them to me. They are male, I think, and old.

Early to bed.

SUNDAY 24 SEPTEMBER A.M. A cool brilliance.

If you examine a shell you find how a creature fits itself to the world. My cabin to me, me to this island. I *will* be austere, be cool. I'll tend this island.

I've started a trail up through the spruce to the knoll. On the far side it's open and falls away in a steep flowing of grass and short blueberry, patches of lichened granite. This island is very old.

MONDAY 25. Rain. I saw it coming across the channel, then saw it on the water, the rings it makes. It darkened the wharf. It beat at the windows for a while. Read all day.

WEDNESDAY 27 SEPTEMBER. In the afternoons the lobster boats go by—four, five of them—it varies. My instinct still is to run out the moment I hear one. Going past, bows lifted, heading in. Processional. A hand lifts, waves, when they see me. Bill Eaton's boat I know because it's small. The toys they leave behind—those glittering buoys.

P.M. Restless—thinking—sitting down at the wharf. Lap-suck of water at stone, a ledge down the shore it drives in under, coughs, grunts, in some rhythm I can't measure or count—snorting, sucking with wet lips at a rock—yes, and reminding me—seeing a distant white feather brushing and brushing the sky. . . . I got to wondering why I feel that the Herne thing might not work, a continuation of it. It does for GH.

I keep having that image, of how she pulled back his shirt to exhibit him, as a statue, him with a smile—yes, and by the fire how he lifted his arms for me, held them up—even turned so that I could feel his back . . . beware the man who shows you empty hands—nothing up his sleeve. I remember him shut away, mindless, intent, until he wanted me awake to know what was happening. But to him—he danced for himself! I was used.

Herne obliterates, he's a killer.

No, not only that—he had an experience. You let him become himself. It might not happen again.

What *is* it that I want? I know what I ought to want—the power to give myself, to be pleased, as a child is pleased, by whatever comes its way, to say yes to anything, to water sounds, star silence, light—dark, too—or to Herne. I think perhaps I'm wrong; he danced for me; he gave what he had, played in the shower. It embarrassed him, though always he hopes that this one or that won't be repelled. Some women like that, you know—didn't he say that? I let him become himself.

Star light, water light. Rustle of water lapping under wharf, rubbing against pilings, wooing me, great watery bearded thing, and the stars watching overhead—and on that tiny beach of shells the waves: *whrassh—rash—risshh.* . . .

JOURNAL. Handfuls of rain dash at the window, flung. It silvers the water out there, sweeps in long veils across it, enters the spruce. No boats. I paint, I read—I cook.

I need more lamps. I need to be able to paint at night if I want. The cabin is cozy and warm, smelling of coffee, of kerosene. Reading *Saturday Cove*—Shorty Gage, Pud Hall, Cap'n Perc Sane —it has the charm that certain children's books have—brainless— a delight.

THURSDAY 28 SEPTEMBER. Trail blazing. Exhausted. Cutting dead branches of old spruce, sharp, dry, dripping with reindeer moss, lichen, old needles. I'm a mess. I kept thinking, If one could snip away dead branches of the mind.

Moon golden, ominous—too rich—there's something in the air. I hear water sounds—sea words—wet lips at rock, insatiable. That sea will finally eat this whole island.

JOURNAL. An event . . .

One of those afternoons when a fog comes in—a wall of it that I could see swallowing up the big island, mountain and all— it reared over it, poured down like a giant amoeba. I watched it come across water, a lobster boat, racing for its life, before it. It seemed to billow up from underneath. Then island after island engulfed, disappearing, and the first of it blowing rapidly among my spruce as if hurrying to some gray destination, then the spruce on that far promontory disappearing, like trees on a Chinese screen. Then it reached the wharf where a gull had perched; then the gull flew away as if scared by it. My boat at its mooring (an outhaul Mr. Brawn had fixed for me), a slim dark shape on the water. I sat and watched it for a while, and when it grew too damp I went indoors to light the lamps, make up a fire in the stove, and think about supper, a casserole, and when I would have it. I was somehow very excited, much alone, oddly happy. It was like being in a storm. But then I heard the sound of a motor out in it.

You can't tell where they come from—they rebound from islands, the sounds of them, float across water, sometimes from quite far away. I often hear their radios and the voices on them, ship-to-shore, even music. This one seemed quite close. It was moving slowly, since the fog was now thick. Then it seemed to stop out there.

And like some siren on her rock, I listen a moment, then walk down to the wharf. Vaguely I think, Deleau, and imagine a black craft hovering out there, eyes peering under bone and wild hair through fog.

Hellooo! I called out, and heard my own voice echoing through the fog, caught in it somewhere, palely . . . ooo. I barely see my own boat, Pennyless, out there—dark. The water is very smooth under the fog—silver. And then a voice comes back—Ahoy. And after a moment or two the motor speeds up. It seems to have spotted land, seems to turn a little; then I see it, its outline, nosing in. I'm suddenly agitated, unsure. Him? I think—that thing Gertrude seems afraid of?

At maybe a hundred feet I recognize it, and feel wonderfully relieved and pleased. I think that they're caught and are putting in. I'm delighted. I'm of use. I watch it pull in to the wharf. Then I hear his voice from aboard. Can you hear me in there? can you hear me, John? Over. Sound of radio voices, mechanical, not human. This is Hale—Elmo. Call Ethel—tell her I'm all *right*, not to worry none. Over. Radio voice. We'll see you, John. Out.

I watch him down in the fog moving around, fastening a line at the bow, then one from the stern. He seems to be alone. He's greeted me. Hiya, Helen—mind if I tie up? Then he's climbing down to the raft. And up he comes.

It's a mite thick out there. How are you?

Fine, fine, I say. Where's Richie?

Over to shore. It's only me this time. Am I welcome?

Well, of course you are.

He hugs me—That's my girl.

He's in a fine mood, is pleased to have made the landing, has some beer in him, I guess.

We walk up over wet grass and rock to the cabin, me pleased with its lights—orange, shadowy boxes projecting into the fog—it's grown dark, everything is muffled, obscure—and pleased to have him there. I'm already hoping he will stay for supper.

Inside the air seems clear and I hear him say, Now ain't this some cozy. He towers darkly in the yellow light. He wears his knit cap, his lumberjack shirt, his short boots—face shiny and red as a tomato. Ain't this some pretty. Then to me, Got caught out there, de'ah—come up on me quite sudden. Don't mind if I stop a while, do you?

I'm hoping you'll have supper, I say. I've got plenty.

Well, now wouldn't that be nice. Of course I will, de'ah. He goes to stand by the stove, casting a great black shadow against the rafters. As in my rooms on shore, he looks enormous.

I'm over looking in the oven and hear him say, Might have a drink, de'ah, if you got one—quite cold out there. I see him rubbing his hands.

I was going to have one myself, I say.

He's taken off his cap, his wool shirt. Blue cotton work shirt he unbuttons at the throat. He sits on a bunk to strip off the boots. You won't mind me in my stocking feet, I hope. I hear them clump to the floor.

I've turned on the radio, turned the oven down, gotten out ice. I bring a chair and put it between the table and the stove, a wicker rocker. Sit here, I tell him, and I go to fix our drinks.

This is very pleasant, I say. I wasn't exactly expecting company.

Can't tell what that tide'll wash up, he says. There—now, ain't that fine—and a hand comes out to take the drink I've brought over. Like when we're on shore—ain't it, de'ah?

We sit.

How's Ethel? I ask.

Well—you know Ethel—kind of touchy now. I called her from the dock so she won't worry none.

I imagine it's quite easy to get lost out there.

Nothing to it—lose your bearings and that's it. Felt quite lucky to hit the landing like I did. I heard your voice—seemed like I'd landed home.

I watch him sipping at his drink and want to ask about Richie but don't know quite how to—about why he hasn't been out. He's talking, saying that I'm missed on shore and that Ethel asks about me and says for him to keep an eye on me. We have another drink and then a third, though I'm watching the casserole.

He himself says, Richie ain't been out, has he?

No, I say. Is he painting any?

Well—a mite, you know. It's mostly at your place he paints.

Well, tell him he ought to, I say. He's good for me. Come look. And I rise and take him to see what I've done of him on the easel.

He studies it a moment, pinching his lower lip, then turns, looks down at me. Now when are we going to have that naked one, de'ah?—and suddenly hugs a huge arm around me.

Don't mind if I bunk out here? I hear him say. I'd hate to run the old Eth-El up on ledge.

And what can I say (though something stirs in me). You'll be my first guest, I say.

Miserable thick out there—can't see the ends of the goddamn boat.

He eats heartily. The radio's going. How about some coffee? I say.

How we fixed for this? he says, finishing his glass already.

We're fixed for both, I say, and go mix him a drink and set about coffee.

Some *hot* in here, I hear him say, and turn to see that he's removed his blue shirt. And I sit with him as the coffee perks. Going to let me pose for you, de'ah? he says. He's tilting back in his chair, is looking at me in an easy good humor. I see the fog outside, and in my mind the wharf with his boat at it, silent and dark, lifting and falling with the dark water.

I'd rather not, I say—not tonight.

I go to get the coffee.

He sits with hands clasped behind head, tilted back—I smell his sweat, a damp, body smell I admire, respect. I'd like to, he says.

Oh——better not.

Ain't no one around, you know—just that fog.

I say, You frighten me a little, you know.

And as before, the voice broadly reassuring—Now, de'ah— I'd never harm you—I like you to look, that's all.

But I've seen what it does to you, I tell him. I don't think it's fair. To you, I mean.

Fair? Of course it's fair. I liked that.

But it makes me feel guilty.

For Ethie, you mean?

I hesitate. Yes, that, of course—she's my friend—

But we ain't got nothing now—like I told you. And she wouldn't mind—

Of course she would.

She wouldn't know—how's she to know?

She would.

He seems to change subjects and says, What do you think about Richie?

I like him, I say.

You ought to marry him, de'ah.

After a moment I say, Why?

He'd be good for you.

Perhaps I wouldn't be good for him.

Naw, de'ah—he likes you.

Why hasn't he been out?

Ain't got the time. We're working separate some now. He's using the skiff, around shore. You like him?

I shrug.

You do—I can tell. Having him pose up there—I seen him that time.

I have you pose, too.

Didn't get them little trunks for me, de'ah.

I smile, feeling pleased that he doesn't know that Richie poses without them. They didn't have your size, I say.

I see him smile back. We sit. We smoke.

Then I say, That's partly what frightens me, you know.

He looks at me. What, de'ah?—my size?

I nod.

Arms behind head, he looks at me. That ain't nothing, he says. Ethie's small.

I know, I say. I try to tell him, in a simple language, that certain women are timid, certain men too much, that he appalls me, in a way.

I ain't asking for that, he says.

Then for what? I say.

I like you to look at me.

Just look? I say.

He nods.

But *that's* what's not fair, I say.

He shrugs. I like it, he says. His manner is quiet, serious.

His glass is empty and I rise to make us another, and hear him moving behind me and turn to see that he's taking the undershirt off. He's bending, stripping off his socks when I come back—unbuckling his belt, has risen, is peeling the trousers down, and my heart seems to shiver, almost apprehensively.

Get your pad, he says.

He's taken the drink, gone to stand with it by the counter.

Go on and draw, he says—want you to draw me, de'ah—like I am.

I sketch as he stands there with his drink and even as before, while it happens to him. I watch him unbutton the shorts, push the cloth down. Go on and draw, he says. He stands, he drinks. He doesn't look at me. A hand casually pushes cloth down till he's half-exposed and he stands that way for a while with it happening to him. Just draw, he says. He drinks, stands, weight resting on one leg. He's not so round, so barrellike as Herne, though his legs are larger. I see him bending—he rolls and strips down the shorts, steps out of them, kicks them away, then stands back up and leans on elbows against the counter, and I experience, oddly, a sense of relief, at having them out of the way—it's what he wants—me to see. And he's naked there, large, heavy, loose. I only pretend to draw. I light a cigarette and seem to hide behind its frail wisps of smoke, I sip from my drink. My fingers shake, and I find him looking at me and see that his face is unsmiling, serious. And it rises, swells, a thing growing, as Herne grew, filled out. I force my eyes to look at him. There must be a kind of pain in this, I think, at such exposure—at the embarrassment of it. Nothing hides him, nothing is in the way, and it stands massive now, erect, stands up like an arm and clenched fist, and he's moving a little, as if away from it, is moving, holding there. This is different, more awkward, helpless. And then suddenly it's just happening to him, in air—legs apart, braced there, it glistens, flings, flies grayly forth. He stands without moving, letting it—incredible—pole, rod, grown wet—it pours—then seems to relax. I turn away. . . .

He's lain down on a bunk and I bring a quilt. Hands behind head, he watches me while I place it over him. From a need to speak I say rather pointlessly, How do you feel? (I'm feeling guilty as hell, inadequate.) I see the slow spreading of a smile on his face, looking up at me—Give me a kiss for good night, he says, and purses his lips. I bend and his arms come up and around me and I feel myself pulled down; I feel his mouth, then his tongue. He's never kissed me before. Easy and fat it moves at my lips, reassuring; easy and slow it goes in. He holds me there. It removes. Lie down by me, he says, and moves to make room. I look up at the rafters, orange and dark. What do you think? he asks from beside me—Didn't mind none, did you? comforting me, himself. I shake my head, I say, No—but I feel guilty again. No, he says, and rolls to kiss me again, holds over me, lifts and looks down. Let me feel you some. I won't harm you, de'ah.

We lie there making love, a kind of love—he's undone my blouse. You scared of me? he asks. How come? You know, I say, and he laughs and hugs me again. It ain't nothing, de'ah—just woman and man—you feel I'm too big? He rolls to me and his tongue comes easily in again. He lifts away, looks down. Don't worry none—I wouldn't harm you—and he hugs me to him, kisses, holds, withdraws. I like you, de'ah—it feels good when you look at me. Then he whispers down, as if people were around somewhere, I liked you looking when I come—I like to shoot for you, de'ah.

I'm afraid, I say, and he quickly withdraws.

I know, I know, de'ah—I won't harm you none.

He kisses again, bends over me, and I feel it against me down there, hard as bone. Let me up, he says. He rolls up and over me, stands by the bunk, erect, stands over me, and I watch while it happens again, him looking down at me, moving his hips, arms held in air. I hear him breathing, the breath coming on intaken rushes of air—he twists, moves, dark dance of him there against light and the orange rafters—breathing like steam engine now, the air gasped and forced out, becoming hoarse—I'm coming, he warns—thrusts forward then holds, has gone rigid—I turn quickly, hold out my hands, my breasts—Get it, get it!—and he strives to reach me.

When he sleeps I blow out the lamps and go to my room.

Fog outside, still blanketing the shore—I watch it blow past a spruce, see the spruce vanish, in a moment darkly re-emerge. And I'm happy-depressed, both at once, and imagine him lying out there in satisfied sleep and think, Yes, odd, it is odd, wanting to be watched like that, to be looked at—it must give him a sense of himself, his body in my eyes, his nakedness.

I think of the fog again, drifting along water, rolling up over stone, catching like smoke in the spruce—I lie back and drift with it into sleep.

In the morning it's still around. I make coffee, watch him stir awake. Morning, de'ah. He rises, stands and stretches and yawns, ambles over to where I'm laying out bacon by the stove; he stands with an arm around me—Don't make none for me, I got to get back, he says. I pour out coffee for him—sugar, milk—he goes heavy and naked with it to sit at the table and smoke, and I bring the bacon anyway, with bread.

They think I'm over to Isle au Haut, he says. He's made a sandwich of the bacon. He says it matter-of-factly, meaning not to worry. He seems indifferent to me now, and I let my hand rest on his back. Still eating, his arm comes around my hips and hugs a moment.

Then he's dressed, he's Elmo Hale again, a lobsterman. His face has lines of sleep on it that I want to rub away. They seem pitiful, strange to me, are husband lines.

I stand at the cabin door and watch him walk down to the wharf, then out on it. I hear his boat start up, see him untie his lines, wave. He'll go in to face himself and Ethel.

There—I've written it, I've put it down—I feel relieved, guilty.

Well, Beth—was it "cheap"?—cheap little tales of sin? of men visiting me? too strange? What would my journal, my day, be if they didn't? Some modest little travelogue. A New York Lady Moves to Maine—Her Experiences There among the Fishing Villages, Making Friends with the Natives, Who Come Finally to Love Her. Decorous, prim. But I am, I am.

You marauder.

SATURDAY 30 SEPTEMBER. Worked at the path all morning, though kept coming back compulsively to look at the journal, liking it, hating it. But what is a journal that will not tell the truth? All Cretans are liars, but that I'm lying is not itself a lie. I don't think he'd mind that I've written that. And it freed me for work. I worked hard, too, lopping off branches—about one hundred feet of branches (neatening up as I go, building small fires), which is a lot. It will be good to be able to make it easily up to the top.

Afternoon into town for supplies. Gin—cigarettes—kerosene. A piece of halibut.

Back in a wind under gray sky, depressed.

SUNDAY 1. October's child is born to woe and life's vicissitudes must know. I am an October child, though to me the month has a great sweetness. Fall, with its promise and threat, when the year hovers, turns, to plunge through November into death.

A late and orange-gold moon, lopsided, and the islands dark under it. Seals or something around, those things that break water. A boat somewhere, over behind Hog Island—they seldom move at night—perhaps someone is ill. Moose Deleau, who cruises at night when lonely, desperate. Is that my dark twin, my soul?

THURSDAY 5 OCTOBER. I must not let this happen. I am a crow, a stealer from life, picking things up for my hoard, word hoard. I'll lay low. This may not last.

Ah—but it may. The "merely pornographic" can sicken seriously. Then I'll try to find Herne, I'll see him again.

And have him screw you silly, de'ah?

My—aren't we elegant tonight.

Now don't you pick on me. You know he would.

Marauder.

FRIDAY 6 OCTOBER. Among the spruce over there, are those birch or larches—tamarack?—hackmatack? Gold. These islands are flecked with it now, and on shore the red of maples. I noticed flowers in town. How the women here love flowers. Petunias, marigolds. And the puffs of the snowballs still, the hydrangeas. Behind flaking, white-painted picket fences, cut granite walls. Chipped, dry, flaking white paint—old bones—the fading life of that world.

SATURDAY 7 OCTOBER. Walking my shore in sun I see things— mussel shells, like chips of sky from some prehistoric past—sea urchins the gulls have picked clean—dried, green as old jade or like chalk, and some still with spines. And a dead gull, too, with crumpled feathers and empty eyes. I made the mistake of picking it up. The air reeking, brilliant with promises.

But the shore quiets me with its vast indifference, its ageless, imperishable beauty—its deaths, its life. I look for a knucklebone, a part of Ellsworth—to put on a shelf, or bring back to Carole Bean, who would cherish it, put it in a box.

Let the sea have its own. Looking into its glass-clear depths, I think of purity, cleanliness—all I am not.

JOURNAL. Heard a motor around the point. I was down on the wharf—leaning against a piling, at day's end, looking at a lovely sky. An outboard.

Did I know who it would be? Almost, it seemed, I had wished him out. I had been watching the sky change—muted tones of pearl—pink, gray—a great wing of luminous cloud, as of gases burning, dying. And below it, down here, as if in vast shadow, the spruce, the opaline water, the wharf.

Yes, it was he again. And more of the same was in store, and unfolded. How to set it down, to show it was the same and yet different?

Whizzing in, sitting erect in the stern, docking with a kind of flourish shaped like a question mark—Hi there, de'ah—his voice coming up to me, water rocking the raft. Walking up the steep ramp (tide out).

He had brought a quart of Gordon's and four small lobsters.

For a moment we stood there, looking (him, too) at the last of the day. I remember now the cove, dark, presided over by spruce—the wharf—and high up a faint trace of pink in the sky that even as we watched seemed to ignite, achieve its minor glory.

And then him, taking over—broad baritone voice that resonates from throat and belly—bulky dark in fall clothes—Just thought I'd come out, see how you was. And I'm excited, and against my will pleased. I've established my role and he has accepted it, understood.

We make our way up over the rock.

Inside I go at once for the ice—the pattern, the pattern!—he to the sink with the lobsters, which are in a large red can. He disappears out the door with the can. Comes back with rockweed and sea water. Leaves them at the sink. Standing by it, in a black-and-white checked wool jacket I remember from Christmas, knit cap, his boots—red, beaming face.

The lamps are turned on and the gray-pink windows reflect an orange yellow, close us in. Oh, yes, I am pleased to have him here again.

Cap off. Jacket off.

I bring him a drink. Leave it on the table.

Let me light that fire for you, de'ah.

We're both moving around. I have muffins I will heat, bring out a head of lettuce, butter.

We sit. We drink. We talk.

Was a fight in town last night he says, Frank Bullins and Archie Brawn—one of Shirley's boys.

I'm listening I say. My Shirley?

Ay-yup.

Yes? A fight?

Well I guess—and a good one. He pauses a moment to see how to tell it. They say Archie been fooling around Frank's wife—it generally *starts* like that—and finally Frankie took after him, down at the landing. Beat him half to death, they tell. Archie in the hospital now.

He pauses—goes on. Ay-yup, they get like that—liquor, women.

Frank Bullins? I say—short man?—has that fast boat he's so proud of?

Ay-yup, that's the one—nice fellow—looks like our Richie some.

I'm fascinated.

Have you ever had any trouble like that? I ask.

He appears to think. Well—I did once.

Yes—?

A fellow from up the bay come fooling around Ethel like. We were all at the dance one night. Asking her to dance, and she not wanting to much, and then giving me some mouth. So I took him outside—and I whipped his ass proper. And he come after me, week or so later, and I whipped him again. And once more. And that time I got mad, and I beat that bastard *prop*er!

He's suddenly excited, it's welled up. And I say, And liked doing it?

Well, of course I did, de'ah.

Why?

Why? Now how in hell am I to know why? Because he come for me—and I *knocked* the *shit* out of him!

I hear him add, I see him now and then—don't hold no grudge.

All of which bothers me obscurely—something direct, un-equivocal; and I ask him about it. A fight like that, a battle—do the men like it?—do they like to watch? or be in it?

Well, some do—some don't.

You?

Me? Again he considers (he's interested). Take like screwing —you get into it. It ain't *liking*—it's more something you got to do, and then want to do. It's inside you, de'ah—it boils up. Men's like that—they like a drink, like a good time—get excited, you know—and want it.

And you're like that? I say.

I see him hunch. Some men are mean—they'll look for that— not me. That time—it ain't *liking*, de'ah—it's—He shrugs, doesn't have the words for it. It's like fucking, de'ah—you get into it—I can break my back fucking—Ethie's small, you know—I got to be careful—but it's something I need—it goes deep. It ain't in the mind. It's like in the balls—you get hot—you want to get *at* a man, get him down, hurt him.

The lobsters, which he steams for us in seaweed, are marvelous. I've made a small salad. We sip at martinis in glasses I've chilled. Sharp bright fingers reach down in me and play there a moment, pick strings, tingle certain nerves.

I ask, How much of a living do most of you make at fishing, the lobstering?

He thinks a moment, is spooning "tamale" out. Ain't none of us rich, de'ah. I watch him eat, face coming forward to the spoon, shining and bronzed in the lamplight, short, dark hair glistening. Fishing ain't what it used to be. Too many of us—and we lay out too many traps—and some say the water ain't clean—like them clam beds you can't dig in now.

It is a poor place, isn't it?—Orstown, around here.

He nods—Ay-yup. Used to be quarrying, shipyards, all that. In a while there won't be nothing.

And I think, as I have so often, they are the last of something beautiful, in the richest country on earth, and in one of the grandest parts of it.

I bring him another drink, and coffee, and set about clearing away. From over at the sink I see him taking off his shirt, his boots, and hear him say, call over, cheerfully, Going to pose for you, de'ah.

How do I explain how different it is from Richie? Elmo *wants* me to see him. And suddenly, very strangely, looking down at the remains of the lobsters, I wonder, Would old Bill—Bill Eaton— whom I've talked to now twice—show me himself, let me see? A glimpse of the father, of the old bull-bellied male, with his grizzled jaw and his huge work-broken hands, somehow more even than Elmo a piling of this place. And standing there at the sink, I imagine that it's Bill Eaton who is behind me.

Richie don't know I'm out here, Elmo says as I come back to the table.

It's half a question and I say, as I have before, Please don't tell him.

Not me, he says. Told them I'm going to see Charlie Stinson over to Isle au Haut. He's selling his traps.

His face shines with good health and well-being. When he lifts off the undershirt, belly hair swirls into navel in its circular rush, nipples expose, hair glistens like black glass. He bends—trousers are stripped off. He sits down.

I get my drawing pad. I've made us each another martini and welcome its cold glow.

Across the table from me he already seems to be spreading himself, making himself a stage on which an actor will appear, and my eyes go secretly to his chest, to the nipples in black hair, raw, as if chafed. I see a black-haired hand rub slowly over his stomach and see him smile as he catches my eye. And the hand rubs up, finds a breast, loose-muscled and haired, and fondles it.

Where you want me? he asks, when he's finished his drink.

I think a moment. Lie on the floor, I say. (Did this happen?)

He rises and by his chair unbuttons and pulls down the shorts, steps out of them—heavy at the buttocks, the legs—haired buttocks, and under the curved belly, dark (almost inscrutably), the heavy genitals.

I watch him coming around the table, past the chairs, watch him squat to his knees and both hands, seat himself on a rug that's in front of me. He stretches himself out.

And I draw him there, lying with his hands behind his head, a knee raised, a leg loosely out.

How I look to you? he asks, as he always does.

Very grand, I say.

Now see? he says?—I ain't all that bad, am I?

He's turned his head, is looking at me.

Now lie on your side, I tell him. Rest your head on your hand.

Something has burned away from between us and I'm able, almost to look at him directly, see how the genitals fall, how the belly does, in a gentle great curve. He is splendid—even the old scars on his legs I had once noticed are right.

I like you to see me, he says.

Why? I ask, still drawing, to hear what he'll say.

After a moment he says, Well—it ain't just wanting you and all, like that—it ain't quite that. It's like with you watching me I'm different somehow—like I feel bigger—or free.

Would other men, do you think?

Well, I never heard them talk—but when you asked me to pose that time—I liked that, taking off my shirt for you and you wanting me to. I wanted to strip right down, Helen. I could hardly stand it not to.

He lies with his arms back and his legs apart, spread out, and I see his stomach and his chest rise and fall. And then I watch it happening to him and sit back quietly to allow it to—the slow rise and arch of it in the quiet around us. He doesn't touch himself as, in dips and rises, tiny jerks, it thickens, fills. We're both almost innocent of any involvement, of anything to do with it. It is trembling and swelling, and I think, Is it painful to him?

And then it is standing up over his belly, flesh against hair, and his body is rolling a little as though away from it, as if it were hurting him. You like that? I hear him say. I see how it quivers, leaps, falls back—he's making it, showing me—he's pleased, he's proud. It curves toward his belly like a bone, seems heavy, swings. He lies back. Then—Take your blouse off, he says.

I'm not afraid of him. We've been through this, in another form. I undo myself. His hands go behind his head and he looks up at me, watches.

I feel exposed and my skin seems to try to hide. You look fine, you look fine, he says. Take that other off, too. Be like me.

He watches me approach. Now ain't that fine, ain't that sweet and fine—so that I stand a moment for his eyes, as he has lain for mine. I feel them on me with a good frankness, and I let them have what they want of me. Then his eyes seem to smile at my own. I hear him say, You're some fine, de'ah—come lie by me.

And I do, my head on an arm he has stretched for me, soft, rubbery-hard pillow, thick muscle-bone. He's letting me get used to him, letting my fears, if they will, flow away. He rolls to murmur things to me—have me feel him (taking my hand down), which I do. It doesn't seem to belong to him, seems foreign, separate. And he lies letting me. You do that to me, de'ah—make me hot—take your hand away or come, I'll shoot—and he rolls to me and whispers what he wants. I can't, I say. His leg comes warmly, heavily over me—Ain't you got that stuff they use? For a moment it lies heavy, weighty over me, a threat, too big.

We stand and for a moment he embraces me, holds himself to me, nuzzles my face.

He's going to try it and I'm afraid.

Which side you like, de'ah?

And lying on the bed I make love to him, seriously—I swarm over him. I take him in my mouth; he wants himself in me but I prevent him, and finally he sleeps.

Late, late, I see the last of the old moon, a tired glow from it filling the room. I would hate to lose him, in any way, and the thought of it lies coldly on my heart. And why else would he come out here? Richie and I have something we share—what else *would* I be to Elmo, who has his family, his home? I'm an object, a cunt, though I'm more by far to him than I was to Herne. My mind wanders into sleep. . . .

When I'm making coffee, frying bacon for him, I hear him behind me and I turn. He comes over (I've turned back) and kisses my neck. He's got a cigarette. Morning, de'ah (I turn around), and see his big, sleep-marked face and short, rumpled hair, which I reach to smooth, at which he takes me in his arms and hugs me, kisses my mouth in morning feasting so that I feel wanted again—then lets me go.

He stands looking out a window, then goes to the door, steps out—and I see him out there, one hand on a hip, holding himself, the glassy stream arching away into grass, yellow and solid against light. Where he stands, hands on hips, for a while, looking out at the water, easy, content. The tide has gone out and the wharf looks tall and slim, somewhat frail—he's looking down to see how his skiff is, where it rides at the raft with its outboard down. Hog Island has risen, exposed its weedy shoulders. I see him amble down to check his lines, hoist the outboard up, fool with it.

He comes back in saying, Nice morning—cold. Goes to the sink and washes himself. I go get him a towel, which he uses, then wraps around his waist.

I bring him coffee and he sits at the table with it steaming in his hand (I lay the bacon out on paper towels—I've put bread in the oven, buttered, to toast), smoking, and I go to join him. I smoke, too—rich tasting of a morning cigarette, with coffee, strong.

I ain't been out trotting around in quite a while, he says. I like coming here.

I don't really want to say it, but I do. Have you other women? I ask.

He shakes his head. Not now, he says.

But you have had?

He shrugs. Maybe one, he says.

Not Gertrude.

A woman over to Swans—some time ago. She took a shine to me.

When?

Oh—might be last summer. And he adds, Then you come along. Which pleases me. Do most men here—have women around?

Well, de'ah—some do.

He's gone to stretch out on a bunk, knee up, a cigarette in hand, towel gone. Sit here, he says, and pats beside him.

He undoes my blouse, removes my clothes—and then kisses me—draws back to look—returns—settles to me, wrapping me in his arms. Going to do me again? he murmurs down to me—kisses again, eats slowly at my mouth, working himself to me with his big muscular tongue.

My jaws ache from him.

All morning, when he'd gone, I walked the shore, thinking of him but letting things have their say. Water sounds. Bird sounds. *Da dee—dee dee.* Redwing? Sparrow?

I sit on a rock, watching the mist scale away, watching the molten water the sun is silvering. My lake, my pond—and I have so little to say about that. Others would tell how things live out there, what rhythms are kept, would wonder about the relationships, think about life.

Why don't I study the gulls? determine which are which, peer at them through field glasses, record their nesting habits or their cries? Or collect algae, seaweeds, learn about lobsters? Of what *am* I keeping a record? *Only* my obsessions? *Only* A's and B's?

Yes, but how can this hurt anything? My private world, my imagined one—why is the writing of it vile? I do seem to accept that as valid. My tough and sanctimonious ancestors—who arrived on these shores at Newburyport three hundred years ago—what would they say of me now and here? God will cast thee down, woman, in thy pride and luxury. You have gone astray. But they believed in something else, *had* something else. *Their* God is dead.

JOURNAL. What date? I have been thinking.

Art ought to approach, to stir, the higher emotions, our intelligence—our sense of pity and pride. It ought to rebuke, or criticize, is a schoolmaster; art is a gilded pill. . . . But Titian's nude women, Rubens's, Michelangelo's great-bodied men? They were celebrating, singing for the joy of song, the glory of the rediscovered flesh. Elmo Hale showing me himself. I was *not* vile about it—my paintings are not vile. Ah, but the paintings do not deal with the other, that *lower* emotion words draw us to. And it *is* lower, and too much time spent there, *down* there, cannot lead to health or to pity or to pride.

But Elmo and I—what *can* that accomplish? And feebly the answer swims up for inspection: pleasure. I can't get *in* to their houses, their lives, I must look through windows, watch, and imagine.

I'm after the beauty. These stone shores, these difficult waters. I wish to exist here. I will not grow mad. Only mad for a moment, a time.

Within this golden, guttering light, reeking and warm from burning kerosene, fluttered around by moths, alone, and ringed by enormous solitudes, like this planet itself. I'll better than survive, I'll survive gaily, and well.

WEDNESDAY 11 OCTOBER. In shore for supplies. Saw Ethel. She calls me Mrs. Crusoe now. You've got to have a cabin-warming, de'ah. I feel guilty with her, but realize she can't know. And think to myself that as long as she doesn't she'll be happier because he would be. I'm displeased, though, by my elaborate, clinical account —though I will *not* throw it away. For Beth's eyes only—she will *let* me be vile, still accept me. I'm *not* vile. I'm mad, that's all, at times. The island promotes it—I know it.

A cabin-warming, a small one. And why not?

We discuss it—who ought to be there, what I ought to have, how they'll get out. And what about weather?

Pass the word, she says. If it's poor, they can stay home and you'll try again. But, she says, this time of year can be handsome. They'll come in their boats or with them who has boats.

We're already planning, and she likes this, being an arranger. Yes, all my lady friends. And Shirley Brawn & Son, plus wives. We decide about children. Children, yes. And Mr. Williams—and write up to Percy Blair—yes, and who had to do with it—and Avard what's-his-name, to show him and talk about the fireplace. And the quarry people, too, the McGoverns, though they might not come—but ask, invite. And Mr. Wilson at the landing. And the McFarlanes, the Williamses, because they're on my road, or I'm on theirs. The Procters? Rufus and Mimi? I write to them anyway—tell them the time and place and to ask around for a ride.

We add them up. Something like twenty-five, not counting the children.

Elmo and Richie have come in. Howdy there, Helen. Elmo seems odd to me for a moment, remote, but businesslike, a little heavy and slow, jovial self takes over. Richie nods. Hello, Helen.

We're going to have a cabin-warming, Ethel says.

Now there—are we now? Elmo says. Won't that be fine.

Ethel and I discuss food. Lobster, of course. And hot dogs. Potato salad. Baked beans. Yes, and beer for the men—coffee— Cokes—something sweet. Ethel says, Elmo'll help and we'll lend pots. We'll cook some things here.

Only bad part is all the mess they'll leave behind, she says. I'll send Richie back out to clean up. He will.

I'm growing excited, pleased—and a bit scared. Will they come? Will they have a good time? Or will it be like Charlie Chaplin's birthday party that frightened me once?

De'ah, de'ah, she says—of course they will. We all like a party.

I'm to decide in the next few days.

I don't stay to supper, since it gets dark and I'm not good enough yet to get back through it.

Elmo's sitting in a chair under a lamp with an arm around Anne, who's showing him something in a magazine. He's put his horn-rimmed glasses on to peer at it, and looks suddenly different with them on—a husband, an older man. I see a great leg heaved up on a knee. Why do I see him as a scamp? Most people are masked.

Richie still has his beard; seems secret, withdrawn. Has Elmo said something? I avoid him—and yet he seems to be there for me. *Do* minds communicate?—waves—all that—does flesh talk to flesh, bone secretly to bone? Oh, he *must* know something, feel unwanted now. I shall have to be patient, though. For the time, I seem to be after bigger game.

FRIDAY 13 OCTOBER. Chill, beautiful morning. A soundless falling of light on the shore. I went to the cove, stripped to the waist, lay on a rock, watched the gulls, interested yet avoiding me, heard the crows—marauders. Then a breeze found me, blew my flesh into sandpaper.

Painted. I'm almost finished with the Hale-at-sink. My best thing so far. Much green has crept in, but the shape, the substance, of the body itself is solid, sound, three-dimensional—that belly has innards, that chest ribs and a heart—I know how the navel goes—I know how shoulders work, how a hip cocks—how the hands grip and support. It's good. And next a nude—lying on a bunk by a window—smoke in the air—a lobster boat out beyond it through panes of clear glass.

And exciting, yes—the cabin-warming. It will be fun, and they're behind me. Of course they will come, most of them. Yes, and whiskey for them as *wants* it—me.

I step outside. Silence. Water. The dark islands. Many stars. With a kind of sisterly wonder my mind goes to Cobbins Cove—wonders who's there, if anybody is. I think for a fleeting moment of that dark one out there, of its odd and crippled soul, that I seem to know.

MONDAY 16 OCTOBER. Elmo out last evening. All this is a great fling for him, I can tell—for any man, I guess—a new woman. Brought lobsters again, what he calls short ones, which he cooked. Has lotion, which he keeps on my bureau. Posed for me naked on a bunk, propped up on pillows smoking, drink in hand. My drawing included the boots, the checked woolen shirt, the window behind him. And it happening to him as I drew, and his hand down at it as if showing it to me, carefully, deliberately, exhibiting, gently squeezing. He likes the game of it, my timidities, which he engulfs, pets, wraps in his arms. He brought something, left it on my bureau—an offering.

Gone, early in the morning—the big boat (not the outboard

this time) sliding away across calm water, leaving its ripples behind to lap my shore.

After he'd left I cut brush like a madwoman—the crows off screaming at something—gregarious, belligerent. Saw a great hawk, or sea eagle. I think it nests here somewhere.

I did a new thing. Went swimming at the cove. Cold green fire. It obliterated me; but something terribly exciting about it. Back in the cabin, I longed to again; my flesh, my skin yearned toward it.

TUESDAY. Into town. I tell Ethel, Let's go through with it.

We have our list. We write notes: Next Saturday—come at noon—if weather poor, rainy, grim, don't come, we'll try again.

They'll be there, she says, even if it ain't perfect.

I stop by Betty Caster's. Not in. At Carole Bean's—in. So good to see her swarthy little face.

I'll be there, she tells me. What can I bring?

Bring yourself, old dear. Come with the Casters—tell May, if I can't get her.

WEDNESDAY 18 OCTOBER. Glorious day. Serene. The sky cerulean, turquoise. Hardly a breeze. A late yacht went by, a yawl, sails spread—apparitional—Crane's word—till elevators drop us from our day. I once wrote a song to that poem. I'm a gifted and talented woman, not quite right in the mind.

I explored, looked at plants. I have bearberry. I recognized it from knowing it at the Cape. This is tougher, tighter-leafed. And inches-high blueberry that covers the barrens here (they burn them off), already red as blood. Juniper that grows over rock like green fur. Many wildflowers, though mostly fleabane and asters now, and late goldenrod. In the woods some curious, huge gray mushrooms, big as plates, that seem to have oozed up out of rotten wood. Fleshly, obscene—like the inner thighs of an old lecher.

And constantly I thought of the party. I will like the boats coming. I'm buying my lobsters, of course, from Elmo. I've borrowed two great giant pots. Ethel had. Paper plates, paper cups. I worry about the coffee—must look for an electric pot, secondhand —I remember one at a church sale. In tomorrow with my lists. Only let the weather be good—please.

Went swimming again. I have to steel myself to. And then love it. I fight it—it all around and after me. Wildly cold.

THURSDAY 19 OCTOBER. Flying around on shore. Gathering things. Checking off my lists. Weather good.
Found, for $10, an electric coffeepot, at a junk shop. Fifty cups.

FRIDAY 20 OCTOBER. Into town again. Ran into Richie outside IGA.
I hesitated. I said, How's the painting?
Saw him shrug.
Aren't you doing any?
Well—not to speak of.
Are you mad at me? You haven't been out. You said you would.
Well, I might, he said.
I say quickly, Would you do me a favor? I'm going to need some kind of tub, something to keep the beer and Cokes in, and a lot of ice. I was wondering whether you might bring it out around noon. It's a lot to ask.
He nods. We got a barrel, he says. Ought to do. Get ice over to the co-op. He nods again.
Well, I'd be beholden, I say.
And on the wharf I see old Bill Eaton, all stomach and grizzled hair, a knitted cap like Elmo's, though gray, rolled boots, which I think he lives in, wears to bed. And on impulse I say to him, I'm warming up the cabin tomorrow—would you come?—you'll know everybody.
He's suddenly shy, scratches his neck with a huge, broken paw. Please do, I say—bring your wife.
Can't, he says—she's been in the ground ten years.
Oh. Well, bring yourself—come with the Casters—or Avard. Or just come by yourself.
Wa'al now, oi moight, he says.
Oh, do—please do.
Shy, yet one of the old bulls around town by the look of him. Yes, dear diary, another one. Can't help it!
Tomorrow—about noon, I say after me.
How's the fishing, Bill? I hear someone say. Kind of bad, I hear.

'Tain't bad, he says—it's wuss.
Oh, let the weather hold.

Beth,

So much to tell you that I'll only tell parts of it. I've been out on the island five weeks. Ups and downs, scares, loneliness, problems, but it's grand—a bit like living in a myth, a legend, which I might, in time, become around here. I know they talk.

And Saturday, this last, we had the house-, the cabin-warming. Ethel got me to. I invited the people who had helped, had to do with it, and my friends, my ladies, the Hales, one or two others, and their children. And they *all* showed up! I had thought perhaps they wouldn't. To see them arrive in their boats—lobster boats are all around me much of the time, but to see these coming to the island, my harbor, my own landing, with their families aboard —coming to see *me*.

The Hales had come early to help and we were ready, me nervous —and even them, even cool little Ethel, excited. All their children, four, had come with them and made themselves useful. Then to see our first boat! That's Shirley Brawn's (my carpenter)—had the family aboard, his son's, his wife, two children. They docked, trooped off, then he anchored out and rowed in while they waited. And up they came and the party began. Then another boat, and then two, us all flying around, welcoming, serving, being introduced (me), and the children off running along the shore, mothers calling after them. They wore picnicking clothes, they looked fine, the men slightly unfamiliar at first. Yes, and the Blairs, my lumber people from Ellsworth, came, rather grandly, in their own boat from up the bay, though not the McGoverns, the people who supplied me with the cut stone. So correction: they didn't *all* come.

But Rufus and Mimi Procter showed up—you remember them, don't you?—him—teaches at Amherst now—is on sabbatical and staying up here awhile. Top-drawer New England—they simply refrain from glittering, though a facet here and there cannot be hidden—e.g., the sweater Rufus had on: one more patch or inch of hole and it would have been disreputable—as it was, a minor glory. And—guess what?—they arrived under sail in a Friendship sloop (probably an original). At first none of us paid it too much attention, though saw it approaching and admired it—the men here now associate sails with summer people and let it go at that.

Well, it was Rufus and Mimi, coming to the party, and at word of that they felt free to admire.

The children were back from along the shore and down in the skiffs at the raft, out of the way. The grownups got food, beer, Cokes—I had whiskey for those who wanted it. We cooked lobsters outside, the men did—standing around beer in hand, to help or watch—like a cookout. The women helped me. They're all great helpers at something like this.

And a certain Bill Eaton showed up in his own battered old boat. He lobsters off my shore and we wave. All spruced up. Everybody knew him, paid him, in fact, attention and respect (he's an old-timer). He had brought me a cabin present—a huge lacquered lobster claw, maybe a foot and a half long, of the sort you might see in a seafood restaurant. Inside, neatly printed, was the date and place: Caught off Drunkard's Ledge, November 15, 1921, by M. L. Deleau. I couldn't thank him enough. 'Tain't nawthin', de'ah. I said, Now you've got to come out some evening and have supper with me—I'm a good cook. Wa'al, he said, I moight—bring'e a lob-stuh, de'ah, if I do. (Like my imitation?)

Quite a number of the men had whiskey. Their wives don't mind, unless they're Nazarenes, Galileans, Latter-day Saints, or Jehovah's Witnesses. These didn't seem to be. Certainly not old Bill Eaton, who would have glowed in the dark.

Oh, I can't tell it. They were sweet. It was "old-timey." And the cabin did get warmed. I can't really mix with them, but I respect them, like them.

And as dark began to set in, one by one they departed—boats snorting down at the wharf, mothers calling after children, waves, goodbys, their boats pulling away, gaily, since the men were feeling fine.

Richie stayed to help me clean up. I've told you about him. He got quite drunk (another island tale you might hear if you come up), but worked like a beaver in the morning, so that things are shipshape now.

I feel a real kind of happiness, though I don't look forward to winter. And there is no point—but *no* point—in a visit for me *there*. You come *here*. You must. Come any time, just let me know. I hope you won't find me changed; I think I have, though. I don't know quite how, just changed, altered, maybe a little mad.

Things still sound beastly down there. Is it the magazines that make it all so horrible? With those ghoulish women on the covers,

213

death and destruction, hideous political figures—oh, God—brutes, beasts. Some of the men were talking taxes here—too depressing— they're being killed by them. I said to Bill Eaton, Do you mind if I ask what kind of living you make? (he lobsters as Elmo does, whom I had asked, too). Mighty poor, de'ah, mighty poor. This town is slowly wasting away while they hurl things at the moon and burn down Vietnam.

MONDAY 23 OCTOBER. Beth, if you read this sometime, it was like that, the party. They all did come. They were fine. I had a marvelous time, too busy to be able to talk long to wives I didn't know, and the men were easy (How you like it out here, dear? —things like that).

It was curious to see and hear Elmo among them. In "public" he is a fine man. In other circumstances, another place, he would have flourished. Yes, they're the last of something grand, him especially, and Bill Eaton. Elmo talking with the men—I listened when I could . . . "Goddamn bunch at Augusta—a man can't make a doll'ah 'thout them covetin' the haa'f of it. Yes, an' oi'll bust moi gawddam aahss t' come up with it—an' tol' Gordon—We *caan't* pay—they know we caan't—baas'tids—propitty so hoigh, y' can't touch it, talkin' about oil down Machias . . ."

And then Ethel, as they were beginning to leave—You want Richie to stay? (she is a schemer). He didn't seem to object.

And Elmo telling me, Now you treat that boy good, Helen—a shot or two (or six) in him so that the glow was there and the undercurrent, the touch of knowingness—holding his Ralph by the hand as the others trudged down the path; and then, Get him to pose for you, de'ah—looking at me, a smile buried in his face.

We stood to watch them off, from up the cabin, Richie and I. Ethel waves, the children, too—clambering aboard when Elmo brought the boat in. And then it backed, turned, headed out, and we listened to the sound of its motor receding, roaring at first like a truck, then fading as the boat, and them on it, grew tiny, vanished beyond the point.

We sat down at the wharf dangling our legs, with drinks, the silence creeping back in after the party. Tide going out and the island lifting its golden-haired shoulders, emerging. Water sounds. I hear my blowing noises and he tells me it's dolphin.

I want to ask him why he hasn't been out, but don't, sensing something fragile there. I sit by him, thinking how gross, earthy, and crude Elmo and I are, up to the point of my "timidity." I don't need Richie in my bed; but I do need him, would like him, to love me and let me love him.

I do say, Do you like all this? meaning where we are and what's around us. And I hear him sigh. He says, I lived here all my life. I like being here. And I can see that he does and we talk very little. We sit down there a long time. I bring us another drink.

And then a marvelous thing slowly happens. Just overhead I seem to see a waving as of white, silken banners in a soft breeze—hard to tell how far away, what magnitudes are involved. I say, Look, and point up.

And after a moment I hear him say, Ay-yup—there they are.

An aurora—the borealis. But like none I've seen. These are draperies in the sky, just over us. And slowly a green comes into the great waving sheets, pale, distant—icy—and even a light it sheds on us from them: we are in a great tent. Then lights seem slowly to shoot up, higher, higher, reaching for a point out in space, infinitely beyond us and yet close. And the waving—a motion—they ripple, they stir in a celestial breeze, some great spatial wind. And under them, in the dark we finally talk.

I'm an older woman, I say—but I think for a while you liked me. You did favors for me.

I like you, he said.

I'm a little drunk now, I say—I drink too much—but do you think you might love me someday?—I mean as a friend.

We watch the sheets of light wave slowly over us like heavenly laundry. A loon calls. I'm not a girl, I say, so I don't mean that.

Girls, he says—I don't care much for that. I ain't interested. Talking about their *hair*, about boys they know.

Do they like you?

He shrugs. Some do. And then—I'm a good catch for them—save my money. I work hard.

Is that why you haven't been out?

The lights up there seem to shelter us; without reflecting down they shed light around us, leaving it dark where we are, a little as in a cave looking out—and quiet wtih water noises, lapping, the dull chunk of the tide up under a ledge.

Ain't he been out here? he asks.

Elmo?

Ay-yup.

Well—he has. What do you mean?

Well—then why you need me?

And there it is. He does suspect, and has, perhaps, even been out—*I* might have—and imagine him, fleetingly, looking in through a window.

I don't know quite what to say, to tell him. And we sit while overhead that great thing goes on, ripples and waves with a faraway ghostly brilliance.

I do need you, I say. I don't have anything *with* him, you know. With you I have painting—and I love that—I might even be dead if I didn't—because it's hard for me here—I don't belong—never will.

But you got him, he insists.

I think that's in your mind, I say, brazening it out. He has his family, you know. You're young. I like that. I wouldn't intrude. We can *be* friends.

I ain't all that young. I'm getting on thirty now.

And don't like women.

Not many.

Me?

And after a moment—I'd say as I do.

Up in the cabin, from scraps, I fix us a supper, and another drink. I'm surprised that he does like to drink.

He says, You don't understand about Elmo. It's like he's my father.

After a moment I say, And since he comes out here now and then, you think . . . I shrug.

He shrugs, too. Well—like that.

What makes you think that?

He looks at me a moment, vaguely, distantly. Well—ain't it?—like that?

Has he said?

He ain't said.

But that's what he's like, you think.

I see him shrug.

I have the radio on, to fill in against silence. We don't listen to it, it's just there.

You think if he visits a woman, he's making love to her.

Well—I'd say. He likes women.

Me?

He shrugs. Comes to visit, doesn't he?

So do you . . . or you did.

But I ain't like that—I don't care for them like that.

Why?

He shrugs. Ain't interested, it seems.

After a moment he says, He took me to that Gertrude's once— he used to know her.

Well?

And with the drinks in him he suddenly says, He laid the be*jesus* out of her—and shakes his head at the memory. I'll never forget. I couldn't do it—and I sat there, them two on the sofa, half-drunk—Ain't *never* seen nothing like it, him laughing like, then going at her. He shakes his head again at the memory of it. I went out and got sick, I got drunk as a bastard, them going and going and him wanting me to—she made me sick, there like that, drunk—disgusting.

And now you think he does *that* with me.

Wouldn't know.

Well, he doesn't. And then I say, If I ever did, I'd rather it be with you.

We lapse into silence, and after a few minutes of it I say, Do you like me again?

And with a flicker of humor, of imitation, impatience, he says, Of course I do.

I bring him a quilt. I say, This is where Elmo has stayed. You'll be sleeping in your *father's* bed.

We'll clean up in the morning, I say. If you're cold, there's another quilt over there.

I won't be cold.

In my room I lie restful, appeased. Tiny fugitive thoughts, like fish, dart through my mind, but the waters they swim in are placid now, easily contain them. Hale and Hardy—but I more or less knew—and him watching them—yes, and hurt by it in some way, it seems—as if watching his father. . . . Doesn't like women now, or that way. . . . But likes me, is not afraid. . . . Why am I frightened by Elmo? Ethel, of course. . . . And I am timid. My own father, perhaps. . . . Bill Eaton—why doesn't he frighten me? Old—older man—timid—I know him to be—I know.

In the morning he's still asleep (huddled under the quilt, short, gold-brown curls) as I go to build the fire, to make coffee, to begin to clean up.

The coffee boils in its pot—the cabin fills with its smell, the smell of Maine. A fresh bright morning outside, damp with a blue heavy fall of dew. A mist hangs in long blue bands over the water and the islands show through. Low tide again. I'm happy, almost suddenly, and take coffee outside, and wrapped in a sweater out there I think how the weather did hold and that they had a good time—yes, and that I've kept my hands *off* him, but that we've had a talk, are back in good graces, whatever he thinks.

I sit smoking, sipping coffee, watching the tide flood in— a long silvery slick on it they say fish cause and that I think of as trails—sea trails. And the shores of that island over there wet gold. And what I think is that with a man at my back, a friend, I'm fine—easy as that. Though I need Beth, maybe others, to talk to. I do miss that, at times rather desperately.

I go back in to find him awake, in T-shirt, lying hands behind head, looking up at the ceiling.

He lies there awhile as I work at the sink, clearing away paper cups, plates, lobster claws. Then I hear him stir, and turn to see him come rolling up out of the quilt to sit hands in lap with it half over him.

How do you like your coffee? I ask.

Oh—regular'll be fine, he says.

I bring it to him in a mug and go back to the sink.

I hear him say, It's me supposed to be doing that.

Finish your coffee, I say.

And then we do go to work, and have a nice time doing it.

I take him in in the boat; he sits beside me, my teacher, and I show off for him a little, dodge a few pot buoys. And we whizz into the cove and I even make a fair landing. We tote stuff up to the shed where he says to leave it.

Went on up and talked to Ethel. Who says, Well, now—he work for you? Weren't too bad, was it?

The party a great success, she thinks.

I'm anxious to get back and don't say. I check in to see Buster— no Buster, of course, but his little saucers are there, picked clean. Maybe skunks. My garden looks almost embarrassed to find that it's let things grow up. Sunlight blessing things—touching them, an October farewell—the air winy—leaves glorious. I know that I'm missing things here. Beth really must come. I've given the Hales her telephone number, and her theirs, if she should call.

WEDNESDAY 25 OCTOBER. In for supplies through grim weather. The water a dull green and choppy. But I wanted that. I'll not be a fair-weather sailor, or islander.

Yes, and for luck, who was at the dock but Mr. Eaton himself—shy, secretive (or to me), hands in pockets of green pants held by mustard-colored cloth galluses—talking lobsters and taxes with two men. Came to help me carry things down. A five-gallon can of kerosene. Boxes of groceries (gin tucked underneath).

Now, don't forget, I told him—you're invited for supper—just come.

Well, I might, de'ah. Weren't that some fine party.

We're standing down by a set of large, green-painted old iron scales on a raft they keep lobsters in. The scales are used to weigh the iron basketfuls they bring in. Water rinses gently over old boards, and silky, slippery, green-haired seaweed grows, awash in ripples of clear water.

Do you happen to know the man who caught that lobster you gave me? I ask.

Why of course I do—were Myron Deleau—lived out to French-boro, what they call Long Island. Dead now, poor de'ah. Got a boy around somewhere—maybe still out there.

What would he be like, the boy? I ask.

I see him scratch up under his cap.

Old man was a big chap, somewhat like me. Dark.

And the son?

Well, I see'd him once, quite some time ago, out by Marshal. Weren't quite smart in the mind. Folks kind of scared of him, so they say.

He's not around here, though, is he?

Not that I know of, de'ah. Why? Someone said something to you?

Oh—not exactly.

Oh, he wouldn't harm you none. Now, who'd harm a pretty young woman like you?

Old sea beast, barnacled, ponderous, who likes me.

THURSDAY 26 OCTOBER. Finished the trail. Up there a great saucered stone I could lie on. Late October sun. The boats looking small—inconsequential.

I can see my cove. Down in the spruce above it I hear crows, sea ravens having a hassle; their sounds drift up on a breeze. They are the wives of fishermen in Capri, quarreling over the evening price of squid.

Great news! Beth to come in November—will let me know exact date. Will fly up to Bangor, etc. This refreshes me. I'll be on shore by then, most probably depends on weather. . . .

Elmo and Richie offshore—waved. Yes, and Bill Eaton, lone, hulking in yellow apron, hauling up a trap—my secret love. I like his grizzled jaw, his shy but furtive eye. Secret as fish, our minds communicate—in his salt dreams I sing from a rock for him. Naked, he swims through sunlit water caves in search of nereids. He's aware of me.

But, oh, Beth. I shall call Saturday.

FRIDAY 27 OCTOBER. Cold but clear. Elmo out. Late yesterday p.m. Didn't stay. I asked him not to.

And told him a little about Richie, that something was perhaps happening there, that I wanted to give it a chance.

I wouldn't want to lose you, he said.

But I've got to give it a chance, I told him. Don't spoil it.

He was good about it. Let me pose for you, de'ah, then I'll be gone.

And did; then in on bed, where he did the act of darkness over me.

You can get me like that, de'ah.

That's not being a real woman, I say. I'm sorry.

You are—he's suddenly over me, has swarmed at my breasts, holds at me sucking them—comes back up, says, panting and fierce, I'll kiss you all over—your tits—your cunt—I'll suck you *dry!*—and wildly his mouth finds one again and he rolls me to him and we lie like that, me feeling him heavily nursing. I touch him and he's suddenly spurting in my hand, heaving his body at me. . . .

Can you get back in the dark?

All I got to do is miss a few toggles—nothing to it.

And with dark coming on, off he went.

THIS EVENING. No Richie. I sat on the wharf by the water, more or less waiting. Loons were calling. I heard the sheep from that bare Scottish island over there.

I go up to read, but the light tires my eyes. I'm tired anyway. Early to bed, between cold sheets.

SATURDAY 28 OCTOBER. Spoke to Beth. (Did I?) How good to hear her voice. Just the same—undemonstrative, cool—but there, as always. She thinks the 9th—a Thursday—which will give her until the 14th. I'm already planning. I'll have the Hales to dinner, take her around to one or two of my ladies—Carole Bean. Putt her out to the island. Hope that the leaves won't *all* be gone.

SUNDAY 29 OCTOBER. And guess what, guess who? Guess who joined my party, my pages? Ay-yup. Old Bill himself. Came gliding in, pretty as a picture, about four. I went down to the dock to meet him, very pleased. Helped tie him up to the raft despite an I'll get her, de'ah.

He was all spruced up, as at the big party, and had brought two lobsters, which I admired—in a bucket with seaweed.

Well, now ain't this nice, I said, in my new Maine accent.

Told you I'd be out, and here I be, he said.

Well, come on up, I said.

Up there I said, I've got beer, I've got whiskey—and I've got a little of both. What'll it be?

Well—a little of both, I should think.

So I fixed him that, a shot and a beer, with a cube of ice, and a highball for me, and showed him the cabin again. Let me get some corn bread going, I said—we'll have coleslaw with it.

I talked from the sideboard, and when the shot had gone down poured him another, saying, I'll be with you in one minute—and he, Take your time, de'ah, take your time.

Portrait: a large face, square-jawed, and shaved now so that the lumps of muscle at the jaw's corners show—small-nosed (it seems broken, as so much about him does, broken yet indestructible)— a strong and wide and weather-lipped mouth; a man rough yet gentle-seeming, as if he had not been around women for a while and had grown a bit afraid of them. Bellied like a bull, he, too: of course, of course, and with a bull's shoulders, rounded, powerful. A face difficult to picture in the stress of passion (what would happen to it?), as most grand and simple faces are, crowned by a shock of unruly hair, iron gray, he has tried to comb. The forehead, where his cap has been, is white against the weathered brown of the rest of it. He has broad cheekbones, small eyes—direct, when they strike yours.

He's come over to where I'm fixing things—admires the icebox, a gas one, that I'm proud of, too.

And he sits, we talk. And since he's a Mainer and from down here, and an older man, he's good at it, though not much of a listener beyond being polite. I fix his drink. I've turned the radio on and put it where it's not too close to us. And he expands, sits back. No one's treated him this well, I'd guess, in quite a while. And I'm like a child, a kind of daughter, to him, so that his stories come out as if he were at home telling them, his old tales—new to me, hence new to him again, too.

Wa'al, an' when that sou'west'ah set in, we near lost her, de'ah —we come that close—that sea out the'ah, some wicked—an' the two o' 'em drunk, loiin' on deck with their bottles. Oi give 'em the rope, stood an' lashed at 'em till they come aloive—one of 'em fought me an' oi knawcked him through the cabeen do'ah, went in ahf-tah him an' pulled him out—I beat him till he come so'bah agin. . . .

That whale—he come roight alongsoide, loike we was jist an-other—many toimes our soize, y' know—an' rubbed hisself on the bo'at, an' Bob layin' at him with the gaft—oi cun't he'p it, I staa'ted t' laa'f an' the bo'at feelin' loike she'd run aground in a sea. . . .

Scrimshaw? 'Cuss I know, de'ah—didn't m' faa'tha go whalin'? An' didn't I have a piece o' it myself? 'Cuss I did.

I pour him another shot, bring an ice cube, get him another beer. Scrimshaw . . . the term has stirred some of the old dream fibers in his brain. Whale tooth ivory—sperm whale—the men carved . . . when oi was a boy—yis, an' m' daddy come home an' brought us a box he made with fids in it an' all, an' needles an' a crimpin' wheel f' m' moth'ah. Oi see him still in his big black clothes— some foine—an' how he liked to go down an' talk to the men he knew, oi rememb'ah that, a great whale o' a man himself, drank rum—wan't s'posed to 'round here then but the ones 'at went away'd come back with it an' the habit. It's always been loike that down he'ah—some do—the wimmin's agin it, y' know—men gits too rough—nawt me, de'ah—don't drink t' home.

And since he knows now I like him, a tale with a girl in it—men hoverin' around her like gulls around a dragger—him, too. A pretty girl—long hair—such a quiet voice. And wicked of him, he tells me—but she liked him. Oi was young then—was a foine big fella, trim an' all—oi was, de'ah. Had my own boat. An' out she came with me for a day o' lobsterin'. An' I stalled her, he'ah, the'ah, and it come on da'k—but I knew a moon'd be up. . . . Nothing happened, but nothing—it all in his mind (or was that the way it *had* been?)—but sweet to him still.

Oh, Bill, how I understand your making it up, how I do!

I ask him about himself. Lives with a son now—older children all gone off. Five girls and a boy, the boy being the youngest. And since he is happy now, and more than a little drunk, a touch of bawdiness comes out.

Foive gi'rils—one roight ahf'ta the other—so m' daddy says, Now, Bill, you *gawt* t' git us a *bo'ay*. You're fishin' in the shallows, de'ah —won't kitch *nawthin'* the'ah—gawt to go out deep. Haw! So oi done it. Woife says, Why, oi ain't never felt so undignified in m' loife! An' I says, Oi'm gittin' us a boy—you've talked me outa foive an' oi'm doin' it moi way now.

You been married, ain'tcha, de'ah?

I fix our meal and he comes to help. And he's drunk now, because he's not used to the whiskey, and stumbles a little. Whoop, de'ah! An arm goes around me. Oi loiked that, what Daddy said —Won't kitch much in th' shallows, Bill—gawt to go out deep. Know what oi mean, de'ah?

Well, and I guess I do, I say, speaking Maine.

An' oi did—give the old lady hell—fer a fact—an', yis, out come a foine boy.

Did you have other ladies around? I ask.

Me? Naw. I stuck it out with that'un, de'ah—wan't much f' chasin' around—though oi wun't moind to now, with her gone, poor de'ah.

It's an offer. And he's standing there not much taller than me, bellied like a Silenus. Gimme a kiss, de'ah, he says. And I say, I will if you'll sit down and eat. Well, oi'll do that. And he kisses me—bends forward, closes his eyes—kisses me awkwardly on the mouth, holding me at the waist as awkwardly—so chastely, somehow. Huge, brawny still, and simple of heart.

Now you sit there, I tell him—and I tie a bib around his neck and bring him things, the corn bread, crack his lobster, and see that he eats, which he doesn't much.

And finally help him to bed—to a bunk—drunk and stumbling.

And I take off his shoes, undo his shirt for him as he lies there, make him shipshape and comfortable—him half watching me, and speechless now, his face gone slack. He wears BVD's but a button is gone—and I peek as shamelessly as Lot's daughters at a snarl of gray hair, reindeer moss on old stone, thinking, I was right, a hairy-bellied man. He's reaching a big arm for me, and I let him pull me down to mouth my mouth with his own, sleep, drunkenness, loosening him, and to take my hand and pull it down to him; and for a moment in the cloth I feel him. He murmurs, almost in sleep—I hear him say, You like me? Moves my hand and carries it down the inside—warm, dark in the hair of him, inactive, lying speechless now, moving away into sleep. I crouch by him and wait until it has engulfed him, then softly, exploringly, I feel over him, his belly, its great old indentation there, birth wound, buried in hair, in fleece, feel down to his soft genitals warm in male darkness. I crouch with an arm over him under the cloth to let his old warmth come into me. Then I arrange the quilt over him and bend and kiss his sleeping face.

In the morning it's he who apologizes, mumbling, embarrassed, a little bit confused—to let me know that he's not a taletelling man and that if he bothered me he hadn't intended to. I ain't like that, Mrs. Calder—don't intend no harm. I say, You didn't harm anything, Bill. He doesn't remember exactly what happened but blames himself for whatever. Finally says, And what them folks ashore don't know won't hurt them none.

I've made coffee for us. I see him off.

Old, weathered, much-painted boat—all he owns, I think—I watch it pull out—fish-scaled old rope lying around, old barrels, barnacled, seaweedy, like him. And he waves—himself, on his own again. Already thinking, no doubt—Now, wasn't that something—that young woman back there—she likes me. She did listen to my talk.

I see him in at the wheel—he turns, lifts an arm, and I lift mine.

I hear the gulls crying. The ever hungry gulls.

MONDAY 30 OCTOBER. Martini in hand, fire in the stove, soup making.

I read that over. Keep your A's, B's, C's straight, dear!

I sentimentalized him, didn't I? And can't quite tell where or how. The word "old," perhaps—the word "big." Touches that blurred the reality of him. My obsession with fathers—which he is. But he's more, I think—like Elmo he's abundant, there's so much to him. I keep saying, All man—meaning what? Meaning, I suppose, that he's strong still, but gentle, and very much himself—not merely a type, not simply picturesque.

WEDNESDAY 1 NOVEMBER. Back after Halloween on shore, where I *did* provide this time and was visited—fire roaring on the grate, two martinis roaring in me. Two little bands of children. I had the mothers in, too, Mrs. Williams, Mrs. McFarlane, and joked with them about doing a little better this time. I went early to bed, glad I had made the effort.

Today—walking the shore and feeling that this is the last of it.

And always the gulls, the gulls—sheer-winged, impervious—yet their feathers wash along the shore. Death, I feel in your midst out here. You're all around and that water is your sign. Washing these rocks, rising and falling, like a thing that breathes.

THURSDAY 2 NOVEMBER. Went in for supplies, and heard some awful news. Young Buddy Caster's boy, out fishing, drowned. Ethel told me. Age eleven. Awful. Though I could not be properly touched by it, not knowing them or him, I sensed how Ethel was. Later, down at the wharf, accounts of it were flying around, conflicting, self-importantly told. They don't learn how to swim. Water too cold, the older ones most often in boots, heavy clothes. They struggle a moment, then go down.

Poor Jules, poor Elizabeth. I'll send a note.

Something in me that has not faced life, doesn't know yet quite what it is or means, its pitifulness, its grandeur—it loneliness. Why I'm here, perhaps, why I've exposed myself to this solitude, these folk, who *are* so close to it, in the midst. And Elmo—at the peak of his vigor and needing to bestow it, share it, and me constantly refusing, drawing back, when it's what he needs.

That ironstone bowl—twelve-sided, a lotus shape—zodiacal—with a chip on one of its twelve points, that tells me I am imperfect, too—a spirit wrapped in this imperfect flesh that foreshortens all its dreams. I'll put my pomanders in it, sea shells, the claw of that great lobster.

Oh, I *can't* leave yet. Not with days like this.

This is life not death. This contains death, is not contained by it. Life, that blue sky. Overcome by my own sentimentality.

I want to see Bill Eaton again, old man of the sea. I'll be careful about his drinks, and as he's dozing off dreaming of a lobster girl, I'll come to him to warm his body with my younger one. A Shulamite.

It's this weather that unsettles me. Gold moon coming up. On the wane. Don't worry, de'ah—we'll say we had motor trouble. See the moon?

I see the moon. It just seems to arrive. Gold bubble in the sky and all the islands darkly laved by it. Do you see the moon?

Yes, and those men fighting; that, too, sticks in my mind. Elmo's account—And then I whipped the be*jesus* out of him. Do they get each other down? I see them as rolling around like cats, going for the throat. That's just in you, de'ah, like wanting to fuck.

FRIDAY 3 NOVEMBER.   In straightening up for Beth. Did see Buster, who acted standoffish, not particularly charmed by my gracious return. I wear a thick jacket out on the water now.

SUNDAY 5 NOVEMBER.   A proper farewell to Pennyless, I must say!

Gray weather, rain—a southeasterly—and in the midst of it, wrapped in oilskins, a gray knitted stocking cap, a boat that seemed tossed, washed over, barely holding its own—Bill Eaton. My heart made a dive for him. I snatched a jacket and ran down, to help if I could. As if he needed it. Grand, how his old boat put in—seeing his face through one of his windows, glass half-covered with white paint—a hand lifted to wave. Just *touched* the raft, which was frisking about.

Hi, de'ah—I hear his voice. Then he's wrapping a line to a piling, another to a cleat, has dropped two old tires over. Made fast.

I'm back, he says, and I lift my arms and we hug.

Mr. Bill Eaton, I say.

Now, it's Bill, you know—Helen.

He's got a pail—I see seaweed in it.

He stands to look at his lines, check the tires. The cove is partly sheltered from the wind.

And suddenly the weather feels good—vigorous.

She's blowing, he says, looking with me—shakes his head.

Just thought I'd come out, see how you was—if I'm welcome.

Which he seems to know he is; and I put an arm around him and hug him again, as if we were old friends, or uncle and niece.

He follows me up the ramp to the wharf carrying his bucket, and on up to the cabin.

And there we are again. And remembering about not getting him drunk, still fly instantly for a beer, a shot, a cube of ice. He's taking off the yellow slicker, his cap. Let me help with those boots I say.

A fire is going—the lamps are on—everything cozy. I've been reading, drinking coffee.

And he says, Now ain't this some nice. And it is.

Yes, and I ain't getting drunk this time, neither, he says. Wasn't that some miserable, me stumbling around like that. I brought you a lobster, de'ah—I'll steam him up for you.

We sit, we talk. I ask about the Caster boy.

Know'd that boy since he wasn't no bigger than a "short"— made boats for him. Ay, it happens. Wendy Cory last winter. Found him on Bear Island, the back side of it, half eaten up by sea fleas and fish. I ought to be dead myself, many times. . . . He talks, sits back.

I go to make corn bread. I don't have much in the cabin now. I listen, I join in. And yes, he expands again, and more readily, knowing that he's liked. I bring him his drinks, having watered the whiskey. At one moment he puts an arm around my hips. You're some good to me, Helen, he says—I felt a mite chancy coming again. Didn't know as I'd be welcome. And I bend and kiss him on his forehead and he turns his face up and I kiss his lips, weathered and chapped and freshly shaved. He's dressed for it, rigged himself up. And he kisses back, an arm holding me. You like me, don't you, de'ah? My fingers go to his gray hair—how good and clean it is—springy, vigorous. He's fresh and clean as a bar of Ivory soap, which he smells of.

And I bring on the lobster (a big one), the corn bread, the melted butter ("marge"), and we eat energetically, me hearing about a way he knows to make chowder, to make biscuits, and how he once cooked on a fine coastal schooner, fo'c'sle and cabin. Little wood-burning stove. Wishes he had it now. He remembers all of it. He can't read or write and you gather that by the telling he remembers it, his things, where he's been. A powerful memory for names and dates.

I fix us a drink, his mild—and he's off on old words. He's a talker and I like it that he is. One of those men with that touch of the feminine that likes words around it—would chatter all night if you let him. There *is* something about him, something that would like to cook and keep house, be neat, be clean, as perhaps old sailors are, old fishermen—in the midst of what little they have, very proper. Yes. I wonder if Mallek had that sort of pride, that touch of the feminine. Mallek—I write the name as that of a stranger now. How different from him Bill Eaton is—stronger, burlier (my old word)—yes, more male, and more female, too.

And when it comes time to, I say, Were you comfortable here? I've this big bed in there—you can have that.

Me taking your bed? he says. And then gallantly—Not without you in it, de'ah—I'd keep you warm, I would.

And why not? I say. I've been clearing mess away, blowing out lamps. And I say, Well—

But for a moment he's doubtful as to whether I mean it—as to whether he does.

You wouldn't mind none? he says.

Why should I mind?

Well then—he hesitates—I'd say that's fine—that's fine.

Go on in, I say—I'll blow out the lamp.

He's sitting on the edge of the bed when I come in, in the gray, moon-behind-clouds light, still dressed. I say, Don't look, and go around to the side of the bed by the window to take off my things. Then I see him unbuttoning his shirt.

And we lie there feeling strange to each other, him in his BVD's, mound of him under quilts. I say, I hope you'll sleep—is it too quiet for you? Silence has come in around us, though there's still the wind out there and water sounds, a dancing of waves on the shore. I like it quiet, he says. I have a cigarette but he doesn't smoke.

I say, Do you mind being here?

Well—I am unsettled, he says, to the rafters. Ain't used to it—this—like this.

Do you mind?

'Tain't I mind, de'ah—I feel—like I shouldn't, you know.

Be with me?

Ay.

Would you rather be out there?

A pause. Would you rather I be?

I'd like you here, I say.

He rolls, he turns to me. You like me, he says.

I do, I say.

Can I kiss you?

I turn to him—and he does—awkwardly, as before. Then he rolls back. After a moment I hear him say, with a kind of sigh, I ain't too young, you know.

Wind outside and the constant muttering of small waves on the shore. The wind worries up under the eave, rattles a window, wants to get in. I've put my cigarette out, and lying with my hands behind my head, I make something up for him. My husband was older than me—I don't seem to like young men especially.

Ay, but I'm getting on sixty, you know—ain't so lively as I once was. And I'm timid now, somehow, being alone so long.

I turn to him. Turn here, I say; and after a moment he does, and I put my arm over him and hold him, till his comes under mine, and awkwardly, uncertaintly, we seem to settle toward each other.

His body, under the soft, deteriorating old cloth, feels warm and bulky hard in my hand. I push him back a little and find the buttons and undo them, and after a moment and almost as if reluctantly he helps me roll his underwear back, strip it away, till his shoulders and chest are bare. And for a moment my hand wanders over him, learning who he is, what is there. Warm flesh over old muscle, great bone. Warm, sweet in my fingers.

And after a while I hear him say, You like that?—and when I say, Yes, he says, I ain't been naked with a woman—hardly even with my wife. And I feel a sense of pleasure, surprise. Do you mind? I ask.

I think he's surprised that I'm naked and his hand is tentative at first, touches a breast, touches away. I feel big fingers moving over my skin—they touch at a nipple, which seems to shiver and freeze so that the fingers play at it. I hear him say, You do like me, don't you? and I move him back, move over him, and kiss down, and he lies with his arms back letting me. And then an arm comes around and then the other, holds me to him, hugs as something stirs in him. His arms are warm, they hold me with a kind of tentative power and I can feel how strong he still is. Want me to take 'em off? I hear him say in a hoarse, unaccustomed whisper; and the bed dipping, clanging, he wiggles and twists out of them, rolls them down, kicks them away, the BVD's—whispers again, as if people were there, I'm all naked now.

And something grows in him, though slowly—hidden, long done without. His hand is a poem of bones and stiff, work-hardened skin, that crochets, makes nets, goes to my breasts, fondles one as it would a child it felt might be fragile. And then is over me and kissing down and my arms go around his back—flesh-muscle-hair of old male, complex in my hands.

He holds himself looking down as I feel at his chest, at his throat and jaw, at his face, then around and down to the small of his back; he pushes up till the muscles there wrinkle and ridge; and I work at them for him, knead in to buried spine. And then with his knees he's pushing mine apart, is over me, enormous, though I'm not afraid as I would be of Elmo. Help me, de'ah—help me now. I do, and he comes in as I seem to receive and enfold, and I hear him sigh as he settles over me.

Under the shaggy warmth of his belly, that root that stretches me, that something in me seized as with a fist, constricted, gripped —till at my ear his voice grown small and hoarse is whispering, Work me, de'ah—and he holds for me to, that part of him hard, unyielding—thick—that I feel down there as with a hand, seize and release, root of him in me—mutters, Work it, de'ah, work it for me.

Then after a time the strokes of his body begin (I'm his wife now) and I find myself helping him as I can, and hear, as one suddenly hears a clock, the bed banging the wall methodically, crash, crash, as if the earth were shaking, as I am shaken, and want to cry out and perhaps do—crash, crash—metal banging against wood, crashing and jangling—which he doesn't seem to hear as he labors, works. And I feel it all through him now. His body, a ball, seems all muscle working within my arms; the bed crashes and rocks; his breathing in my ear—and I feel him hold hard and quivering to me, feel suddenly warm inside, him totally down on me and he shoots and throbs—shoots, shoots—to hard, hoarse snorts of pleasure in my ear.

When he rolls away he's still breathing heavily, is saying, Fine —that were fine, de'ah, fine—is patting me.

And in a minute or two is talking again. I ain't been with women, you know—didn't harm you none, did I—I tried not to— you all right, de'ah? I tell him that I'm fine, just fine (which I am, though restless, unsatisfied). He rolls to me, puts an arm across me. Were it good for you, de'ah?—you liked me?—did you? I feel his breath on my cheek, damp, smelling like my own of food and drink, whiskey—grain—and I turn to him. He's fatherly, affectionate now—*he* feels fine—fine—having emptied himself—back in a world of simple emotions he's good at, at home with. And after a while he's asleep, and the sound of him beside me is good, too—a snore—soft, or tentative, at first, then snorting, eruptive—and I lie listening to it and to the wind outside rattling things, blowing coldly, erratically at the eaves, and hear beyond it the water sounds. I drift toward sleep and feel the shape of him beside me, the warmth of his back, and hear his guttural snore.

In the morning I know that he's going to be awkward about me seeing him, so I say, Don't look while I dress and I won't at you —though I do, at his broad white back, streaks of hair, enormous, his brown and grizzle-haired bull neck, his thick arms, as, creaking the bed, he puts on his BVD's. . . .

Do I *want* to be Pasiphaë? Am I insane? Am I lying?

It's still windy, choppy outside, but I know he wants to get away by himself again and he pecks me goodby and I watch him walk down to the wharf, carrying his bucket. His boat down there, much painted, much repaired—and I see him look back and wave.

Spray dashing over its bow, it heads out, veers to the left, fights at waves, and I think, He's going the long way round so that they won't know where he's been. Good for him.

It *was* good. Bill Eaton—my secret love out of all of them. I won't spoil it. I won't talk about it to myself any more. Old drunken bitch, one of your happier inventions, all of this.

MONDAY 6. Weather still bad. And this was to be my final day here . . . this year. I've enough here to hold out, though cigarettes are low, gin low—me low. Beastly how it keeps up, as if no love were left in the world. Gray wind, gray rock—gray water—and my crows reduced to a petulant silence, or wind-tossed bundles of black rags.

Read. Climbed the knoll for a look at things. Universal desolation—windy, shadowless gray dotted with whitecaps. But perhaps Beth will bring good weather.

TUESDAY 7 NOVEMBER. Letting up a little. Of course I *could* make it in. All it takes is nerve, but I see myself crashing against a shore.

Bill Eaton—who liked me. His talkative old soul, his awkward apprehension, and the fine way he went through with things—I think he liked it, though isn't used to it. It *is* that female streak, something that likes the feel of things, unlike the conquering-hero type. He would share the experience, let you feel him, feel back, would learn. I like that in him. Do men like a touch of the male in a woman? I would. Will he visit me on shore? Yes—we'll manage, during those long winter months. It will help to keep Elmo out, Richie in place, or Herne away, whom Pasiphaë could really come to depend on, even go looking for. Oh, I'll quilt like a mad woman, I promise, I'll have people in; I'll learn, I'll learn, I'll become this place.

Oh, Beth, be there, please. Don't fail me.

4

WEDNESDAY 8. On shore. *Back.* And good to be. Dead stalks of goldenrod, the fields blowing, leaves gone, but the spruce, guardians of this place, staunch, unchangeable. A few rusting clumps of chrysanthemums left, and the dahlias fallen. I'll go out again to lock up the cabin. Mr. Williams to haul the raft up on shore. After Beth has left.

TUESDAY 14 NOVEMBER. Well, she has gone. She restoreth my spirits, that woman.

And even the weather held. It was fun. Thursday night all we did was gab, eat, gab, drink, by the fire, talk—talk!—I, like a starved thing to whom words were food. N.Y.—old times—what's happening—her—me. She is just the same. Though I, she told me, had, in fact, altered, grown a bit weathered—yes, more blousy (not her word) but she said, Well, darling, you have expanded here and there. The men love it I said—I do it for them. She herself was looking a *little* haggard, but trim as a bone.

The big thing was just to have her here, to listen to, to listen. My God—the sound of an old friend's voice!

Certain differences—the old ones. She's committed to all that down there, feels we have to do something, not just face it, actually *do*—get a uniform on and get out there, march, write letters, lash around. I say, It's not just the hoop-de-la I'm running away from—not *just* students and blacks and Vietnam, China, poverty (Lord, I say, we've got our share of *that* right here, these people, a lot of them, can't afford to eat). But not *just* all that, I tell her. Something more mysterious that I can't quite define. I can only say that the new technology is behind it, creating it. It's the *numbers* of us I'm afraid of. The figures—well you've seen them —appalling—but absolutely appalling.

I said, As you know, I used to love modern art, contemporary, to call it that—art being made, then, there; I dislike most of it today intensely—so that I'm not even on *their* side—I don't seem to have a side.

She said, Because you're a backslider. You want to go back, to return—and there is no going back.

But what's forward? I asked. Need everything change every year? New this, new that, year after after year? It's been doing that for at least the last fifteen. And now they're sweeping up little piles of dirt and leaving them on the floor and calling it Object No. 7. A box is art. A building wrapped in polyethylene—any smarty gets attention, and serious attention now. Why?—tell me *why*?

Oh, you know why, she said—don't play so dumb. You're giving yourself airs, old thing.

I imagine they're saying, It's *all* beautiful—the whole goddamn world we're about to blow up—the art that embraces all. And why must *both* nature—all that out there—*and* man be left out?

You've lost your sense of humor, she said. They're against everything you are—fancy packaging, lousy content—commercialism—random sprawl. . . .

Well, we argued, discussed. I'm no longer intelligent, she lets me know—the wilds have taken my wits. But it's as if they were sick of things, I say, not in love with them—sick of man, of themselves, bored by nature—mildly interested in mechanics, in making little things—but nothing so good as a boat, a fish net, a wooden barrel. They're interested, I told her, in blowing up the past, dissociating, as if the past had its hands around our throats.

I said, I think "art," in quotes, has had it—and if mine is, theirs is, too—the brains are somewhere else now—into computers—systems.

Herb said something like that. I don't agree.

But, darling, you and I can make half the things being turned out. Okay—so they're making fun, debunking—the selection and arrangement of junk—instant art. Art now is simply an attitude.

And you don't see that it corresponds? she said—that if Greek art mirrored a respect for order, *their* art reflects the disorder of its times?

I sat there twisting my hands—backed off—I said, Oh, dear—all those beards, that hair, that posturing, costuming—the whole damn bit—I *hate* it—they dress *up* so! They're cheap, and vulgar. So self-conscious.

Well, it is a little hard to take, she agreed—the young always have been. And it's they who're behind it. It's their world. They don't *like* ours, any more than you seem to, you know. . . .

Friday I took her around to look at things, called on one or two of the ladies—May Stinson—Elizabeth Caster (told her about the grandson). And into Carole Bean's little white kitchen, and over to meet Ethel. She liked my ladies. And has, of course, a fond and loving eye for things around her, so that I didn't have to keep saying, Look at that. She saw, and I saw it again with her, could feel her own excitement, approval.

And since the weather was expected to hold, put off taking her out to the island. But we walked, picked little things—a good, *long* walk—that got her blood going, she said. I tried hard not to make it a travelogue. I drove her around, showed her Gertrude's landing —no Gertrude, of course—and did tell her something about that. And said, in my mock manner, And that's Maine for you, de'ah— making do—to which she said, Merciful heaven—and told you the whole thing? You hear of it, but you seldom . . . She shrugged and I added, Get the beauty of it hot? That's not what I was going to say, she said.

Ethel, Elmo, and Richie to dinner Saturday night. A good fire, drinks (my special for Ethel). I was anxious for Beth to meet them. Elmo a *little* reserved at first, but looking splendid—massive—red-faced—glowing with health—not "de'ah"-ing us but most pleasant. I kept wanting to say, You should see him when he's more at home. Another city woman around seemed to quiet him down. Richie, of course, said not a word. But Ethel and Beth and I chattered—me at moments a bit feverishly. Oh, it was nice. Good food. Left about eleven.

She and I sat up and talked. You seem rather taken, she said. By which one? I asked. I'd say the older one. I said, He's got four children—and that nice woman for a wife. I know, she said.

At which point I said, Wait a minute, and went upstairs, rummaged around, found the first painting of him (standing facing the sink), one or two sketches, plus several island ones.

I have another over at the island, I said, that's better—but this *is* coming along, as painting—don't you think?

She did. Was generous about it, in fact.

I said, He poses for me when I ask him to. Doesn't seem to mind doing it.

The sketches (of him) were the ones I had done late last summer, at the sink, and one sitting at the kitchen table. Seeing them through her eyes was difficult for me—I could tell that I had over-emphasized here and there—and she remarked on the fact, a *bit* caustically—or warningly.

I'm surprised he did sit for you, she said.

He enjoyed it; I did, too. I think no one had ever really looked at him before.

Admiringly, she added for me.

I told her about Richie, and went up and brought one or two of his things down, the ones he had given me. She liked them at once, just as I had.

I was evasive—really dumb as a stone—couldn't share any of it.

Down at the wharf whom should we meet but Bill Eaton, sitting on a bench sunning himself like a walrus. How full-fed he looked, hands folded in lap (seeing him with her eyes—how difficult). I introduced her. Ay-yup, pleased t' mee'cha. I said, Bill and I are good friends. I keep m' oi on her out the'ah, he said. Do you? she said. Ay-yup, oi do. Some of his traps are offshore, I told her. Oh? she said. We gabbed for a minute, him friendly, shy.

Now don't go too fast, she said, as we left the dock.

What do you think of him? I asked.

He's fine, she said. He's this town thirty years ago, I should imagine. And very much your style. I know you, pet.

Can you see him, seriously?

How do you mean?

I've been to bed with him.

You haven't, she said, and looked at me, and I nodded.

Well— she said. Yes—I can see it—in a way.

He came out bringing me lobsters one evening—I had suggested it—and we got quite drunk—and one thing led—I shrugged and she said, Oh, dear. And then, But no Fifi Lavernes—please. Don't feel you have to be queen of this water front.

Oh, it was just a fling, I said. And he *was* marvelous—in a way.

I suppose he must have been—in a *way*.

I think I shocked her though. And I mustn't. I found that I could not confess, as I used to threaten to in my letters—as perhaps I may, in my letters. But I couldn't, directly to her. Something held me back—some protective instinct, I think. Because I *have* to protect things, conserve—no cats out of bags. Yet of course I longed

to let them—but this next winter ahead scared me, does scare me.
But I shared what I could with her.

Island marvelous—as she had known it would be. Much larger
than she had expected. She had expected to find me perched like
a gull on a rock, I think.

Oh, the wharf, the cabin, the cove—the whole splendid thing
was there, as if I had never left it. I could see *me* up there,
watching us come in, waving, running down across ledge.

Yes, she loved it.

They lobster out here, I say. Elmo Hale does, Bill Eaton does—
others. They wave. They are beautiful.

We look—we smoke—we drink coffee—are silent. And she's
good at that—she's an old pal—we don't have to talk, or always
explain things—even the things I leave out.

Yes, it was good having her here—splendid. And now she does
know, or some of it. I *almost* furnished her with a moon.

THURSDAY 16 NOVEMBER. Frost. And not the first of it either.
Cabin still open out there. Elmo and Richie dropped by. Elmo is
going to a meeting of the Lobstermen's Association in Augusta tomorrow. Richie not. Come over and paint with me, I say to Richie,
if it's a good day.

I have a fire going. I've fixed them drinks.

Now Richie, you hear what the lady says, Elmo says.

Oh, let him alone, I say, rather sharply. He can come if he
wants—and not if he doesn't.

Well, of course he can, he says, as if surprised.

Did you like my friend?

Ea'ah, she's nice—and good-looking. Wouldn't you call her good-
looking, Richie?

He shrugs.

We prefer our Helen here, don't we, de'ah?

Let him *alone*, I say again.

Elmo in a frisky mood. Going to the city. Though actually it's
a sober matter—they want the lobstermen to agree to limit their
traps, etc. They're afraid of fishing this place out—which would
mean the end of them. And it may be in sight.

They leave about eleven.

I write a note to Beth, filling in a few gaps, explaining, sending
love. Out once more tomorrow.

SATURDAY 18 NOVEMBER. He did come, in the outboard. Brought his box of painting things along, which touched me somehow. I had the stove going. He pulled out a sketch I hadn't seen and tacked it to a space on the table I had cleared for him. Boats, island and distant hills, all in some perspective of his own. You going to draw me? he asks. Do you mind? I say. He strips down to his shorts. These, too? he wants to know. I hesitate. Oh, you don't have to, I say. And I see, sense, some complicated inner shrug, and off they come. He doesn't mind, it's just that he knows it's odd of us. As before, the sight of him without his clothes is like a fine present. I say to myself, My *God*, some of us are beautiful, fine to see.

We talk, intermittently, as we work. I say, Elmo likes you to come out here, doesn't he?

And after a moment, Why you ask?

Oh—something he said. Then I say, I wish you'd tell me something. He's daubing with his brush at his palette and I say, Has he said anything to you?

About what?

Well—about me.

A shrug.

Has he?

Well—some, you know.

And what do you think?

I'm behind and to one side of him, and the late-afternoon light comes in, shadows his body, which seems to me more beautiful than I've ever seen it.

He's like that, you know. Likes women. I don't mind.

He's been here, you know.

I know.

You don't mind?

I know'd him a long time, he says. He likes you.

Then why would he want you to come out?

At which he shrugs.

It must be to protect himself—you know, from Ethel—the town.

Might be.

You don't like women much, do you? I say.

Slight shrug. You've said that before, he says. I ain't used to them, you know.

Do I seem old to you?

You? Naw. That don't matter to me.

Which interests me and I say, You don't have many friends your own age. A question, to which he says, Ain't got any I know of—don't care for them.

And later, You're going to stay here, aren't you?

Well—can if you like.

Which makes me happy, so I fix us a drink.

I can't paint and drink both, he says, almost petulantly.

Well, have a drink then, I say. We're losing the light.

But in the failing of it, the last of the sun slants in to embrace him, lay on his limbs, it would seem, a film of gold cloth—a stocky Ganymede, some indolent favorite of a god—privileged, sweetly spoiled. His nakedness seems totally natural, even to him, I think. Light catches, ignites hair and beard—copper—bronze—genitals nestled in hair, the cock stubby and short, looking small against his body's curves and masses.

I've made martinis. He sniffs at it suspiciously.

Try it, I say.

It'll plaster me to the wall, he says, with a touch of humor.

He puts the shorts on—a white skin that obliterates details. Goes to sit on a bunk.

I fix a supper of beans and toast. He's had a third drink by then. Yes, how curiously indifferent to his body he seems—but isn't there a certain arrogance involved, a knowledge of how the sight of it pleases me? He knows, he knows, with some side of him that is sleekly sensual, and intuitive. We've finished supper and he's back on the bunk with coffee, lying on pillows he's heaped up against the wall, gazing with vague, luminous eyes at me, or through me—but he knows I'm looking at him, permits.

My eye falls on a book I've been reading. Do you ever read? I ask, and see him shrug again.

That book there—it's by a man from down here. It's about this place—what it was like a few years ago when all they had was their own skill and strength to depend on. About winds and tides, fishing, sailing—about making do. I sounded like a blurb.

His eyes shift to the book.

I think you need more than you have, I say—other paintings to look at—maybe a book or two. If I lend it to you, will you look at it?

And somehow negligently, or absently—or even knowingly—he looks at me. Might, I hear him say, sounding faintly impertinent.

No, *not* impertinent—*confident*. Yes, Elmo has said things to him.
Well, I will then, I say.

And hear him say, I read a paperback once about fish—cod, and haddock, hake—the kind we catch—and sea birds, and small things that live alongshore. A woman wrote it. Seemed like she knew more than a man who lives here might. Science book.

Did you enjoy it?

He shrugs. Parts. About a bird she called rinkops—and things I knew—herring—seining for them. It was a little like poetry.

You still like poetry?

He shrugs. Can't understand most of it. Others'.

It grows late. He seems absent, or uninterested. We're only sitting there drinking—me asking questions, giving the answers.

What about turning in? I say.

He merely lies there.

I blow out a lamp, another. I throw a quilt to him, which he catches without moving. I step up on a chair to blow out the last lamp, and seem to blow us into darkness, blow him away, though he hasn't moved.

And as once long ago, it seems, I lie hearing sounds out there. The wind, a dark breeze, is from the east, and I hear water lapping along the shore, splashing a little. Some sort of bird—Rynchops, nicticorax—flying past. Through my window I can see stars, which surprises me—I'd been thinking that fog was out there. It was moisture. It was moisture on the windowpanes.

SUNDAY 19 NOVEMBER. Well, old girl.

Well, what?

How did it go?

You know.

Was he mad for you?

Why these questions?

You know.

Yes, he was.

You lie.

All right. He permitted it, he allowed it.

Permitted what?

I'm attractive to him.

Allowed what?

He'd never been with a woman.

He'd been with Gertrude.

240

With Elmo. Watching.
You don't know that.
He said so.
Watching what?
You're vile.
You are vile.
I'm not.
You're evil, corrupt. You contaminate.
I do not!
As with Bill Eaton, whom you sprang at.
I did *not!* He was old, forlorn, he needed me.
Forlorn! You're gathering them—you amass, collect.
They *come* to me!
You seek them out. You eat men like air.
Who said that?
Some great poetess. But you would have snitched that, too. You
take things that aren't yours.
They intrude—*they* contaminate!
You deceitful whore.

Was it that bad? Was it simply luring him in, going at him?
I was breaking through ice, cracking a shell.
But from bits, flakes, you elaborate. That Elmo business, wanting
Richie to watch—you don't *know* that.
He *told* me.
Sending him out there.
No, he came, he wanted to—and *he* came to my door. I only
petted him because he wanted me to. (Do you mind that? . . . Why
should I mind? . . . Do you like it? . . . I don't know. . . . Shall I
stop? . . . No.) He lay there, he let me. For Elmo. And did like it.
For Elmo?
Have I spoiled it? We used to paint, look our own ways at life.
I'm a kind of lover now. To both of them. Which is what they
want.

TUESDAY 21 NOVEMBER. On shore. Each day something to be faced,
coped with. The hot-water heater went out. Called Jules. Buster
came limping in. Something had been at him, maybe the crows. I
patched as best I could, made a bandage. Storm windows to get up.
Wood to be ordered. Last winter I burned three cords. Life rattling
the door, trying to get in, or out.

But promise—*promise* control—Beth sensed, almost knew.

FRIDAY 24 NOVEMBER. Event: Thanksgiving with the Hales. It was good to repeat. Them all there, as before, almost the same talk. And good to have the children around. Neither of the girls will be pretty, but they'll do. Betsy does have a boy, a long gawky one trying to look grown-up. Sideburns. No love beads, though, no beard. He came in about four o'clock as we, all bloated and fat with good food, were finishing. Fishes with his father and already has an air of confidence. He's not hanging around, waiting for rich drafts of the higher wisdom to be poured down his throat. He works, helps earn money. Robbie Stinson. I liked him.

Richie—whom I observed in his habitat more closely. Wordless connections with Elmo, who spoils him, too. Yes, I see that side of things clearly now. Elmo owns him, has him as property. I begin to see into Elmo, under that jovial exterior—how he almost lets his own sons go in order to concentrate on Richie Hayden, who is everything, child, friend, son, worker, companion.

Handsome they all are in their home. How good it all *smelled*. Onions—the turkey—them. Warm, vigorous. I wondered, fleetingly, where Bill Eaton would be, having turkey somewhere? Or a dried bit of cold cod?

A good day. I had one highball, read, and went to bed, fat with well-being and food—a memory of steamed onions.

SATURDAY 25 NOVEMBER. Drove out to that promontory—almost to get away from something. Images: blowing grass; a stone wall; a brier rose with its withered summer apples left—a house *had* been there—whose?—Captain Bass? some bits of rusting iron were left—a bedspring. Boulders along the shore they say the ice moves. Those same logs—in the sun a soft, silvery gray. The sea—that great friend, great enemy—mindless, indifferent.

I seemed to be standing at the world's edge, alone, seeing, as I did in the fog that time, the remains of things, our leavings, a painted board, a bit of rope; and for an instant sensed how small we are against all that, how frail, marvelous, and impermanent.

Again I could see swells out there, undulant, silent in sunlight—green here, malachite—blue (lapis), perhaps, in Greece—white houses. I found a lucky stone, red with two white bands, and the bones of a small animal, white, dry.

I would not mind being washed up on that shore.

SUNDAY 26 NOVEMBER. Talk with Elmo, who came around. Our most serious, most direct talk.

We talk for a while about the meeting at Augusta (that, of course, is what is actually serious, not me and mine). Didn't go well. They cannot agree—factions—opinions—no real knowledge of the problem, which is simply: How many lobsters are there in one place? As, somewhere else, How much gold is in one mine? Whole new concept: of farming lobsters, growing, cultivating them. *Necessary*—but no agreement. Short of sight. I've been reading about it, I've listened to them talk.

Screw them! he says—meaning change—it—the new world. We can't beat them, de'ah.

And then, with a second or third drink down us, we talk about Richie. I accuse him, good-naturedly, of sending him around, encouraging him—really, of using him.

You do, don't you?

Richie ain't had a woman.

You've told me that. You want me to be it?

Well—it might be good for him, Helen. He's a nice fellow—you know that.

Did he actually go to bed with Gertrude?

He shrugs. How would I know?

You'd know. He just went there with you, didn't he?

Well, he did that.

Why?

What you getting at, de'ah?

You have mixed motives.

I have what?

You have reasons for getting him to come here—you're using him.

Well, I might.

Then he says, It's a small town, de'ah. I like to come here. You like me to. You're a lone woman—what's wrong with a man?—or two—as long as you're quiet. That boy—he does what I like—I'm like his own dad—I *am* his dad. What harm you find in that? You and him likes to paint—I like to fuck—and he'll pose for you, same as I did.

What has he said about that?

Look of great innocence—Why, nothing, de'ah—what should he say?

243

He poses for me naked already, you know that.

Look of surprise—Now does he?—ain't that fine—like me.

No, not like you—I think you asked him to.

Me? Now what makes you think that? He's unbuttoning his shirt, stripping it off. Raising his undershirt—for a moment I see it peeling up like skin. Drink in hand again, on his knee, he sits back.

Now what would make you think that? he repeats.

Well, please don't, I say—don't sic him on me. Let him alone. I can't marry you.

No—but you can love me some, de'ah. I ain't been nowhere since I seen you last. We been hunting, you know.

You *tend* to think it would be nice for the three of us—all to be quite friendly—don't you?

Well, of course I do, de'ah.

But he won't really admit it, not yet. He's patient. I'm trying to think of something Richie said, but it evades me. Come sit, he says. Come sit. Pats the sofa. I rise, take his drink, and mine, replenish them. Patterns. Help!

He's down to his shorts when I come back—I've heard him in there—sits—with a leg up and an arm around me. The whiteness of the skin, never, it seems, exposed. You worry too much, de'ah. Let him come around. There's Ethel, you know—there's folks. You like him, don't you. Drink in hand he turns, turns my head. Kiss.

I just want it kept open, I say. No, he doesn't like women—but there's a chance. He doesn't mind that I'm older.

Well, of course I will, de'ah.

He unbuttons the shorts, leans back.

In a while we're naked under the lamp, which he's turned down. I feel his head, his back, as he sucks at my breast, and look down to see his lips there—I feel his tongue brushing my nipple, circling it. He moves my hand so that it holds the breast for him and an arm goes around me to pull me more to him. For a long while he sucks—peacefully, with closed eyes. . . .

WEDNESDAY 29 NOVEMBER. My ladies again. Our quilting group. I'm busy collecting and swapping scraps. Making a design. This one to be colorful, of squares in squares, *in* squares. A big one, four little ones inside it, and in two of those four littler ones. Red, white, and blue, to match the last. My guilt at lost patriotism.

These women *are* like old floor boards, two feet wide and twenty long—they're like old furniture, built to last, like their quilts. Me—

like my own, badly sewn in spots. I must not lose their respect.

JOURNAL.   Took off for Bangor—pretext, looking for cloth. Really just wanted to drive before the weather sets in, see a movie, stretch.

Found a bit of scrimshaw at a roadside place called the Blue Mary—a crocheting needle with a curly design on it, of I think olive leaves, some whaler had made for his girl or his wife. Three years at sea. They tattooed each other. Who was it told me his grandfather had had a clipper ship put on his chest by a friend and a mermaid across his stomach? Yes, and who told me they buggered each other more or less regularly, paired off, squabbled, made up? Like prisons. Well, they had to do something—without old Ffii Laverne to cheer things up.

At any rate, I did not make the rounds of the Jed Prouty, and arrived home sober, though plunged fairly quickly into the blue pitcher.

Reading *Finnegans Wake* again. He dreamed all that and the dreaming sustained him. *He* dreamed history—me, I dream of bawdy nights. But he was a giant.

JOURNAL.   Buster sick. Dragging around. Poor little thing. What can we do for them when they are? No vet around. Funny, how I remember last year him looking up at me from his little dish of food—how it touched me.

Richie Around to Paint. And we did paint—he with his clothes *on* for a change—but I had no sense of having frightened him off. That island thing—inconclusive.

December–11?

Beth,

It's just me. Nothing much to report. Weather so far bearable, in fact darn good.

Sorry to hear about sniffles at home. *Down* here we're impervious, a hardy crew.

You persuade me that a visit *is* in order. If Herb and Sally do go to Nassau for a few weeks, I will come and use the apartment, and you can come over and share it with me. We'll see some plays (joy) and a few people and have fun. I'll let you know. I'm writing to Herb in a minute.

Wrong—my fling with old Bill Eaton not a case of misdirected

245

romanticism; and I am not role-playing, as Herb would have called it, or succoring the needy. I was lonely, for one thing, and intrigued, for another—and crocked for a third. Yes, intrigued. For a *kind* of person—type—object (check one)—he is fine—*superb*. Old as he is, and he's not that old; ugly as he may seem, he's still hale—hardy (personal joke)—and what shall I call it?— affectionate. *Not* a dirty old man—there is *nothing* of that there.

Why am I going on? Obviously, Beth, you bugged me, knocked away at a prop. He's almost my only real and clear thing. With him I feel no guilt at all. His wife is dead. I'm not poaching. And I'll see him again, too.

Listen—let's count on it, begin to, a visit to N.Y. I feel stirrings, as in the old days: Let's all go to Capri.

TUESDAY 12. An adventure, of sorts. Out walking, and perhaps half a mile down the lane that runs back by the Baptist cemetery came upon an old wreck of a farm with a woman out front splitting wood. Two children were carrying the chunks up to the house porch. It was one of those fine old houses—Greek Revival—fallen into paintless disrepair—that had had style. Fields ran back toward encroaching woods. I had a main impression of rusting equipment long abandoned. Among dried weeds lobster traps stood piled into latticed walls near the barn.

She stopped to watch me as I came by, she wearing a faded, navy-blue, bunchy, buttoned-up man's sweater with holes in it, and seeming vaguely familiar. A small, rather peaked-looking woman, of indeterminate age—and since she seemed friendly, or ready to be, I went over.

That looks like good wood, I said. I'm splitting mine, too. I'm no good at it.

I ain't much myself, she said. My husband and the boy help.

How much do you burn in a winter?

Oh—I don't know, she said vaguely. Six, eight cords, I should guess. We ain't got oil or nothing. It's an old leaky house.

It's a lovely one.

She turns to look with me at it a moment and says, It was. It's kind of gone down on us lately. Burt, my husband, thinks he might paint it next spring, but he thought he might last spring, too.

Her tone suggests that she accepts this, has acquiesced to certain limitations, to mere possibilities. She sounds tired, a tiredness that is perpetual now. Her flat shoes are too large—might even be his, or a boy's. She wears a cotton skirt that could be anybody's.

I'm at the old Stinson farm, I say.

Nodding her head she says, We know—our kids was around Halloween with the Williamses. I'm Ginny Beal.

Oh, I say—yes—I'm Helen Calder. Vague disturbances in my mind, the stirrings of memory.

She seemed to hesitate a moment, then said, You want to come in? I got coffee on the stove.

I felt pleased at being asked and walked, chatting, with her and the children, who followed us, to the porch.

It was not one of your Carole Bean kitchens, I'm afraid; looked cluttered and dark when we entered, but was warm. She seemed to notice it with me. I ain't much on housekeeping she said—things pile up on me. What I need is a maid. Move, she said mildly to a child who was eating something at a table, let Mrs. Calder sit there. Another child was over at the stove making itself tea. I heard a small child crying somewhere. You give Lou her bottle? she asks. The child nods. Go see to her, will you.

Old printed muslin curtains at the windows permitted a dull gray light to filter in. A calendar is on the wall, and a picture of a lake with an Indian canoe drawn up to shore, framed in birchbark. Oilcloth on the table.

How you like it? she asked. I thought at first she meant the kitchen and for a flurried instant wondered what I would say. The coffee, she says.

Oh. A little milk, please, or what you have.

Canned—will that do?

I notice cats around, quite a few, comfortably tucked here and there. They ain't good hunters, she says, noticing that I'm noticing. We got mice as big as them in the barn—maybe that's why. She brings the coffee over, saying in her tired little voice, Now and then we'll miss a cat and I'll tell Burt, my husband, they got it. Another stir in the tides of memory, at the name.

I'm afraid to go in my barn, I say. I think I might have some of the same breed.

I used to take Burt's shotgun when I went in, she said—now I just don't go in—I tell him it's their place. My father used to farm and we had cows and things then, but Burt hauls and you can't do both, she says.

She's joined me at the table. You can't raise much down here anyway, she says, so we all just run to the store. It seems easier.

I ask if she minds if I smoke and she says that she doesn't.

I know the Hales, I say—I suppose you must.

Oh, sure—Burt and him trade at the co-op, she says.

He wants his boys to work with him, I say. I should think most of the men would.

Most of the men do, she says, but most of the boys don't like to work, it seems. I don't blame them. But my husband says the boys will come in handy by and by—he says if we feed them now they can feed us later. He wants another.

I shouldn't imagine *you* would, I say, sympathetically.

I see a truck wheel in to the semicircular mud drive and pull up by the woodpile. A man wearing a cap and carrying paper bags backs out. A boy gets out the other side and disappears. We watch the man walking across the yard.

Beth, open the door for him, Mrs. Beal says, and in he comes, filling the kitchen with himself, his bags, a draft of cold air. This is my husband, Burt, she says to me, and to him, who is putting the bags on a table near the stove, This is Mrs. Calder, Burt—lives at the Stinson farm.

Nice to meet you, Mrs. Calder, he says. Hello I say.

I realize I've seen him in town—one of the wharf "elders" in rolled boots, though maybe not forty yet. Two children I hadn't seen stand in a doorway. They all appear to be about the same age, wear nondescript clothes, don't talk, are lovely.

Did you get sugar? she asks.

He fishes in a bag, brings the box over, goes back to stand by the stove. Some cold down there, he says.

Some cold up here, she says—I been out splitting wood.

The two children in the doorway have come in and are picking things out of the bags—loaves of Wonder Bread, a large jar of Skippy peanut butter—which they seem to have been waiting for. They set about spreading it, and I study them intently till she says, You want some? I tell her no, and that I've got to be going along. Where's Henry? she says to her husband—I'd like him to meet Mrs. Calder before she goes. He's gone to clean them spark plugs, he says. How's the cabin coming?

Well, I'm in, I say. I've been staying out there.

He takes his blue jacket off, which looks like Navy to me, and hangs it on a hook on the wall; brings his coffee over. Sit here, she says, getting up—I've got to get the chowder going. I'm behind.

You been here some time now, ain't you? he says to me, stirring sugar from the box into his coffee. We see you around.

Another child comes in, goes to the peanut butter. I nod, then ask, rather forwardly, but I'm curious, How many children do you have?

Oh—ten, I guess. You ain't married?

I was.

Sometimes I wish I could say that, Mrs. Beal says from the sink.

You can say it any time you like, de'ah, he tells her, looking across the table at her. Square, rather expressionless face—large —with something young about it, something, some trace, of the young husband still there. Straight blond hair.

Well, it is hard, she says, to me—children and feeding—and never getting out. I suppose you travel and all.

I feel his dark-blue eyes slowly switch to me. I have, I say— but I'm staying around here these days.

Where's there to go? he says, somehow to her—one of their arguments, I suppose.

I'd just like to stay in one of them big motels for a while—and I wouldn't care which one, she says.

Well, you get the money, he says.

She's come over to stand by him, and almost absently a hand goes to his neck, the back of it. We don't get out, she says over him to me. I ain't been to Bangor in a year.

You get the money, he says doggedly. Strong, fleshy-young blond face.

I suppose I could take in boarders, she says—or maybe move down to Gertrude's.

Ha, he says—and I think, Gertrude—my one?—and as if in answer she says, I don't suppose you know her—one of them women the others know about, but don't call on. The men do.

Now, don't start that, he says.

The children are after the peanut butter again.

Mrs. Calder here's bought that island, Pennyless, he says to her. How do you like to be out there?

If I was on an island, she says, I believe I'd sleep all the time.

You do here, he says. Chops wood, he says to me—two licks of the ax and she's in at the coffee again, or them cookies.

Children and feeding, she says.

At least you *got* food.

I hear the child crying again. Go see to her, she says to a girl twisting open a jelly jar, who says, It's Bethie's turn.

Go see to her, he says, and with a little toss of her head the girl goes out, and in a dispirited voice, to herself, Mrs. Beal says, Oh, God. She goes to the sink where she's peeling potatoes. Mr. Beal watches her. We get in that motel, de'ah, and you can sleep till the horn blows, he says. She reaches for a potato, rinses it, says, I'd like a restaurant meal, too, sometime.

He waits for her.

And not hake. And not halibut.

Steak, he says, to me.

She shakes her head. *Quiche Lorraine*, she says.

Now ain't she got plans, he says. What in hell's that?

It's growing dark and I'm beginning to want a fire, make a drink, though I've liked being there.

I'm out on the porch beside the fresh stacked wood. She's come to the door.

Now, you come visit when you want, she says. I'm always here.

Not at one of them fancy motels, I hear him say, standing behind her, filling the doorway.

No, not traveling, she says.

And I did go home and have a fire, stirred up a martini, and set about fixing a bit of supper.

I picture them to myself—is there something mean in him?—I decide that he is mostly exasperated, certainly that—and she just overpowered by it all, and perhaps *some*thing, a little, of a slattern. I think also maybe he's made her like that and likes her to be, submissive, put down, with a feeble kick or two left in her.

How typical that house is, of a certain "economic level" here. With just a touch more initiative, how handsome it all might be. That fine line of house to kitchen to shed to barn. Give it a lawn, a coat of white paint, lilacs, a dooryard rose. Yes, the Hales thrive by comparison.

Burt Beal—did Gertrude once mention him? Local, ex-Navy, I'd say. A touch of the brute in him—quite sexual, I think, in a kind of point-blank fashion. For the Collection? Maybe not.

JOURNAL. Richie around—a Friday, though I'm losing track of the days.

He didn't want to paint, right away. Had brought a few pages he had written (he had read the Gerald Brace)—showed them to me. As in the poem, I felt something caged, inarticulate; he was imitating, though trying to add something of his own, something real that he knew about and had felt. It was about being out there —hauling. It was about being with Elmo, and how he feels about the boat, and the way things feel to him on a good day, the way they look. All misspelled, ungrammatical, the handwriting fifth-grade with a strange, carved look to it. I could see him licking and biting the pencil.

My fire is going. Buster sprawls in silken grace on a chair. He's better now. I'll finish this and walk out for a look at the stars. I keep hoping for an aurora—remember sitting on my wharf with Richie while that thing flamed over us. Why can't I keep it at that?

WEDNESDAY 27 DECEMBER. Christmas gone—including a party of my own here yesterday, Tuesday—the Casters, May Stinson and Carole Bean, Joe and Helen Curtin, whom I met quilting, E E & R, and the Williamses, the McFarlanes, and the Beals—all wearing their good clothes, in which they resemble dressed-up farmers and wives (nothing wrong with that). Men in the kitchen, women in the parlor, as though they had entered by separate doors; but then the women went in search of the men and the men came in, for a while, joined before gradually separating again. The talk: weather, fishing, taxes, local events, the new gym—with me always just a bit on the sidelines once it gets going. But I put my two cents in when I can.

And the Beals fit in all right, since everybody at least knows who everybody else here is. She in a rather meager little dress that was somehow just like her, and he in his suit—one more towering male in this house. Yes, he knew Elmo and Richie, knew Jules, as Ginny seemed to know and be accepted by the other females. She had some beads she displayed for us that he had given her (simply awful), and I tried to imagine him picking them out. (Note: of *course* Gertrude had mentioned him—spoke of him as mean, advised me to keep my distance. I will.)

In a bunch like that they have fun, and with the liquor flowing in the kitchen (out of sight of the ladies, though not out of ken), the men get noisy—lots of "gawddamns" and "baa'steds." The ladies like Elmo, who maintains the pretense of liking them back, a bit ponderously, I might add (out of pique?—Now, Elmo . . .).

But the great concerns hover visibly in the background: money, weather, food, and work. Politics, too. They let themselves out on short leashes, working as hard as they do. Picnics are still their game —cooking and eating—church suppers. Why so many of the ladies carry weight and the men grow portly. They like me, but properly consider themselves superior. After all, they've been here a while; I've just arrived and will always be "that new woman." Mr. McFarlane had brought an accordion and played it for us. I am not mad about an accordion but it added a note of cheer.

Christmas itself much like last year. The boys gave me a model of their father's boat, the Eth-El, complete with his numbers penciled on its bow, and two tiny little traps they had made out of broomstraws. I was much pleased. I gave Richie and Elmo each an outdoor lighter that works on butane, and they seemed to think they would be useful, ignited them all evening. And Ethel a fine little pin more expensive than I think she realizes. And the children things. We all went to church again, dressed in our best. Another energetic, tireless performance from the pulpit, which bored them (I saw great, wide, unabashed yawns) but which they seemed, nevertheless to approve.

I can understand religion here. It allows them to gather. Yes, and to hear the old wonderful story: Creation, Temptation, Carnation—Incarnation. They like the Old Testament and find themselves in it—strong, backsliding people who want God and need the fear of Him in their bones, with promises of love thrown in to do what you can with.

Lights strung across Water Street, yellow—red—blue—white—a few green—a few broken, the houses shadowy beyond—that slightly squalid, carnival look to things that I also love.

And now begins the long hard haul to spring.

DECEMBER 31.   New Year's Eve. I've been watching it on television and feeling very demure, and a bit left out. Crowds in Times Square. I always think it's the same crowd. Hurray, hurray! Fizz. Pop. To bed. I wondered a moment who might be at the Jed Prouty.

SATURDAY 6 JANUARY.   A warm day for this month, though swatches of snow are around like dirty laundry, sheets—so walked in to town and down to the landing. Found Bill Eaton there on a bench in a patch of sun, boots crossed, hands folded in lap, leaning against siding of gray shingles. The wharf—he clings to, haunts it. He's one of the few who still go out when the weather permits, and even when it almost doesn't.

He wears one of those knit caps, skullcaps, that Richie and Elmo often wear—his gray. His face is mahogany with a silvering of bristle on jaws that are massive and square. He has the fresh, gray eyes of a child, the body of a patriarch.

We watched the water, gammed, till I felt the cold.

I got some coffee home—would you care for a cup? he asked. And in his rattly old truck off we headed through town—then down a little road I didn't know, where the houses were very small, the yards sparse, fishermen's houses—and finally 200 feet or so down a rocky, grassy lane that led out to the water, where three shingled shacks were silvering on the shore, one of them his. A wharf stood out from a cluttered bit of ledge.

Poverty—poorness—being poor—not the same thing. Poverty the abstract term—something one wars on. Poorness, being poor—not always depressing. Though I was flabbergasted by that kitchen, where they cook and eat and live, he and his son, who not having a job and nothing to do was there with a tiny radio he had, turned on. Clothes were hanging to dry over the stove, an old wood-coal burner partly converted to kerosene; the table had an oilcloth on it, plus newspapers, a bottle of ketchup, a half-eaten can of sardines, a box of crackers, plain old wooden chairs around it. An iron sink stood on thin iron legs with buckets and dishcloths around—they wash not only dishes there but themselves, apparently, after heating the water on the stove—oh, and nameless objects in corners, under things, hanging, leaning against a wall—yes, poor—all cluttered, a mess, yet not depressing—perhaps because of Bill, who didn't seem to notice, who pushed things away, sat me down, got out a punched can of Carnation milk, brought over two mugs, introduced me to his son, who nodded, but didn't speak. The coffee was already warm. Just out the window I could see a great heap of cut wood and broken lobster traps against the pink granite of a ledge with a trace of snow on it. I was warm, my feet were thawing; I saw things that I seemed to respond to, broken, mended, used, and used again, until ready for burning.

I sensed the water out there and through a blue-clouded window could see it; I was in the midst of something; and looking around me at that tiny, dark, cluttered and crowded room I felt at home, and felt, mysteriously, at the brink of an understanding of what it is we all need: *less*, and not more.

Just a glimpse, not to be thought out by me. Yes, because there *was* that boy with nothing to do. But how little Bill seemed to resent him there, as though why should he need to do anything? Something small and quiet about him—Chuck—whom Bill calls Chuckie de'ah. That's Chuckie's pile out there, he told me as I looked out at the wood—he keeps us warm, he does.

He showed me their one bedroom and another tiny room where they simply "keep things." No apologies.

He drove me back in to town (Now you come for coffee with me, I said, you and Chuck), and we parted.

TUESDAY 9 JANUARY. Snow flurries, presided over by sun through breaking clouds. Sudden gusts of speckled wind would swoop in, surround you—you in a glass storm-ball thinking, Oh—oh—look—then racing away to dance at another window, leaving the air clear, the yard dusted with white.

WEDNESDAY 10. Quilting.

I want to know who made that hall. I seem to hear their voices in there—their ancestors, presiding still.

THURSDAY 11 JANUARY. Worked at a painting of flowers in a bowl, zinnias, from memory. Trying for a bolder style.

Note: I'd like to paint children, I think—this prompted by seeing two of them walking this morning, which reminded me of seeing them in summer, along the road, in yards. The children here are often beautiful, especially, it seems, the girls—blond, tiny, blue-eyed, frequently ragged, barefoot, unkempt. The boys tend to be round-faced, pink-cheeked, sturdy, also blond. But it's the girls—because of their hair?—who seem so lovely, a bit waiflike, delicate. They are very friendly, almost always speak if you pass them walking. They remind me of what I have lost (as, almost, what does not?). . . .

JOURNAL. The rash is back—goddammit. Out with the calamine lotion again. Maybe if I rub gin on it . . .

JOURNAL. A dash up to Bucksport and the Jed Prouty. No excitements to report, no boozily friendly millworkers dancing me off my feet. Home safe and sound and disappointed—rattling my old pearls.

SUNDAY 14 JANUARY. Guess who came creaking in last evening in his old cut-down truck.

Much like a cabin visit. Slicked up for it (and I seemed to see him at his sink, pots of water steaming on the stove, standing on wet towels, the blinds down—Come give my back a scrub, Chuckie).

How you making out, de'ah? Some cold out, ain't it? Rubbing his hands. I smelled Aqua Velva, which he'd probably gotten for Christmas some years ago, and something that I think was damp wool.

Much pleased, I took his jacket and cap and hung them where they would warm.

I wanted to fix him a bowl of soup, but he waved it away, had already eaten, so I got us a drink instead and built up the fire a little.

I wondered about you at Christmas, I said—at Thanksgiving, too—I wondered where you would be.

Was over to my daughter Mary's family, me and the boy. Husband works at the sardine factory.

Miss you out there. Cabin looks fine—raft's up on ledge—but now, ain't *this* some nice. And for a moment he looked around at the room, and for a moment I saw it through his eyes as against his own little place. Yes, I may look rich to him, though he might just see it all as well lighted and cheerful, neat, ample. Well now, what's this?—he had picked up my scrimshawed tooth.

I listen to him, then fix us another drink; and he expands, grows to feel at home there on my sofa, talking out his memories. He's learned his talk from his father, perhaps, as Elmo and Richie have from theirs, him, the other older men. It comes down. I study his face and realize, from some vantage point, that I ought to be leery of him, as women at one time were of men like that—big-jawed—small-nosed—of broad lipless mouth, and nearly flat of cheek—a face out of history that clubs have rained blows on, face of the earthborn English, Saxon-old—Jute—Briton; his shoulders, next, go with it, as do the eyes, not innocent now, grown secret—as has he; some tone, some look to him, at something in the air that has come around us, since he knows again I admire him (or perhaps I exude some perfume, some female scent, as the civet cat). He's been telling me about lobsters. He has superstitions about them, where they go, why they return. He knows crevices they like.

And after bringing the drink, a cracker or two, which he takes without ceasing to talk (about the sea now), I sit on the sofa with him. And now he pats my knee, calls me de'ah—and an arm lifts, it includes me. Yes, de'ah—storms—and a man'll wash overboard—and they can't last—boots fill—they go down. I once seen one man wave, and it broke my heart.

Shyly, craftily, he lets me understand that he wants to go to my room. And I manage it—by hook, by crook, female cunning, old guile (Do you like apples?). We go upstairs. I show him a painting of Elmo, whom he does not recognize, of course. Surprise. I paint. Yes, and I need someone to stand, to pose. You, I say—on your boat. Well, we might, de'ah. And me, rather bawdily, And maybe here sometime, on that couch. Like *that?* he says. Now who'd want to see me naked, de'ah? Maybe lots of people, I say. We find my room and undress.

Lying together—he talks—talks. But then we kiss and my hand wanders over him, till he rears up and on elbows, is over me looking down, and I see vague light-shine in his eyes and remember the face—it watching me, looking down as my hands go over his back, holding there for me—and I think, Like lion looking at its prey, and am aware of the arched chest and the belly just brushing me. And he stretches, stretches up for me as I rub, pushing himself back with his arms, and my hands go to his chest, slide down into hair as he holds himself for me, something ancient and ritualized in the way he gives me himself, as if offering me in some way his heart.

He fucks me hard, his body grown muscular, thick and alive, working at me.

Very late he leaves (Will you be all right? Oh, yes—we'll make her fine), and I watch his lights sweeping out, and worry a little. Not, of course, that he's that old, but he's had a fling. I see him climb into bed and his son roll over to make room, the two of them like spoons, to keep warm.

JOURNAL. A clear, clean day. Bill Eaton somewhere along with me, I walked out to the promontory—known, I learn, as Old Man's Neck—for a look at the sea. Captain Bass and the "orts"—I find what I take to be foundation stones and remember GH's account, and Herne.

My mind simplifies out there—lovely things write on it. Wind and water, rock—a tough grass. A tiny, rutted road winds down to the very point where a backing-turning place exists.

But all so washed by weather, sun, by salt wind. I look at the water. I think, Ah—a few of us—some lucky few—could know this properly; and I realize, for a kind of honest moment, that I'm an aristocrat and believe in that. They *are* aristocrats up here, too, oddly—poor as they be.

I stand and look until the wind, the motion of water have scrubbed my mind clean as the beak of a gull.

January 18 Thursday

Dear Beth,

Herb thinks they *might* go traveling, but isn't sure. Will let me know as soon as he is, etc. Goddamn it to hell. I had begun to count on seeing you, New York. Down there perhaps I could talk about something that worries me. I couldn't here. Worry isn't the word. Concerns—threatens. When I'm with you I can't talk about it and say to myself that I'll write, and when I'm here I can't write and say that I'll talk. Which means I guess, that it's not to be forthcoming. Not yet. I write about it in the journal, which has become intermittent but goes on. Well, it's *work*, for one thing, turning life into words. (Words into life?)

Hale and Hayden—Elmo and Richie—stop by fairly often and are comfort to me; two bears in my parlor I dance for as best I can. A large moving around, a settling by the fire, then the room, a little rockily, settling back around them, including them within its chintz, its warm, yellow-dark, light limits. They sink back, they talk. And through their talk a sense of their world floats in. They live on a margin, never very far ahead, often behind. So that I see how I do fit in, for these two—an oasis, slightly unreal, comfortable, reassuring, someone they can come visit. I am a rich woman to them—and one they can make free with, too.

Hale—yes, darling, I am, as you guessed, a little taken, and like to think that I could have been happy with him, having his children, keeping his home, making a place for him to come back to out of the sea, listening to his complaints. I would have belonged to this place then, as Ethel does.

And the other, Richie—he and I paint (you saw his things, one or two). Unfortunately, for me, Elmo has a kind of hold over him and won't, I think, let go, except for purposes of his own, which

257

are slightly obscure. So that it's complicated, since without Elmo I just might have (might have had?) some sort of chance. He doesn't seem to mind an older woman—apparently does not feel threatened, or whatever. Did I tell you he's posed for me? Nude. He seems to do it as a favor, of sorts—terribly nonsexual. Oh, and we've talked, evasively. He comes around, comes here, I mean—but at times I think because Elmo has told him to.

And old Bill Eaton paid a visit—very decorous—and I one to his shack, where he lives with a twenty-year-old son in what might seem like squalor were it not for the water at his front door, the pyramids of lobster traps in his little yard, a great flow of granite littered with twine, rope, *beautiful* old pot buoys—all a mess, and all lovely. His kitchen, dark, grimy, with a large iron stove—and two tiny rooms, one filled to the ceiling with furniture, old clothes, tools, sea things, instruments—probably mice—the other containing a large brass double bed they share—large, comfortable, nice.

Yes, Bill Eaton does appeal to me. I had intimations of this toward the end in N.Y., when, desperately, I went looking for something I felt I had lost—dressed as Fifi Laverne. I know much more clearly now what it was I was looking for. He's the bedrock of this place. Without him it could not have existed. And I like feeling close to it—as I do to the water, the rickety little wharves, the lobster floats, the woof and warp of this place. Don't worry for me there, I won't charge after him in the old high heels.

All I meant to say was that about the visit. We'll wait and see. Love to you and yours.

WEDNESDAY 24 JANUARY. Quilting. Snow around, in tiny flurries but ominously. We forget it by the stove, stitch valiantly, have a coffee and doughnut break; certain husbands arrive and are welcomed, and we emerge to gusts that are chill and beautiful and dash for cars. Drove down to the harbor to look at lights, then home for a hefty drink and a fire, a magazine, a poem—Roethke—the old woman.

THURSDAY 25. Wind gone but snow is falling out in the blackness of this night. I'm in some sort of mood but will not give in. A sudden longing to see N.Y., to watch snow streaming down the East River.

FRIDAY 26. Worked at my zinnias. I'm getting a dust color in—

dusty pink, dusty apricot. I have to cheat to do it, by using white. Worked at the Hale-on-couch, at certain dangerous parts of it I must not exaggerate.

Made a great casserole—mushrooms, olives, and apple chips, oysters, shrimp, tuna, the works. Who cares how fat I get? Old Bill Eaton, looking down, admired me as I rubbed his back, his chest, arched forward, watching me while he let me feel—walked himself up on me with his arms like some huge paraplegic. That aroused him, didn't it?—I caught a glimpse of his face in under that gentleness, saw something brutal though buried still, mix of the female-male. I—oh—yes, lights. One of them out there plowing now. I am watching them sweep over snow, pause, sweep back, flakes suddenly visible. Good. Which one?

SATURDAY 27. What to say about last night? That Hale plowed me out?

Came in shaking snow off. He seemed serious.

Ethel headachy. I say, It must be hard on her, it is on some women. He agrees. Not that she picks on him, just seems to reject —or so I gather from what he says. And I say, That must be hard, too—to *have* to separate, even for a while, from someone you've been close to. And apparently certain women do.

He doesn't understand—but then, no more do I, not having reached that yet.

We go upstairs, he taking the bottle with him. He wants his clothes off, mine—wants to lie and talk, smoke, drink. He passes the bottle and I take from it—old Fifi Laverne—and we warm to each other.

But we talk and I get my licks in, about Richie. I say, You have him on a string—you have him moored to your landing—and he'll go along with anything you decide on. Do you just send him around?

At which he rolls to me. Who got you? he says. Did he?

Apparently he doesn't know about that evening on the island— which wasn't much but *was* us, Richie and me.

Hmmm?

Nobody's *got* me, I say, a little impatiently.

He looks down at me from an elbow, sips from the bottle, then bends and kisses whiskey into my mouth, sips again, kisses again— we share it, sharp and strong, then growing sweet as it seems to melt away.

He been with you yet? he asks, lying back.

The answer, presumably, ought to be no. In fact, is no.

No, he hasn't, I say. He's shy.

Shoi? he says. He does what oi tell him.

Why?

Because, he says, he's my boy.

So you're not going to give him a chance?

An' whoi should oi? I'm the one gawt ya, y' know. Got him t' come around, pose f' ya—I knew ya loiked that. Did he?

Not especially, I say, but feel chilled at his statement. And I don't think you did, entirely—he came around to paint because he wants to paint—

Paint, he said.

And posed for me because I needed someone to.

He painted befo'ah y' gawt he'ah, de'ah. An, oi was the one who posed fust. I stood the'ah f' ya—oi loiked to.

Why?

Oi wanted ya t' see me, de'ah.

He's putting me in my place, but I resist. See what?

Wha'cha think?

See what?

M' *balls.*

And then you told him to?

Ay.

Why?

I've tol' ya, de'ah—the town—ya lady frien's. 'Cause I loike t' come he'ah (and he rises, turns, comes over me)—an' you loike me to. And he takes my mouth again, forces it open with his tongue in a thick, deliberate probing as his head turns—asserting himself, and again I think of Bill, spruced up, wanting a little love, though I remember, too, that other thing in his face, leashed.

But he *doesn't* know about Richie, that he came to my room, allowed me to make love, and did respond. At least I have that. What would he think if he did know? But gradually my mind drifts away, drifts back to him, who is over me now in a close, hot worrying, has sunk onto me, rhythmically, his body moving. I hear him murmur, Go git it, de'ah, what I brought ya—go git that stuff. I can't, I say—I know I can't. And he's after me again, rubbing my breasts, my thighs, nuzzling. Go git it—go git it, de'ah—his voice quick, hot, his hand taking my hand down. He bargains— I'll be good f' ya, de'ah, oi promise—I'll git it f' ya—I'll git it. He rises suddenly, moves away—leaves the room. I see a light turn on. I hear him in there. It goes out. Then he comes back.

I'm scared. It will damage me in some way. But he has me now. My hands claw at his back. Wait—*wait!* I say, and he holds, pauses.

He talks to, murmurs at me. He comes in in a thick, hard parting of me—wider, wider—Wait! I cry, *wait!* He holds—on shoulders and arms up there (he's watching me). At moments my hands dig at his back. He's careful, slow, holds on his arms, his knees—Easy, de'ah, easy, I hear him say—he comes down, comes in—more—more. I feel him to be enormous down there, no end to it. More, more. I hang on. . . .

Then somehow I seem to unlock. I give in—give in—and he sighs, is talking, murmuring, has entered completely, and my arms go around his back as his have come around me. . . .

Oh, Beth, it was good. It was. It only sounds bad on this cold, white page. I'm more than I was—I know more, I've learned. . . .

TUESDAY 30 JANUARY. Coffee with the girls. We gossip, we chitter like mice, gorge on pie, talk about dieting. I admire Carole Bean's geraniums, which are blooming insanely there at the windows against snow.

I do see other ladies, too, and an occasional man at the laundromat—the Wash-A-Teria—their voices a little like the washerwomen in *F.W.*, the Annaliviaplurabelle part. I feel left out.

NIGHT. I'm drunk, a wreck, staggering around. Elmo here again. Just appeared, or it seemed. Oi had t' come here again, de'ah. . . . Who cares? Who'll ever know? When he left I stumbled out to the car, martini in hand, drove to Old Man's Neck—stood in wind and darkness, hearing the rush of waves out there. *What am I to do?*

JOURNAL. My own geraniums—the rose especially—look lovely at the window of the borning room. I like to pick the dead leaves off. They smell so good—in my fingers, withered. I like to read in that room. I can look out and see the barn. I suppose I should make that into a garage. Come spring and I'll have a good look at what's in there.

SATURDAY 3 FEBRUARY. Richie around to paint.

He changes into the trunks without saying anything. It frees him to do that, I think; something is shed other than merely the clothes. An old self. I work on a nude of Elmo—of Hale-Hayden —lying on a bunk, boots beside him, checked shirt on a chair. A window behind. Bill Eaton now in it, too—the belly. All my men rolled into one. But the drawing is sound, I know where things go.

We work without talking, he at boats in the sky, to call it that —strong colors, a freshness. We're happy up there. And I know that Elmo is slightly misinformed about things and that Richie is now freer of him than he thinks.

He comes over a moment to look at what I am doing, and after a moment says, Ea'ah, that's him—got them big balls, ain't he? Which surprises me that he would say that. And then, You seen him, huh?

I nod. He knows you've posed for me, too.

Yes.

I say, Do you come here just because of him?

He's gone back to his own painting.

He say that?

Well—I think he likes you to—so that people won't talk when he does.

Ea'ah.

Do you? I say.

I like it here.

I did not pounce on him. I know he knows about Elmo now. He seems to accept it as in the order of things. I asked him again about Gertrude. *Apparently* (he was reticent) Elmo had him watch more than once—in fact perhaps fairly often—poor Gertrude crocked out of her mind.

The weather tightens its grip on us. At times nothing moves, no one is in sight. You admire the gulls, perched on the canning-factory roof, so superior, in their way, to us, who perch so precariously under ours. They stare, cold but superb, at the world, waiting for better days. May they find them.

JOURNAL. House-snapping cold—nothing moves—certainly not me.

JOURNAL. Subzero. A dead sparrow out there where I put seeds. Death in a snowbank, only a tiny one but it touches me, who am God, since I do nothing but watch.

JOURNAL. Richie *is* publicly visiting me—I'm sure. Has come twice just to sit, apparently, and let his truck be seen. I ask him about himself, I manage to keep a little conversation, like a kindling fire, going, but conversation is not what he's about and my feeling today is that he is here on behalf of Elmo. Father Hale himself around twice—to sit, drink, and be merry.

Thus far my ladies don't seem to have noticed. They would accept Richie, I believe, are curiously not prudish about that (life must go on), might even be glad for me—it would give them a topic, among other things. Elmo would be a very different proposition.

JOURNAL (don't know the date). Long walk in a brilliant day. Down to the harbor. Color—light—air. Watching the tides, the boats (old Bill's still out there, among others).

Walking along Water Street. Smoke rises from the black chimney of a lobster shack. A figure moves over snow, past a latticed wall of lobster traps, walks to the end of the wharf, I think urinates. The gulls seem, rightly so, indifferent, though two sail over him to investigate. And the sun is going down, is sliding out from behind a slate-blue cloud; I look away a moment toward it, see that the houses are in the shadow of the hill, and when I look back, a lovely thing has happened—the boats and the island shores beyond them have all turned pink and orange. Richie is right. They do, they are.

A woman near me is out, unbelievably, hanging wash, which plays a moment, like children, in a breeze, before freezing. Beyond her I notice how separate, or contained, the little houses look—empty, waiting—though I know that a life goes on within them. Up on the hill behind them the trees look stark against a sky that is taking on color as the sun goes down. The grander houses are up there, some fine early Victorians, some Greek Revivals. I remember handsome cut-granite foundations, an iron fence, a widow's walk. As I do, they watch the sea, though for different reasons.

In the waning light, when I got home, I worked at the painting of Elmo. A good looseness to the figure—so at ease, so simply there, as with strange, luminous eyes he looks at me. Not quite him—a cousin, perhaps—a touch of Herne, or someone I imagine. And through the window I will suggest the outdoors, that other

I saw this afternoon that is all around me, now fixed in a silence I could shatter with a scream.

JOURNAL. Note from Herb. They *might* go in late February—things are uncertain, though he is on sabbatical. Worry about a book—dynamics of something. . . .

My book, my journal. I am becoming immensely cunning. Witness that about Beth, for instance. I still know what is "real"—will others?

JOURNAL. Richie here painting. Changed into trunks. Admired, a bit reluctantly, the nude Hale (which *is* finally good). I asked him to pose. Lie over there for a few minutes, will you? Like this? he said. I shrugged, and without more ado he pulled off the trunks, not even bothering to turn.

I was able to check on a line here and there, a shadow.

JOURNAL. Out walking. Just to *be* out. Weather grim. No shadows, no light.

Walked up to see Ginny Beal—in her kitchen with children, cookies, coffee. She's pregnant again—and didn't seem to mind. Burt was out in the barn building a skiff with his boy. We walked out to watch them a while. They had rigged up an oil drum, made it do for a stove. We brought coffee for them. Poor or not, successful or not, Burt works. Big, strapping young man, you wonder why things run down on him. Maybe not too quick in the mind.

Elmo waiting for me when I got back. My heart, something, leapt at the sight of him—undershirt off, shoes off, drink in hand. Hope you don't mind none, de'ah, me making myself at home. He had a fire going. His face shone like a berry in it, his hair gleamed black into mussel-shell blue, pelt of it over his chest. He rises, comes toward me, opens his arms and hugs me to him.

But what am I to do? How to survive in *this* without *that*? I was with my ladies for hours, walked through a dead world, visited the Beals. And I do need a drink. My good ladies. I need it to come back to sometimes.

Our dialogue:

Richie been around? he asks.

On your behalf, I say—and his own.

His own what?

He was here twice to sit, and twice to paint.

Now ain't that nice.

Where is he now? I ask. I suddenly remember not seeing the jeep.

Driving around.

While you're here?

Ay-yup.

You complacent son of a bitch.

Why you say that?

You had him drop you off—just like that?

Just like what, de'ah?

He's bending to take off his socks.

Where does he go when he's out like that? I ask.

Just rides around.

Hasn't he any friends?

He knows a fellow or two—sometimes he'll go see Harvey Grindel.

Who's he?

Lives over to Oak Point—he hauls—same as me.

And Richie just rides around.

What's wrong with that?—he don't mind.

How do you *know* he doesn't?

I know. He's holding out his glass and I get up to make us another. I hear him in the parlor, thumping around. And I realize how easy it all is for him now.

Next time you might as well tell him to come and wait here, I say, handing the drink down to him, him sitting there in his shorts. He pats the sofa for me to sit with him. That would be nice of you, de'ah, he says.

I'm curious, of course. I say, You wouldn't mind, would you?

He turns to look at me. *You* would, though.

I might feel confused, I say.

About what?

About how to feel with him here.

Why should you feel confused, de'ah?

Come on, don't be d-u-m.

He wouldn't mind.

You don't know that.

He looks at me again.

You mean because he's been to Gertrude's with you—I know.

He still looks at me. Round, weather-reddened face, black hair.

And you—made love to her with him there?

265

Ay—yup.

Why?

And he says after a moment, I want that boy to *learn*.

Is that why?

Why you think?

I don't know—maybe you like to.

I did that time. He's put an arm around me; he picks at the buttons of my blouse. Fucked her proper, de'ah.

So he could *learn*?

I want him to *learn*, maybe get married, get his own place—people ain't married gets kind of queer after a while—I seen them.

Like me.

Not like you, de'ah. He unhooks the bra, runs a hand up under my breast.

Why not let him have a chance with me, then?

I will. And adds—When I'm through with you—but says it with good humor, fondling me.

And when will that be?

Maybe never, de'ah—I like you—and then says, with a kiss at my ear, I like to fuck you, de'ah.

With him watching?

He looks at me, a smile broadening. I might—could be good for him.

And you would enjoy it.

I would.

Why?

Oh, something this way comes—something dark. I see a face, big-jawed, forehead brute, over eyes encased in bone. They peer through fog, for me. Of my own making.

JOURNAL (WEDNESDAY). Quilted with my ladies like a madwoman all afternoon. I watched them to see whether they were watching me. And in that cold old hall, of dusty, white-painted wood that has heard its own stories, huddled as near to the stove as we could get, smell of coffee around, something clean brushed my soul, almost got to the corners. Boats, water, tides, rocks—storms, deaths, winter births. . . .

They sustain me, these women—knowing they've had their own times with their husbands cuddled under quilts like these, giggling and whispering in those old beds with the children nearby asleep.

Now, Fred. Small are the houses they have to survive in. They're real women—as girls, pretty enough for some man to pursue and fondle. May Stinson—she is pretty still. Shadows of the girl about her—way she parts her hair.

Perhaps I could have been one of them once. Talking economies. Now take a tomato—*peel* it, I say—put an onion with it—biscuits—an egg. . . .

Driving home. The sun had come out below a long plate of leaden sky. And the spruce black, and the water with a long trembling red streak on it—and the shore, the rocks, hard—crevices filled with snow and ice.

Why does it suddenly come at me, get in my throat, all but blind me? I'm caught, that's all, in some trap not of my making. Not of my making?

February 20 Tuesday

Beth,

Tell me something. Our dreams—do they ever become real? Adam woke to find that his had. Sometimes I'm afraid that could happen to me.

It may be, dear, that I don't quite belong in this world. I try hard, too, but maybe at the wrong things. Once I met someone I called Mallek (have I told you?), whom, in a way, I liked; but then, somehow, he, it, got out of hand; he began—I suppose you'd call it appearing. Something like that seems to be happening here, getting out of hand. And I can't control it, and I know it isn't right. What I am coming to suspect is that, in ways I don't know about, *it* is controlling me, right along. I seem to live in a dream. I seem possessed.

Probably it was wrong to think I could live up here. But if not here, where?

And I'm so *close* sometimes, I am—I can see it, touch, *feel* it almost. Then I'm ecstatic, so that anything, even a rock, strikes with the force of light. Then shadows form and the night comes on.

Nothing in nature is lone. And I think I always have been. Why? Herb and I—nothing really worked.

Why can't I fashion a *good* dream? It may be I have no love, and nothing else will keep the world going, and perhaps now not even that.

Though you, of course, I love.

JOURNAL. The famous winds of March blew Richie in as I was
having a drink. To sit, to talk.
Me: Well, well—what brings you around? (I was in fact having
a third martini, or a fourth.)
He: Well—I was out driving—thought I might stop by.
Me: And welcome, welcome—it's a lady in distress who wel-
comes you. I could use some company. Take your pants off.
He: Mighty mean out, ain't it?
Me: But my fire is going. My cat is lying before it. You've met
little Buster, haven't you? We've been talking about the weather
—the famous winds of March—perhaps bringing a little aerial
garbage our way.
I fix him an incredibly strong drink, which he eyes askance but
accepts (doing his bit for old Dad).
So wha'cha think? I say.
About what? he says.
Well—pick a subject—wha'cha think about anything?
I think you been drinking, he says—not critically, he's only ob-
serving.
As a matter of fact, I say, I *have*. And I add, Didn't you know
that I was an alcoholic, an original member of AA?
What's that? he says.
It means that I'm partly out of my mind—not responsible—
but I'm of the older generation, so that's understandable. Fuck
'em all, we've always said. Take your *pants* off.
He looks at me a moment. Helen, he says, you're crocked.
Say that in dialect. And when he says, What? I say, Say it in
Maine, talk Maine—because I've got to learn—loin—no, ler'n—
I'm going to blow this whole joint apa'ht.
You are some drunk, de'ah.
Where's Elmo?
Home, I giss.
You *giss*?—don't you know?
He's home.
Well, so wha'cha doin' he'ah?
I told you—nothing—driving around.
And where do you drive to, may I ask?
Where's there to go? I just drive.
Droive.

Stop picking. I'm going to knock you on your ass, de'ah.
You wouldn't.
No—I wouldn't.
At which he stood up. At which I said, in time-honored phrase-ology, Sit down, sit *down*—and gave the time-honored wave.
You're drunk, Helen—and it ain't good for you to be. I'll go.
Because I love you, I said—that's why I'm drunk.
I watched him standing before me, still with his cap on, the knitted blue wool one.
Oi'll see ya, he said.
Oi'll see ya, I said.
When he left, of course, I laughed in my great merriment and washed that down with another martini, then drunken tears. Old fool. When they try to help, what do you do?
But it was for Elmo.
It was for *him!*

JOURNAL. Who was around again? The great Elmo. Nonjovial—businesslike. Apparently bothered by something. A windy zero outside. Blazing fire, before which he stood and stripped, clothes thrown to the side. I said, What's the matter with you? He pulled the socks off, the pants. I said, My, aren't we elegant tonight. The long johns. Going to bring me something? he said. You didn't ask. Aw, stop your blathering—go get me somewhat. Somewhat? He looks at me. I don't scamper away but I leave him alone—because he *would* knock me on my ass.
And he fucks me there on the floor in point-blank fashion. Sounds come from him steadily—grunts—unh!—unh!—and I am finished by him, as he in a moment is finished by his own passion. No special excitement to it, a machinelike performance.
We lie by the fire. I've brought us another drink.
What's the matter? I ask.
Nothing.
Something is.
And after a while I hear it, as if grudgingly at first. Money—bills—work. And for what?
Ain't got a goddamn nickel. Davie's sick. Aw, Christ—I can't make it. I try—and can't get one penny in the bank.
A man works, he tries—up in Connecticut they get thirty, forty dollars a *day*. Down here—nothing.
And I like it here. Born, raised. But can't make no living, de'ah.

I work, I bust my *back*—and there ain't one fucking *dollar* in the bank! I got a good house, a good boat—man to help me and all, Richie—but can't make a goddamn dollar is mine.

And Ethie—been home all winter, and I wanted to take her out, buy her a meal, let her see folk and all. Yes, and I had seven dollars free money. And she said, I got some—and went and got it. And I worked—I worked like a *bas*tard—all summer, all fall. And who *gets* it? *Who?*—who gets it, who *gets* it!

And I suddenly feel him shaking and I'm frightened. I try to hold him.

What am I holding? Maine? All this. And I want to, and it scares me that I can't, can't possibly.

But I try, and feel him trembling in my arms. He's hurt, he's mad. He wanted to take his wife out, my friend Ethel, who must have said, Seven dollars is plenty, El—or, It doesn't matter, I don't want to go. And now he's here, because it's away from all that.

We lie still. He says. But I *can't* make no living. What I'm going to do?—*ain't* no lobsters. And that's all I know.

And Ethie, and sick, you know. And here I am—drunk, lying here—and she—Take me upstairs, de'ah.

And up there it isn't love he makes—to me. I'm an object he's come only to hold—I'm worry beads, or an old rag doll he might once have had.

March 12

Dear Herb,

It didn't matter. I might not have taken it anyway. A difficult winter. Me against all this. I'm concerned.

I don't know how to define it. Something up here is losing, that's all, and maybe me with it. Going down, going out.

I guess New York would have been fun. But now I'm trying terribly hard to manage up here. If I can, I'm safe, will have made it.

Oh, Christ—news everywhere a disaster. More effective and destructive nuclear weapons—the MIRV—or, motto: The sooner you get your birds in the air, the better (your birds!). Dismal attempts at building new cities.

We are shitting on this world most poisonous turds, farting into the atmosphere. And now, most beautiful us, we are about to desecrate the moon. Most beautiful us—the new men: totally con-

ditioned, physically flawless, cunning beyond belief. Oh, basta—
you know it better than I.

But these men down here—they can't make it now—a man can't
work for himself, with his family. They're obsolete. And taxed the
hell out of existence, too, because they know it in Augusta. The
villages are going, the coastal towns. In a very short time it will
all be "summer people" here—then hotels, marinas, gift shops,
mobile homes. Oh, yes, I'm watching the end of something.
Fond regards and all that. Hope the book goes better.

JOURNAL. Richie around to paint. I apologized at once for my
beastly behavior, which he seemed indifferent to—the behavior.

I am finishing up the Hale. How come you put that belly on
him? he asks.

Does it spoil everything?

I wouldn't say that—it ain't him, though—not quite.

How would you describe who it is?

He looks, purses his lips. Well—like an old-timer—like your
friend Bill Eaton.

Won't Elmo be like that in a while? He's big.

He might. He eats enough.

He goes back to his own work.

Supper at Ethel's. Little David well again—bronchitis, but they
seem to have whipped it. I brought him a little ship model I had.

Boots by the kitchen store. Family scarves, jackets, coats bunched
on the wall on hooks. We're getting there, she says, about the
weather.

News: Betsy's engaged. To the Stinson boy. Course they won't
be married for quite some time, she tells me.

And her big dad says, She'll be flying away first thing you know.
And Anne says, I don't like boys, and Elmo says, Now what's
wrong with *boys—I'm* a boy. And Ralph says, She does, too—I see
her with Reggie Coleman, who's a jerk. And Anne says, He is not
—at which Ralph crows, See! And Anne says, *You're* the jerk.

Supper is beans and chowder and bread that Ethel has made and
a pie I've brought. I help with the dishes. Later we all watch TV.

JOURNAL. The winds of March are justly famous. Foul over the
scabrous remains of snow.

But blew Bill Eaton in for a visit. Just thought oi'd stawp by, see how ya was makin' it. Nasty out, ain't it? Vaguely we itch toward each other. I offer him a drink, which he accepts, mellows over. It's weather we talk about—he has stories about that, too. And we talk, too, about being alone, though of course he has his boy.

An' I like him there, de'ah—we don't squabble none—got the TV—an' we'll sit up to watch the Late Show now and then—like them Westerns, y'know—an' them spook shows, loike the woife an' me with the radio once. Oh, he's a comfu't, de'ah. But oi ain't been out much—down t' the dock an' t' haul traps is about all.

Accepts another drink from Fifi Laverne. It was a party—and I needed one, and so did he. And we *had* one. Came upstairs—still talking, him as if talk were a second suit of clothes.

He undresses, still talking about Chuckie, whom I can see he worries about. He ain't been with wimmin, y' know. Fools with hisself when he thinks oi'm asleep, loike they'll do.

I'm curious. Masturbates? I say.

What, de'ah?

Plays with himself?

Yis, de'ah—loike I do myself sometimes, when he does. He loikes us to, poor de'ah—'tain't nawthin'.

But—You do that together? I ask, as innocently as possible.

Wa'al, we do now and then. Oi wun't want him runnin' around gittin' some girl into trouble.

But what is it you do? I ask. My curiosity is aroused.

Well, de'ah—just jerk off, loike a man will—ain't gawt nawthin' else.

We roll toward each other. Comes over me and I rub at his back as he holds above me; my fingers go lightly up and down, all over. Get me good, he says, get what you want. My legs go around and I cling to him, his belly between them. I pull him down on me, we kiss, me at his back with wild fingers, I moan, I feel him down there, inch down to get at him—still kissing me, he comes in and I cling, I work at him as I did that other time and he holds himself there for me.

We separate, lie together again, him kissing me, talking a little, till I feel down for him. I want him in my mouth. Which surprises him and for a moment he prevents, but then lies letting me—and after a while moves a hand to feel down at himself and my face—Y' loike that? I hold his big legs in my arms, I feel how they work, lift, stiffen—his body moves, struggles—I feel his belly with my hands and his legs clamp, hold me, hands at my head—and he works, rubbery thick mushroom in my mouth, till his hands suddenly grab at my head and hold—Nawt yit. We play for a long time. I go at him till we're wrestling in each other's arms—kissing, breaking apart. He pushes me down to him and I take him again, him holding my face. I push his hands away and he lies letting me and moving till I taste him suddenly moving and hot in my mouth. We lie apart.

Seems—loike it were too much, loike m' insoides all come out. Did you like it?

Yis—yis.

I lie with my head on his arm as he talks to the ceiling over us. Boy done that to me once in moi sleep, he says, an' I slapped him for it. But oi let him.

Later he climbs on me, and in light from the hall, faint shine of his face, ancient and brute, looking down at me—Gonna fuck ya now.

APRIL. Deceitful weather—first this, then that. One day of sun and scudding clouds, then lank chill winds with purple hands and blue noses. I look at the weather, with eyes of the purest hate.

MONDAY 1 APRIL. Carole Bean says, Now hold on, de'ah—before you know it we'll be there. Dear woman, I say, we're months from it yet. It's April that's peckish, she says—turn your back on it to boil water and you're apt to be under snow.

WEDNESDAY 3 APRIL. Went for a walk around the harbor by a brisk chopping sea brilliant in sun. High tide. The skiffs frisking at their moorings out there. Great gulls swooping in—then lifting on the breeze, lifting and turning—wind-blown, heavenly trash. Silver. Greens. The low dark of islands.

Wrote this when I got back. At times I feel as though films of dust have fallen on the lobes of my brain, smothering clear thought, clear feeling.

My poem: Like water in a bay
Where ships have settled, we
Do not bear close scrutiny.
Our tides from some slight distance—say
A gull's cry—flow

273

More cleanly, flaws appear
But seldom,
To the eye our currents show
No sign of what the gulls are after
Down below.
Be wise, or kind,
Do not approach too near.

FRIDAY 5 APRIL. Long talk with Ethel. Depressing. Apparently things are not going well. Are even considering moving away, leaving. Elmo might work where a brother of his works, at a Grossman's lumberyard.

Is it that bad? I say.

After a moment she shrugs. They can't keep up, she says. It doesn't seem to get better, and El does as good as most. He works hard. They just ain't out there. And we hear the taxes are going up again. They're after the shore property, them, up in Augusta.

I feel chilled. But move? I say—leave here?

We can get a good price for the house, she says, and some land we have.

Oh, but you can't, I say—I mean leave, go—this place would die without you—I would.

We aren't anxious to, she says. Harvey Robbins is going, y' know —has that house near the cannery. Others are. Junior Bass.

And you're serious? I ask.

I'm afraid so, dear.

I suddenly long, am wild, to tell her, to cry. But I need you, him—you are this place—I must have *some*one. I say, I couldn't bear it if you did.

She merely shrugs. We'd all get on, she says. Things would be different, that's all.

But she's tough, able to accept.

She says, You don't understand. This house, this place—in the old days they could make enough—no one was rich, but enough. We can't now. They aren't out there.

She means the fish, the lobsters.

And in her kitchen, sitting at a table, a window by us, I begin to know—and my bones grow chill. I can do nothing now but watch the clouds form, roll over everything I love.

You can't go, I say—you *must* not leave. I look at her, the woman, the friend I've been unfaithful to, over and over in my mind. I say, I love you, Ethel, I love your family. You must not leave.

And she looks back. She says, I know you do, de'ah. We like you, too.

I blurt it out, I say, I make use of you, I sponge off you—someday I'll tell you—I'm evil, I'm wicked—but I need you here—you.

She simply looks at me—plain little Ethel Hale. I could tell her. I could tell her all. But of course I can't. I can simply look at her and nod. I do say to her, You're all I have.

She says, Well, you found us, de'ah—and we found you. We love you, too.

SATURDAY 6 APRIL. All day, more or less stunned, moiling it over. What would be left? Bill Eaton could not be enough—everything swings around them, my family.

MONDAY 8. In the afternoon out walking, mostly just to be out, sniffing at spring, looking for the signs of it, depressed, worrying about them. A red pickup drove by, an old one, barrels and things in the bed of it, went by, then stopped up the road and came backing toward me. I suddenly knew who it would be—that big bullethead, white shirt—his Sunday dress-up shirt. Drew abreast of me. I could see his big moonface (it was he I saw that time, not Elmo) through a broken window, and shivered—the bangs of an old boy. He opened the door. Where you going? he said, in the high-pitched voice that sounded immediately familiar. He had a jug on the seat beside him, a cigar in his mouth. Where you going? he said.

I was just walking, I told him. It keeps me in shape.

Yeh? Shape for what?

You can never tell.

I look for you—never see you around—how you been?

Pretty good, I say—for me. How have *you*?

No different. Kind of lonesome's all. Want a ride?

And in the midst of that depression, I got in.

Where'd you like to go? he asks.

After a moment's thought I direct him to Old Man's Neck, which he seems to know—as I guess he would—Ea'ah, I been there—and off we go. And down through the sapling spruce and out onto that grassy, barren knoll the sea surrounds. Where we park and where he offers me the jug and warns me that it's strong as skunk piss.

And it is—or like kerosene at first—I feel it instantly, burning my throat, then making its nest of fire somewhere within my ribs. The ocean out there, brisk in a late breeze, those pink boulders on shore—I perceive it freshly and with mixed emotions as we lean back, jug between us, talk; we smoke (he a cigar), we share the jug. And the light settles, it purples the boulders, touches to pale pink the foam of a spent wave. I see a freighter quite far out, heading up the coast. We talk about Gertrude a little, that she ain't quite right in the mind but that he's known her since before she was married. About the fishing, which he admits is poor—he's had trouble even getting bait. Price is high, though (he means for lobster)—dollar twenty a pound. And more soon. The shrimping wasn't much good—scalloping neither.

And when it grows dark, he puts an arm around me, pulls me to him, says, Nice to see you, de'ah, and kisses me. I feel the back of his head. We're suddenly clamped in arms, clamped mouth to mouth; we've been waiting, we're instant and fierce about it. We let go, sit back, his arm around me still. Night coming on, sound of wind. His arm has pulled me to him where I rest against a warm bulk of white shirt, sensing, feeling him under it. We're comfortable. He's still smoking a cigar. He doesn't talk, just holds me in an arm and smokes. Finds the jug and holds it for me—lifts and drinks himself—replaces it on the floor. The arm comes around me again.

Let me feel you, I say; and obligingly he unbuttons his shirt for me to, a hand from around me picking at the front of it.

Oh, I'm *not* a whore, I'm not.

Cozy in that little truck of his—a baby shoe dangles from its rear-vision mirror—rags, wire, tools, beer cans around—a moon-clouded window something has shattered, maybe weather—he's found my breasts, has fondled them a while. We drank, we smoked. I took off his shirt, found myself in arms that seemed to be sweatered in that rough wool, felt his mouth on mine, felt his body bending over me. I wanted us to be naked in there with the heater on, the night, which was coming around us, my sense of the sea out there, us parked in that truck at the edge of it, and he was willing—so we got out and undressed by the truck—sudden sense of the air, moving and cold on me, the grass rough to my bare feet—I see the pale shape of him across the hood, bending, coming erect—I'm excited, feel free, feel that I'm in for it, too—and then get back in to a mingling of bodies with him suddenly bent over me, me rubbing his back, thick wool.

He lies back, me crouched ludicrously on the floor between his legs, one up on the seat, him patient, accepting it, lying back, almost dozing, it seems—wind outside, it suddenly buffets the truck —a hand falls on my shoulder, pats. I hear him say, I wanna go to your house, de'ah—lies letting me suck, emotionless though aroused.

Want to fuck ya some, I hear him say—no hurry—take your time if you like that. He's hard as wood, calm, comfortable, lying there—his leg adjusts around me, his hand pats. He has a radio he turns on, lurching forward a little—tiny jangle of sound, music—he lies back listening to it.

Then and without bothering to dress he starts up the engine, and we drive back bouncing up the rutted, curving road, grass blowing in the headlights, silky yellow brown from winter, reminding me of his bangs. I'm smiling inside—I think, We're crazy—he is. In a broken dashlight I can see that he's still partly erect between spread-apart, round thighs—bare feet down there on the pedals, in shadow—the light turns his stomach and chest to gold wire—big moonface above, the round jaw of it lit by faint glow. By back roads he knows, through headlighted trees, a pile of cut logs, a sudden granite whale, he finds my road—I'm surprised to learn that it is when he stops, turns; I didn't recognize it. Before long we wheel in to my drive.

He comes into the house, having left his clothes, the jug in the truck, bringing only his cigars—portly-hairy body, flexible—he walks with his feet out in a kind of springy bounce.

After many drinks and a kind of dancing he does for me, by himself, he came upstairs and stayed almost until dawn. No "love" to it. He left about four, me a wreck, he still himself—went out to his truck, peed against it, dressed, me watching from an upstairs window. Then drove off. . . .

I wonder who or what it is he loves, if anything—a stranger, that one—a satyr. I could have sucked at him all night, and he could have held there for me to, reaching down for the jug, grown finally bored.

And that's enough—you *are* a whore, a writing, inventing whore of the mind.

But an honest one. No fundamental lies. It's only that other you lie about, isn't it? Richie? No, I do not. Bill Eaton? No. I lie as little as possible. About that one, Herne, I don't have to, I omit. Can I say he doesn't exist? For me he does.

JOURNAL. An incident, slightly amusing. Elmo around. B, not A. In a grand mood, it seemed—chores of winter over—repairs, replacements—and behind him now the sense of confinement, though spring is by no means here, is a month and half away (maples still leafless, the alders mere sticks). But he's going out again. He's behind with that—boat troubles, I think. And me with that shadow across the path. I want to ask him about it, talk, when I say, Ethel says you're thinking of leaving, he waves it away. Now, de'ah, I ain't come to complain—maybe they'll be in again. He doesn't want to think about that, he's in another mood.

We talk. On my way in with another drink I find him over at my desk, propped on his arms, reading. Instant sense of dismay, of being caught out—I've left the journal there, open to that fling with Gertrude's old friend. He's turning a page. I manage, without snatching, to get it from him. I laugh, awkwardly—Now, now, I say.

What's all that? he says.

Something I made up, I tell him.

Made up? Let me see.

But of course I can't.

You got *me* in there, ain't you? he says. I nod, I admit. He's seen his name.

And who's him, that one you're talking about?

No one, I say—I write for practice sometimes.

What did you say about me?

Oh—things you tell me, that's all.

About me posing for you that time, I'd bet. (Shrewd.) Have you, de'ah? Let me see.

But I dodge away from it, though I say, I *will* let you see something if you promise not to tell—I mean *promise*. He nods—I promise. I mean not even Richie, I say. I promise.

So I unleaf and bring out for him the Bill Eaton passages, from the cabin-warming on, playing with fire; and nervously I watch him pick his way through them. Then I go to the kitchen, not wanting to be there as he reads. Let it work its effect pure. (Pornographer!)

When he is through he looks up at me with a queer, almost puzzled smile.

You been *seeing* him? he asks. I nod, thinking, Suppose he had seen what I'd written about us, him and me—I have still the sense of an escape, though he says, And you put all that *down*?

It's a diary, I say—it's just for me.

Who's that Beth?—that friend was *here*? When?

I half nod. She'll probably see it someday.

I see him shaking his head, frown, hear him say, Well, I *never* read nothing like that. How come you make such stuff up?

I'm instantly defensive, feel exposed. But what do you think, I say—about him. Is it like him?

Like him?

The way he talks, what he looks like, is.

I see him shrug, as though that were no matter. It's *like* enough. He *kiss* you like that?—want his *back* scratched? I *never* read nothing like that—Helen!

You don't read, I tell him coolly. Books are full of that now. It's permitted. You may write what you like.

You don't say. Seems kind of nasty.

It's what people do.

You mean *them* people—marching around naked, keeping away from the draft.

It's more than that.

And I guess it is—wearing that long hair—I'd beat my boy silly if he come home like that.

I say, But it's *more* than that—it's the whole thing, the new world—they're excited about something.

And *I'm* saying it ain't natural—books like that—people reading what he done—like watching him do it to somebody. Not some-body—you! People as got nothing else, them's the ones. It ain't *proper,* Helen.

We've gotten off the track and I take the pages back from him, chagrined, annoyed, and go to fix us a drink.

And we blather on for a while, till he says, Yes, and you got me in there, ain't you? Let me see—come on. He insists. So I find a place where he's posing and hand it to him and watch while he reads. He's shaking his head. When he's through he hands it back, he says, Why you write all that?

Because it was like that to me.

Seeing me? That's just a man, Helen. I thought you needed to see for your drawing, that's all.

I did. At first.

Yes, but setting it down, having me talk and all—why you want all that? Why do you have to make up so much, Helen? Ain't the truth enough?

I think a moment. (What to say—in fact, why *do* I? "Truth"? Yes, why not enough?) I like to, I say. I'm alone much more than you think. It cheers me up.

You write like that about Richie?

Not quite.

He's looking at me. Something is shifting him back into good humor. He shakes his head. I never seen *nothing* to beat that— you worked up a storm in that old man, de'ah. And I'm glad you did. I always liked old Bill. And then, and slightly to my surprise —Why don't you write something more like that about me—I'll pose for you—you can get it all down.

I'm suddenly confident again. (I am?) I thought you didn't approve, I say.

Well—it ain't I approve. His smile broadens slowly out. Gets me kind of—shook up, you know, seeing all that. Put it in—get it all down, like you done with Bill—and let me see. I'll do it good for you, de'ah. Yes, and I'll get Richie to, too.

Don't you say one word to Richie about it, I say.

Amusing—in a way.

He didn't seem to mind my having that fling with Bill. On the other hand, why should he? I did have it, didn't I?

TUESDAY 9 APRIL. The last quilting tomorrow. I'm anxious to see them, my ladies, and afraid to again. Something *must* be writ on me by now. If only I believed in God. That graffiti from a men's room Herb let me use: Nietzsche Is Dead—Signed, God. His was the world that is killing mine. To be merely human, to be monstrous. I won't lose my grip on things.

FRIDAY 12 APRIL. Still cold as Billy-be-damned. But you can smell the difference, and here and there a green thing pokes through— the return of life, the miracle. It drives me to my vile practices. Each bud a birth, a new start down that old path, constantly offering choices that must be taken. And then certain choices are made (e.g., to write about Mallek), and you're on the way down. Where is the point of no return? How would science describe that? I wonder when *I* passed it?

Saw Mr. Hale at the P.O.—seeming like a familiar stranger. I feel instantly a little shy.

How you makin' out, de'ah?

Great burly, booted shape of him—that blue knit hat—rolled so that it fits his head like a skullcap—suits him. They always wear the same clothes. We gab a while. The boat's in the water. They're out now. The island is still there.

Looks good, he says. When you figure on going out?

I'm on my way to see Avard Bunk, I say—about the fireplace. Good time to, he says. Summer work ain't started yet. Well, we'll see you, Helen—come have supper; Ethel likes that; and with a friendly look at me, almost a pat, he clomps off, thick-legged, broad of back, patches on the seat of his blue pants.

Odd to see him out in the open like that—I realize that I seldom do. Yes, my word, how handsome some of these people are. If circumstance narrows them, it chisels them, too. Elmo Hale in bed? I wonder.

Standing there in the sun, watching him move off to his truck, some sadness comes to me, at the gulf that separates. How can I learn to accept that fact?

But I'm up, I'm stirring again.

SUNDAY 14 APRIL. Mr. Bunk is available. Great luck. We drew up plans. He remembered the cabin very well, from the warming. Has a friend who will boat over the stone, the brick. Will start this week. I'll go with them. A joy to be active again.

Richie around to paint. I'm putting the finishing touches on the Hale, nervous about exactly where to stop. And I ask him and he says, sensibly, Right there, now—he ain't just a cock, you know.

I'm going to do one of you next, I say—you painting, in those trunks.

And he says, You mean you ain't going to paint my balls? And I say, Ha ha. But it's his round.

In the kitchen I ask him about the Hales leaving, whether they might. He's evasive, shrugs, and I sense how hard for him it might be if they did. He'll see how it goes this summer, he says. He don't want to.

What would you do if they did? I ask.

Well—stay here, I guess. I don't know.

My mind blazes briefly with fantasies and yet the mere notion of them leaving is too much for it; it retreats in confusion.

JOURNAL. Buds—fat, turgid. Imminence, signaling the great conversion. I walked in my woods, broke off twigs, examined the clenched leaves, ate them. I destroy, I create, my hair a tangle of wind. Girls waking from sleep—hamadryads.

Called on Betty Caster, whom I hadn't seen for a while. We gossip. Another fight in town—one of the men badly hurt—over, she thinks, that Janice Hutchins who lives out past me. Do I know her? I shake my head, feeling a not unfamiliar touch of guilt. I generalize; then I say, a little brazenly, I wonder if Elmo Hale has ever had a fling. Elmo? she says—well, there's those that would like to, I know—big, strapping man like that, and Ethie—seems like she couldn't care less, at times. Of course, she's had the best of him hot, as they say, and is past her time.

I see quite a lot of her, I say—they've been very good to me. You do wonder though.

Ea'ah, you do wonder—could be a slyboots, one of them quiet sort. You wonder about that Richie, too—don't manage to get out amongst the chickens at all.

He comes to paint with me, I say—he's good at it.

Ethel said something about it, that he was.

I'm going to try to sell some of them for him this summer.

Are you now, de'ah? Have some coffee—it's on the stove.

April 27 Sat.

Dear Beth,

April on the wing, though little evidence of spring up here as yet. Signs, stirrings—a crocus or two, a snowdrop, but still mighty cold. If I were a bit woodsy-er I would see more, and the tiny, scurrying life that Miss Carson saw so vividly.

Bill Eaton by again, of whom you don't quite approve. He is my one bit of luck, though Richie Hayden comes around quite often to paint and has done remarkably. I envy him his gift, I who have to work so hard for anything. Perhaps my talent is with words. Well, at least I can make some things with them—unfortunately *not* of your "Summers in Castine" variety, with lists of plants, birds, and typical events. The Hales are not great picnickers and my other friends stay fairly close to home, being workers, all. Would it have been better had I gone after the summer people?

—the Procters. They, I am sure, do picnic, with gangs of children, dash off on little excursions, go antiquing (so do I).

Did you realize that the cabin is shortly to be graced with a fireplace?—my current project. And that I'm contemplating a front porch—deck—and that soon my little boat, the Pennyless, is to be launched, and that I will be out there again, hearing the dolphins ride past, rolling and wheezing—

I *am* through the winter dumps, which is something. And soon the seasons will smile, the lupines will be back, fields of daisies, sun, fog, the sounds of the fishing boats. I've got it all. And yet dreadfully at times there steals in a sense of total emptiness (please, this only for you), as if I were moving over something that could give way at any moment (the idea that the Hales might have to leave here, for an example). And wildly I do what I can. I write, I draw, paint, I invent—I make a life for myself that seems inordinately rich, oozing with plenty, dripping, complete. I hate to say it but I lead, at times, a very satisfying inner life—secret— utterly private (which was almost crashed in on the other day— Elmo Hale here, reading some of the journal, which I managed to snatch before he'd got too far).

It's that that I'm growing leery of. I create it, indulge it. And have the feeling at times, a bit scarily, that it begins to create me, that something retaliates, that dreams do become true. But what is one to do? How to live with a gap in things? I'm trying to. An alcoholic of the mind, an addict—so that at times I rush home to my dream, unlock it, let it loose; like a thing one keeps in a cage, I go to play with it. I saw Elmo on the street the other day and found myself suddenly shy. Mad, mad.

Enough—love from this beautiful and desolating land.

TUESDAY 7 MAY. How I leave you, old friend, to lie alone for long stretches now.

Why am I not dazzled by the other commonplaces? Why are the others so endlessly intrigued by the notion, say, that metals can be annealed, sand melted into glass, or that certain stars are dead, have been dead for centuries? Yet they know what I know, that words cannot produce love, that the uncreating word is the word of the intellectual playing at love from a distance, that at the bottom it is grunts of anguish, ecstasy, and pain. And that work is our only salvation. And the love that springs out of life.

On this fine spring evening, why all this?

Guilt? Remorse? Who has the word?

Mr. Bunk comes on apace with the stonework. I have the weird feeling that it is being built for reasons beyond my ken. That it is a mental event, not a real fireplace in which sea wood would burn green and gold and give off an odor of things perishing.

FRIDAY 10 MAY. Odd, to see Elmo in town again, coming out from the hardware store. Yes, as though he had emerged from a dream, detached himself from it.

Hiya, Helen—standing a moment to let me come up—that broad sun-reddened face, the wool clothes. And again I'm shy, self-conscious.

Richie appears—the two of them. They are this place. With an effort I break from my own dream of them.

What *weather*, I say—it's a little more like it, isn't it?

Some nice out, Elmo says. Ain't seen much of you, de'ah—come for supper. His friendly, direct eyes—I see them as containing him, them and the network of wrinkles, the gleaming smooth skin, around them. How simple and dignified he is. What a fine man.

How's the lobstering? I ask.

He shrugs. Well—it ain't too bad—we catch one now and then —don't we, de'ah? he says to Richie.

And I'm thinking, with some corner of my mind, This is what I have, this friendliness, here, in the street, where the sun presides, the water laps at the shore, the houses stand around. I hear Elmo say, And we'll stop out to see you, de'ah—we're running traps out there again.

We part, we go our ways, and they stay in my mind as presences.

Wood, water, sun, fresh air—a house with peeling white paint— a glimpse of the boats out there—a car going by—voices—my packages. I want to walk down to see Bill Eaton, and do, but he's not there. The gasoline pumps. The skiffs tied to the raft, nestled against it. The water, where seaweed sways at a piling.

JOURNAL. Out walking. I used to think of it, see it all in words— passing an old farm, or down at the harbor seeing sunlight on cut-granite blocks, blotched mustard gold with lichen. A mere listing of flowers—what is that? and that?—would help, used to help. But the days pass over me now as if I were something alien in their midst.

But soon I *will* garden. Oh, yes, burst out there to disturb that peace of weeds, of dreaming plants, of things whose names I know no more than they know mine. I will live as a member of that congregation that watches, listens—tends, moves on. Think of Bill Eaton, imagine that he— Oh, imagine *nothing!* Let be.

JOURNAL. Supper with Ethel and them again. A general chattering of family life, Elmo in the midst of it, taking it for granted. In the kitchen where I'm sitting with Ethel a moment, he comes in, takes off his shirt, his undershirt. I watch him washing himself at the sink. Ethel's talking about something at school. Anne passes through the room, is touched by sunlight a moment. Sound of splattering water. He washes under his arms—fat, immense broad back of him—white. I don't want to look, and feel an illness grow in me. And he turns, rubbing himself with a towel—Didja git them flashloight batt'ries? he says—to Ethel—who stops, realizes she's forgotten—Well, oi need 'em, de'ah—Christ—nob'dy remembers nawthin'—stands there rubbing at his chest with the towel. What is it? I say, to her. Batteries? He's turned back to the sink. Could I get them at Bartlett's? It wouldn't take me a minute. And I do, I scoot out, taking him with me in my mind.

JOURNAL. Here last night. He comes in and the house seems to ally itself with him, cease to be mine. Not him of the street, of that kitchen life. Something of himself he sends forth, that enters my receiving mind.

Mostly, our talk, about Richie—yes—of whom I feel now I ought to protect what is sound and simple in him, even if selfish—his talent, his gift. I don't *want* it drawn in. Elmo's plan. I want you to marry that boy—keep them from talking. That's what it amounted to.

I said, I will not use him as an object even though you do.

I ain't using him. Then, in a kind of wide innocence of tone, I'm trying to help him, de'ah.

Oh, stop it!—he's a thing to you, a tool. So am I.

I'm a tool, you're a tool, if you like to call it so—and we'll help that boy, and help ourselves, too. Stop your talking so goddamn much—come help me off with these boots—my back is sore, hauling them traps all day.

Poor you.

Well, I am. There—take a hold of it—help me, de'ah.

And get my shirt for me. Pull it up, de'ah (holding up his arms).

Anything else? I say.

You can help me with them pants.

I bring him a drink. I want my chance with Richie, I say, and not in your way, whatever that is.

You'll get it, de'ah—I promise you. Let me see what you're writing about me now.

No, I say.

Why?

I'm ashamed of it.

Go get it, de'ah—I can guess what you got there. You got me showing you myself.

I rise, and after some thought I do bring him parts, the pages that start with April, spring. And somewhat nervously I wait, I watch, as he reads—he reads slowly, has his glasses on, almost piecing out the words. I see a smile. What? I say.

Me reading that about Bill—you got me talking like him.

You do.

He reads slowly on, without looking up says, You like looking at me, don't you, de'ah—and a moment later, What's "pornographer"? Looks at me. What you getting at?

Skip it, I say. I'm going to cut it out.

Why I look strange to you in the street? he asks—what you mean by that?

Well—out in public—not here—you seem like two people to me at times.

He grunts. One would be enough, I'd think. Reads on—smiles again—reads out loud, He ain't just a cock, you know—and him saying down here (pointing at the words with a finger), You mean you ain't going to paint my balls. I like that. Looks up at me and seems strange to me in his glasses.

He reads through to the end, scratching his head, licking at his lip. He finishes, shuffles the pages together, hands them to me, takes off his glasses.

What do you think? I say.

It ain't like that other. It goes along better.

Which do you prefer?

And I see him smile—knowing and slow. Well—I kind of like to see Bill getting it—if he did. You ain't making *that* up, too, are you?

A shrewd question.

What would make you ask that?

Well, him getting so hot and all—though I can see how he might. Lot of them old boys never did get it proper—women thought it was nasty, against the Good Book somehow. But he smiles, puts an arm over my shoulders. Lord, de'ah—you did kick up a storm in him. He turns to unbutton my blouse. Kiss my belly, de'ah, like you done his. He unbuttons his shorts. . . .

I'll burn this, I swear—my image of him, lying under me, arms back. Get me like you done him, he says, I lean forward, take his flesh in my hands, my breasts. I watch him watching me, I see him smile. Get me, de'ah. I work at his flesh in hair, I fit myself over him. You're like a flag on a pole, de'ah. I work at his stomach, him up in me—his face smiles—Get me, de'ah—grows tense. Like a fury I work at him, snakes in my hair, eyes ablaze, and through what has come on me see his face as if bathed in wet fire, eyes closed—then opening, watching me—see his head roll, feel his body under me writhe—his head rolls, goes back—I see the underside of his jaw—his arms back, fists clenched—I ride him like a wild horse. . . .

The power of my own pornography. Potent far beyond its own words. How very strange.

What has *happened?*—where has the *rest* of it gone? The trips to the laundromat, walks into town. You saw Carole Bean yesterday, with her bandaged fingers, felt good in her kitchen, warming like a cat at her stove; May Stinson dropped by for a gossip and chat. You talked recipes—a way of using cold cod and milk (which sounded perfectly awful). You've been reading a lot. Sarah Orne again, dipping, browsing—as if her cleanness of soul would whiten your own. You've been painting. The days go on. (It's the nights.)

But you write only certain things in the journal now, as if fundamentally obsessed—which you are. How filled it used to be with pieces of this place, like a quilt. Even Bill Eaton—you cut him off, you go right to the end of a visit, as helplessly as he comes to you with his good rambling talk, his need, his gentleness, the sense you get from him that you matter to this place, are a part of it, since he is—all *that* you have been slighting, as if you cared only about something grotesque, that odd lust you have for certain parts of his body—letting him kiss you like that, for the strange excitement it causes him—*that* is your dwelling place now. Can we still say it's not pornography? Yes, we can—still. But you do monsterize. You could even damage Bill in some way. He's at a time. In another day, had they known, they might have burned you for a witch. Yes, and the rash is a good deal worse, strawberries along an arm.

FRIDAY 17 MAY. I am excited at how the fireplace comes along. Stone after hand-hewn stone—big as Bibles—good to touch—rough, simple in the fingers. I help them as I can.

Avard Bunk—who looks the name—who looks like a stone man, too, a mason—dark and squat, with big blue-veined hands, black-haired and broken-nailed. And a wonderful hat of some sort of duck or canvas, dark blue, that might have looked perfect on Mrs. Procter. Talking down-East—slightly different from the speech of Elmo, or Bill Eaton and the others. He's from Stonington, worked at Crotch Island under old John Goss, whoever he was. Or was that his father?

Stonington—I want to go down there. And almost did last summer in one of my getaway drives to anywhere—a long furious careen (half intending to see the Procters) got me to Deer Isle—which had captains' houses, a white Grange Hall, several stores—a shop where I bought a knit-noddy, outrageously priced but worth having. Whose woman told me of another place in Stonington—the Alphabet Shop?—which she said was very good.

The same way I got to Jonesport a while ago, too—town so sad, Godforsaken, barren, and ultimately exquisite, like almost nothing left in America. Why didn't I write more about that?

The tiny houses down tiny barren lanes to the brisk chopping sea, Homeric—islands offshore, the whole thing perched on the borders of disaster, yet braving it out and there to stay.

And they come, in the end, to one or the other of their tiny weed-grown cemeteries, which are everywhere (sometimes of one kind of stone—or several)—a gathering underground, to continue there (more slowly perhaps but together still) that chattery gossip that carried them through their days.

Avard Bunk and his good helper—another Elmo—Elmo Tucker—who giggles when I come too near.

They, like Mr. Brawn & Son, have their secret language away from me—a continual gossipy flow. Now hand me that stawn the'ah, El—ea'ah, that close-cropped 'un. She did pay, just as the groceries was runnin' out—as I knew she would.

It will be slim, a bit elegant—and serve the purpose. Which I continue to suspect is the stuff of dreams. Dream fireplace, dream mantel. Which Avard says he can make of an old piece of chestnut he has in his barn. That, too, a dream.

MONDAY 20 MAY. I'm going out Sunday, I think.

And suddenly so much that I want to do here. Gaze at the advent of spring, a religious event, an earned one—merely to have survived that winter earns one a spring—this spring—which glows, glitters, broods, alternately. And though nothing here is lazy-long, the great summer approaches, as if on bended knees to worship itself.

I want to clean out the barn, do things to my garden—make way for the delphiniums.

I shall take Buster with me.

SATURDAY 25 MAY. Drove, stopped, parked, got out, walked, drove on. Not many flowers yet.

That feeling of having made it through followed me like a friendly dog. I felt as blithe as laundry in a wind.

Saw Elmo, who said he'd be around.

But you *have* asked him not to come out there, for a while—a month.

I said, Please understand—I have to try it alone, be alone—if I can't, I've had it. Him sitting in the kitchen watching me in a vast good humor. And he promised. If Richie wants to come out to paint, that's different. We do paint. But give me time—give him time.

He stays. We drink. We do the deed. He leaves. I write it up with frightening embellishments—too frightening. This time I do rip it up—all of it.

Yes, tomorrow—I'm going tomorrow. I'll be free out there. I'll have a chance.

5

SUNDAY 26 MAY. I'm back, I'm here, on the island. I am free. Nothing to write but that. . . .

JOURNAL. So— Yes— Yes—am here. Am ready now.

And life out here begins again—with tiny things—inconsequential—of vast importance. The way a rock I knew from last summer looks—the way little things have changed—pockets of sand, the broken pot buoys wedged in crannies, pink, orange, spotted or striped, smashed, tatters of rope still fixed to them—from the winter storms when it was wild out here, a battering and smashing of things, where I should have been. The way nothing has changed.

The cabin weathered the seasons like a fine boat. It has only improved, aged, slid toward belonging. Innumerable small things to be done, such as sweeping out the paper husks of moths, dead bees, a million flies. I suddenly find I have to go back to get shelving paper, to get flashlight batteries, groceries (things have frozen and gone bad—the potatoes in cans—not the carrots, though). I'm reabsorbed into this place, this life.

The filling and the lighting of the lamps, that dark ritual. Light fails and familiar shadows return. I greet them with a friendly nod.

JOURNAL. What was I afraid of? Of loneliness? I'm no more lonely here than a stone. I'm a part of this place, my blood flows to those rhythms out there—star rise, cloud form, water run, drift of fish, of bird. Gull cry.

JOURNAL. (WHAT DAY?) TUESDAY 4 JUNE. A secret dash into town for supplies, the mail. I wanted to see Bill Eaton. Not around. My sense of momentary disappointment down at the dock—but seeing the boats, his among them, moored—the old wharfage—things my eye fell on, approved. Then back here through sun-struck islands that seemed to make way for me, to part, to close behind. I was a gull.

SUNDAY 9 JUNE. Happiness.

My ravens, my crows, have followed me over.

Buster, whom I saw vanish, instantly, into an undergrowth of bayberry, to emerge, looking furtive, fierce, with a mouse.

Will Bill Eaton come out? Do I want him to? Him, yes.

JOURNAL. I'm back to it, I'm painting again.

The easy settling of the dust.

At evening a martini out on the ledge where I overlook the water. I have to wear a sweater still. The air loses the sun, loses its warm hold on summer as if summer had not arrived. Oh, and the light—a transparency—a huge jewel I am living in the middle of, like a princess in a tower.

Crow call, gull cry. Above me now a great burning cloud, as of enormous wings.

I have a pair of loons. Will they leave soon, fly north? Ducks are around, all kinds of them. I want to know their names. What are those quick-winged little black-and-whites?

JOURNAL. Nothing, I begin to think, is impossible to me. I have control. I did need them, and may again, but just cutting spruce, getting ready for the fireplace when Mr. Bunk comes out again, is enough. I asked for two weeks. I've arranged our stones for him, into small and large.

I am going to make shelves to put things on, the urchin shells, the bits of wood, of lichen, reindeer moss—things that I find I can love again. The way a shell grows, a mollusk lives, these trees, and in them the self-important crows—and all around the water, coming and going in its great tidal movements—I am a part of that, and by knowing I am, accepting the fact, I belong.

JOURNAL. Swam at the cove—through nets of green fire that entangled my limbs. An act of will is required. Entering the green furnace of the sea—immolation. At moments I wish it were even colder. Then out to sun on the coarse-grained sand.

Good for the rash, which is better.

FRIDAY 14 JUNE. Dash into town, for a fling, of just seeing it, walking around, looking at the flowers—lupines, lilacs—is it mallows that resemble hollyhocks? The little houses still there, very quiet in the sun. I wanted a moment of company, of feeling people around.

And suddenly in a truck passing by there was Bill Eaton, who pulled over. I came up. The hugeness of him there in that decrepit interior, the friendly eyes under that iron-gray hair that springs out from his cap. How are you making her, de'ah? Something flows between us, secret, immediate. I hoped you'd come out, I say—I've been looking for you. Had a mite of trouble, de'ah. Oh? Wasn't nothing. At the window his massive, unshaven face, blue cap, swirl of gray hair. You home tonight? I nod. Might come around. It's a question. I'll be there, I say. He nods. I see a six-pack of cola on the seat by him. For Chuckie de'ah. I'll see you. I cross the street as he drives off.

And walked to the IGA, got bread, etc., carried it down to the car. Decided to leave it there and to walk home. And feeling on a lark, I got out the Toro and went at the lawn. Bill to look forward to instead of merely hoping, wondering. My supper—Mother's Last Resort, or Swillpail Surprise—odds and ends and a can of chickpeas, onions, a potato. And what a fine feeling to be waiting there with a drink, a magazine, the evening outside mellowing toward dusk. I sat feeling that I had made it now, with work and luck, patience and love; I could sense it all around me, they in their houses, me in mine, with a friend coming, who would talk (I imagined us sitting in chairs on the lawn), who might tell me about lobsters or his life out there (Moighty mean, de'ah, that nor'easter at m' rear, an' the toide s' high haa'f th' toggles was un'dah).

Lights sweeping in. He's there. And slicked up, bathed and shaved, covered with Aqua Velva (That bait'll git on ya, de'ah— toimes was m' woife wun't sleep with me). And in the kitchen after a hesitant moment of shyness he spreads his arms for me and holds and hugs me. Noice t' be back, de'ah—oi missed ya.

I've made us a small fire, since it's cool. And we sit, we talk, we have our drink. He seems to feel fine, and I ask him about what bothered him. He waves it away. 'Twan't nawthin', de'ah— had headaches loike. We kiss, we embrace. I unbutton him, and he lets me—he helps, and we roll that old cloth down—and yes, though he's sixty now, he is grand—and laughs and hugs me to hide himself at first. And I sit leaning against him within a warm arm. Y' loike me, de'ah? He means (is beginning to mean) love, but the word is too much for him. I kiss. His face turns. I undo the belt while he sucks himself in to help me. Under his ribs I can hear great thumps of his heart. I draw back, and I look at him; his head turns again—Oi'd loike t' be upstairs with ya, de'ah. It's too light for him here; he needs the dark.

And up there, as before, it's he who has me, the shyness gone, and some of the gentleness—over me on his arms and knees, I who am prey, and I suddenly clamp up to him, as before, and he holds letting me.

And he whispers down to me, secret things that he's probably never said before, love things, with a coarseness to them, a guttural urgency—and I say up, What will you do? and he says down, Oi'll do it, de'ah. What—what? I say. Oi'll git ya. I whisper up, having pulled his great head down, I whisper it in his ear—and the word is electric, hot, and I feel the head nod and feel him come down on me.

I rise over him. I hear him whispering at my ear—Gonna *fuck* ya, de'ah—the word seems new to him, it means we're now one and the same, or parts of a single whole.

I wouldn't let it happen to him then, I didn't want it to.

Later, lying within the pillow of an arm, I said, Do you love me? And after a moment heard him say, I do, de'ah.

We lie feeling each other, as exploringly as young lovers—he lets my hands go where they will, and me his—huge, gentle, moist, finding me out. We doze, wake, talk, whisper, play, through a darkness that pales. And finally he holds me down though I fight like a Sabine—crimson dawn at the windows and him on me holding my hair in tight fingers, his belly and thick thighs pinning me there and me clawing his back, raking it with merciless fingers as he gets in and has me with short hard thrusts of his whole body.

Exhausted, we sleep.

After coffee I walked into town, in early-morning light watching the swallows strafing fields and road, seeing a pile of cut wood, then that church, with a peculiar clarity. My mind needed those things—an openness, a clean, nonhuman freshness; elsewhere it had been satisfied, so that partial images accompanied me as from some vague and splendid dream; yet in calm, summer-morning air (gulls around, men working down on the lobster rafts), I found my boat nestled among the fishing skiffs and welcomed it with a kind of smile. To the island.

JOURNAL. I sit on the wharf and hear night sounds—cry of bird flying past (rinkops?)—water sounds (soft *hrass-whrash* of waves on mussel-shell beach)—and watch the moon—not golden yet, a slimmer, silver one. I love ya, I do, de'ah—he did say that. Images fly at me like night birds, uttering cries.

Whrash rash (then softly, *hriss*—a tinkling of shell). And below the wharf *slip lip lap lop*. When it clunks up under a ledge some-where, I think of Herne—of that one—yes—bullethead on haired shoulders working in . . . *Grawk!*—a night sound, harsh and pained —there's black in it.

I'll give Bill something—him—who has so little. I'll leave him something.

JOURNAL. Out touring among islands in the boat—my first time for that. Seas strange and beautiful to me—it was morning. The water was glass, was molten. I saw sheep on one, I saw crows, gulls drifting down for the mussels they drop, I looked for deer. I saw a long sprawl of stone like a sleeping woman, saw great boulders lying on the shore. I passed a lobster boat and the men waved to me. I wanted to go aboard, to watch them at their work—saw how one hauled up a trap, silver and dripping—saw no lobster in it. Sea urchins, which they picked out and threw away—a crab. Aren't they around? Are they shedding? But the morning was blithe. Other boats were out, six, seven of them. And everywhere the stone islands, as I first came among them with the Hales.

I like the things in my boat—the orange life jackets, a compass, a galvanized-iron horn, a coiled length of rope, a flashlight, a pair of oars, odds and ends. I suddenly gun it and feel myself lift off the water and feel the water under me in rapid pattering, and hear it splashing against the hull. I am powerful—as long as things work—and in me, always, that slight fear that they won't (do I have enough gas? is there a ledge ahead of me I can't see?). But the morning *was* so blithe. I'd like to find Bill Eaton, go aboard, watch his huge hands handling things. Foine—it were foine, de'ah —through a vision of islands my mind goes back to him, to the bulk of him in my bed, lying half under a quilt—Do you love me, de'ah?—then he vanishes as one approaches, and I chug slowly past—and know where I'm heading now—that big island that I've seen from my knoll, quite far out, sometimes only in haze. I check my gas. I loiter to watch a wave swell toward that fat flank of stone, rush lazily up it—whitening, sprawling over it a moment—falling back. Then I head out.

I cross deep water. I can tell that it's deep from the way the swells have formed. The great ground below. It smells different, too, and the air out there is cooler. Molten, undulant water—strong feel of the sea. It frightened me a little, but I kept my nerve up.

The island was much larger than mine. People had lived on it. Several houses were still standing at the edge of its bottle-shaped harbor, and I had a terrific sense of the past, of a tiny ghost town out there, watching me as I moored to the remains of a wharf. How still and clear the water was, gold rockweed in it, like brains, how washed and weathered that old wood. Who had been there? I wondered. I peered in windows.

From the houses tiny trails led up past a barn. Stone walls, fences—the grass away from the spruce was nibbled down—sheep trails, sheep droppings everywhere. I wandered up over a rise that resembled moor, stood looking directly out past one or two small barren islands to the sea. I could imagine fog rolling in and blowing across the field—though everywhere now sun. My boat down there glittered a moment, reflecting it. On that outer shore the headlong waves crashed in, on a small beach reaching almost to a line of silver logs. And then I saw them—eighteen thick-fleeced sheep on another rise. I counted. They were as wild as hawks and fled from me when they saw me coming their way.

Off among old spruce I found a tiny shack of rotting boards, a double bunk in it, and a bed, a broken and rusting iron stove. The mattresses were cloth and straw. Calendars on the wall—1937 —1939. Three old chairs, utensils, broken bottles. Weather had come in, had munched on wood, licked paper off the walls. Bleached old buoys and toggles lay around—rotting rope. I saw what they had had to work with, live with, and was suddenly fiercely in love with them again—what they are, the ones who still are left—up in the dark of a cold morning, raw wind, cold hands, cans of gasoline, dampness, foul-smelling bait, a chop just out from the harbor—all day out there, and often not enough to pay for their gas. It's the very homeliness of them that I love—they're tough, they're weathery, lean or large, and know their work. I'll ask Elmo about this place, about them.

JOURNAL. The moon rises from behind a black island and slowly floods the world with silver.

The blue pitcher is filled, the lamps are lit. I think of Bill. I want him here, I say to myself, I'm his lobster girl. I love ya, de'ah. Bill who has taken me for his own.

THURSDAY 20 JUNE. Went into town for boards and metal supports, sandpaper, odds and ends. To the P.O. Nothing but bills and brochures, and Lilly Talbot, who said, It must be lovely out there. I had hoped for a letter from Beth. Then, at the dock, I asked a man if he had seen Bill Eaton and learned that he had gone to a hospital. Knew nothing else. Thought it was last Saturday. An immediate, frightening sense of dismay. But no, no, no . . . To a hospital? Why?

Putting back, thinking about him, worrying. But I *can't* go see what has happened—it might *make* something happen.

I'll go see him. Soon. (Why he hadn't been out. Perhaps?) I have no way of praying. Please—whatever—let nothing happen.

FRIDAY 21. Okay—now write. But God—how to say it—Bill is dead. Bill is dead. Had died *Wednesday.* A stroke, another—they called it apoplexy. I couldn't believe it. I went outside and stood by the car in the sun, feeling it under my hand, hot, dusty; I was crying.

I wanted to hide. I got quickly in the boat. I saw his old boat, tiny, forlorn.

Sick with it all day. Nothing to say, though I try. Sick and a little scared. Try praying. Can't, I don't know how. The funeral is tomorrow.

But what have I done? Why this?

I find myself having things to say to him, and his funeral is tomorrow.

SATURDAY P.M. The Church of the Nazarene: a few panes of colored glass, a country church, a poor one. Not many people there, but enough—the men he had worked with and lived among, their wives, young men who had known him since boyhood—the Hales, Richie. Chuckie. I went by myself. A simple service; good words for him; all dressed in our best and gathered to see him off on his journey out of this world into whatever. May it be better.

Not many wreaths. A cemetery on a small bare hill (cheap little plastic flowers in glass jars by certain stones, a few small flags hanging quiet over others)—sunlight everywhere—pebbles, clamshells, dry grass. We listened to the great grave words, not many; then we left him there, among the weeds and wildflowers of that place. The sunlight seemed a rebuke to me. I went back to the house. I wanted to remember him as clearly as possible. I worked at the delphiniums. Down on my knees I weeded.

MONDAY 24 JUNE. Thinking now of the disservice I've done him in this—a man of such simplicity. To listen to him was to hear a child. Forgive. Please, Beth, I loved that man, just wasn't good or patient enough to get it down, give him his life; had to dodge and lie, make up—go for the exciting parts.

Old man, old child, forgive.

WEDNESDAY 26 JUNE. The crows are angry at something. Cawing away in the spruce.

People (who?) out there picking up his traps. I watch as they circle one, haul it up, stack it in the stern. Then the boat disappears around my point. Faint glimmer of a wave—ripples breaking on rock.

Something has gone that I need.

SATURDAY 29 JUNE. Elmo's boat—that long low line of it. They waved and kept working, laying down traps. So, they'll be in these waters again.

I see them impersonally from here, clad in their yellow aprons —orange caps—indistinguishable—two dark shapes.

No Bill out there. We did belong together, made acceptable love, gave and got. . . . Y' loike me?

I did—and liked the way you slicked up, got yourself ready for a visit. Shaved—wild hair combed as best you could, your good shirt on, your cleanest BVD's. You were elegant. What can I leave you now?

JOURNAL. Doing dishes. Cleaning things up. I remember saying once, Cleaning things cleans me.

JOURNAL. Lines come to me. I don't know whose they are. Many ingenious lovely things are gone . . . and gone are Phidias' famous ivories, and all the golden grasshoppers and bees. I've been saying that over to myself, the way one repeats things gardening.

THURSDAY 4 JULY. That was unfair, and terrible. Bill's boy. I saw the boat—didn't recognize it at first, just knew that it was familiar. And then did, and stood up at the cabin watching it, supposing that someone else was using it now. It came in to the wharf, then I saw the boy on the raft tying up. I don't know what I felt— thinking perhaps I ought to have gone to see him after the funeral. I stood waiting for him, watching him walk up to the cabin. I saw him bend down, pick something up. He got quite close before he stopped. I saw him looking at me. Then he flung something that broke a window and turned and ran back down to the wharf. Wait—wait! I cried after him. But he was already on the boat, pushing off. I could only stand and watch it head out.

I felt sick.

JOURNAL. Things have become more serious—clearer, sparer. I see with another eye—*through* things, I almost think. Rocks have a transparency—flesh must—have lost the old look of finality, as though lines terminated there. Are more lovely for it, too. Everything flowers—stone flowers, grows radiant, filled with light. I have a sense of wonder at the moss by my spring—where *can* such green come from, or such *tiny* flowers? I'd never seen them before, never noticed.

JOURNAL. Fog today. A kind of flesh over the bones of this world. I am isolated, shut in to an infinite gray.

Despite a coolness in the air, needing to feel something strongly, other than loss, I took off my clothes and walked the shore, realizing I was invisible—clambered, clutched, hearing motors around. Even in this they will work, compasses in their minds. Was that Elmo?

JOURNAL. Sorrow flew at my heart as I stood on a rock in the fog. It nests here now.

JOURNAL. Everything flows—rock into earth into sea. Sea flows into rain—rain back into sea. Stone flows. Everything flowers and returns. My hands are grass. What does it mean? The end is not here.

JOURNAL. Fog. It may go on for days. I go naked in it again. I wander the island, wet, tennis-shoes, thinking intermittently of Bill Eaton, as of something I once found. Was it that that killed him?

JOURNAL. My mind ranges and wanders. I try to sit in the cabin decently with a book, but the fog beckons and I shed my clothes for it.

My white twelve-sided bowl, filled with crab claws and stones, a pomander I made—the pink and the white. Not beautiful enough. But nothing is.

JOURNAL. The fog, gray ghoul—and suppose I lost my way in it and came to the sea out there just beyond these islands. Portugal.

I no longer feel a desire to walk in it. The fog holds the water down, creates a heavy listlessness. In my cove an undulant silvering of brown kelp. The gulls haven't moved from the pilings all day.

I can't see it but somewhere the sun is down. In town the boats that went out are coming in, work done. Are they sitting in Ethel's kitchen? Do they talk of me? Elmo washing himself by the sink? But I do see one of them down beyond the landing now, starting a motor. He bends to adjust the choke—an arm tugs, tugs again.

I'll do a page of FW. That was dream, too. No martini for you, old gal. Stop panicking. The fog will rise and like a ghost depart and the sun smile again.

JOURNAL. Sound of a motor through the fog, which had thinned a little, as if to let something in. Early afternoon (I think it's a Saturday). I went to the door to listen, compelled. An outboard, by the pitch of it, slowing down. And my mind is instantly ablaze. Then out beyond the wharf, just by Shawl Island, a shape nudges its way into the cove, a dark figure erect in the stern. I go down to see who it is, not hoping one way or the other. And even down there I can't tell—around me, the dripping air, below me water, the two almost of a piece, graying to a vanishing point. It's Richie, and my heart welcomes.

He says from down in the boat, I brought you out this—some package he has. He moors, tilts the motor. Wearing his orange hunter's cap, he comes clambering up the steep ramp, bundle in hand, which he gives to me. It's cigarettes, a bottle of gin.

When I say, Did you have trouble finding your way? he says, Ain't it some thick. Ethie's sent you a pie—I forgot. And he walks back down the ramp, comes up with it, wrapped in aluminum foil. She thought you might get lost out here.

I almost did, I say. I'm relieved to have him there; sense of being abandoned vanishes.

The cabin seems warm and friendly with the lamps on, soft orange rectangles, like boxes, luminous, which we see through fog as we come up to it, early as it is.

Inside he says, looking a moment, Nice in here, ain't it? Unusual for him. A fire is going in the stove.

He goes over to look at the easel: white curtains, bottles along a sill—an arrangement of objects. Leaning against a wall is the half-begun one of him, standing brush in hand at another easel—I've just sketched it in, sized some of the canvas.

Is that me? he asks.

As far as I've gone with it, I say. Did you come out to paint?

I see him nod. And then the first thing he really says: You hear about Eaton's boy? Took off in the old man's boat. On the fourth. They ain't see him since.

No—I hadn't. (Why is he saying this?)

Fleet as fear I think, Have I killed him, too?

And I realize I can't tell him that he came and stoned me (only Elmo knows about Bill Eaton). Fear glimmers at me as from the shadow of tragedy, at someone's daring to face the great mind-less sea—needing to; and pity—whatever—seeing him in that crazy little kitchen as I had seen him once . . . *you killed my father . . .* Did he say that?

I ask Richie if he knew him, and he shakes his head.

He wasn't quite smart, they say. Bill took care of him. Nice fellow though—I guess.

What do you think he's up to? I say.

Can't say—been foggy quite a while.

So it's all gone now, tiny family, or at least that's my sense of it—and I think of them nestled in that old brass bed keeping warm, or watching the television together. Bill under those few flowers now with the ribbons weathering—and that boy—where? He came to see me first.

He was going to sit for me, Bill was, I say. I go to take my

bottles down, get out the paper and paints. Down at his boat—
I was going to have him sitting on the side of her.

He's stripping down to the shorts. Strange, automatic—after
all this time. How long has it been?

I say, Why don't *you* try a sort of impression of him? You
could. I'm going to myself, later on, at least I'll say it's him.

I might, he says. Seems to consider it a moment, then—I'll
have to get the drawing down first.

He comes over to the table where I am and I help him make
room.

I sit and look at my painting of him. I've made the back too
broad for the rest of him. I study it, waiting for him to be at the
table, but think, Bill's boy—and find myself saying, I'm not bad,
I'm not—I loved him, too. Richie seems not to hear.

I'm still so aware of the fog outside, its gray face at the
window, and I rise to go look at the wharf; and seeing a dark
shape of boat down there, I am suddenly and enormously aware of
a ghostly loveliness to things, a huge sadness—I'll go back, I say
(I've been talking to him lately), and write it more proper for you
—I'll let you talk more if I can—and I'll be better about how I
felt that first time, you drunk and muttering. You were a fine love.

Richie is drawing now. Yes, he does lick the pencil—considers,
chews, then seems to pounce. And I go to look.

His face lifts and he seems surprised to find me there. Beyond
his shoulder I see a boat against a wharf, the dark figure of a man
near the stern. And it is Bill—somehow—a kind of angular blob that
suggests the power of him. And the boat, I see, will not be beautiful.

And then he's at the easel with it and I'm correcting my drawing, allowing the back more curve, seeing how it swoops down
into the taut skin of his shorts—backs of thighs, round calves.

And we work silently for what seems like a long time, me
touching the foundations in, him working rapidly, so that already
the sense of it, the painting-to-be, his, is there, the character it will
have—much black—the sense of things in silhouette against brilliant
water and small, distant boats. And suddenly I realize how subtle it
is—Bill, our friend, in black—only a shadow now against a world
still brilliant for its loss of him. And I remember how he puts boats
in the sky, and remember that page of his—a phrase that says
they're the same, just in different places, slightly different forms. I

think he paints boats that are gone now, as well as those that are here.

And later I fix us supper—beans and corned-beef hash—and a drink, saying, Can you stand a martini? I've turned the radio on so that we won't have to talk—Radio Rockland (Gertrude's old station)—weather—though of course no word about the fog. And we talk about Bill Eaton, me trembling on the verge of a confession, him remembering him from his boyhood, like someone's old dad, talking, talking.

He had stories for everything, he says—his whole life was yarns— and the boys, the kids, liked them. He was gentle with them, liked them around—the men, too. I knew his wife—homely woman, good-hearted.

And more and more I realize how far from getting him down I've been. I didn't take the time, or simply couldn't have, so I say, obliquely, I loved what I knew of him—and the liquor helps and I see him nod. He was what this place, Orstown, will *never* be again, I say—he was the past, and the best of it.

He nods. He was, he says. An old-timer—a good man. Then he says, Why are you crying? I don't know, I say—at death. But it's an easy tear and I say, Did Elmo know him—I mean know and like, all that?

He hunches a little, almost squirms. Seemed he was—what you might call a bit jealous of him. Yes—he liked him—but seemed like —like Bill was something he might not get to be, and yet might like to. El stays to himself, like me—can't sit in the midst of them the way Bill could. El ain't so easy as he looks, you know.

I know, I say. At times all he seems to have is you—apart from his family. Men like him, though, respect him.

He wants to come out here, you know.

I asked him not to, for a while.

I know.

And then I say, Does he want to come out here with you?

And after a moment he nods. He wants a time. Wants to get drunk again, you know, on the side.

Did he tell you to ask?

Well—not like that. He hinted around—laughed some and nodded when I told him I was.

Would you like that, him to come out with you? I said.

I'm aware of a moment of hesitation, diffidence—almost, it might seem, out of loyalty to Elmo.

I don't know as I'd *mind,* he says. Him and me's that close, you know.

(Oh, the floodgates. No. Yes.)

Do you think that would be proper? I ask.

Proper? Well—that depends, don't it? Like what's proper and all?

Do you like being here by yourself?

Like now? I see a wry, crooked smile. I wouldn't come if I didn't. But would like him, too.

Well—if you would. Yes—I most likely would.

I cease to catechize. Yes, he is tied. And why should I resent? So am I—to all that's made me what I am—whatever led me to feel in on sleeping Bill—get Elmo to pose—dodge responsibility, flee the mainstream, hate change, invent.

I rise to put the dishes away, clean up; and when I turn from the running water I see him stretched out on a bunk, propped up on cushions. The table lamps stand between him and me in their mild orange radiance (I see him between blackened mantels), and see with surprise that he's removed the shorts, and now lies with a knee up, a leg dangling, self-aware—almost seductive. And through the light I see that his eyes are closed. And I realize he's lending me himself. And I turn off the water, go to sit at the table with coffee, the remains of a drink, to be quiet and watch.

I do love his body, the sight of it—very different from Elmo's, or certainly Bill's, but as if he were a leaner son to them. He stirs— an arm lifts and crosses his forehead and eyes as if to block out the light. His body stirs as though something were constricting it, confining. Orange light—shadows—through which I see what is happening, and I watch quietly while it does, him shifting and stirring occasionally—what I had not seen, had only known about in the gray light of another cabin room, taking place here.

And I watch while it seems to come into being, complete itself. I am surprised, as before with Elmo, and wonder, How? from where? though I find this very beautiful, a kind of fulfillment of him, of what his body is. He stirs again—murmurs—I watch, but he doesn't touch himself, lies shielding his eyes—I see his body move, hear muttering, a sigh. And finally I rise and go to him; and hear, to my pleasure, welcoming sounds as he shifts to let me beside him.

Later I rise to blow out the lamps and go to my room, leaving him asleep.

I lie watching the gray-white light at the window, thinking of him—an object—yes—but something that needs me in its way. Yes, Richie does make himself an object for me—as if he were a book, a stone, or something he has found and is lending me. He's mine, if I want him. I'm not his—I'm Elmo's—which makes him a servant to me, of sorts.

I doze, and wake to feel him sitting on the bed.

Smooth curved masses of his body in my hands, his back, his legs—he lies in a kind of indolent repose permitting me. Not love, though love is in the neighborhood, I think, around some corner he's never been yet but knows about. And I do treat him as an object, since he expects me to, and play with him again for what seems like a long time, a giant doll, full of responses that I love and hate him for and prolong, finally viciously, so that he sighs and mutters to himself, twists, heaves up, finally at just air.

And in the morning I sneak out to fix coffee, comb my hair—start a day that I can live within.

JOURNAL. He's gone, and the fog with him. A cloud has gone.

How did I weather it? Not well. Still sick about that boy who stoned me.

Oh, but the sun—and the islands, as if awake again. I hear sheep and remember those wild, woolly ones that fled from me out there.

Looking at things—the wet, creeping juniper, like some green cape of feathers Montezuma might have worn to please Cortes—the crowberry; and in the cove sea peas, pale, purple, watered-down royal blood.

I brought back things I had found to put on my new shelf—shore things, island things. I listened to the music of the boats, busily at work in the morning, far off and in their guttural roar sounding like distant trucks on some sea highway.

Yes. But what am I doing here?

JOURNAL. Richie, who depends so entirely on Elmo. Elmo, who wants to come out, or so Richie says. I think it may be Richie who wants him to.

Give it up, give it *up!* You *can't* go on like this—you can't *make up* a story in place of your *life*—let Elmo alone! Let Richie come out to paint, just keep your hands off him, your mind. Elmo, seeing that piece about Bill Eaton—he's told Richie, they're talking it over, would like me to be a Gertrude for them. I'm losing control—my mind.

Yes, and the rash is back. And doesn't it enhance that lovely round arm of yours!

JOURNAL. We worried about you, Ethel tells me. We sent Richie out to see how you were coming. That fog hangs on sometimes, though we're used to it.

It does, I say—I'm glad he came, I needed the company. And thanks for the pie—I needed that, too.

I find myself noticing her things, as if I hadn't seen them for a long time. China and glass (not much, but her best) in a white corner cupboard—pictures on a wall—a sampler in a pine-cone frame. After the island they seem civilized to me—which explains a lot about these interiors.

I'm in to look at my garden, spend a couple of nights, recuperate.

July 21 Sunday
Stinson Farm

Beth dear,

All my news is July and weather, the look and feel of it. I'm on the island but take a day now and then ashore to tend the garden. Cool mornings, dew on the grass and those little cob-webs like unburnished silver plates we loved as children—on the privet hedges, as I remember. I won't bore you with details— you must have it there, too, and your garden must be heaven.

One long difficult week of blind fog that led me to the blue pitcher too often, but I survived, more or less intact, though that rash I used to have is back. Well, it's part of things; we are very weathery up here and notice it more—a continual play, whimsical, erratic, or the elements, with its own rhythm, its own unity.

Perhaps my one bit of news is that Bill died, Bill Eaton of whom you disapproved.

I've written about it as well as I can, which is all I can do. His death demolished me. Secretly I had counted on something there, had created a fantasy that grew real, so that the things I tried to say, what I wrote about him, were not good enough. And one day, in the midst of the fog, young Richie Hayden came out; and we talked and he painted him—it was fine—a dark shape on a boat against heartlessly bright water. I said to myself, My word, that *is* Bill.

His funeral was a simple affair. He's now in a simple plot of ground. Going back to the earth from which he came (though I think of him as belonging to the sea), and I'm having trouble accepting it, or much of anything. He had a son who lived with him. He came out to the island one morning and threw a stone at me—at a window, but really me. I heard later that he had run off that same day in his father's boat, and still later that it had been found wrecked on a shelf of rock quite far from here. They haven't found him yet.

In a way that's quite a bit of news—one more lovely thing gone—and what worries me is that I might have had something to do with it. The boy told me so. He was right.

Drop a line soon. Tell me about *you*. Love, as I say, from this impossible world.

JOURNAL. Washing dishes, my ironstone. Pots and pans. At least this cabin will be clean. I will not shame this place by letting it grow sullen.

And I'll learn that, I will. I *almost* know.

Went off to sun myself on another island. An adventure, since there is the business of landing, of watching the boat, the tide. But the sun is good for me, good for my skin, my soul. Found a sheep's skull at the water's edge—foam in its bony, hollow eyes. Said to it, Ah, death. That's what I said.

Painted on Richie. I shall try for a certain stance he has—feet planted, legs apart, sturdily there confronting things—his things.

Seeing them this morning offshore, at work—a wave—hand raised in salute. I wave back—the boat circles its trap, one bending, pulling in rope. Gulls around—mewing—the ever-hungry gulls, filled with hope. I think they come from another world—perhaps one lovelier than this but less vigorous.

JOURNAL. Richie out in the morning, quite early. It must be Sunday. Gone now.

We painted, and talked. He would like me to let Elmo come out with him, I could tell. He asked me to ask, he said. So beautiful there in the shorts—painting at another impression, memory, of Bill Eaton—on the dock, barrels around, which he has Bill resemble—again, in silhouette, very dark—which lets him avoid details, though much is there.

And the new game. On the bunk—Let me sketch you there, I say—and he hoists around, removes the shorts, lies back. Not in innocence now, and I sketch as it happens—eyes closed, lying voluptuously back in the pillows, he lends me himself again. Narcissus. I remember Elmo saying that he would be shy about that. Not so, not now.

He leaves late in the afternoon, me down at the float wanting to see him wave, which he does, a raised arm, from quite far out, so that I know I've been in his mind, at least that long. With his absence, suddenly that world—bubbles—foam.

JOURNAL. Trying to recall bits of Hopkins—Crane—how many dawns chill from his rippling rest. . . .
Everything poetry—metaphor. Which means, I suppose, a belief in God. Impossible *not* to believe. Or *to* believe.

JOURNAL. Swam at the cove. Therapy.
I think of Elmo as I first saw him at the sink. Something tremendous. Seeing him in town—I have the sense of things receding—of being eaten away, though I could wear him away as water wears away stone. I will. I'll get even for his keeping his distance. Only that other one could reduce me, who fucked me all night, hardly moving at times. Not Elmo—he can't hold back, goes wild from the excitement of it. Soon. Dark joy. Then I'll burn it.

WEDNESDAY 24 JULY. I am working toward something. When I read back, as I do now, I notice the direction. Though I never would have seen much of Bill Eaton (probably), his loss was serious; *he* would have provided sanity with his occasional visits; somehow, when we needed one, he would have known I was there, would have slicked up and come out; and all that other would have become an occasional fling. But now it will *have* to be Elmo, whom I've been keeping away, but who is there, patient, with his great jovial boom—putting in to call—though not to land—from his boat this morning, Richie innocently at work in the stern with coiled rope and traps. (Innocently?)
Yes—everything so beautiful here but me. The dawn. To the east the water often has a heavy molten look with incredible colors, magenta, pink, silver, plum, and blue, all painted on silver.

I'll have coffee and walk. And later—to see the whole bay from my hilltop quickens the blood, the white boats everywhere, and the sounds of them, a winking of buoys. I'm ringed by islands, pink and green. Fresh as Eden.

But something this way comes, some dark prolusion. It can't last. Those nights when the blue pitcher and I talk and my mind goes, and I'm wildly happy, knowing I'm destined for wide seas, some great voyage—and write it down, write it all down, then destroy, so that not even I know what has happened, or will. Though I've heard that boat—lightless, at night, low, and black as a catafalque. And at times all I'm fit to be seen by are his eyes, him crouching, down at my wharf. (Why do I see him as timid?) He keeps me company, though I'm afraid of him.

SUNDAY 28 JULY. Nosed around on shore day before yesterday. Coffee with Carole Bean. How's life on the islands she asks, and then, rather casually (though it surprises me, I had forgotten), You ain't run across Ellsworth, have you? She means some trace— a shoe, or a bone. I shake my head, secretly pleased that she has her fantasies. But like their boats these people weather it, tough as old planks, horsehair sofas.

Yes, and saw Gertrude. Seemed just the same. We have mugs of coffee and sit with them down by her wharf, legs dangling. The afternoon light is lengthening, slants from behind us into the cove. I admire a tiny clump of evening primrose growing by a rotten board—lemon yellow, brisk, gay against the green water.

I say, Do you ever make things up—about your life?

How do you mean, de'ah? she asks.

I explain a little that I write, compulsively, and that at times, usually at night, I find myself—well, telling myself stories—a form of art, a questionable one. But the trouble *is*, I say, that it tends to become a sort of habit, a sort of false true life.

Daydreams, she says.

Night ones, I say.

She shrugs. You got to get yourself a man.

I have one, I say. (Lie?) I explain a little about Richie, watching to see what she'll say, and see her nod.

I know him, she says. I thought I told you—that friend of yours Hale brought him around a few times—maybe five, six years ago— we got drunk and your friend got—sort of lively like they do— crocked, you know—was having some trouble at home. That young one didn't take to it—but that big one screwed hell out of me—if you'll pardon the language.

Has he been here since then? I ask. Hale?

She shook her head. I don't think he runs around.

It's him I see, I told her—I paint with the younger one—the big one has posed for me. I got him to.

Yeah? she says.

And his wife is my friend—I see his family.

She looks interested.

Well, it's a problem, I say.

I can see.

I give in to it, now and then.

Yeah?

I make things up, about him. Invent. She's watching me. I keep telling myself, promising myself, not to, and then I'll have a drink or two and work at the diary—a journal I keep—and then somehow he gets into it. He likes me—or I think he does—likes to drop by, anyway, have a drink, sit and talk. It's generally innocent, though I can feel—well—that he's interested. He posed for me in his underwear. It—pleased him.

I can imagine, she says.

I'm afraid of spoiling it.

You got a problem, she says. Why don't you go for that Hernie—the one with all that hair. He's crazy.

We hear a car and she turns.

Jesus—that one, she says—and I see someone drive up under the spruce. Owns a sawmill up toward Edsville, she tells me. Now just *sit*.

We see a man get out—he's spotted us—come ambling down across the ledge to the wharf. Another of her big ones. There's something wrong with him I can't account for at first—then do, as he nears—only one hand. His shirt is open halfway to his belt— V of brown hair. He's one of hers, all right. One of mine, too, I think wryly, though I only stay long enough to get a whiff of him—one of those loungy, easygoing ones, all belly and balls, a wife and five children, a business, a house, and a quiet yen for the lower things.

Meet a friend, she says to me. I suddenly realize again that she and I are *totally* dissimilar—I live in the mind—little of that bothers her any more. I think she lives with her father, though. I wonder what he may be like. I rise, make excuses, and leave.

At home my delphiniums are still up—standing against the wall like aristocrats waiting to be shot.

Clouds have come over and the sky now is filled with black angels, rushing to some battleground not too far away. I decide to stay on shore. As I'm having a drink I hear the rain.

Met Elmo leaving the wharf next morning, this morning. He pulled over and we gammed. Then he said, I'll be out to see you pretty soon, Richie and me—we'll bring you lobsters. Any time, I shout across a widening gulf of water. We have drifted apart and I start my motor up. I move on, over a silver mirror that four ducks are winging across, two upside-down.

JOURNAL. Fog around this morning, one of the warm ones, though pea soup. No boats. I walk in it.

I'm in a round gray room furnished with granite, a driftwood log, crab shells, gray lapping water. I move and the room moves with me, the furniture shifting, altering. Gulls up ahead. With sudden hunching of shoulders, alarmed lumberings. They know enough to be frightened. But of me?

They belong to a different order of being—not lower, quite different, that's all—as the fish do, and the seals, the barnacles. It is I who am less complete, so awkward, exposed, so dependent on mere cunning. I frighten. Another woman could have held bread in her hands and they'd have come.

Strong sense of it around, the brute, beautiful existence I dream of belonging to. I cast a long shadow before me across these things. . . .

And I know what I have to do, and I make my way there, clambering. A rock, a handful of sand—wild iris like purple butterflies arrested in flight. And there I undress. The water grips at my heart with a hand of ice. I'm in fire. I thrash away from it as from whips. I carry my clothes back in my hands, longing to pacify the gulls, to tell them I'm not dangerous. And find a boat at the landing. Richie. Who is standing up at the cabin— pale, white, in shadow—in shorts. We go inside and go immediately to a bunk, and are, it seems, there for hours, him lending me himself but without hands on me. I smoke, I wait, walk around as the cabin finally grows dark—go to him again, who lies there heavily, passively.

Beth,

Wildly happy. It may be momentary but I am just now.

Fog, fog, fog—I've walked in it all day. I swam, when to swim here is to suffer death. I am becoming a poetess of these rocks, love. I am an island and these waters acknowledge me. Old Father Sea whose long beard tangles its green hair in my legs. Oh, only a note to say hello. To say I love you, wish you were here. Wish you would write. I can't write much now. I am an island but mail comes out even to them. Or I go get it. Wish me well. (*Have* I told you I own an island?)

JOURNAL. Fog again. It brightened once and the whole world miraculously turned *burnt orange*, the water molten, Hog Island over there pitch-black, an outline only. And my wharf—the gulls sit on it as if in conference. A boat out there. I wave, am waved to. Humans signaling to each other. Ripples come to shore from its wake; they clash delicately on the rocks, stir seaweed.

Cooking (a cauliflower—creamed tuna). Reading—Brecht—*Mother Courage*. Why on earth!

JOURNAL. Sunned on the rocks and swam again. I'm getting to like it. Brutal.

Then went in for mail, supplies, a short visit with Ethel; who talked about the children—Betsy—David, who's becoming interested in shopwork, carpentry—and then Bill Eaton, whose boy's body had been found. I talked about him, too, Bill; I tell her he paid me a visit and yes, that I know his stories, too. She was making bread. I'll send Richie out with a loaf, she said.

A great calmness of sun and water going back.

Catadromous (there's a word)—it's where life comes from, that water. I try to imagine it. Great warmth, I suppose—a kind of slime—and then? Sunlight impregnating stone under water—the god.

Catadromous—back running—needing to spawn in the sea. Mark that.

JOURNAL. WHAT, THE 6TH? I don't know how much longer I can keep him away. I've been trying to live without that, being afraid of what might happen to me. But this island's after me now. I prowl, I try to surprise it, catch it out at whatever it's up to. I'm playing a game of chess with it. All my pawns are gone, my bishops, my knights. I have only queens and castles left. But I'll win.

Worked at the painting of Richie again, which changes now that I know more of him. That endless energy—as if he were nineteen. This is something he's never had. He comes whizzing out now almost before he's left—takes a few hours to rest, recuperate—returns. I drain him to the dregs. Because of Elmo—it comes from Elmo, I'm sure of it.

JOURNAL. Bird song. *Da dee—dee dee dee dee.* Simple as sunlight, pure as air. I sat in the sunlight smoking, listening . . . I was that bird.

JOURNAL. SUNDAY 13TH—*I think.* I picked marsh rosemary—lavender—I don't know which. I put it in a slip-ware bean pot—I have, gold—brown, encircled by a pale, cream-colored serpent. Uruboros. Purple and gold, the colors of royalty, of Crete.

JOURNAL. I'm making it. Cut spruce till I was dead. Clearing up behind the cabin. One drink—*one* (I promised)—before supper, then to bed, though restless—smoked like a fiend. I'll cut spruce tomorrow, too. Etc.

JOURNAL. Richie out. (The other, first one—almost.) We painted Almost like old times, though I've lost something there. That young lobsterman I used to know, that inarticulate one—something I represent has altered him, or what is there now—perhaps it was always there. But so lovely, standing at the easel, sunlight outside, the windows filled with islands and water, his body. He works, indifferent to me. In our way we are in love, love each other. I think he could learn. I discovered a small mole by a shoulder blade. Nothing is perfect.

And when the painting is through, he (my sweet invention) lies on a bunk. We never talk, he's just there. I'm always surprised —so thick—pale blue with carved mushroom head, inverted, red brown. My lips seem to enfold it, my tongue finds its curved surfaces, explores—he sighs, lies lazily there. His body working a little, he gasps, works, lifts—his legs stiffen, he fills my mouth— sweet pungent flow of him—we meld—his hands go lightly at my hair. And then later again—again—until nothing is left but his tough jerking body. It's I who give up.

JOURNAL. Trip in to shore for supplies—mostly gin. Decided to stay the night, feeling I had things to do, or that I ought to be there. Sitting out by the grape arbor under a pale and yellowing sky, faint, purple scent of them around. I was depressed. Traces of remorse, a sense of inadequate supports, sneaking fear of winter, another. Thinking of Bill. Yes, and then lights from the road sweeping slowly in—a small truck. I thought it was Elmo. . . .

Oh, I won't write it—what's the point?—and yet there it is, was. So, yes.

He sat by me a while eating grapes that stained his lips and gave his mouth the look of a maw. Got up, went in the house— in a few minutes came back out naked, great portly-hairy body walking in its springy roll toward me. His body's center I see in that light is that blond navel from which gold hair curls back. Like Bill's, I think—great birth wound, source of his body's nakedness. A kind of sun. He picks grapes, comes over to lie at my feet on the lawn, spitting out seeds and skins—finishes the bunch, rolls to remove my sandals—lies there kissing my feet, sucking my toes —bang of white hair—boy-man. When he lies back he lifts my feet and rests them on his stomach—soft, unresistant—and he lies, hands behind head, and watches me. I feel with my toe at the navel and his belly suddenly balloons for me.

Who is he? I wonder—why is he lying there? Because he knows how strange he is—because he lifts, comes on his knees to rest between my legs with his arms around me, his face on my stomach. I feel his hands unbuttoning me. When I'm naked my legs go around him and he holds for me, I rub, I pat, he nestles within my arms. I give him power. I moan and he's suddenly still, face buried, holding for me to rub at his back—he wants me to, something from me pours into him.

He's suddenly pushed himself away, rolled to his feet. He's frisky, cavorts, is extraordinarily flexible. He exhibits himself, holds for me to see. Then from his back he's pushing himself up, like a crab waddles toward me.

I straddle him, rub at his stretched stomach, his chest, as he holds for me to. I lock my legs under him, hold fistfuls of hair, feel the straining of his arched body as he waddles away across the lawn with me up on him. I see that he's heading for that tall grass under the apple trees. Lurching and rolling, we enter tall grass but he moves on until the yard is lost behind us. We're in under the trees. Where he collapses on his back, deposits me. You gonna git me? he says—high-pitched little voice, surprising—he's lying there for me. A hand reaches up—he fondles me, fondles himself, lying there in the tall grass as in a nest. I feel myself pulled down. He rolls, shifts—then suddenly is at me. I cry out, once. I'm eaten, munched like a fallen apple, his head hard and working—yes, those water sounds, they were his, those wet lips— I'm crying, or singing, my legs cling to his back. I see the stars, brilliant in a pale field of blue that shades off toward black as I come. I'm lifted, doubled back—I'm held against thick-haired shoulders, then savaged as something wells in him and he eats.

In my kitchen we drink, heavily—he takes me into the dark and is back at me like a dog, again. Oh, yes, a satyr god—we couple for hours—he has complete control.

Was a woman once, ov'ah t' Haa'pah's Row—one a' them summ'ah wimmin, had a cabin the'ah—come in an' bought crab one mawnin'. An' she koinda gimme th' oiy. An' she come baa'k, bought mo'ah crab—gimme th' oiy. Wa'al, t' make th' stary shawt, I went visitin'. An' the'ah she was—had that noice little cabin, had a bottle, took me roight in.

Wa'al—so we gawt t' talkin' an' all—could see she loiked me— I was youn'gah then—frisky. She seen it. An' seen how I was so—hairy loike—oi let 'ah—talked about it some—wanted t' see. So took the shert off t' show her—an' jes sittin' the'ah, jes' havin' a drink, lookin', an' *me* lookin' back, she come twoice she tol' me—was that hawt—jes' lookin' at me. Well, de'ah, she wanted t' jur'k me off—an' I let'ah—an' I stayed in the'ah that whole noight an' she done it fo'ahteen toimes oi could remem'bah. 'Cuss oi was youn'gah then, could come all noight.

But how, I want to know—why?

He shrugs. Hawt loike—

But what is it?—for what?—her? And he shrugs again. Dunno —it's more like an itch—like somethin' in there wants to come out, a—koinda *lump*—somethin' itchy—an' oi got to get it out.

Fuckin's different—gits ya baa'k—tho' oi 'druth'ah fuck—y' kin git inta it—loike a woman in Tainesville—summ'ah folk—I go visit. Oi kin fuck her till oi caan't git off—it gets *in* me—oi caan't *git* enough—don't come s' much, jes' go an' go—loike with you that toime, oi could keep it jes' on edge loike, jes' on *edge*, loike it were the'ah, loike—loike it *were* comin'—droives me crazy, de'ah, 'twere loike comin' steady—can if oi'm keerful. An' that woman'd get her teeth in me—I gawt scaa's—boite me some fierce, an' oi'd *slap* 'ah, an' she'd *hang* on, an' oi'd go an' go—she boitin', chewin' at m' shoul'dah, me *bleed*in' all ov'ah—seemed.

Funny, he says, scratching at his chest—Been loike that since oi was a kid jur'kin' off. Had a frien'. He usta come stay with us Sad'days. We slep' in a shed Daddy kep' his wood in an' such—had a bunk out the'ah. An' we'd git t' playin'—an' oi gawt t' screwin' that boay—loiked me to. Only the comin' paa't sca'd him—figgid he moight git somethin' from it, loike a baby, if he let me. So tol' him oi wun't if he'd lea'me—an' yis, oi'd hold away from it an'd go on him all noight. He loiked me.

Do you have children around? I ask.

He shrugs. Mus' be some. Loike m' daddy—screwed haa'f th' county.

Did you like him?

He nods. Oi did.

And your mother?

He shakes his head. Mostly him.

He is remarkable. I wonder how many others are like him. I think perhaps he doesn't really *like* women—that they do something for him, and that he has that energy.

(Herne. *Would* he be like that? Do—I get a sense of things from him? Only a sense, I think, of the unusual. No love, as far as I could see. Except—who knows? the parents?)

No, nothing to build on there. An occasional bawdy night. I'll throw this away. It's kept me company. Let the gulls have it. But not right now—later.

JOURNAL. Dolphins rolling past, playing out there—silver humps that emerge from the water a moment, submerged. They talk, I've heard, sing songs, play games, are wonderfully gentle. The most gentle life of all. You see Greeks riding them, naked youths. But those are dead—*the* dead.

JOURNAL. Dug clams lustily—at the bed down the shore. Low tide. In a minute, it seemed, I had filled my basket. Covered it with rockweed—let it sit in water. When they've washed themselves out, I carry it back.

JOURNAL. Beth, oh, Beth—this should be to you, *is* to you, though I can't write; you don't know enough of it yet, But horrible. I'm frightened now. He came out here yesterday, Elmo. Just suddenly there was his boat nearing the wharf—it was afternoon—he was on his way home, I supposed—I don't know why I hadn't heard his boat.

And suddenly I was flying to the mirror with a comb. I was a mess, had been clearing out a trail on the hill (I hardly dare look at myself these days). I put on a dab of lipstick, did what I could—rolled down my sleeves, since my arms are now solid red. Hardly finished before he was at the door and heard him calling, Hi, in there!—anyone home? I ran to welcome him. He was holding two loaves of bread that Ethel had baked for me. There he was with them—Simple Simon, huge, good-natured, holding them out—apologizing for having *intruded*.

I was so pleased, having seen no one for days except—oh, never mind. And then suddenly everything seemed to congeal, to form into a solid. I knew him, knew every inch of him. I said, with a mock bow, Come in, come in. He did, and I put the bread away.

I wouldn't let him go. I talked, I babbled, and could see him looking at me as if in curiosity, though his face tends to be impassive. I said, What about a drink? I smiled. But you see, I knew him so *well*—that face—the look he had given me, the body I had seen, the back. I said, I've been *dying* for company. I won't take no for an answer—things like that. Coquettish—*awful!*

It seemed so familiar, I had been through it a hundred times, was enacting a scene.

And there he stood, knit cap and all, brawny, impassive—Ethel's husband—my friend. Now, you really must stay—but really. I was crazed.

And then I think he saw that I was. I saw his eyes grow evasive, heard him mumbling—I couldn't hear what—I was talking, saying things—things like, I've been wanting to talk to you, Elmo—then terrible, ghastly things—watching him begin to retreat, to turn, to look for the exit—me saying, *Please* don't go, you don't have to, stay here a while. Beth, he bolted—simply left and hurriedly, leaving me there with my lipstick and my raveled hair.

How could I, how *could* I?

What to do now? Sit tight. Go to bed. I can't think it out. I've become a serious mess.

JOURNAL. My hands are shaking. Think—how bad was it? Who would he tell? Ethel? Richie? I can't go there now. Where can I go?

He looked—as if I had frightened him—no, startled—at the unexpected. *Why* so unexpected? Didn't he know I was in love with him? Am I all that bad? Nor did he "bolt," as you put it—he simply exited—as if he thought I weren't well, were drunk, didn't want to embarrass me. Yes—more like that. Oh, he *can't* tell Ethel—he won't.

But something else has gone now—it is another death. The lovely shine it used to have is gone.

JOURNAL. Quick, necessary dash into town. I looked furtively at faces, wondering whether I'd been detected in their midst (I wore my sleeves rolled down). I said good morning to Lilly Talbot, snatched for the mail, and quickly left, clutching a letter from Beth.

I should wear a boa to town, or an emblem saying, *Amor Vincit Omnia*. . . . No way to make believe any more—no way to make it less real, or more.

How can the world cause this pain? What have I done to it?

JOURNAL. I can't bear to think, but must. What have I done? Smashed something.

I'm seeing him in church. I'm seeing him reading something to Anne. Bringing me those loaves of bread from Ethel. Why did I think I had some claim on him, that he was "interested"? And what if he *was*? I must have looked like a harpy, some ghastly old frump—coming at him. You'll have to live with that now.

JOURNAL. Question, if I may: What made you think these people were anything *like* you? For one *moment* what made you think that? You're hollow, dear—you're a shell, a leftover—from Newburyport (wouldn't *they* be proud of you now).

JOURNAL. Suppose, since he knows me now, he comes back. He must be thinking it over. And he did have that fling at Gertrude's. Would I want that? Would I want the first time to be *that* way?

I could explain things—he'd understand—I *know* he's not gone blabbing around.

JOURNAL. Walking the shore. Looking for feathers. To make a wing of, perhaps.

Seeing them out there.

JOURNAL. Walked all day on the shore. Lost in that devastating light.

THE 22ND? Thinking, thinking. What do you know about them? —him—Richie? They're only objects to you, aren't they? forms of pure decoration. You're a collector—first one, then two—then three. Not people, dolls—things you dress and undress, since their nakedness shines on you. Elmo at the sink that time. Getting Richie to paint naked for you—for *you*, not him. How do you know what *he* wants?

But people are only that to you, entities seen from the outside, aesthetically, *functionally* satisfying—seldom with that network of timidities, aggressions, hopes and fears, and dreams, that makes them what they are. Even Ethel—an object—picturesque. What *does* she feel about life? or me? or her best things? They have feelings I never consider. I'd be a bad novelist. Solipsistic.

This is serious, isn't it? Do I treat this whole world like that? —as an object, there for my observation and delight? Did I treat Herb that way? He begged me not to divorce. I said, But I need something else—it's not working for me. For *me*. Yes, but what about him—for *him*? Why couldn't I have *made* it work? But I had to go careening off like some lady adventurer in Arabia, to get fucked by the natives, or at least to make it up.

You love nothing but some dream of your own mind, a world of objects you manipulate. You have a bad habit now—you want to make the world what you *want* it to be. It is wrecking everything!

Wait. This *is* serious. Think now. Wanting Richie Hayden naked in here—but what about *him*? A person's not like that, a man's not—a man works, he makes love—at proper times.

You *cheapen* the world. You own things, buy them, have them sent—Beth, send me books—this—that. Because I love them. Like this place—I see it far more intensely than any of them do—I'm its watcher, its guardian. At times I feel that I sustain it, that if I weren't here its sunsets would cease to exist. I've *created* Richie and Elmo—without me they would be nothing, hidden in some dark room of the world. I've shown the world what they're like.

No. You've shown it what *you* are. You don't know what they are like.

It's all need with me, isn't it? What *is* it that I haven't learned? Something deep—something simple, and hard. The world hears us, knows about us in some way—that gull that flew from you—we must go lovingly to it, not looking, not even hoping, for some reward, since the reward will be in doing that.

JOURNAL. Was I being honest?—or just jotting down attractive words? Word hoard. Their power to deceive or to illuminate. Listen—only with Bill Eaton were you almost honest, woman to man. Because he *let* me be! Yes, you were lucky that *he* needed *you*, that he wanted a woman and thought you were one.

Learn. Learn! Get off this island!

JOURNAL. Bird song: *da dee—dee dee*—simple as sunlight, pure as air. I sat in the sunlight smoking and listening, holding my knees. I was that bird.

JOURNAL. Richie out. (Surprise.) Much as if nothing had happened last time he was out. I'm not sure what to make of it. He seemed to want to paint, undressed, and did paint for a while. Then was on a bunk as if tired, or resting, leg up, forearm over his eyes—yes, and finally—I went to him, again, almost with a sigh, and fleetingly I thought, again, He's still mine, even without Elmo—if I want him. Without Elmo? Wondering what it might mean. His hand rests on my head—he's stroking it. Again. And then, again, he lets me know that Elmo wants to come out —with him. I lift away. Did he say that? He nods. He told me to ask—says he wants a "time." What else did he say? Nothing— he wants to cook lobsters for us—he told me to ask.

A faint shiver inside—I know what is happening. A "time"? I say.

Well—a party. He gets that way.

He takes my head in his hands, gently pulls it back down (who's the doll), saying, He just wants a time—ain't nothing.

I hold back a moment. I say, Do *you*?

I wouldn't mind. He gently pushes me down, and after a moment I hear him say, Might be nice—the three of us. I hear him sigh.

JOURNAL. Richie again. He wants Elmo. Mulling at it all day. Elmo has sent him, I know. I'm to be used, as they used her. But I won't be. I'm a woman still, eaten up maybe, sick, but not mad.

JOURNAL. Painted. No good. I couldn't see. My hand shook.
Slashed at alders. Swam at the cove. In the water I held still to let its fingers take my throat. Richie here when I got back, standing up at the cabin. He leads me to my room; round back and legs of him. Indolent, yet he keeps me there—at ease in pillows, sighing, holding my face in his hands.
He wants to come out, he says. Got some noice lob-stahs he's savin'. He wants t' cook 'em for ya.
Do you like to look at him? I ask suddenly.
Wha'cha mean?
Did you like being at Gertrude's? You said it made you sick.
Stroking my hair with his hand—That was some toime ago—I dunno—'twun't be loike that now.
Legs go around my waist.

JOURNAL. I'm giving in.
I drink to the moon—I sing to it. To the dolphins rolling past.

JOURNAL. Because I've tried everything. My books, my painting. Were I on shore now, would it be different for me? Coffee at Carole Bean's? Supper at Ethel's? My garden? What have I lost?

JOURNAL. Richie again. Didn't paint.
He knows he's all I have now. Luminous blue eyes that gaze at me as if from a million miles away—the beard. In smoky cabin air, clothes on the floor, light touching soft curls to copper gold, he lies propped on pillows, hands behind head, muscular. His sensual, spoiled face. Not my type, I would have said not very long ago.
Enough gin?

JOURNAL. Gulls were down at the landing, guiding the fog in, and crows cawed angrily. Things turning around, reversing. Cove settled to a dish of mercury. Low tide—rocks, the heads of drowned men. I'm afraid of it—cuts me off from people on shore, my ladies.
The ghost of Hog Island across the water, long, low, and black

—radiance lifts, for a moment undulates—gold-shouldered; lifts, sinks, tentacles, island disappears, fog battening on it.

I hear it finally, their boat, *a* boat, but having the power to summon, I know. And for a long moment I think, No—I won't let them in. I can't live like this, I'll say—you must not come to me—please. One supper at Ethel's, a loaf of her good bread, worth more than anything you can give me. (Control, now, control.)

I see delphiniums—stately women in sunlight; smell coffee, hear gossiping tough old ladies—finger quilts in a hollyhock world of white and sagging clapboards—and find myself walking casually down to the dock as it enters my cove. I've walked down to see the fog, that's all, to look at this elemental world, thinking in some foolish formal way, Beauty is involved with Death; only the light that casts strong shadows is brilliant enough—it glows a last moment through the fog and turns their boat black so that I think, Deleau. (I *must* begin to call them that.) Silver and black, a radiance and a silhouette—yes, and it's that, too, that I've gone down to see, old Bill—it's what I shall paint next, if my hands don't shake. (Describe!)

The boat takes on colors as it drifts in—tones of white, of green, dull red, gray, black, burnt orange. I see how solid, sound it is, how fine its lines, its sheer. With a low throaty gurgling, it turns out there as if to let me look at it, drifts sternward toward my raft, faint blue smoke at its exhausts.

They're carrying things—a bucket with brown seaweed, a paper bag. The silence breaks as Elmo booms up, self-consciously, We brung lob-stahs—Richie said you wun't moind—holds the bucket up to show. Yes, there are at least two Hales—he's as schizoid as I am. Nothing seems to have happened—nothing—just that he's back. Dark, muffled sense of joy. Clumping up in knit caps and yellow rain jackets, Elmo and Richie—my mind swarms at them.

In the cabin, totally himself again, but as if for a last time, Elmo holds the bottle high. Gonna have ma'*tee*'nies. Helen, de'ah —go fix us one. A party call. Richie takes the lobsters to the sink. I put another chunk of spruce on the fire I've had going all day. It's been damp and cold. And quickly we settle in; Elmo, in one of his great party moods, sits by the fire presiding, priming himself. He's already had a few—whiskey in the boat.

Nothing has changed, so it seems. Wha'cha think of our lady

he'ah, Richie? Ain't she some foine? Gonna pose for ya, de'ah, soon's we've had that lob-stah—see if oi don't. Ain't had lob'stah in quoite some while—and to Richie, Gonna eat her, shell an' all. (Clever Elmo, he feeds my text.)

I've made them martinis—I am having my third. Gawt t' have lob'stah, don't we, Richie? Moi mouth's all *wet* for it—gonna suck her *droi*. How's it been goin' out he'ah? Been quite fawggy, ain't it? Some thick.

The cabin is orange, the air blue. I've turned the radio on—Radio Rockland. News of the world comes in.

You been out, Richie? he calls. D'ja pose for our girl? And to me, confidingly, Richie likes t' pose, loikes t' show ladies his body—and over to him—Don'cha, de'ah?

Now, ain't all this some noice—wah'm's toast, ain't it? Don't moind none, do ya, de'ah?—and off comes the shirt, then the undershirt—a great ballooning of flesh when he swells his chest. Oi feel good now.

Over at the stove Elmo stands looking in the pot from which Richie has taken off the lid—clouds of steam—Elmo, holding him in an arm, hugs him—suddenly ducks to bite at his ear, Richie only hunches a shoulder. Oi could eat this boy *aloive*, he says back to me—he's m' de'ah.

The lobsters are marvelous. Elmo sucks the meat from the clams, the little ones, cracking them in his teeth—melted butter —his face glistens as he worries them, sips at martini held in delicate paw—lamps gleam—chest muscles twitch and jump as his arms move. His mouth is red. He eats heartily.

Now, Richie, he says, cajoling, don't be so formal—and get that shirt off. We want to look at you, de'ah. Got skin like a baby—not like me. He rubs at his chest—seems to show it to me, almost privately. I'll make us a drink—don't mind, do you, de'ah? Ain't that some fine. Now ain't all this nice.

I see him standing behind Richie's chair unbuttoning his shirt. He allows him to. Helping him off with it, then pulling up his undershirt. Then standing to feel at the flesh of his shoulders, kneading it, looking down. Richie's got a good figure, ain't he? he says—feels like a baby. He bends and feels down at his chest. His hands go up to the throat, circle it, stroke up under his chin, smooth over his cheeks. Richie's my boy, he says—I'm his dad—ain't I, de'ah?

We have another drink, Elmo talking compulsively. He rises,

322

comes to my chair, bends and kisses me—suddenly feel his tongue like a sponge at my ear. Gonna get him for us, de'ah? I hear him whisper.

I'm aware of the radio—of Richie, flushed, still slightly withdrawn—light catches in his curls, coppers his beard—sitting with a drink in his hand, not quite watching us, but there.

I have enormous control (I have to in a world all of my creating). Elmo vanishes, reappears in his shorts, drink in hand. I *got* to feel at home, he says. How I look to you, Richie? He stands swelling out his chest, arms raised and cocked. In the firelight the genitals stand in massive relief though without detail, mere potency in stretched cloth. The body gleams and bunches as he flexes, turns, swells his chest again. He lies on my wolf-fur robe, holds his glass on a broad knee. I see Richie at the sink, pouring himself a drink.

Lamplight, firelight—the radio—Rockland—voices—my own, theirs. I'm talking with Elmo, who's stretched out by the fireplace. The terrible loveliness of a drink, feeling it occur, warmth spreading through me, silver as fog. I stare at the rafter overhead. And timelessly and as if from nowhere, out of the dark, or my room, I see Richie. He's sitting naked now in a chair away from the fire. Elmo talking, ramblingly. That drink gets in my belly— get me another, de'ah—lifts his glass to me, lying on the rug. I do. Hoisting up on an elbow, he spies Richie, crows, I told you, de'ah—there he is! Come here, come over here, de'ah. He beckons. Lie down here. Richie standing above him looking down, Elmo looking up. She seen you like this? he asks. He reaches and feels Richie's thigh, rubs up, feels his balls. He stands letting him. Git a haa'd on, de'ah—we wan'cha to.

I watch them lying there, Elmo with his shorts still on, Richie naked—arms back, a drink by his side. I see Elmo roll toward him, look at him, rub with his palm, his chest, his stomach, rub down, then roll back to look up at me. (Control, describe.)

Richie's my boy, he says. Yours, too, de'ah—like I am.

Then rolls again back to feel over him, squeeze an arm, to feel at the smoothness of his chest, reach down to finger his genitals—Richie lies letting him, as if indifferently. Strange surrogate—doll. Got to get it up for him, Elmo says. He himself is already enormous under the cloth—which he finally rolls back to unbutton; lifts hips, strips down, strips off—and lies back to look up at me, rubbing his shoulders on the fur. Come down and join us now, de'ah, he says. Richie ain't had this before. He needs it. We got to help him, you and me.

My breasts feel like flour in silken bags, oddly loose still and heavy. I stand over them, powerfully, and Elmo's hand reaches up for me as the other wanders over Richie, fingers his gradual stiffness, as he lies still, head in hands. (Could I paint *this*?)

Elmo is kissing me with full mouth, head turning, slow, me between them now. He murmurs things. I told you I'd get him, de'ah—we got him now, you and me. And then he's over me and coming in, and I make room for him, him on his hands, his arms, looking down—and we look at each other as he enters me. Then, mounted, he lies on his elbows and slowly moves at me, lifts to kiss, Richie lying beside us, turns my head, goes up to his arms. Kiss her, de'ah—kiss her for me. Richie lifts and turns, moves on elbows over me, and does; the first time he has; and secretly we know each other a moment, like saying secretly, Hello —Elmo in me, deeply, moving again, holding himself on his arms above both of us. Kiss her, de'ah, he encourages—one of his hands is on Richie's back. I have both of them. You ready now? —I got her right here, de'ah. I feel Richie lift away, Elmo withdraw, feel knees and thighs down there. I help as he clambers over me, I help as he feels down and feel Elmo's hand—and together we manage him. And then it's him who is over me and I feel his relief and excitement—his first time. I hold him in my arms, I spread for him, I feel his body on me. Elmo on knees is watching us, then lies beside us, moves Richie's head away to kiss me himself, a great taking of my mouth with his, murmurs, He gittin' ya?

My head is in Elmo's lap, who behind me is sitting legs out, holding my face in his hands looking down. And I look up as Richie moves on me. He gittin' ya? he murmurs down—Ya gittin' her, Richie? Git her good, boy. My head goes back and back— I lie seeing his face upside-down, looking at us—chest, round arms. He bends and kisses me and my mouth opens for him. Withdraws. Takes Richie's face in his hands, murmurs to him, Ya gittin' it, boy?—git her good. And he is moving harder in me, Elmo directing, saying, to me, He's comin', and to him, Git it, boy—leans back to brace himself on his arms as his legs go around Richie's body, my head pillowed on his stomach now—Git it, boy—the frantic body seems to come in both of us, Elmo saying tensely, Git it, git it!

And gradually I am covered by them, lapped and warmed, and distantly hear the soft sound of the fire licking, see rafters, orange and black, as they move over me, first one, then the other, talking, murmuring—a soft laugh—muttering of surd lips—Richie's beard.

What more, what more?

JOURNAL. Walked all day on the shore looking for something I have lost. Feathers. I've begun to collect them. I will have to keep that other journal now.

Martinis, and I settle at the table to summon them again. Writing. Something precious I approach with care. . . .

Word hoard unlocked, and the images tumble out, a blind fury of them that I'll burn, hide away, firelight and bodies, gin, Elmo holding my head in his lap while Richie goes at me, and at me, tirelessly. Like worms on the body of a bird, they crawl over me. Let me say it, tell it. Never *mind!* I promise, I'll burn all this. But first, just let me say it to the end!

Yes, Richie is the worst. As if he had always wanted this, bathed in Elmo's huge naked laughter—brutal, fatherly—he has me and has me. And me—I'm sucked toward it as toward some absolute reality. I'm a chalice. I burn all night. But they separate me, this does, from everything.

JOURNAL. Out again. In a flash, it seems, we are naked, on the floor, the three of us. Want to see me jerk Richie off—Elmo on his knees over him. And you get me, boy.

Richie lies on me—I whisper up at him, in an ear, Do you love me?—do you?—and hear him, in my ear, say, Yup—yup—rhythmically, abstractedly, Elmo lying on his side watching us—Get her good, boy, or you'll get my cock up your ass. I gradually disappear beneath them.

Write to Beth now, confess, tell her everything, that I am "infinitely ill." (Are you?)

JOURNAL. Royal Stinson's boat off there. I didn't wave. They didn't. I can't go back to shore. It's written on me. The world, my world is ablaze. I see stones, pieces of wood. I can't look at the stars. Buried myself in water today, held still for it. I need it badly. Eaten up.

JOURNAL. Dark joy (will that phrase do?), that I have given in to this, though it absorbs and separates. I am rare and strange, still human—beautiful in my way, for having paid this price.

In morning light—

Would I want to return? Not in this form. Something in me, what I was born to was imperfect. Let me come as a gull. Because I *would* want to revisit this world—only in a more perfect form. Where would I find a more beautiful one? Oh, but it's just that beauty isn't enough.

AUGUST. Wandering my shore waiting for them, who will not leave me alone, no more than they would Gertrude once, though we've surely transcended that. She had her father—I have a father and son—and have had a grandfather, who gave me the wound of his entrance into this world to kiss as I pleased. Old thing, I've made a cross for you—I went and dug you up. You were less scarred and eaten than I.

My live ghosts arrived at evening, with a setting sun, under clouds of fire. A game. Elmo came up from the landing naked, as if he had arrived from the sea—Ulysses—lumbering—letting Nausicaä study that crude body bursting with health, full-blown, those genitals, heavy as lead, swinging like weights at his legs—Richie behind. Whom we undressed on the rug, him loosely indolent, his dumb little game, helping a little, allowing us, though he smiled, like some spoiled Greek slave—then they me—who then watched Elmo do me royally, the chief, captain of the ships, giving orders—Get her head in your lap, Richie—driving down into me to the soft steady music of grunts—Hold me, boy. Richie worse than Elmo in some soft brutal way—permitting, allowing—endlessly there for both of us—it's he who has Elmo, I see now. He owns him.

JOURNAL. AUGUST PAST. My delphiniums dead, lying in their royal blood by my wall. I didn't water them or weed them out. Little Buster gone—who used to look up at me from his dish of crumbs, as if to ask, Why don't I use a spoon?

JOURNAL. Washing myself in the sea. It flays me, peels off my skin. Sunlight can, too.

Gods need us, to hurt, to remind.

JOURNAL. I clean the cabin as if it were a shrine. I love doing it. I clean seriously—not to wash them away, off the paper, oh, no—to make a finer place for them who are works of art, imperishable, if too costly for me to own long. I've entered bull world. I bed them on golden straw, hang chains of rosemary—on my knees under them, Pasiphaë, fondling, I feel their knees shake like stone weakening, my forehead warm against bull-smelling shagginess. They descend, their hoofs trample me in their eagerness. I am Io, pursued in a cloud of fog, who will be punished for this for a thousand years to come. Ethel, forgive my mind.

They watch each other over me, almost jealously—no, it is I who watch them, rock and water mingling, like weather creating a world of which I am a part. With strange, slow smiles they mingle above me. Watching, as water watches sun, I mingle them.

Something enters me, comes in; that island undulant with fog, which rose and sank on it. Oi'll git her now. I partake, I am eating stone. *Oi'll* git her, the hawt bitch! the haze thins—moon-smiling face looking down, seriously—Herne?—have they brought him out?—the sun through clouds of silver mist that are voices—fades—something muffles my mouth, which has been uttering, More—I need more. Oi'm gittin' her now, de'ah. I am rock, they swirl on me, they require me. Together, on knees, they shower down on me. I am Danaë.

JOURNAL. Buster back. I scooped him up. I purred. I made him a marvelous little cat dinner. Where have you been, where have you been? I cried.

JOURNAL. Gathered feathers.

Then rushed in to shore to see Ethel, to confess—to my ladies—anyone. Bought cigarettes, gin. Went to Bill Eaton's old shack—no one there. I lay on their ragged and empty old bed, drinking and looking at a moon through a blue window.

Was that me?—staggering through town, humming and drunk?—so involved with the beauty and loneliness that nothing mattered—me? Louisa? Some horror, perhaps.

Perhaps no one saw. Or perhaps I'm unrecognizable now.

JOURNAL. They were like animals, muttering, snarling. They fought over me. They battled for precedence. I fought back, looked fiercely up at them while they grunted like brutes, reduced me to meat and bone. Now you—change of bodies—Now you—rhythmically, till Richie fought Elmo off—She's mine, she's mine now! Yours? you bastard—*mine*.

I ran down to the shore, insanely drunk, but Elmo laughs and catches me at the wharf. Where you going, de'ah?—we ain't through with you yet. And he holds me in his arms while Richie has me—Take your time, de'ah—and he does, as Elmo in some vile way has me, too. I stumble back up to the cabin—they catch and carry me. Got to have our lady, Elmo says. Come here —hold her, Richie. Uncouth laughter—grunts.

JOURNAL. Read *Finnegans Wake*—a page—he was dreaming of all, for all—Adam and Eve in their glory and shame, sucking his sons off, or them him. When will I wake?

JOURNAL... When will I *wake!* Dreaming of feathers, some savage glory of flight. I am possessed.

Here again, all night. (Must it be *every* night? My God—soon there will be nothing left, nothing left to write, nothing left to write *with*.) Yes, it was Herne out here with them that other time. I knew I'd seen him. Naked they wrestle, they fight, are rough, and quick, get one another down, a moil of them—wild laughter —partly for my sake, yet they love the hotness of it. Herne is the strongest—sudden, wild-bull energy—has Richie down, has wrapped him in arms, Elmo at him in some way. I preside. Then at me. Look—look at her! Quick—now you. I looked back. Let me, let *me!* The hot bitch—look—*look!* I convulsed. Let me, you bastard, let me!

Indomitably I look back as Elmo comes into me again, watching my face. Herne is at Elmo—gold mesh of fur—they squeal, lurch away. I'm under them—flesh—I'm slapped, I'm held. Now take a turn. Elmo says. They laugh. Jesus. Herne dancing in kerosene light—belly-dancing—Richie under him on floor—Elmo in me watching him—later them all dancing over me—I lie looking up at bellies, genitals, hands, round faces looking down—the hot bitch —I reach for them.

JOURNAL. Oh, yes, oh, yes—all day.

It happened.

Some wild thing—unexpected—unhoped for, even.

How to say. Like stigmata—maybe that. Or perhaps the fact that it was a lovely day, of sun and light on soft water, blue sky, white clouds. An innocence.

I was sitting on a granite ledge. I heard gulls mewing somewhere, I heard crows—my black and my white—and somewhere my white-throated sparrow—*da dee—dee dee*. And just suddenly, with no effort, no will, I was in it—I *was* all that. *Dee—dee dee dee* —sweet—prolonged. And was seeing the wildflowers on shore as if I were there, the fields of daisy and orange hawkweed—field grass bending to touch of breeze. I was there. I was seeing around me, too, my things, these things. My hands were on rock, then were in rock, yes. My eyes filled with water, in a sweet drowning were water—yes, were light, too, were sky. I saw the sleek lifting of a dolphin's back, and could touch it with my hand, which was rock. Waves came over me. Seaweed was my hair. I was all those things.

And it lasted, it lasted—a minute—an hour. All day. I became a part.

And I know why. I don't want *any*thing now.

And how close the gulls came, swooping, tying their white knots in the sky—yes, and I flew with them. And heard the crows and went and cawed with them, and fought for a mussel.

I saw things with utter clarity. A bit of dried seaweed. I said, I'm that, that's me. Yes. And I knew that if I picked it up, so much as *moved*, it would disappear—perhaps into me. I sat letting it happen.

I had done something with my mind—I had put it away, as if it were a ball, an old toy, put it to one side. And my hands grew down into rock—my hair became feathers. By willing it I knew I could fly. I said, Not now—this is enough. For today.

But I rode a dolphin's back. Smooth and lovely—I was that lazy, gleaming arc, that Greek boy.

Something that was always there has come back, come in.

Day breaks and the shadows flee away.

And I sit here now, scribbling it down, to tell—to tell of the glory.

JOURNAL. I've lost a little of it. Be still—it will return.

———

329

JOURNAL. I begin to learn. . . . How to say it? Say it—control. I learn that I am an intersection of lines, from all points in this world here. They draw me. I'm them. I could not arrogantly claim that they are my product, that I produce them. Not that. But while I'm here attentive, loving, they produce me, define me, and realize themselves in my being. That tree: it imprints itself on me, in me—that rock—that wave. I *am* those things, I become those things—and become this place, as I did for a while with Bill Eaton when he found himself with me, old soul, who was himself this place. So that a sea gull cracking a mussel cracks me; yet I am that gull, that soaring, that falling. A wave breaks and I break with it and am lost, and re-form, secretly, to break again. I could leave and these things would remain. While I'm here, they constitute me, make me up, I'm them.

Through the eyes they come in. Through the listening ears.

I am little, or nothing, without them. I participate.

How to know what is enough, and settle for that.

The veins of this being end in my heart.

6

Beth—dear heart,

So much to tell you that I can't. I will someday, I'll confess and you'll listen and understand. Let me just say that I've been involved, not with monsters (except me), but with the monstrous, somewhere down in Hell, on my long voyage out. Something came in on me, got to me. Never mind.

But forget *every*thing I've *ever* told you—I can't remember it all—forget and listen. Something has happened.

Remember Hale?—Elmo Hale? You must—Ethel's husband, etc. It involves him, with whom I seem to have fallen in love, seriously.

Because, like old Bill Eaton (I forget—do you know that name?), he is this place, as those women I told you about are—only he the man of it. I admire them, love them, as I love everything up here. But Hale typifies. Eaton's dead.

I don't know if I told you, but once, quite a while ago, he looked at me. He had brought something around from Ethel, probably a pie—and that's all it was, a kind of serious look, from a man to a woman. And once I came into his kitchen as he was ready to wash; and he went ahead with it while I was there; and it was (in some far-down, dark, and subtle way) a showing of himself; he let me see, he showed; and the sight of him like that made me ill. Leave it at that. A look, a show. And I went after him, got him to pose for me. And that's about it. It sounds so Victorian—lone female, neighboring man, father of four.

And for months, for years now, he has inhabited my *mind*. I've used him there, battened on him, sucked to the marrow, like a vampire. Only it was I who suffered. Dear heart, there's nothing *left* of me, I'm eaten away, mind gone, heart gone. Except—that I've had a wonderful morning. I became a stone, a gull. Darling, your old friend can fly!

331

I had to say it. I am not a lie, I'm me—twisted into a bit of driftwood now, washed up, but me, your old pal, my angel.

I am free now, cured of a flawed heart, because of one wonderful morning. I can look at a dory now, with its bailing can, its layers of chipped and cracking paint, its unassailable lines, and become that dory. I have become this island.

Don't be surprised to see me on your sill one day. I'll be small and feathered. I'll go, Dee—dee dee. Don't let me in.

JOURNAL. Another good day. One by one they will build me back. I am careful not to ask too much of them. The reading. The painting—flowers again. I have burned those others, the monsters, except for that one of Elmo from the back, which is good.

Is there a "pure" life somewhere?—one better than another?—as a country one opposed to an urban? I'm no longer sure. I don't believe in Eden any more. But I believe there are places where, conditions under which, it might flourish, might not. That dream that I didn't understand—love among the ruins, that was all.

JOURNAL. Day breaks and the shadows flee away.

It is certain that I feel too guilty. In my mind I harmed, perhaps, Ethel. I have foisted on others desires that were not their own, or at least as far as I know. What sin is in that? Misrepresentation. But whom has this harmed except me?

I'll study control. I *will* not feel guilty.

JOURNAL. Gulls out there. How fitted to their world they are. I've burned that journal, the other one. I read it first. What struck me was the thinness of the margin that separates the real from the merely imagined, desired. It could have been like that. I'm sure that at GH's it is, with that what's-his-name (the one I did that to in the truck). But I'm learning control. They haven't been here for days. I feel so much better, cleaner—more honest. Yes, I'll survive.

Only, Lord, I'll need to have things to do.

A slippery world, a difficult one—but what's good that isn't?

JOURNAL. Elmo. Been and gone. Odd—first time. What to think of it? Reality?

When I saw his boat I felt scared but quickly rolled down my sleeves, touched my hair, bit at my lips.

He had even dressed for it, fixed himself up. And was embarrassed at first, self-conscious. You got that drink?

I wept, I broke down. Cruddy old blousy me.

And we had one—two—not quite as in the old days (very little of your coastal Maine wit). But he wanted me. And on a bunk, with most of his clothes still on, went at me. Stolidly—though at the end did speak—I'm comin', I'm comin', I'm *comin'*—methodically, over and over—a habit, from saying it on his husband bed to Ethel.

Then did up his belt and left. So *that* was Elmo Hale?

JOURNAL. I find myself listening for him—that one. I tend my hair, keep a bit of lipstick on, my sleeves rolled down. It wrecks everything. Gulf widening between me and all that—me and everything. I hate to light the lamps.

Because out there—it darkens, it flows.

I'll begin to make wings, consider a trip.

JOURNAL. Elmo back again, as dusk was setting in. No blithe chatter, as at Gertrude's, perhaps—though he had fixed himself up again and asked for several drinks. Went to the bedroom, stripped, and in that comparative dark went at me brutally, was tough, and hard. Some wretched fragment of me feasted on it, too, tried to say, I have him, I have him. No victory. Made me do what Richie lets me do—I gagged—he held me till he was through, then let me go. That's what you been doin' to that boy, ain't it? he said—suckin' him dry. I like that, too, y' know.

I said, Don't tell the ladies—I have to go in to town.

Who'll tell anyone? he said. Come down here.

He didn't kiss me when he left.

Of course I can't go to his house again, his home—Ethel's.

I don't think he'll be back.

JOURNAL. By looking at water, I grow watery. I'm Daedalus, I can make wings. My boxful of feathers. Perhaps he'll come back. I'll tell him everything. Please forgive, I'll say—I made a terrible mistake—a way, it was, to keep that fog, that solitude, at bay. It was only a game, a dream. It was just a game. Forgive.

Ah, but then it happened, didn't it? The dream came true.

I watch them out there. They still wave when they see me. Something perfect about them—the boat, the water—how they circle a trap, haul it up, fling it back, move on to the next, the morning light over them, its grace, granting them approval. I am free to go back. I'll become a great quilter, a gardener.

JOURNAL. So happy today. I became a stone. It took almost an hour, then suddenly I felt it begin to happen again, my hands rooted to the rock, interpenetrating, then me *in* the rock and growing down, until only a husk like a dead moth was left and I had gone in and was rock, was this shore. Though if you had seen me, perhaps I'd have still been there.

JOURNAL. Them out there this morning—a sail up—the jigger—diaphanous brown-gold sail against sun—going past. I didn't wave. I stood and looked at them as if they were part of some marvelous object I can't touch but can merely contemplate. One of them did wave (was it Richie?) but I still didn't. I want to be an object, a mysterious part of this place. What was my name, that woman's?

JOURNAL. That black boat—I saw it again, under the moon last night off Hog Island. It moved slowly, seemed to hover, like some timid hungry thing. I've got that claw! I yelled to it. It had no lights.

JOURNAL. Every feather—precious to me. Elmo—why did I ever think that I needed him? Or Richie—self-contained young man. I have a god. I go naked for him, he will allow me to inhabit these shores disguised as a bird. When the fogs are in, I'll perch on my wharf, wait for a boat, hope for scraps.

A kind of hail and farewell is going on. I'm making amends, though hear motors at night. I call out to them. Oh, let me stay, I cry, give me more time. I'm trying.

Waters will wash these shores, rains dribble my footprints away, the cabin will rot.

JOURNAL. My heart—my mind—something, won't let me alone. It makes decisions, then ignores them—betrayal. It lacks the power to abide, but wants to, desperately. That boat out there—why do I know it so well?

I sang on the rocks.

JOURNAL. A rock—a wave— I flew over them. So simple.

JOURNAL. He's gone now . . . day breaks . . .

It coasted slowly in, the black boat—tentative—unsure—not quite a lobster boat, though I seemed to recognize it and went eagerly down to the wharf. That face—broad as a frying pan— it spoke up: I seen ya loight, it said. But he was frightened; crouching shape in black slicker down there, crouching away from me; and I realized that I was scaring him as I used to scare my gulls. I beckoned. I said, Throw me a line. And finally he did.

In the cabin he sent shadows reeling around the walls away from us. Is this yours? I said, pointing to the claw. When he picked it up, I saw that he couldn't read. It says, M. L. Deleau on it—caught off Drunkard's Ledge, November, 1921. Turning it in huge paws—I could tell that he had no mind. But the fingers put it carefully down—hearing him say, My faw'thah's mebbe. I took his slicker off and a hat, crushed, oil-stained, with a broken patent-leather visor to it, oddly jaunty, that seemed familiar to me, too. I made drinks. I sat and smoked and watched him watch the fire with eyes set deep in bone. When I said, Have you eaten? his face looked at me, so I fixed us something, made another drink.

I stood behind him, feeling at the base of his skull, then bending over him I undid his shirt, him sitting immobile, as if helpless, as I pulled it back and off, then unbuttoned an undershirt of stained yellow and wool—yellow on black (his shoulders, back, bristled like a hog's; my fingers felt at them as they might have at something I had found, could do as I pleased with). I undid myself and sat across from him, firelight on my breasts, heavy and golden, a goddess, and saw how his head stood on shoulders that were mossed logs; and I realized with pleasure that he was deformed—no real neck—everything too big—bones got in the way of each other, the muscles, what could be seen of them under the hair, were too large, too abrupt. I thought of Gertrude's fear of him, but I have left her behind. He didn't look at me; I was still scaring him, and I wondered how that was possible. I wanted to say, I'm not a witch, you know—I won't *eat* you. I made him a third drink.

Is that your boat I've been hearing? I asked.

As if dreamingly his face turned toward the sound of my voice. Been watchin' the loights.

Where do you live?

'Board the boat.

I smoked and looked at him. The chest, too, was deformed—grotesquely muscled—too thick. I went to stand behind him again, and bent and ran my hands down it, feeling my fingers like mice enter fur, burrowing, seeking him out—barnacles—felt and moved on as over seaweedy rock, down to a square of brass, him motionless though I could hear a sound that he made, like whimpering, as I undid it. And felt in for him.

I took off his boots and saw horned nails like seashells. I unbuttoned him—struggling, on my knees. I removed cloth coarse as canvas, him looking away from me at nothing. I saw legs white as stone.

I put on my lipstick, my cologne—my pearls. I danced for him and he sat looking straight ahead, dazed, mindless, tranced. I blew out a lamp, another. In the orange light of one last lamp, in firelight I danced before him. He sat erect. He followed me with dark eyes.

With a glance at the lamp, the table, the empty glasses, I led him by my hand to my dark doorway—he shambled, stumbled after me.

And in there I let him worship me—whimpering—then suddenly squealing like an ape. I dreamed of fishing nets and lobster pots, wharves and white boats, delphiniums—ladies and quilts—kitchens and coffee and pies—I had all my old power back. I know. I am this place, a part of it, starved or mad in its midst—ghost lady of Orstown.

He'll be back, wanting me on his boat; and back and back, going mad with me in there, gibbering and squealing, until finally I'll have to, I who finally let him in.

October something, 17th?

Beth old girl,

I'm going on that trip we used to talk about. We always said it was what I needed. I'm going to fly on some homemade wings I have. I've been practicing. And it will be marvelous, divine—from one to another perfect vacationland. I'll fly over all that junk.

I've got to leave this place. They've taken possession. One has been here for me fourteen times according to a journal that I keep. He wants me to go with him but I won't—I refuse and refuse. And now I won't let him in though he cries like the wind at my door.

How did it happen, you wonder. I don't know, angel—it happened—a martini or two, a great solitude—I let them in—the last one seemed to come from the sea. He's not what you would call intelligent. Elemental is more like it. He beats me, blacks my eyes.

Me—this place—we stare at each other now. How do others manage it? Who knows? They have their families, supports. That's what it takes. I made demands on it that finally emptied it of all but me. So that's all I see now, me looking back at me, and not much of that left either, some little final sliver that lets me write to you.

What hurts is the thought that I *could* have made it—a bit of luck and a squeak—that I almost did. A lot of little things, *little* events, that's what it takes. People, families, a fair. The rest, without that, is junk.

I tried to break the silence with words but there's a barrier that even they can't cross. And then the words take on a life of their own. Such *power* they have.

There are husbands and wives, there are children, there is labor, work; there are old friends, and ladies made out of pine boards—there is all this water and rock, and those angelic birds, perfectly indifferent—they pass and repass, trailing invisible threads to knit us a tapestry. Words written in air that I can't read any more. Goodby, angel. Consider this with love.

Five gallons of gas—I'm heading for Portugal. I'm taking Buster along.

Dear Herb,

I found her. That is, I found where she had been all this time.
I don't know what to say to you. My sweet old friend. I've known
her for as long as I can remember. But now I don't know what
to do, what to say.

I found the Hales as soon as I got here. They were the ones
who had called about Helen. They were all there in that odd little
house she wrote about to me, every bit of them she had collected
and saved. They seemed like a wax museum she had made,
down to the last stitch and button. Still, they were marvelous,
even though I hate them now. No wonder she fell in love with
them and had to move in. That boy Richie was there, sitting in a
corner silently, a nutty little son. Elmo Hale did seem a fine man
and a good father. What she saw in him was there, a genial look
to him, a fine man.

It seems they know very little. He said that the last time they
saw her she didn't wave to them as she always had. "It worried
us," he said. "We used to see her out there. I've put in more than
once with a pie or bread from Ethel here." (That's practically a
direct quotation.)

Ethel, the wife, said that they had gotten to know her well,
that she seemed to like it there with them and liked her children.
She used to paint with the Hayden boy, Richie.

The awful thing of it is, Herb, that there is no way to tell
what they knew, or didn't know. They kept their own counsel, and
probably hers, too; and of course I did. They told me they'd be
leaving this place soon, as she had partly guessed. There seems,
in fact, to be no way to make a living any more.

I met two other women, a Mrs. Caster and a Mrs. Bean. When

they heard I was here, they came by. And then a few others, older ladies she had quilted with. I went here and there. I "researched" the whole damn thing.

And the town; still as I had seen it once before with Bill, long ago, just the same. And then that island, finally. It broke my heart. It had broken hers. That tiny wharf and that cabin. That part was all quite real. There were only the beginnings of a fireplace, started some time ago. Another crack in my heart, Herb, when I saw that it wasn't all there. Oh, but the rest of it was, it surely was! I sat and cried. Everything. Even a spruce and a log some men she knew had sat on once—before she scared them away. She had described it all quite precisely.

And then her journal. Apparently she couldn't throw it away, after all. I found it wrapped in a quilt, neat as a pin, except for certain entries scratched out or worked over. I really can't bear to decipher them.

I haven't read it carefully and I probably won't ever be able to. But, dear God, I did read with love. If she needed those men there, they were there, in all those horrifying ways. And I could imagine it. Herb, that cabin, that whole place, was so filled with them and with her. I kept speaking, kept saying to her, I know you're here—I won't hurt you—I've finally come to pay that visit you asked me to. But she had absconded, flown.

I'm going to send this journal to you. And you consider it with love, old friend, you. There is so much there. So much of her. Such love, such . . . I don't know what—failure? Well, I've failed, too. Most of us have. She didn't want our world, that's clear enough. She wanted God, she wanted it all, what women do want, and words finally failed her.

Well, Herb, good night. I'm exhausted and sad. I want to lie under those trees out there and dream that that sweet lady will come back to wake me and say, "Stay for a while, I've got things to show you, wonderful things. Help me to make it all work."

But I couldn't have, not possibly. What could?

Beth